STILL HOOD

K'wan

STILL HOOD

St. Martin's Griffin 🐾 New York

STILL HOOD. Copyright © 2007 by K'wan Foye. All rights reserved. Printed in the United States of America. No part of this book may be used or reproduced in any manner whatsoever without written permission except in the case of brief quotations embodied in critical articles or reviews. For information, address St. Martin's Press, 175 Fifth Avenue, New York, N.Y. 10010.

www.stmartins.com

Library of Congress Cataloging-in-Publication Data

K'wan.
    Still hood / K'wan.—1st ed.
        p. cm.
    ISBN-13: 978-0-312-36010-8
    ISBN-10: 0-312-36010-X
    1. African American beauty operators—Fiction. 2. African American musicians—Fiction. 3. Brooklyn (New York, N.Y.)—Fiction. 4. Street life—Fiction. 5. Hip-hop—Fiction. I. Title.

PS3606.O96S73 2007
813'.6—dc22

                                            2007021197

D 30 29 28 27 26 25 24 23 22

Acknowledgments

I'd really like to thank God for two very important reasons: one, for blessing me with this gift; and two, for allowing me to hold my head when I wanna jump out the window and do something stupid. It's an uphill climb, but nothing worth having comes easy.

I would also like to thank my mother, **Brenda M. Foye,** who left before I got signed to Triple Crown back in the day. Though you may not agree with some of the things I do and have done, you know my heart is always in the right place. I cherish this gift you have given me and will continue to use it to enlighten and uplift those I can.

Before we get into all the traditional things that go into the acknowledgment pages I would like to take this time to acknowledge **Ms. Kia "Caramel Diva" Smith,** a young life that was taken far too early. No one can say for sure why God takes the young and innocent and leaves the old and scornful, but I believe there is a method to His madness and would never question it. I am just very glad to have met Ms. Smith at the Harlem Book Fair in 2006. She was by far the most dedicated supporter of my work I have ever met and I was honored to be able to thank her in person. Have a safe journey, Kia.

To **Ni Jaa, Alexandria,** and **Star-Quan.** The world is a cold and unforgiving place and by the time you reach adulthood it will probably be worse. Watch, learn, and understand what and why I do so that you will be better prepared for what's coming your way. Keep your hands close to your chests and always remember that just because someone smiles it doesn't mean that they are your friends.

My wife, Charlotte . . . Thank you so very much for being the sanity to my madness and the calm to my rage. It takes a hell of a woman to be married to someone who can at times be emotionally unavailable, or just plain out of touch with the world at large because he's so consumed with his work, and still stick around. I knew there were a few good women left in the world and I was lucky enough to get the best one out of the lot . . . wink.

My grandmother **Ethel** and my aunt **Quintella,** whom I love so very much. Thank you for being the strengths of the Foye clan and for trying to hold it together for everyone. You've lived most of your lives for everybody else and now its time to start living for *you!*

Now for as much as I love my aunt and uncles, **Darryl, Frankie,** and **Leslie,** I gotta take this time to shout out my uncle **Eric,** aka Uncle **Elroy.** For as much as I mess up, which has been a lot lately, you've always got my back and I not only thank you but love you for it, real talk!

Ramona Holder, oh you thought you was gonna slip through the cracks, huh? There has never been a time you haven't come through in a clutch and did whatever was needed with or without being asked. Charlotte is blessed to have a friend like you, now stay y'all asses out the club . . . ha ha.

Ms. Tabitha Hamilton, you know I couldn't forget you. You make the seemingly impossible possible and I'm glad to see you enjoying life again.

To the Staff at St. Martin's Press: Monique Patterson, you are a super editor and always cool under pressure. It went to the wire on this one, but you know I'd never turn in a book that I felt was half ass. I pride myself on quality material, even if we dance on the fine line getting it turned in. **Abbye Simkowitz,** you're a beast, kid. I need to hit at least fifty to sixty signings with this one, and that's just in the first few months. I'll rest when I'm dead. **Kia DuPree,** who catches hell when I drag my feet but always takes it on the chin. No more missed deadlines. **Matthew Shear,** thanks for always giving me the ball in the clutch. This year I'm going for the MVP award!

A'ight, now on to the shout-outs: I've said it before and I'm gonna keep saying it until somebody starts paying attention; FREE **Tony** and **Tyrone Council, Albert Javier, Ramon Pequero,** and **Michael Wilson!** It's one thing to convict a man based on guilt, but when you can lock somebody up for damn near the rest of their natural lives based on the words of drug addicts, liars, and cowards, it really makes you take a long, hard look at the judicial system.

I'd also like to thank my loving in-laws, Valroy and Ralph Milan (I didn't miss you this time), Cousin Koo-Koo (who isn't the best navigator but a damn good drinking partner), Honey Wagon Mike, Val Castro (the official ambassador of Bedstuy), Party Tyme (Stunt 101), Mark the Shark, Cousin Shae, Page, my baby mama Denise (even if she don't read my stuff no more), my pops, Tommy "Tom-Ice" Greene, Sharif Jackson (Congrats, kid), Jermaine and Elan Brown (It was good to have the old crew back together. Delta Force Posse was in the building!), Aunt Cookie & Uncle Robert (don't sit at a card table with these two unless you're *ready* to play), the Johnsons, Councils, Wilders, 7K (thanks for the memories), the whole 70 west, the whole Douglass Projects (where champions are born and alcoholics are made).

For the Game: I've met so many people since I've been published in '02 that I hope I catch everybody, but if I don't, my fault. Nakeya Murray of As the Page Turns and the Literary Consultant Group. When the time came we took it back to the streets and burnt the Turnpike up. Thanks for helping to make *Hood Rat* #1. My Dude Erick S. Gray (keep pushing fam, they'll get it right sooner or later). Derek Vitatoe (Though we didn't do heavy numbers I'm still confident that you will go on to have a successful career in this. Keep doing you kid!). My folk J. M. Benjamin (Real recognize), Al Sadiq Banks (The mayor of Newark), Mark Anthony (Q-Boro), Anthony and Jay from Augustus Publishing (y'all know I don't claim many, but we're always gonna put it in the air), K. Elliott, Brandon McCalla, Thomas Long (you were the first one to see your work on the screen and one of the few who never changed up on me), Treasure E. Blue (we're bringing Harlem back), Tu-Shonda Whitaker, Tracy Brown, Kashamba Williams, Keisha Erivn, Shannon Holmes, Vickie Stringer, Nikki Turner, Caleb Alexander (this kid is gonna be a problem), Teri Woods (it was a pleasure to finally meet you at the BEA), my brother from D.C. Darrell King (you still can't see me in Madden), Brittani Williams, Anna J., Coast2coast readers (y'all been down since forever), Joe-Joe, Meja Books in Delaware, Source of Knowledge in Newark, all the magazines, bookstores, vendors, and online groups that have stood behind me over the last few years that I might have missed, and *most* importantly the readers. Without you guys the majority of us will still be on the streets trying to get by and praying to see tomorrow—at least I would. You will always be my first thought when I write a novel.

In parting I'd like to say this for those who whisper behind closed doors and take petty jabs at my character; nine joints in five years and I haven't run out of gas yet. Can you say HEADACHE?!

Contact info:
Black Dawn, Inc.
c/o K'wan
P.O. Box 1728 Lincolnton Station
New York, N.Y. 10037
e-mail: Kwan@BLACKDAWNBOOKS.COM

Chapter 1

"YO, THIS MUTHAFUCKA IS GONNA BE POPPING tonight!" Roxy said, louder than she needed to.

The midtown Manhattan block had started to resemble a parade more than a club line. Women pranced back and forth, scantily clothed, preying on the men who ogled them. Cars were bumper-to-bumper, either looking for near impossible parking or trying to holla at the chicks. It seemed like damn near everyone in the city had turned out for the event. It was going down and as usual Roxy and Sugar were on the scene.

Roxy and Sugar, or the *Good Time Girls* as they were called, were notorious for sniffing out a good time. From video shoots to parties, they had to be in attendance and dressed to the nines in fashionable hoochie wear, if there was such a thing. The performance at the nightclub was supposed to be the one to kick the summer off properly, so you know they were on set and planned to let everybody in the joint know it.

Roxy was the stallion of the duo. At five-nine, with long legs and enough breasts to smother a brother, Roxy could turn up the temperature of a room considerably. She wore pink fishnet stockings beneath her denim miniskirt, accented by a chain-link belt that hung just right over her full hips. Topside she rocked a cropped jacket to match the skirt over a pink T-shirt that read *University of Good Pussy*. Her weed-slanted eyes searched the crowd for someone she knew so she and Sugar could skip the line.

Sugar was the G of the crew, nice with her hands and no qualms about cutting you. Her compact but very well proportioned frame was stuffed into a leather cat suit, with stiletto-heeled boots that stopped just above the knee. Little did anyone other than Roxy and Sugar's brother, who designed the boot, know, but the clear heels screwed off to be used like daggers in case of a problem. Sugar was the pretty-thug bitch that any cat would love to have riding for him. Separate, both girls were a handful, but together they were an accident waiting to happen.

"These hos ain't got no sense of style," Roxy said, eyeballing a girl wearing a knockoff Dior dress.

"Fuck the bitches; I'm trying to see what niggaz is out here. I'm trying to get my freak on tonight," Sugar said, standing on her tiptoes to see over the crowd of people. "Yo, let's walk to the front and see who's at the door."

"And lose our places in line?" Roxy folded her arms.

Sugar sucked her teeth. "Bitch, do you see how fucking long this line is? By the time we get in there the party will be over. Bring your silly ass on." Sugar led the charge towards the front of the line. When she peeped who was watching the door a broad grin spread across her face. "Yo, ain't that the nigga from Flatbush that always be pressing you?"

Roxy looked over at the six-five guardian and frowned. "Yeah, that's his ugly ass. Every time I see him he trying to get me to slide. I ain't fucking wit him."

"Yo, why don't you go holla at son so we can get up in here?" Sugar suggested.

"Hell nah. You know if I ask him for a favor he's gonna be pressing me to leave with him later."

"Fuck that, Roxy; we can always slip out on his ass in the crowd. Stop acting like that and go work that magic." Sugar patted her playfully on the ass, drawing lustful looks from some of the guys watching.

"The shit I go through for your ass," Roxy said, making her way towards the bouncer. When he turned and saw her his eyes immediately lit up.

"Baby girl, what's the deal?" The hulk smiled, opening his arms for a hug. Roxy reluctantly let him embrace her. He smelled like cigarettes and liquor, which made her wanna gag, but she held it down for the greater good.

"What's happening, Big Daddy?" She ignored his hand brushing against her ass. "I ain't seen you around in a minute."

"A nigga trying to get a dollar." He nodded at the club. "I got my management thing popping during the day and I do this at night to stay in the loop, ya know?"

"I know that's right, and don't forget the little people when you blow up," she said, stroking his ego.

"Never that, ma. You know you'll always have a special place in my heart, even if you ain't got no love for me."

"You know it ain't like that. I just be on the move," Roxy said, acting like she didn't notice the two cats standing off to the side trying to take pictures of her ass with their camera phones.

"I be trying to tell you to fuck with a nigga, but you act like you don't hear me, shorty. Ma, I could get you on some album covers and make you that bitch on the video scene. Let me get ya number and imma take you to breakfast or something so we can chop it up." He looked at Roxy for an answer and she desperately searched her brain for an excuse. Fortunately she didn't have to.

A 1971 Lincoln Mark 3 eased down the block doing about five miles per hour. The car was the color of a Hershey's Kiss, trimmed in gold. The back of the car dipped so low that it almost touched the ground as it coasted to a stop on gold wire rims. Smoke billowed from inside the passenger side door when a man who stood a hair over five feet stepped out and walked around to the driver's side. He tugged at his jacket and gave a quick look around before opening the driver's side door. When the driver stepped out the whole block openly stared. The Ice Man was officially on the scene.

Black Ice seemed to almost uncoil, stepping out of the car and onto the street. The coal black young man was dressed in a blood red suit, with a black silk shirt beneath it. A heavy cross decorated with red and black diamonds hung around his thin neck, clanging slightly when he moved. Ice made sure to pop the sleeves on the double breasted jacket so that the onlookers could get a taste of his wrist game. If you looked closely into the iced-out frame of the watch you could see that the hands were designed to look like a woman spreading her legs. The two heavy red diamonds in his ears were overkill, but Ice was known for being over the top. It came with the job.

Extending a manicured hand, Black Ice proceeded to help the first of his tenders from the rear of the car. A peach-colored chick who wore a short, feathered wig oozed out of the vehicle and stood next to her man. Though you could just about see her ass cheeks under the short red dress, she made no attempt to pull it down. The next girl was a white broad who had to be damn near six feet tall, with fire-engine-red hair. She had lips like Julia Robert's and fierce green eyes. Her breasts looked like steroid-pumped cantaloupes, fighting to escape from the black leather dress that hugged her frame. Taking a lady on each arm, Black Ice strutted towards the front of the club.

"You just gonna leave that pretty muthafucka right there and tease the rest of us working stiffs, huh?" the bouncer asked with a half smile.

Black Ice looked back at the car as if he was just remembering it was double-parked. "It ain't gonna be there but a minute. What's popping, Daddy-O?" He slapped the bouncer's palm, leaving a hundred dollar bill in it.

"You, as usual." The bouncer stuffed the bill into his pocket. "What's good, Shorty?" he addressed Ice's partner. It wasn't a slight towards his height; Shorty was actually his name.

"Ho money," Shorty said good-naturedly.

"I know that's right," the bouncer agreed, as if he had a clue. Unclamping the velvet rope, he nodded for Black Ice and his crew to enter.

"Ice cold!" someone shouted from the line, drawing a nod from the Ice Man.

As Black Ice passed a starstruck Roxy he stopped and gave her the once over. Leaning in close enough that his diamond-filled chain brushed her chest, he whispered, "You got a million in cash between yo legs shorty, let a nigga help you make your money grow." Without waiting for a response, he disappeared inside the club.

"You don't want none of that poison, ma," the bouncer said, not really feeling the attention she was giving Black Ice.

"Nigga, please. I wasn't stunting homey like that," she lied. "So, what's up boo? Can me and my girl get a look out on this line situation?" she asked, cutting to the chase.

"One hand washes the other and two wash the face, ma," the bouncer said in an almost sinister tone. "Will I see you later?"

"You know I got time for you, Daddy." She patted his cheek.

"That's a bet." He lifted the rope for Roxy and Sugar to pass through. There were angry mumbles from the people who had been waiting on the line, but the girls paid them no mind. Once they were inside the club Sugar asked the sixty-four-thousand-dollar question.

"Who was son with all the shine?"

NOT MUCH COULD BE HEARD over the roar of the crowd. Exit was packed with partygoers and they were all screaming for blood, Bad Blood. For those who don't know, Bad Blood was an up-and-coming rap group discovered by rap superstar Don B. They were supposed to be the rebirth of Harlem-based hip-hop, but alas, the streets weren't ready to let them go. One third of the group had been murdered over drug money and two more members had been dropped from Big Dawg Entertainment, leaving only one.

The front man, and one of the last surviving members of the group, paced the stage looking out at the crowd. A white gold chain with an iced-out rottweiler head, which was the logo for their team, swung freely from his neck. The overhead lights bounced off the piece, making the diamonds look like a rainbow. Dark blue Red Monkey jeans hung slightly off his ass, making him walk sort of like a penguin as he moved across the stage.

He had just finished performing the group's single, "Slap Yaself," which had rocked the streets the previous summer, assisted by a hype man. Just thinking of his fallen comrades had suddenly made him very emotional. True waved to get the DJ's attention and signaled for him to shut the music off. At the abrupt stop of the music there was some grumbling and a few choice insults, but for the most part all eyes turned to him for an explanation.

"What's hood?" True said into the microphone. The crowd roared as if he had said something noteworthy. He swayed for a minute as if he was drunk, then walked from one end of the stage to the other. "Yo, if y'all fucking wit Bad Blood, let me see you throw ya fucking Bs in the air!" In a massive wave the crowd started touching their thumb and index fingers together to form the letter B. "Now, if I may quote one of the greatest rappers ever . . . this is strictly for my niggaz!"

The DJ switched the beat and he went into an unreleased track from True's album called *Blood of My Blood*. It was a song he had written and dedicated to the memory of his crew. Shouts of "Bad Blood for life" and "Rest in peace, Pain and Lex" came from the now-emotional crowd.

Sweat trickled down his face and onto his once-crisp white T-shirt. Careful not to get the damp shirt tangled in his chain, he pulled it over his head and exposed his chiseled stomach. When he tossed the sweaty shirt into the crowd they went crazy. The bouncers had to separate two girls who had gotten into a fist fight over the sweaty garment. Just like Don B had told him, he was a natural star.

"YO, THAT NIGGA IS KILLING it!" Sugar shouted over the music. She was swaying to the beat, sipping on a glass of Hennessey.

"That lil muthafucka can get it!" Roxy said, damn near drooling over True.

"Bitch he don't want that raggedy ass pussy," Sugar teased her.

Roxy looked at her like she was crazy. "Ain't a nigga alive that can resist a shot of this." She slapped herself on the ass. Roxy was about to tell Sugar about herself before she was caught up in True, onstage, stripping. "Girl, he about to throw his shirt! I can get a grip for that muthafucka on eBay," Roxy said, bumping her way through the crowd.

"Girl, you better not!" Sugar shouted, but it was too late. Roxy had made her way into the crowd and was elbow-to-elbow with four or five other females anticipating the shirt.

As soon as the shirt left True's hand all hell broke loose. A girl built like an SUV laid two chicks out with sharply thrown elbows before they even had a chance to reach for it. Roxy went up for the shirt like Dennis Rodman going for a rebound. She managed to snare the neck, while the big girl caught it at the bottom. For a minute the two girls sized each other up, each wondering what the other was going to do. The girl flexed, but before she could throw a punch, Roxy had laced her twice. The blows seemed to only enrage the big girl, and she charged Roxy. Before she could connect, security had rushed to the spot. Two bouncers restrained her while another one dragged a kicking and screaming Roxy towards the exit. Sugar lowered her head in embarrassment and slipped quietly out behind them.

Chapter 2

IT HAD BEEN ABOUT TWENTY MINUTES SINCE
True had finished his performance, but you could still hear
people chanting the chorus from "Blood of My Blood." He
had managed to track down a fresh white T-shirt, but with
the heat in the club, that one, too, would soon have to be
trashed. A swarm of eager young ladies tried to rush him
when he got off the stage, but the bouncers managed to
keep them at bay long enough for True to make it to the
VIP section. Normally True would've welcomed the advances of a dozen pretty young women, but not tonight. He
just wanted to sit in peace and reflect on his accomplish-
ments.

True had come straight from the gutter and was slowly
making his way to the top of the food chain. Born the son
of a hustling-ass mother, the streets had been all he knew,
until Don B came along. The older head had taken True under his wing and showed him that there were far safer ways
to get rich than throwing stones at the penitentiary.

True had been a natural on the mic and it was obvious
from the beginning that he had star potential. With three
solid MCs and two pretty boys, the quintet was destined for
greatness; but one night had changed all that. A petty debt

had shattered their dream and taken a piece of him in the process. His friends were dead and he was left to carry the torch.

"You did ya thing out there, kid," Don B said in his gruff voice. True had been so lost in his thoughts that he hadn't heard Don B approach. He was dressed in a black T-shirt and black jeans. Like True, he also wore the signature rottweiler head around his neck, but his was much bigger.

"Yeah," True said, halfheartedly.

"What da deal, my nigga?" Don B asked, sliding into the booth next to True.

"I'm good," True lied.

Don B just stared at him. Even through the blacked-out shades he wore, True could feel Don B's disbelieving gaze. "True, I've known you since you was a shorty, so I know when something is up. Talk to me."

True hesitated for a minute. He thought about insisting that it was nothing, but he knew Don B would see through the lie. "This." True spread his arms.

"This what?"

True searched for the words. "The crowd, the music . . . all this shit, man."

Don B picked up an unopened bottle of champagne from the table and popped the cork. He turned the bottle up and took a deep swig before responding to True's statement. "I don't understand you. You just went on stage and turned this whole mutha fucka out and you're sad? Help me out here."

True ran his hands over the stubble on his freshly cut head. "I know I should be happy, but it doesn't feel right. Pain and Lex should be here for this."

Don B let out a sigh. "Here we go with this shit again. True, how long are you gonna beat yourself up about this shit. Them niggaz is dead and gone. I miss them too, but there's only so long you can mourn the dead. You can kick yourself in the ass until it bleeds, but it won't bring them back."

"I know," True said sadly. "I'm just trying to make sense of all this shit."

"I got something for you to make sense of." Don B slid closer to True and threw a muscular arm around the youngster. "In a few weeks your album is gonna hit the streets and sell like crack. We already got a guaranteed fifty thousand shipped, and that number is gonna double with this tour popping off. You're the man, kid, like it or not. Now, you're gonna get the fuck up and come fuck with some of these fine little bitches that came out to see you, smell me?"

True managed to muster a smile. "Yeah, man."

"A'ight then, tighten up." Don B patted him on the shoulder. A small cluster of people had begun to form around the entrance to the VIP, drawing Don B and True's attention. When the bouncers were able to clear a path, Black Ice came sauntering over with two of the baddest bitches either of them had ever seen.

"The great and powerful Don." Black Ice gave him a half bow, never relinquishing the arms of his women.

"Don of Harlem, kiss the ring," Don B joked, extending his gaudy pinky ring to Black Ice.

"Nigga, don't play with me. I don't kiss nobody but my mama, and that's only on holidays. Show the proper respect." Ice shot back. He spread his arms and he and Don B shared a manly embrace.

Though their lives had taken two different paths, Don B and Black Ice had been friends since back in the PAL days. Even then it was apparent that neither of them would grow up to have regular nine-to-fives. While Don B's uncles were teaching him about the drug game, Ice's father was turning him on to the art of macking. Ice was in and out of the game all through his teenage years, but it wasn't until his father was murdered that he jumped in the game headfirst. At twenty-three years of age, Black Ice was a respected and recognized player in every circle.

"I'm glad you was able to make it out, Ice," Don B said, reclaiming his seat.

"You know I wouldn't miss ya boy's coming out party. What's good, True?" He gave the young MC a dap.

"Trying to win," True said modestly.

"Looks like you're doing more than trying, baby boy. All these bitches do is pop their fingers to ya shit." He nodded at the two girls. "Damn, where are my manners? Fellas, this is Wendy and Lisa." He motioned to the black, then the white girl. They waved, but neither spoke.

"Don't talk much, do they?" Don B mused.

"Not if it ain't about a dollar." Black Ice said flatly. "Ladies, take young True out there on the dance floor and let me and Don B rap for a taste."

"Hold on, man," True tried to protest, but the ladies were already pulling him to his feet. Giggling like two schoolgirls, Lisa and Wendy led True out to the dance floor.

IT TOOK A MINUTE, BUT after True had a few drinks he managed to loosen up a bit. He had a bottle raised in the air and was sandwiched between Lisa and Wendy, getting his swerve on. Don B and Black Ice watched from the sidelines in amusement.

"Look at that nigga trying to step," Black Ice snickered. "Your boy is cold as hell on that mic, but he ain't much of a dancer."

"Shit, he ain't gotta be. As long as that nigga move them units like I expect him to, he's gonna be straight," Don B replied. He had a blunt pinched between his lips and the last few swigs of his bottle dangling in his hand.

"Don, you know a lot of niggaz thought you was gonna fall short when ya boys got killed, but you've turned shit to sugar once again."

Don B grinned. "You know I'm known to do the impossible, my nigga. I know how to smell a dollar."

"Indeed you do, playboy. I swear you rap niggaz is shinning like you on the track or something."

"All it takes is a little dedication and hard work."

Black Ice looked at Don B as if he had lost his last mind. "Shit, I'm allergic to work, man. The hardest part of my day is counting that trap money every morning."

Don B laughed. "Yo Ice, I never understood how a bitch could sell her pussy all night then turn around and give you every dime she made."

"It's a gift, baby." Black Ice winked, downing the last of his drink. "See, a square nigga is always trying to get into a bitch's drawers, but my interests lie elsewhere. I conquer a woman's mind before I lay cock to her. That's the sweet science of sin. I could give a fuck if you had a gold pussy and platinum titties—that shit don't move me. Like my Pa used to say: "A bitch is only as good as the bread she checks in." All I'm interested in is that cold cash, daddy."

"I know that's right." Don B gave him dap. "Yo, speaking of cash, I got a proposition for you."

Black Ice gave Don B his full attention at the mention of a dollar. "Talk to me."

"You know, ya boy Stacks Green is in town shooting his video and promoting his album, right?"

"Yeah, I hear they been throwing money around like its water." Ice nodded.

"You know, niggaz think they stunt game is up, but this is still the Don's city. We got a few events lined up on some costal-love shit."

"Costal-love, last time I checked you niggaz was supposed to be rivals? I even heard the mix tape with you and one of his boys going at it."

Don B shrugged, as if it were nothing. "Just a little friendly competition. Personally I think the kid is an asshole, but you can't deny the fact that both our camps are blowing up on the music scene. Big Dawg got a crazy buzz, but this nigga got Texas in a stranglehold. I'm trying to rock this nigga to sleep so we can see some of that paper down south too. While the nigga is in town we gonna show him a good time on some welcome to New York shit. We're even having a celeb barbecue and basketball game. His five against my five on some winner-take-all shit."

"Sounds like you got ya hands full, baby boy, but I know you didn't wanna talk to me about no basketball game. Shit, I ain't touched a ball since I took to the track," Black Ice told him.

"Nah, I ain't talking about you playing, I'm talking about you investing. Son, we got fifty gees riding on this game!"

Black Ice eyed him suspiciously. "So you called me down here to crack for some bread?"

"Black, you know I'd never come at you like no pauper, the Don ain't hardly popped," Don B said, flashing a large wad of money. "Dawg, I got wild paper tied up in True's album, not to mention the advance I fronted Lex and that stupid mutha fucka Pain, so you understand my situation."

"How much you trying to get me to throw down, Don?"

"Son, throw in twenty-five and we bust the winnings down the middle. I'm telling you, throw in with me and you're guaranteed to make yaself a nice piece of change."

Black Ice took his time responding. He did this partially because he was weighing it, but mostly for the theatrics. He wrapped his pack of cigarettes on the bar before coolly sliding one out. With slow and deliberate motions he took a deep pull of the cigarette, before addressing Don B's proposal. "That's a lot of bread on the table, Don. I'd sure as hell hate for them niggaz to be getting their grills upgraded on my dime," he said seriously.

Don B looked at him like he had just said something foreign. "Man, I got some of the coldest young niggaz from New York playing on my squad, Ice. Ain't no way we can lose!"

Ice thought on it for a second, and then nodded. "A'ight, Don, lets trim these suckers. Twenty-five apiece and we're partners; but you gotta do something else for me to sweeten the pot."

Don B grinned. Ice had a lot of nerve asking for more than he was already getting, but Don B knew that's what he was used to, so there was no slight. Ice made his money off the backs of other people, so in his mind everyone was a stepping-stone to further his own goals. Don B would've been a fool to think otherwise. Ice was pushing it, but for the sake of winning fifty-gees, and bragging rights over the Houston crew, Don B would at least listen.

"What you need, Daddy?"

Ice spoke to Don B, but kept his eyes focused on the swirling clouds of cigarette smoke. "Me and a friend of mine been throwing these locked door events. We get twenty to thirty of the freakiest bitches we can round up and turn em loose on suckers who don't mind spending for a taste. Every party is thrown at a different location and by invite only. It'd be nice if you make sure them Texas boys and their money were in the spot Saturday night to spend some of that paper."

A broad grin spread across Don B's lips. "Come on man, I thought you needed a favor?" Don B joked. "A'ight, send the time and address to my two-way and I'll make sure I get Stacks and them to the spot. As a matter of fact, come through the block tomorrow. Stacks is shooting his video in Harlem and I'll introduce you to him." He gave Ice a pound.

"Not a problem. I'll roll through with a couple of my bitches so these niggaz can see what I'm working with. As far as the twenty-five stacks, Wendy will drop the bread off to you Friday."

"Damn, you don't do nothing for yourself, do you?" Don B teased him.

"Not unless it's wiping my ass." Feeling a presence at his back, Black Ice spun around on the bar stool. Standing directly in front of him was a five-two, cinnamon thing, with what could only be called childbearing hips.

"What's up, big time?" She took in his red suit and heavy jewels. Shorty knew she had it going on, and was hell-bent on showing the well-dressed cat at the bar.

In his most sincere tone he said, "Cash, bitch. If you bout that then I'm bout you." The girl looked at Black Ice like she didn't know whether to slap him or continue the conversation. Both Don B and Black Ice fell over the bar laughing.

IT WAS ABOUT FOUR-THIRTY IN the morning when the last few partygoers came staggering out of the club. Traffic was so thick that the cars couldn't get through the block doing more than five miles an hour. Men and women paired or tripled off in search of whatever other mischief they could get themselves into. True's listening party had set the summer off properly.

Across the street, huddled in the shadows, two sets of eyes watched the crowd. The first set belonged to a dark-skinned kid whose head looked like it was too heavy for his gooselike neck. The second kid was dark, but not as dark as the first. A tattered toothpick rolled back and forth between his large lips. The line of his jaw looked like a stone carving as he bit down on the toothpick.

"You see that nigga?" Gooseneck asked.

"Nah," Toothpick replied. "But I know the nigga ain't leave yet, we been watching the door for two hours."

"Sha, it's hot as hell out here man, how long we gonna wait?"

"Until I say, Charlie." Sha took the toothpick out of his mouth to make sure he was clear. Charlie didn't press the issue. Sha was someone you didn't want to argue with unless you were ready to get physical.

Ignoring Charlie, Sha went back to watching the front door as he had been for the last few hours. He was beginning to wonder if maybe Charlie was right and they should come back another day, until he saw his mark. A low growl escaped him as a red haze formed over his eyes. He wanted to run up on the man and make him strip before he popped him, but there were too many people. He had to do it as he had planned or it was pointless.

"Come on," Sha said, checking the clip on his .380 before tucking it back into his pocket. Charlie followed, but made sure he didn't get too close just yet. It'd look funny if they both approached him. Sha kept his eyes on the young man as he moved coolly in his direction. From the way he was swaying and trying to balance himself against the wall, Sha could tell he was drunk. It would take the fun out of it, but oh well. By the time the young man even noticed Sha, he was right on top of him.

THE MAN OF THE HOUR came half stumbling out of one of the side doors. Don B had told him to stay close until they gathered the rest of the entourage, but he had managed to slip off. The Hennessey was mingling with the champagne in his gut and it wasn't a pleasant meeting. If he was going to throw up he damn sure didn't want to do it with hundreds of people watching.

True managed to maneuver himself over to the wall and lean against it for balance. The world wasn't spinning as fast as it had been, but his head still felt like it was wrapped in plastic. The sound of crunching glass drew his attention to the street. He looked up just in time to see a dark-skinned kid coming in his direction. The kid had a square face with a wide, flat nose that looked like it had been broken a time or two. Drunk or not, True wasn't foolish enough to let a stranger roll up on him like that. He didn't have his gun on him, but the butterfly knife he had slipped from his pocket to his palm would have to do.

"Got a light, money?" Sha asked, tapping a cigarette on the back of his hand.

"Yeah," True said, using his free hand to dig in his pocket for a lighter. He handed the Bic to the stranger, careful not to get within arm's reach of him. There was something about the kid that made True uneasy. He wasn't sure if it was the fact that the kid kept staring at him or the fact that he looked familiar. True was about to ask what he was staring at when a voice called from behind him.

"Yo, fuck you slide off for?" Don B asked as he approached. He was flanked by two large bodyguards and about ten people bringing up the rear. He glared at Sha, but didn't acknowledge him. "You a'ight?" Don B was talking to True but he kept his eyes fixed on Sha.

"Yeah," True said.

"Thanks for the light," Sha said, giving True back his lighter. He gave Don B and his entourage the once-over before disappearing back across the street.

"Fuck was that all about?" Don B asked, watching Sha leave.

True just shrugged. "Nigga said he needed a light."

SHA'S LEGS THREATENED TO GIVE out on him before he had made it completely across the street. It wasn't because he was nervous; it was because he was angry. Rage shook Sha's body so intensely that he looked cold. He could almost taste victory, but the unexpected arrival of Don B had snatched it from him. He could've kicked himself in the ass for toying with True instead of just handling his business. He had wasted precious time and undid his own plan. It was okay though. The next time he would be swifter and True would be a statistic.

Chapter 3

THE BLOCK WAS QUIET THAT MORNING, WHICH was a relative miracle for the Brooklyn strip. The first pigeons were beginning to gather in front of the buildings to pick over the scraps left from the night before. Somewhere in the distance a tattered shade flapped in the light wind, applauding the coming of the new sun. The warm breeze washed over the curb, spinning a lone Budweiser can that had been abandoned by its five brothers. It wasn't even eight o'clock and the air was already humid. Just another sign of what a hot summer the inhabitants of New York could expect.

In the doorway of the fourth building from the corner a figure appeared. She was a brown-skinned cutie who let the front of her shoulder-length hair flop over her high forehead in bangs, while the back was flipped and pinned in place. A pair of cream-colored Capri pants hugged her hips and thighs as if they had been designed specifically for her. Removing a small mirror from her Gucci knapsack, she examined her face, making sure she didn't apply too much eye shadow, nor that the lip gloss was painted on too thick. To her, appearance was everything. Confident that she was killing everything on the streets, Dena Jones stepped off her stoop to face the world.

Dena was the youngest daughter of her mother's, and hadn't spent enough time with her father to find out where she fit in on the chronological scale of the scores of bastard children he had fathered. To her, the only siblings she had were the ones who had come out of her mother's womb, regardless of who their fathers were. She was the youngest child of three, and in her opinion the only one not like the others.

There was Shannon, her hotheaded older brother. He was what you would call a career criminal, spending most of his teenage and young adult life in someone's detention center. Shannon was amongst the elite, as far as street niggaz went in Brooklyn. Everyone knew he wasn't to be fucked with and tried to steer clear of him for the most part. Standing at about five-six, Shannon had what some people called a Napoleon Complex. He had long ago earned his hood stripes, but being insecure about his height made him feel like he always had something to prove.

Dena couldn't say that she agreed with Shannon's lifestyle, but she also couldn't knock his hustle. He never shitted exactly where he lived, and he broke his mother off before the weed man or one of his bitches ever saw a dime of his money. Since Joe, Shannon was the closest thing they had to a man in the house.

Joe was a guy that Dena's mother had hooked up with a few years after Dena's father had taken off. He was a Puerto Rican cat who made his money between driving a delivery truck and slinging cocaine uptown. He treated all of the children as if they were his own, never trying to overshadow their fathers, no matter how fucked up they were. Joe had lost his life when Dena was about twelve or thirteen years old. Nostrand Avenue, formerly known as N.A. Rock back in the day because it was always rocking with one thing or another, would be Joe's final resting place. He had been on his way to visit them one night when he lost his life. A young man shot him in the back while he was coming out of the Nostrand Avenue train station. He didn't take Joe's money or his jewelry, just shot him and ran off. The police would later discover that it had all been a part of a gang initiation and Joe had the misfortune of being a random target. Though Dena never admitted it, the scars from Joe's murder had never really healed.

Then there was Nadine, the oldest of the three. Behind her back Dena referred to Nadine as one of their mother's greatest mistakes. At the time she had become pregnant with Nadine, their mother had been in her last year of high school and scheduled to leave for college in the fall. When she found out that she was pregnant things changed considerably. In the beginning she planned to just go to school at night and work during the day, but when Nadine's father took off she was forced to work two jobs just to make ends meet. By the time she realized what was becoming of her life, Nadine was four and her mother was pregnant with Shannon.

Nadine was well into her thirties but still couldn't seem to find a place of her own, or a clue as to what life was about. She was content to coast off government income and an on-again, off-again supply of sugar daddies. No one could deny the fact that Nadine was fine—ugly was something her family didn't do—but she had about as much get-up-and-go about her as a six-hundred-pound man looking at a Stair-Master. Dena saw her as an example of what she didn't want to become.

Careful not to twist her ankle in the high-heeled Gucci sandals she wore, Dena made her way down the stairs. On the last step she almost tripped over a beer bottle that someone had left on the stoop. She looked down at the almost empty bottle and sucked her teeth. It was bad enough that the building was fucked-up and the landlord refused to do anything about the recurring rodent problem, but the nightly stock-pile of trash was getting ridiculous. People would party on the stoop all night and leave their trash wherever it fell. It was just one more reason why Dena was determined to finish school. She knew that completing her education was her best chance at getting off Jefferson Avenue.

A few buildings away were two girls that Dena didn't care to see first thing in the morning, Yvette and Mousy. Yvette was a transplant from East New York that had moved to the block a few years back. She was a mixture of Dominican and Black, giving her a skin tone that was a shade deeper than caramel candy. Her face could've been considered attractive had it not been for the lingering war scars from the many scraps she had been in over the years. She wore her long hair wrapped and tucked beneath the ever-present scarf on her head, more so to keep her hair from being pulled out in a fight than to preserve whatever hairdo she was sporting.

Mousy was short and dark-skinned, with large breasts and an equally large mouth. Unlike Yvette, for whom there might've still been hope, Mousy had never been very attractive. She wasn't butt-ugly, but it was an effort for her to turn the head of a man who had anything going for himself. Mousy was a skilled boxer, but had made her name in the streets for her willingness to go above and beyond in the bedroom. Though it was never confirmed, Dena had heard that a guy gave Mousy two thousand dollars to have oral sex with his pit bull.

These two were the official guardians of the "Stoop of Shamelessness." The stoop was a platform for all things hood. Most neighborhoods in the inner city had a focal point for most of the bullshit that went on in them, but the stoop had them beat. The things that took place on that stoop were straight out of an episode of *Jerry Springer*. From drug sales to group fights, to domestic disputes, the stoop had it all.

"Look at you!" Yvette shouted as Dena approached the stoop. Yvette let her eyes roll from Dena's Gucci sandals to the matching shades sitting on top of her head. "Dena, I gotta give you your props. For a young bitch you be on your job. Get money, shorty!"

Dena smirked. Though she didn't say it, she knew Yvette was speaking the absolute truth. For a girl that was all of seventeen years old, Dena had quite a bit going for herself. Unlike some of her peers she was about to graduate high school and had a feasible shot at going to college. Dena gave a halfhearted effort at best, but a natural intelligence kept her ahead of the pack. None of her teachers could quite understand how a girl who looked at school with such a flippant attitude could be so brilliant. It was one of the greatest unsolved mysteries amongst the faculty of Martin Luther King Jr. High School.

"I just do what I do," Dena replied, executing a playful cross-legged strut. "What you doing outside this early?"

Yvette shrugged. "Shiiit, waiting on the aftermath."

"Aftermath of what?" Dena asked.

"You didn't hear what happened last night?" Mousy asked, anxious to recount the story. "Them Hancock bitches came over here on they bullshit last night, trying to say that Tee-Tee fucked Tango's ugly ass. You know he got a baby wit that bitch Boo from Hancock, so she be acting like she got papers on the nigga. Anyhow, these hos came over here stunting, so Tee-Tee and them got it popping. Yo, Tee-Tee ragged that bum bitch!"

Dena shook her head. "I knew that shit was gonna happen. Every time one of them bitches walks to the store they grill this building all hard. I never knew what that shit was about, but I always knew it was gonna explode."

"Well it exploded alright," Yvette added. "After Tee-Tee mangled that ho she came back with her brother Scott. Him and those degenerate-ass niggaz he be with shot out Tee-Tee's windows last night." She motioned up to the fourth-floor window, which now had a black garbage bag taped over it.

"Damn, they was popping last night?" Dena said, looking up at the window.

"Yeah, I'm surprised you didn't hear it."

"Girl, you know I be in a coma when I'm sleep. I guess that explains why the block is so quiet this morning."

"Yep, everybody is waiting to hear what happened, but me and my girl wanna see it firsthand," Mousy said.

"Y'all bitches is crazy. I wouldn't want to be out here when the shit hits the fan. Especially as reckless as these niggaz is wit they hammers," Dena told them.

"Man, listen, I'm out here trying to make a dollar. I can't let some knucklehead-ass dudes stop me from doing my thing. These crack heads wanna get high on the wake up, and I'll be damned if my rocks ain't the first ones they taste in the morning. Besides," Yvette dipped her hand into the trash can and came up with a chrome .25, "I'm ready for the bullshit if it comes my way."

"Yo, we about to get high, D. You wanna blaze something with us?" Mousy asked, holding up a small Ziploc full of pretty green buds. "This shit is straight from Five-Six."

"Damn, you rode all the way uptown to get that?" Dena asked.

"Please believe it," Yvette answered for Mousy. "I'd rather travel for it than smoke some bullshit, feel me? So what's up, you trying to get high or what?"

"Nah, I think I'm gonna pass. If I fuck around and get high before school I won't be able to get a damn thing done." Dena lied. Actually, she preferred to get high early in the morning. That way, she'd be floating for the majority of the day. The real reason she turned down the weed was because she didn't want to smoke behind Mousy. She had heard more than a few stories about where that girl's mouth had been, and the last thing she needed was a strange growth on her lip for the love of a get-high.

Mousy shrugged, "Suit yourself." She really didn't care what Dena's reason for not smoking with them was, because to her it was just one less head on the blunt.

A thumping sound drew all their attentions to the lobby of the building they were standing in front of. The sound was distant at first but seemed to be getting closer. It sounded like someone dragging a pushcart down the stairs. They all watched curiously as a pair of legs appeared on the stairs followed by hips, then an upper body. In a matter of seconds Dena's best friend Monique was standing on the stoop in all her glory.

Monique was a big girl. She teetered somewhere between big-boned and fat. A baby or a cheeseburger would likely push her in the direction of the latter. Even though Monique was a size sixteen, she refused to believe she couldn't dress as provocatively as a woman who was a size eight. That morning she had squeezed into a pair of shorts that left little to the imagination and a halter that strained to hold her huge breasts. The noise everyone had heard was produced by her calf-high leather boots that sported a tall wooden heel. The zipper on the side looked like it would go at any minute, but Monique still stepped like a fashion model. In an attempt to preserve some of her decency, she wore a plaid shirt that was tied off at the stomach, but she still looked like she had just stepped off someone's stage. Monique was a big girl, but because she had a very pretty face and outgoing personality, she never found herself short of men who showered her with affection. After all, big girls needed love too, right?

"Dena, I know these hos ain't got you caught up in the drama which is this stoop?" Monique said in a deep voice that didn't quite fit her China doll face.

"Fuck outta here, like you don't spend as much time on the stoop as we do," Yvette shot back.

"What y'all doing out here so early?"

"Bout to get high." Mousy held up a Dutch Master that was still in the plastic sleeve.

"Now, you're speaking my language," Monique said, retrieving a crate that had been left in the building lobby. When she settled on the crate you could almost hear the plastic cry out for mercy.

"Mo, you know we gotta go to school," Dena said, checking the time on her cell phone.

"We'll still be on time, Dena, stop acting like that." Monique waved her off. "So," she turned to Yvette and Mousy, "I know y'all got the lowdown on what happened last night, so spill it." Just as simple as that, Monique was caught up in the gossip network, listening intently as Yvette and Mousy gave her their accounts.

Dena sighed. She knew that it would be a while before the girls finished smoking and running their mouths, and she didn't want to spend any more time around them than necessary. In an attempt to occupy some of that time, she decided to walk to the corner store for a loose cigarette.

Right next to the bodega a group of young men were shooting dice in front of the liquor store. For the most part they were a rag-tag bunch that was known to dabble in one hustle or another around the way. They made up the knucklehead population of Jefferson, with their shenanigans constantly making the block hot. In the center of the group was a young man Dena didn't want to see. She tried to slip in the store, but it was too late, as she had been spotted.

"Baby girl, wha go on?" Roots asked, in an accent that was heavier than it needed to be. Roots was a tall kid, with peanut butter skin and locks that stopped just above his lower back. He bopped towards Dena, smiling so she could see the cheap yellow gold in his mouth.

"Sup," she replied in a very disinterested tone.

"Come sis, ya no sound happy to see me. Put a smile on that pretty face." Dena gave him a fake smile and moved toward the entrance of the bodega, only to have him block her path. "Why you on it like that, sis? You know I check for you."

"Roots, you know I don't fuck with neighborhood niggaz," she said, trying to be as polite as possible. Dena, as well as most of the girls on the block, hated the pushy young Jamaican, but they tolerated him because he worked for Sosa, the local weed baron. Sosa had the best weed in a ten-block radius but didn't deal directly. If you wanted to get served you had to see Roots.

"Fuck you lie for, when I know you used to see the skinny kid down the way?" he accused.

"That was like five years ago!" she reminded him.

"Five years or five days, what should it matter? Listen, I know you like the big-money men, baby, so stop acting like you don't know what time it is." He flashed his bankroll.

Dena looked at the short stack of mostly singles and sucked her teeth. "Son, I wouldn't care if you had Bill Gates's paper, I still wouldn't fuck you." She tried once again to enter the store, but this time Roots grabbed her arm forcefully.

"Fucking tease cunt, you trying to play me?" he barked. "Bitch, I'll—"

"You'll what?" a voice asked from behind Roots.

A cold chill ran down Roots's back. Even before he turned around he knew what he would see. Standing on the curb was the equivalent of a mail box dressed in a white T-shirt and shorts that stopped just above his ankles. The owner of the voice rocked his hair cornrowed straight back, held down by a black stocking cap. Empty black eyes stared at the Jamaican, daring him to do something stupid. Roots had disrespected Shannon's little sister, and Shannon wasn't happy about it.

"Go ahead, Roots, why don't you finish telling my little sister what you'll do to her. Talk some more of that rude boy shit you was kicking a few minutes ago," Shannon dared him. By now the girls from the stoop had rushed over in anticipation of a good ass-whipping.

"Come on, man, it was a misunderstanding," Roots tried to plead out.

"That don't sound like the shit you was kicking when we walked up." Shannon's companion taunted Roots. He was slim with chocolate skin and cunning eyes. Other than Shannon, no one on the block knew much about the kid named Spooky, except that he was from Harlem, and every bit as deadly, if not more so, than Shannon.

"Yo, son, this is between them." A big-head kid from the dice game tried to come to Roots's defense against the foreigner.

Spooky spun on the kid and pointed a 9 mm at his face. "Shut the fuck up, before I dis ya stupid ass out here." The big-head kid did as he was told.

"Like I was saying," Shannon continued, looking from Roots to Dena and back again. "From what I hear, it seems like you've got a problem with my sister?"

"No problems, kid." Roots raised his hands in surrender.

"Dena?" Shannon looked to his sister.

For a minute Dena just stood there. She knew how her brother got down, so the situation was sure to turn out ugly for Roots. She started to tell Shannon that they didn't have a problem, but when she thought about how Roots had harassed her as well as other girls from the block she decided that it was finally time for someone to check his ass.

Dena folded her arms and spoke very clearly when she said, "Yeah, we got a problem."

Roots opened his mouth to dispute what she was saying, but never had a chance, because Shannon's fist came crashing into it. Shannon was shorter than Roots, so he had to swing upwards, but the blow landed true. Shannon hit Roots with a right then a left, and came back with another left. When Roots tried to cover his face, Shannon started working on his body, hitting his ribs with the force of a pro boxer.

The only thing that saved Roots was the bodega owner, Ralphy, coming out of the store. Ralphy was a Puerto Rican throwback to the Beat Street era. His socks were always pulled up to his knees and his white-on-white shell toes were cleaner than a nigga's who had just gotten out of the joint. Back in the day, Ralphy had Bushwick flooded with coke. He and his brother Juan had come down from the Bronx and clocked heavy paper in the fresh Brooklyn hood; but eventually the snitch factor came into play and both brothers found themselves property of the feds. Juan cut a deal with them, offering to take the weight for the drugs and the five murders they had them on if his brother would be shown leniency. He ended up with life plus sixty-six years, while his brother was released after serving ten. Since then Ralphy had been operating the bodega and running numbers out of the building next to it. Both were properties he had purchased before his incarceration.

Ralphy grabbed Shannon around his arms and pulled him off Roots. Shannon snarled at Ralphy, but didn't attack him. The kindly Spanish cat who owned the store had known Shannon and his family since the eighties, so there was a line of respect that he wouldn't cross, even in a blind rage. Spooky went to draw on Ralphy, but Dena gave a quick explanation of who he was, and the killer fell back.

"What the fuck, Shannon!" Ralphy yelled, looking at the bloodied Roots lying across the entrance to his store. "Did you have to beat him up on my stoop?"

Shannon took a minute to catch his breath. "My fault, Ralphy, this nigga just got a big mouth." Shannon kicked Roots for emphasis.

"Come on, come on." Ralphy pushed him back. "Shannon, get your ass up outta here before the police lock you up. Dena"—he looked to the girl—"get your fast ass off to school and stop causing trouble."

"Ralphy, I didn't do nothing!" she protested.

Ralphy looked from Roots, who was having trouble getting to his feet, back to Dena. "You never do. Just go, Dena."

Dena opened her mouth to say something but knew it was useless. "Come on, Mo," she called to her friend and started in the direction of the train station.

Mo hesitated, looking from Yvette and Mousy, who were laughing hysterically at Roots, back to Dena's departing form. "But the blunt ain't dead!"

Chapter 4

"YEAH, YOU AIN'T POPPING THAT SHIT NOW, IS you nigga?" Jah stood wide-legged in the middle of the plush living room. His arm was fully extended and locked in place at the elbow. In his hand he held a high-tech pistol with an incredibly long barrel. The anticipation of the kill made his heart beat slightly faster in his chest. He always got butterflies before he popped off. As cool as the other side of the pillow, he pulled the trigger and hit his mark.

"Blood, that was a lucky shot!" Tech accused, watching the low-bit digital duck go bug-eyed and spiral into the video grass. Busting out the old school Nintendo and playing Duck Hunt was a favorite pastime of theirs.

"What I tell you about that 'blood' shit, Tech?" Jah placed the plastic gun on the table.

"Come on, man, it's just something I say," Tech smirked.

"Dig, I ain't blood or cuz, so stop kicking that backyard boogie shit to me."

"I forgot that the only set you respect is the green side." Tech waived a dollar in the air, which Jah quickly snatched.

"Muthafucking right. Cash over colors, fool!" Jah pushed Tech playfully.

Tech was a few years younger than Jah, but had proven

to be wise beyond his years. It was good for Jah to have someone to keep him occupied, since Spooky was still running wild and kept a low profile. He was on fire in Harlem, so he spent a good deal of his time in Brooklyn with his brother Nate and his crew. The Brooklyn heads were jacking shit left and right, but only a few of them put in *real* work, until Spooky came along. When Jah asked him what was up he simply said: "I'm giving them a swagger."

The previous summer had taught him a painful lesson: Tomorrow isn't promised to anyone. His brother had killed himself in prison after murdering his son's mother, or at least who he thought was his son's mother. As it turned out Rhonda had ran a dirty game on Jah's brother, Paul, and in the end both their lives were the price; and then there was a little boy that had no parents. The grandmother stepped to the plate and took in all three of Rhonda's children. Some say that the guilt of the way she had treated her daughter in life moved her to do so. She got a monthly check from the government, and every so often an intern from Big Dawg would drop money off. Most shrugged it off as True or Don B just feeling sorry for the kids, but a select few suspected otherwise, since the paternity of little P.J. was never really figured out.

Thinking about Rhonda often made him emotional. Clearly, she was a pain in the ass, but Rhonda had her moments. For all her fucked-up ways, she loved her kids and made sure they were good. Rhonda just had a fucked-up perception of life. In the end, greed and ignorance caught up with her and she paid with her life.

All the deaths he had been touched by or brought down on himself left a bitter taste in Jah's mouth. He still made moves with Spooky, but his heart wasn't quite in it anymore. As much as he wanted to completely leave the game alone, he knew he still needed to eat. Luckily, his lady, Yoshi, was a chick whose mind was always on paper, so she taught him a way to capitalize on it.

Her job as a stylist kept her in contact with paper. Yoshi rubbed shoulders with some of the elite in the entertainment industry. A lot of these cats felt like moving around with a bodyguard would damage their street credibility, but muscle was always necessary when dealing with paper. This is where Jah came in. He could blend in with the entourage and didn't mind laying something down if the paper was right.

This kept paper rolling in for Jah, when he chose to work, but he didn't really like playing the roll of guard dog. Some of the cats he worked for were cool but the rest he could do without. To him, most of Yoshi's clients were pussies with money, trying to stunt. Jah was of a different breed and just being around them was a task.

"Why are y'all making so much noise out here?" Yoshi barked as she stormed out of the bedroom. Long dark hair with flecks of gold hung loosely around her face, curled slightly at the ends. Looking at her exotic features, you'd never have guessed she was beaten within an inch of her life less than a year ago.

"My fault," Tech said sheepishly.

Yoshi placed her hands on her almost perfectly curved hips. "Tech, what are you doing by here so early anyway, when you're supposed to be in school?"

"Come by? Shit, he never left," Jah chuckled, gunning down another duck.

Yoshi stormed across the room and stood in front of Jah, blocking his view of the video game. She was wearing a white linen shirt and tan skirt. Over her arm she had her blazer of the same color and a large makeup case was in her hand.

"Jah, why do you have Tech sitting up in here, when you know he's supposed to be in school? Its bad enough that he's getting left back again, but you're encouraging his bullshit."

Jah tried to peer around her to see the screen, but she moved with him. "Tech is a grown-ass man; I can't make him do nothing."

"He's seventeen!" She cut the television off. Yoshi turned her attention to Tech, who was watching the whole thing with an amused look on his face. "Tech, you my man fifty grand, but you know I don't condone the bullshit. Now, you ain't gotta go to school if you don't want to, but you ain't gonna lay up in here all day."

Tech shrugged his shoulders and got up off the couch. "A'ight Yoshi, I ain't trying to get that man in trouble. Jah," Tech turned and gave him a pound, "I'm out." Tech snatched a cigarette out of Jah's open pack and headed out the door. When Jah turned to go back to his video game Yoshi was shooting him a menacing glare.

"What?" he asked defensively.

"You know what!" she shot back.

Jah sighed and placed the plastic gun on the coffee table. "Yoshi, what did you want me to do, kick him out?"

"Yes. Tech needs to have his little ignorant ass in school instead of sitting up in here smoking weed and playing video games with you. You need to be more responsible."

"Whatever," Jah got up and headed into the kitchen.

Yoshi glared at his departing back. She looked around her tastefully decorated living room that now resembled a club house with empty beer bottles and overflowing ash trays. She loved Jah, but sometimes his irresponsibility and lack of motivation got on her damn nerves.

For as much of a pain as Jah could be, Yoshi couldn't deny that he had won over parts if her heart that no other man could think of sniffing. Back in those days she was shaking her ass at various strip clubs and trimming cats for their bread. Her mentality back then was "I don't give a fuck, if it's about a buck." Her outlook was drastically changed when she was beaten and gang raped by a scorned trick and his minions. After that she felt so low in life that nothing could pick her up, until Jah.

Up until then she had never seen him as much more than Paul's wild-ass little brother, but Jah showed her a much deeper side. It touched her how he could give so much of himself and not ask for anything in return, but it was his passion that made her love him.

After the rape, death rode Harlem like a dark horse—with Jah holding the reigns. All of Yoshi's attackers and those close to them met horrible deaths. Though Jah never admitted to it, the word on the street was that his vengeance was of legendary proportions. When he put her mental demons to rest he helped her reconstruct her physical self. He hovered over her like a guardian until Yoshi felt like she was ready to face the world again, but this time she wouldn't have to do it alone.

Yoshi loved having a man to pamper her the way Jah did, but she sometimes felt selfish about it. Jah was a wolf, and she knew the call of the pack rang heavy in his ears; but he still put her first, which was no easy task for a man like Jah. He was a predator, and the block was his jungle. Being away from that was, in a sense, removing a piece of who he was, and it showed in the way he hung around the house smoking weed with Tech. He and Spooky still made moves, but Jah wasn't in the thick anymore.

Once Yoshi was well again she was back on her paper chase, but she wasn't stripping anymore. True had gotten her a job doing wardrobe and makeup on video sets, to try and make up for what had happened. Though he wasn't a part of the act, he felt guilty because they were his crew. It didn't take long for record execs to recognize Yoshi's fashion sense, and she found herself doing plenty of freelance work. Yoshi became known as an up-and-coming stylist and everyone wanted to work with her. In no time, Yoshi was back to doing what she did best, stack cheese.

Being that Yoshi was now in the entertainment business, she rubbed elbows with a lot of heavyweights, some not being the most savory characters. She instantly saw the potential in it for Jah and plugged him. Jah was making anywhere from three to five thousand a night just to hang around. Every once in a while he might have to slap somebody, but hell, he'd been doing that for free since Yoshi knew him. Things went well at first, but after a while Jah seemed to lose interest and withdrew to the apartment. Now, Jah did his part and they weren't strapped for cash, but having him around the house 24/7 was starting to blow hers.

"Where're you off to," Jah said as he came out of the kitchen with a forty-ounce in his hand.

"Work," she said, snatching her keys off the coffee table. "Stacks Green and his crew are shooting a video in the city this week, and they've got that grudge match with Don B's team at the King Dome next weekend. He said he tried to call you about doing security but you haven't called him back."

"I'll get around to it," Jah said unenthusiastically. Jah had indeed gotten the message Stacks's assistant had left him, but he chose not to return the call. Stacks Green was an up-and-coming dude from Houston's rap scene. His single, "Golds and 44s," was getting heavy rotation on every station and he had already shot two videos without even having a record deal. Who needed label money when you had the block?

Word had it that Stacks Green put the *D* in Dope Boy. He had North Houston leaning and rocking off the shit he was putting on the streets. Still, Stacks was wise enough to know that the streets wouldn't be forever, so he ventured into music. He had started out as just being the CEO, but after loosing his main act to federal prison he had to put on another hat. The bugged-out thing was that the boy was dead nice. He had a New York flow, with a twang of the south. The best part was that he never ran out of material, because he was still heavy in the streets.

Stacks and his crew were certified street niggaz and he always paid like he weighed, but Jah just didn't like him personally. Stacks was loud, arrogant, and sneaky. More to the point, he didn't like how the man looked at Yoshi. An admiring look he could tolerate, but there was a hunger in his eyes that Jah didn't like, especially after what Yoshi had already gone through. Stacks was an arrogant muthafucka who thought his paper entitled him to any- and everything he wanted. Jah knew that if he ever got out of pocket with Yoshi he was going to kill him, so he saved himself the trouble and just avoided him.

"What's with this chip you've got on your shoulder?" Yoshi asked.

"What you talking about, boo?"

"Jah, you know what I'm talking about. Every time you get around Stacks or someone mentions his name you get all funny style."

"I don't know what you're talking about, Yoshi. If I don't like the nigga, I don't like him. Ain't no funny business about it."

"I hear that Jah, but let me give you some advice: Stacks might be an asshole, but he's got long dough. For some reason you make him feel safe. Now, I don't know what done crawled up your ass, but you better pull it out and call the nigga back. These lights ain't gonna keep themselves on."

Jah turned around and glared at her. The storm clouds brewing in his eyes made her take a step back. "Who the fuck do you think you're talking to?" He slithered out of the chair and in her direction. "Yoshi, don't I do what the fuck I gotta do to hold us down?"

"Calm down, Jah, I'm not saying you don't, but—"

"But shit!" he cut her off. "You standing here telling about why the fuck I should be so quick to accept a handout from that fat muthafucka. When did you become president of the fan club?"

"Slow ya roll, Jah." She matched his tone. "First of all, I ain't the president of nobody's fan club but my own. Furthermore, all I'm trying to tell you is not to let your feelings fuck with your pocket, that's a fool's move."

Jah bit his bottom lip. "Well, pardon me for not having long dough, but I ain't hurting for no change, know what I mean? Even sitting in here playing nursemaid I do a'ight for myself." He regretted it as soon as he said it.

"Word, Jah?" Her words were just above a whisper.

"Yoshi, I didn't mean it how it sounded." He tried to correct himself but the damage was already done.

"Nah, you meant it just like you said it. But let me tell you something, Jahlil, I am now and always have been an independent bitch. Whether I was shaking my ass or shaking a nigga's pocket, I did it on my own. Now, I love you and appreciate everything you've been to me, but if you don't wanna be here I ain't gonna hold you." Yoshi didn't even give him a chance to respond before she was out the door.

Chapter **5**

WITH THE AFTERNOON FINALLY ARRIVING, SO did the crowd. The quiet stoops were now beginning to draw people as the partygoers and general late-risers were finally coming out of their apartments.

Shannon sat on the stoop of his building between a pair of succulent chocolate thighs. The thighs belonged to a neighborhood tender named Shakira, who was busy braiding his hair. Shakira was nineteen years old and built like a porn star. Her breasts were so big that buying a Victoria's secret bra was out of the question for her. Niggaz on the block had been trying to hit that since she moved around the summer before, but Shannon's game had prevailed where others didn't.

Shakira played naïve but she was far from it. Growing up in Red Hook and having two aunts that sold pussy taught her a lot about getting where she needed to be. She knew Shannon was that nigga on the block and therefore the one she would let break her in. Shannon had pounded that pussy up, down, and sideways and always came back. Shakira had a shot to die for and a head game that put a lot of grown women to shame.

"Damn Shakira." Shannon flinched as she ran the comb through a tangle of hair in the back.

"Don't get mad at me, nigga; take better care of your hair. If you would perm this bitch once in a while it might be easier to deal with," Shakira shot back.

Shannon leaned forward and craned his neck to look at her. "What the fuck do I look like, running around with a perm in my hair? That's some Harlem shit."

"Watch that," Spooky said playfully.

"My fault, Harlem," Shannon smiled. "Your brother take that shit to heart, don't he, Nate?"

"You know he do," Nate replied. Nate was Spooky's older brother. He was six-two and had the physique of a boxer. While Spooky was raised with his mother in Harlem, Nate was raised with their father in Brooklyn. Though they lived in different boroughs and had two different mothers, their father made sure they spent time together growing up.

"Word life, y'all some cool niggaz, but you know I'm Harlem to the heart." Spooky pounded his chest.

"So what you doing down here with these niggaz?" Shakira saw this as an opportunity to pick the mysterious Spooky's brain.

Spooky shrugged. "Ain't nothing, just kicking it with my brother."

"I'll bet," she said, not believing him. Unlike Nate who liked to brag on his exploits, Spooky kept his hand close to his chest.

"What's up y'all?" Yvette walked up. She was wearing a pair of royal blue pajama pants with yellow ducks on them. Her socks were crispy white, but the flip-flops she wore were dingy as hell.

"Vette, what's popping?" Shannon gave her dap.

"Just waking up from earlier," she said, stretching. Because she wasn't wearing a bra you could clearly see her silver-dollar nipples pressing against her white T-shirt. Yvette might've been a rough chick, but her body was crazy. She had no kids, so her stomach was for the most part flat, and she had just enough ass that you could grip a fist full while hitting it from the back.

"Harlem, let me get a bone?" Yvette said to Spooky, startling him. He didn't know if she'd noticed him sizing her up, but she gave him a real mischievous look.

"This my last one." He handed her the cigarette he was smoking.

"That's the best part." She pressed her lips to the butt and took a deep pull. There was a challenging look in her eyes that made Spooky's groin warm. "Where the weed at?" She addressed the entire stoop.

Spooky went to say something, but Shakira beat him to the punch. "How much you got on it?" she asked, not bothering to hide the sarcasm in her voice. She didn't like Yvette because she was always around Shannon. Even though he wasn't her man, Shakira felt like she had papers on his dick, which was absurd.

Yvette ignored Shakira. "I know you got that good shit on you, Harlem?" She addressed Spooky.

"I keeps that Barney, ma. Go get a Dutch and we can burn something," he said coolly.

"That's a bet." Yvette stepped off the curb.

"Stank bitch," Shakira mumbled, after Yvette was out of earshot.

"Fuck is up wit you and Vette?" Shannon asked.

"I just don't like the bitch," she replied.

"Damn, Shannon, you got these hos bout to squab over you," Nate teased.

"Nigga, I ain't no ho!" Shakira snaked her neck.

A little boy with a half moon cut into his hair ran past the stoop, with a skinny light-skinned kid on his heels. The light-skinned kid hurled rocks at the other kid, nearly hitting Nate.

"Booby, you better watch where the fuck you throwing them rocks, before I kick your little ass," Nate grumbled.

"Nigga, you ain't gonna do shit!" Little Booby stuck his tongue out and ran off.

"I'm gonna kick your ass when I catch you!" Nate called after the fleeing little boy.

"These is some disrespectful little muthafuckas," Shakira said, as if she were a model citizen. "They bum-ass mama need to teach them some fucking manners."

"You better not let Shirley hear you talking about her kids. You know she be tripping," Shannon teased her.

"Shannon, I don't know why you think it's something sweet about me? What, do I gotta lay one of these bitches out before you finally take me seriously?"

"Go ahead with that, Shakira." Shannon waved her off as he watched Yvette jog back to the stoop. Her breasts bounced under her T-shirt, giving all the men sitting there food for thought. Shakira also picked up on it, and she only got more irritated.

"I hope you know how to roll a Dutch?" Yvette asked, tossing Spooky the cigar.

Spooky smiled, which was something he didn't do often. "You got jokes, ma. Take a seat and pay attention, you might learn something."

Yvette shook her head. "Y'all Harlem niggaz stay popping shit. Yo, Shakira, slide over some so I can sit down." She motioned at a spot next to Shannon.

Shakira sucked her teeth. "Damn, why you trying to squeeze all between me and my man? Nah, ain't enough room on this stoop."

No sooner than she finished her sentence, the whole block seemed to get quiet. Everyone on the block knew Yvette to be one of the coolest chicks out, but they also knew her to be a warrior. For Shakira to come out in her face like that, she must've had a mean knuckle game.

"Excuse you?" Yvette rocked back on her heels.

"I ain't stutter. It's too tight over here for you to be squeezing between me and my man," Shakira reiterated.

Feeling the mounting tension, Spooky stepped off the stoop and over to the side where Nate was standing. Nosy bystanders moved closer to the center so they wouldn't miss a good fight. Yvette glared at Shakira like she had lost her last mind. She gave Shannon a questioning look and he just shrugged his shoulders.

"What you looking at him for, he ain't my daddy," Shakira said, getting up from behind Shannon and moving down a step.

"Little girl, if you step off that stoop you're going to lay on it," Yvette said very calmly.

"Word, bitch?" Shakira took a step off the stoop, and before the other foot hit the pavement Yvette hit her. She laced Shakira with a left hook to the cheek, knocking her into the gate. Shakira bounced off the gate and came out swinging. Yvette could fight her ass off, but Shakira was a healthy girl. She clipped Yvette on the side of the head, dazing her. Yvette moved to swing, but Shakira was a little quicker. She caught Yvette twice in the face, but couldn't lay her out. Yvette faked a right and came with a left. Before Shakira could get her head right Yvette threw a haymaker and knocked her into the trash.

"Yeah, told your ass you'd lay on it!" Yvette said, sounding winded.

It took a second for Shakira to shake off the cobwebs, but when she was able to focus she saw Shannon looking down at her from the stoop with a smirk on his face. This added to Shakira's rage as she came lunging at Yvette with a bottle in her hand. Faster than anyone's eyes could follow Yvette whipped her blade out and put it in motion. She gave Shakira a half moon across the forearm, producing a wail that sounded like a scalded child. With rage in her heart, Yvette went to cut Shakira across the face when Nate grabbed her from behind.

"Get the fuck off me, Nate!" Yvette snarled, trying to kick at Shakira.

"Chill, ma, its over." Nate tried to sooth her.

Shakira tried to go in for a hit while Yvette was being restrained but Shannon grabbed her roughly by the arm. "Don't even go about it like that, Shakira. It's over."

"I'm gonna kill that bitch!" Shakira struggled against him.

"No, you're not." Shannon fished around in his pocket and came up with a fifty-dollar bill, which he placed into her palm. "You're gonna go to the hospital and get your arm looked at."

Shakira's arm was stinging and blood was starting to drip onto her shirt. She tried to give Shannon a fierce look, but he had an unwavering coldness to his eyes that made her look away. "A'ight." She crushed the bill in her fist. "This shit ain't over though." Shakira stalked back down the block to her building.

Yvette waited until Shakira was out of sight before turning back to Shannon and company. "Does this mean we ain't getting high?"

Shannon just shook his head. "You Jefferson broads are something else."

Chapter **6**

THE END OF THE SCHOOL DAY COULDN'T HAVE come fast enough for Dena. Once again the air conditioning wasn't working and the windowless classes were hot as hell. She would've ditched her last few classes, but she had a math test in eighth period that she couldn't miss. The moment it was over she was out, end of class or not.

As she stepped out of the school's side exit the afternoon sun stroked her cheeks. Squinting, she threw her shades on and made her way to the side of the school where her team always gathered. Sure enough, Sharon was leaning against the brown brick like a ghetto Naomi Campbell.

Sharon was a Harlem chick and wore it with pride. Normally, the girls from different boroughs didn't really click, but Sharon's young ass had a swag that made Dena take to her. She was a tall drink of water with peanut butter skin and long legs and serious attitude. Sharon was young, but carried herself like a worldly woman. She was always fresh to death and seemed to know everyone in her hood. Hanging uptown with Sharon was how Dena met her man Lance, or Lazy, as they called him.

They had been sitting on a stoop off 112th and Lenox, smoking with some guys they knew, when Lazy came out of the building. From the arrogant smirk on his chestnut face he knew he was killing em in a pair of creased, blue Pepe's and a Detroit Red-wings' hockey jersey. The killer part of his fit was the red and white Nike Airs with the Big Dawg logo airbrushed on the side. He spoke to Sharon but didn't acknowledge Dena.

Two days later the location was 115th, but the cast was the same. This time Lazy came coasting up on a motorized scooter, circling Dena and Sharon. Dena stared him down as he did her, returning the vibe. He finally stopped spinning on the scooter and introduced him-self. From the word go, Dena was taken with the young man and he with her. They were from two very different boroughs, but the chem-istry between them was quite natural. She was a smart, streetwise chick from Brooklyn, and he was a young dude with a very bright future.

"Dena-D, what it is?" Sharon greeted her.

"Trying to keep from melting in all this damn heat." Dena fanned herself. "I see you're dressed for the occasion though."

"You know a bitch gotta be prepared." Sharon did a little twirl so Dena could take in the whole fit. She was rocking a short white tennis skirt with a blue-and-white polo shirt and the matching Stan Smith's. Sharon, like her mother and sister, was blessed with a body. The most outstanding part of her outfit was the iced-out ankle bracelet.

"Somebody ass is looking like money," Dena said, eying the ankle bracelet.

"Just a little present from one of my shorties," Sharon said, hold-ing her leg up so Dena could get a better look. "You like?"

"That shit is fly!"

"You know Harlem is the freshest borough; all we do is rest and dress." Sharon snapped her fingers. "If you play your cards right I might introduce you to one of his peoples."

"Listen to your little hot ass," Dena teased her.

"I get it from my mama," Sharon shot back. "Anyway, what you bout to get into?"

"I'm supposed to be hooking up with Lazy," Dena told her.

"Romeo and Juliet, back at it," Sharon teased her.

"Don't hate cause me and my man do more than clock the hourly rates at the Liberty."

"Dena, don't play yourself. I ain't never been no Liberty bitch, it's the Marriot or nothing."

"I know that's right." Dena gave Sharon a high five. "So where the weed at?"

"You know Harlem got that *real* sticky. You ready to take that trip?"

Dena thought about it for a minute. "Nah, I can't boogie just yet. I'm trying to give Lazy the benefit of the doubt." She dialed him on the cell, but got no answer. She hoped that he was at least on the train en route to get her.

"I'll bet. What y'all doing?"

"Probably go get something to eat after we catch *Dreamgirls*," Dena told her.

"That shit still playing?" Sharon asked, knowing that the movie was months old.

"Only in certain spots. I went on the Internet and found a theater in the Village that's still showing it."

"Y'all'd be better off getting the bootleg," Sharon said. "Where that fat bitch Mo at?"

"Better watch ya mouth before she hear you and put them things on ya lil ass," Dena teased her.

"Knock it off, D. Mo is my bitch, but you know I get busy."

"You get busy, but I catch wreck," Mo said as she came down the stairs. She had a burning Newport hanging from her lips and a Haitian kid named Hans on her heels.

"So what's up, baby, you gonna stop playing and come see me or what?" Hans asked in a heavy accent. His slim frame rocked from side to side making sure she saw the gold chain dangling from his neck.

"I'll think about it," Monique said seductively. "As a matter of fact, I need you to do me a solid."

"Whatever you need, baby, I got you." Hans licked his lips.

Monique leaned in and began whispering into Hans's ear, letting her tongue graze his lobe. By the time she was finished Hans was on his way up the block with his boys and Mo had two dime sacks of chocolate in her purse.

"Now, that's how you do business," Mo said, giving Dena and Sharon high fives.

"My bitch is always on her job!" Sharon laughed.

"Somebody gotta be," Mo capped back. "What you bitches doing standing around like you selling pussy?"

"You got the nerve, looking like you fresh off the track." Sharon pinched the front of Monique's shorts.

"If that ain't the damn pot. Your butt is too big to be tucked up under that short-ass skirt." Monique nodded at the skirt that Sharon had to pull down in the back every so often. Had a strong gust of wind came through, the whole world would've been able to see her panties, if she was even wearing any.

"Don't hate, bitch."

"Whatever, ho," Mo shot back.

"Why don't y'all cut it out?" Dena cut in, sounding a little annoyed.

"What the hell is your problem?" Mo asked.

"Lazy got her ass waiting again." Sharon volunteered.

"Why don't you mind your damn business?" Dena snapped.

Mo just shook her head. "Dena, I don't know why you're mad at her. You need to be mad at yourself."

"Myself? What the hell for?"

"Because you let him set you up for the bullshit every time."

"Mo, you don't know what you're talking about," Dena said, dialing him again and still getting no answer.

Monique folded her arms across her large breasts. "Baby girl, you and I both know that's the biggest lie ever told. Don't get it fucked up, D, I got love for Lazy, too, but the boy ain't never on time. Its like I told you before, niggaz don't do shit quick but cum."

"Amen to that!" Sharon gave Mo a high five.

"Fuck the both of y'all." Dena tried to front like she wasn't tight, but inside she was steaming. She hadn't seen Lazy in almost a week, but she understood he had business to handle, so she didn't complain.

Lazy was on his grind, and she was cool with that as long as she got some quality time in with him, but that seemed to have gone to the left. She had been waiting all week to see *Dreamgirls* with him and he had pulled another no-show, something he was starting to do pretty regularly. Lazy had never been the most prompt person, but he was fucking up more and more as of late. Dena's mind told her that something wasn't right, but her heart wouldn't allow her to accept it. Dena had guy friends that she allowed to spend paper on her, but Lazy was her heart. Just the thought that he might be fucking someone else made her nauseous.

"Fuck that. Y'all can stand around here all afternoon if you want to, but I'm taking my ass uptown. A bitch gotta get her sexy on, for tonight anyway," Sharon told them.

"Tonight, what's popping uptown?" Mo asked anxiously.

Sharon looked at her in disbelief. "Damn, y'all don't get cable in Brooklyn? Stacks Green is in town shooting his video, so you know all the ballers are coming out in full force."

"That Texas nigga with all the gold in his mouth?" Dena asked.

"It's platinum now, baby. They're gonna be in New York all week, doing it up."

"Now you know I gotta be there," Mo said, checking her hair in her compact mirror. "Somebody has got to show you Harlem bitches how to stunt. I gotta jet back to the crib and get fly. D, you rolling?"

Dena thought on it for a minute. Lazy was already twenty minutes late, so it was obvious that he was on his bullshit, and it made no sense to stand around and wait on his tired ass. "Fuck it, come on."

"That's what I'm talking about," Sharon said excitedly. "Y'all bitches hurry up though, cause the 40/40 Club is supposed to be jumping tonight, too."

Dena gave her a confused look. "Sharon, you know damn well we ain't old enough to get into the 40/40."

"Stop being a lame, Dena, you know I wouldn't put it out there if I didn't have a plan," Sharon told her.

"Say no more. Lets get up outta here," Dena said, leading her crew to the train station.

. . .

TWENTY-TWO BLOCKS SOUTH, A FAMILIAR face was descend-
ing the steps of the two-thirty Greyhound bus, just arrived from
Charlotte, North Carolina. He had long since shed his braids, and
twenty pounds due to stress, but for the most part Larry Love looked
the same.

For the last few months he had been selling crack out of a housing
project in Greensborough. Marlene was less than pleased with the
stunt Larry had pulled and had spared no expense trying to have him
captured and prosecuted for it; but the hustler was always one step
ahead of her. He'd sold the car and added the cash to the money he'd
fleeced from her and used it to buy cocaine. Larry had a cousin who
was already doing his thing down in N.C., so it was easy for him to
get established; but staying that way proved to be something different. It didn't take long before some young wolves ran in the crib and
put two in Larry's cousin, taking all the work and the money. If it
wasn't for the fact that Larry had been out tricking on a bitch that
night, he'd be dead, too. Not one to take a blessing for granted, he
made tracks back north.

When Larry exited the Port Authority he almost expected Paul to
be standing there waiting for him, like old times, but he wasn't.
Larry's betrayal had helped to contribute to that. Never in a million
years did he think that Paul would off himself, but he had. The strain
of what had happened with his son, or not-son, was coupled with
Larry and Marlene's betrayal. If Larry could've done it all over again,
he'd have never fucked Marlene, because the price that came with it
was higher than he was ready to pay. Every time he thought about
how he had done his man he cried, but there was no amount of tears
that could bring back the dead.

Larry hadn't even known he was crying until the warm tear hit his
cheek. Wiping it away, he made his way out of the station and lost
himself in the crowd.

Chapter 7

THOUGH IT WAS THE MIDDLE OF THE AFTER-
noon, the room was almost completely dark, save for the
thin beam that managed to shine through the small space
between the heavy drapes. The smell of Egyptian musk in-
cense hung in the air, but you could still pick up the sweet
smell of purple haze beneath.

In the center of the room was a vision of a ghetto queen.
Her long weave was pinned to the top of her head, but a few
strands had managed to snake their way loose. Dressed in
nothing but a purple, laced thong and thigh-high hooker
boots, you could properly appreciate her large but healthy
breasts and extra-large booty. She was slowly swaying to
the raspy sounds of Lyfe's "S.E.X," totally lost in the music.

Lazy was resting on one elbow amongst silken throw
pillows like he was the prince of Persia. His ebony skin almost blended perfectly against the black satin sheets. His
hair was neatly braided into two French braids that curved
behind his earlobes. The half-smoked blunt hanging from
his mouth bobbed every time his full lips curved into a
smile. If his boys could see him, they would surely say he
was the man; but they didn't have to, because he already
knew it.

"You like this, Daddy?" she asked, turning around so he could get a better view of her ass.

"You know I do, ma. Make that shit clap for me," he said in a smooth voice.

She dropped down on all fours and cocked her ass in the air. The young lady began popping her ass up and down on the carpeted floor, causing the cheeks to clap together in a seductive rhythm. Wanting to impress her man, she began popping one cheek at a time in tune with the bass of the song. Slowly she slid further down, spreading her legs until she was in a T position. Moving her thong to the side so he could get a better view, she began opening and closing her pussy lips like it was a fish gasping for air. Looking over her shoulder, she slid one hand around to the back and began sliding her middle finger in and out of her gaping sex.

"Do that shit, girl," Lazy hissed, stroking his dick with his free hand.

From the thirsty look in his eye she knew she had him where she wanted him. She flipped over onto her back and began finger-fucking herself from the front. Her finger and inner thighs were wet with her juices, making it easier for her to get two more fingers inside. At various speeds she jacked her fingers in and out of her box, making a sloshing noise. By now Lazy's dick was so hard that the front of his Nautica sweat pants looked like a tent, but his face was as cool as the other side of the pillow. Never taking her eyes off of him, she began to crawl on all fours towards the bed.

"Umm, is all that for me?" she asked, rubbing her palm over his erection through his sweats.

"That depends on what you're willing to do for it," he teased, sliding back a little further onto the bed.

"Baby, you know I'd do anything for this sweet candy."

"Is that right?" he asked, pulling his penis free and stroking it openly. Though Lazy was a slim dude, his dick resembled a blackened salami roll. He ran his hand up and down his shaft while she looked on in anticipation.

"Anything, Daddy, just let me have a little bit." She had gone from sounding like a seductress to a fiend in need of a hit.

Lazy paused as if he was pondering something deep, then looked down at her and said, "Suck this dick."

The command had barely left his mouth before she was on him. She took his thick dick in her hand and gently began running the tip of her tongue around the head. Her mouth felt like a warm spring as she licked and teased him, letting saliva run down the shaft and over her hand. Though Lazy's dick was wide, she had no problems stuffing it into her greedy mouth. The top half went in with ease, yet, getting the rest in proved to be a task; but she loved a good challenge. After two attempts she managed to take almost all of him into her mouth and Lazy felt like he had just stepped into another world.

Skillfully she relaxed the muscles in her throat and took in his entire length. She let him tickle her tonsils before pulling up and going back down again. The wetter his dick got, the easier it got to slip into the back of her throat. Lazy grabbed the back of her weave and began fucking her mouth like it was his first piece of pussy. A less seasoned female would've gagged, but she took it like a soldier, slurping him like a Bomb Pop on a summer day. Sucking dick was one of her favorite pastimes, and she blew Lazy like his was the last dick on the planet.

"Ooh, that's what I'm talking about! Shit, I'm bout to cum!" he whimpered. She tried to pull her head away, but Lazy held fast. With a grunt, his body went stiff and he blew his wad in her mouth.

"That was some bullshit." Michelle sat crossed-legged on the floor, wiping her mouth with the back of her hand.

"My fault, ma. That shit was so good I couldn't hold it," Lazy said with a smug grin.

"I'll bet. Well, do what you gotta do to get it hard again so I can get mine." She attempted to straddle him, but Lazy pushed her off him. "Word, it's like that now?" she said with a major attitude.

"Michelle, I got a move to make right quick. Real talk, I'ma beat that pussy into submission tonight though."

"Lance," she called him by his government, "you know I gotta work the night shift at the hospital tonight, so don't try to beat me in the head." She crawled over to him and started tugging at his sweat pants. "Now, slide back and act like you know, so I can ride this donkey."

"Later," he said, standing up and brushing past her. "I'll come by the hospital on your break and fuck you in the linen closet like we did the last time." He tried to kiss her on the forehead but she moved away. "Why you acting like that?"

"Cause you be on some bullshit. You fuck my weave up and bust in my mouth and you trying to tell me I can't get mine? You know what, fuck it," she said, getting up off the floor. "I don't know why I continue to fuck around with young niggaz, it takes too damn much to train you."

She tried to get a reaction out of Lazy, but at best he just raised his eyebrow. "Michelle, I told you before and I'll tell you again, if you feel like that, do what you do. I got love for you, boo, but I ain't never been the nigga to cuff a shorty."

"I know, cause all I'm good for is fucking and hitting you wit paper," she said scornfully.

"First of all, I was a young, fly nigga when you met me, so miss me wit the bullshit. Second of all, you know I got love for you, but I ain't gonna keep bumping my head against the wall trying to prove it. Accept my love or don't." He shrugged his shoulders and walked into the bathroom.

MICHELLE WAS SO MAD THAT she had to stuff her face into a pillow to muffle the roar she let out. She was horny as hell, and Lazy had the nerve to leave her hanging. If it had been the first time, she might've considered letting the slight go, but he was starting to do it more often. Back when they first met he used to love to fuck her. She could suck him off for a half-hour straight and he would still climb in her pussy and tear the walls down. Now it was becoming a task to get more than a fifteen- to twenty-minute romp out of him. She should've listened to her friends when they told her not to fuck that young boy.

She had met Lazy three months ago when he came through the emergency room of Harlem Hospital, where she worked as a triage nurse. His boy had took a shot in the thigh and was bleeding all over himself. Because he didn't have insurance, the staff didn't move as fast as they could've to treat him. Sympathizing with their situation, Michelle shuffled the paperwork and got Lazy's man taken care of. To show his appreciation, Lazy brought her a plate from Manna's when she took her dinner break. From the conversation, she knew he was trying to get at her, but it wasn't until they got a little deeper into it that she saw promise in the young boy.

Lazy was a young cat with a hustler's spirit. He had a wisdom about him that you didn't see much in men his age. Of course he was a street nigga, but he was still in school. Lazy got so-so grades, but his skill on the basketball court balanced the scales a bit. He was a six-six guard, and was cooking cats on the high school circuit. It would've been a stretch to say that he was one of the more high-profile recruits, but scouts were definitely paying attention.

Michelle immediately saw the potential in giving him a little taste of her goodies. She made her own money and wasn't pressed for cash, but it was obvious to a duck that Lazy was destined for great things. He was a knucklehead that just needed a little direction. In him she saw a young cat that could be molded to be the heroin lover that she had always dreamt about—but she often wondered if his bullshit was a fair trade on the reward.

LAZY CLOSED THE DOOR BEHIND him and made sure to lock it. It wasn't unlike Michelle to come barging into the bathroom to catch him in there for some dick. Home girl was a freak to the third power. He had fucked older women before, but Michelle gave him a crash course in *real* sex. She did everything from fucking him in public to licking his ass. Michelle's shot was without a doubt the best he had ever had, and he'd tell anyone that, but she was moving too fast for him. Being eight years older than him, Michelle was a bit more seasoned and focused. While Lazy was thinking about fucking girls and running the streets, her mind was on building a foundation . . . which, as there was nothing wrong with that, he just wasn't interested in doing with her. For as good as Michelle's pussy was, Lazy's heart was elsewhere.

After cutting on the shower to drown out his voice if Michelle was ear-hustling, he called Dena. He knew she had her heart set on seeing *Dreamgirls*, but he had been so caught up with Michelle that he'd lost track of time. The phone rang three of four times before going to voice mail. The next two calls didn't even ring, just straight to the service. *Yeah, she's pissed.*

Of all the chicks Lazy dealt with, not one of them had his heart the way Dena did. She was smart, sexy, and about her business. Dena, too, encouraged Lazy to do something with his talent, but she also knew how to play her position and leave something alone if he wasn't receptive to it. She reasoned that Lazy would see the wisdom in her words or he wouldn't.

"Fuck it," Lazy said, placing his phone on top of the toilet seat and stripping for his shower. Dena would get over it, she always did.

Chapter 8

"COME ON, GET BACK ON D!" BILLY SHOUTED from the sidelines. "Y'all moving like molasses out there, lets pick up the pace."

"Coach, we've been running the same play for almost a half hour. Can we get a rest?" a young man with tiny boxed braids in his head asked.

"If y'all would get it right then you wouldn't have to run it so many times. Keep running." She popped him playfully in the head. Dressed in a tank top and sweat pants, some of the young men found themselves slightly distracted by their new coach. Billy looked like an Eye Candy model, but carried herself like the Gooch from *Diff'rent Strokes*. Some of the new players looked at the pretty young lady quizzically, as if they didn't know whether to take her seriously or not, but the ones that knew her reputation did as they were told.

Coaching the thirteen-and-under team was something that she had recently taken on. Between coaching, attending BMCC, working, and balancing her personal life she hardly had time for sleep, but it didn't bother her too much. Billy had seen firsthand what could happen to kids who didn't have positive outlets, and it wasn't pretty.

The summer before, she had endured the murder of one

of her closest friends, the rape of another, and the suicide of a cat she had known for ages. All this while trying to make sense of her fucked-up life. After the brutal murder of her boyfriend, Sol, she thought she'd never find love in the arms of a man again, but was shown the light by the most unlikely person.

"Stop talking to them kids like that," Marcus said as he strolled into the gym like he owned it. He wore a tight-fitting red-and-black motorcycle jacket and carried the matching helmet in his hand. A thin film of sweat coated his face, giving him a slight glow, and increasing his already intoxicating sex appeal.

"If they'd run the plays like I drew them up I wouldn't have to scream at them," Billy said before kissing him passionately. A couple of the boys snickered, but a quick look from their coach sent them back to running the play.

"Sweet as candy," Marcus said, licking the leftover moisture from his upper lip. Marcus was a former knucklehead who turned himself into a legitimate businessman. He owned a strip club and a Laundromat, and he had money invested into several other ventures. Though he had long ago squared up, he still had that thug swagger about him, which turned Billy on to no end. That's why he was the first cat to get the pussy in the last couple of years.

"You keep talking like that and I might give you some head tonight," she whispered, brushing herself against him. "What're you doing here?"

"I came to see if my lady wanted to ride on my chariot," he grinned.

Billy glanced at his helmet. "Not if you're on that death-mobile."

"Quit being a punk."

"Call me what you want, but that still ain't gonna get me on that thing."

"Well, maybe I can get you to ride on this thing." He grabbed her hand and tried to place it on his crotch, but she snatched it away.

"Don't do that in front of the kids."

Marcus looked over at the players, who were trying to pretend they weren't being nosy. "Man, this ain't nothing they ain't never seen. Hell, most of them probably get more pussy than I do."

"You keep talking reckless and that's gonna be a true statement."

"Anyway"—he sucked his teeth—"you going to class from here, or you wanna catch a flick?"

"Nah, I don't have class tonight. Me and Reese are supposed to hook up. We'll probably go out for some drinks or something."

"She better be careful; you remember what happened the last time she got drunk," he joked, but Billy didn't laugh. "Boo, you know I was just kidding." He reached for her but she jerked away.

"Well, you've got a fucked-up sense of humor. That girl has been through a lot," Billy said with hostility. Poor Reese had made the mistake of getting twisted with a group of young rappers and letting them run a train on her, which resulted in an unwanted pregnancy and an STD. Thankfully, she gave birth to a healthy baby girl, but the identity of the father was never discovered.

Marcus's head dipped a bit. "Sorry. That was foul."

"Just like a nigga." She shook her head. "I swear, y'all are so insensitive when it comes to certain shit. What if that had been you?"

"I don't think I'd have been too upset if I had fucked five or six chicks at one time," he snickered. This earned him a hook to the ribs.

"So I ain't enough woman for you?" she snapped.

"Billy, you know I didn't mean it like that." He rubbed his ribs. "Why you getting so uptight?"

"Cause you don't know what to say out ya mouth sometimes, Marcus!" Some of the kids were starting to look, so Billy lowered her voice. "Look, why don't you just go wherever you were going and I'll catch up with you later."

"A'ight, boo. I'ma get up outta here," he said, leaning in to kiss her on the lips, but she gave him her cheek. "Oh, its like that?"

"Its how you made it," she said flatly.

"I hear that, Billy," he said as he left the gym.

Billy stared at his departing back so hard that it's a wonder she didn't burn a hole in it. For the most part, Marcus was a very caring and sensitive man, but every so often that ignorant-ass street nigga peeked out. She hated it, but she knew at the end of the day it didn't define who he really was. Regaining her composure, she turned her attention back to the court.

. . .

MARCUS STEPPED OUT OF THE gym feeling like a complete ass. He meant the statement to be a joke, but Billy had caught feelings behind it. The way her moods changed frustrated him to no end. Sometimes they'd be laughing and having a good time and in the next instance she would withdraw or become angry. He tried to be understanding, in light of all she had gone through, but it didn't make it any easier to deal with.

When he stepped out into the afternoon sun he peeped two young ladies admiring his red-and-black Yamaha. One wore a short skirt, while the other had a pumpkin-sized ass stuffed into a pair of jeans that were so tight that they looked liked they might rip if she bent over. They didn't look to be more than seventeen or eighteen, but they turned very seasoned eyes in his direction as he approached.

"This your bike?" the one in the skirt asked.

"Yeah," Marcus said, easing past them and mounting the motorcycle. Though he tried to ignore their stares, they were both eying him like the last supper.

"Why don't you spin us around the block?" Jeans asked.

Marcus pulled his helmet on, leaving the visor up. "First of all, I ain't never heard of three people on a bike at the same time. Second, I don't think you could handle all this horsepower." He patted the bike.

"I never met a horse I couldn't ride," Jeans shot back.

"I'll bet," Marcus snickered.

"I'm saying though, why don't you give me a number or something so I can get at you later?" the skirt cut in.

"Nah, I don't think my girl would like that."

"What ya girl don't know won't hurt her," Jeans said.

"Yeah, but if she finds out she might hurt you. One, shorty." Marcus revved the engine and peeled the bike into traffic.

CLICK. CLICK. CLICK. JAH SAT on the couch flipping his phone open and closed, as if through some miracle it would make things okay. Yoshi had been gone for hours and hadn't called. He thought about calling her, but pride and lack of courage wouldn't allow it. It was amazing that, as assertive as he was when it came to the game, he couldn't quite get it to carry over when it came to his lady. The statement he had made to Yoshi was fucked up, but he didn't mean it like that.

Jah was still a young dude, so he really didn't understand affairs of the heart. He knew that he felt for Yoshi what he had never felt for another woman and it scared the hell out of him. For someone who didn't know what it felt like to be in a relationship with a woman, love was a totally alien concept, so at times he regressed and hid behind his hard-rock persona. He knew he loved her but wasn't quite sure how to articulate it.

His mind spun back to Stacks Green, who was, in essence, the root of the argument in the first place. Jah understood Yoshi wanting him to go out and get money, but what she didn't understand was that it was hard to do business with someone you despised. Granted, a check was a check, but when it was coming from Stacks it felt more like a handout, and Jah was never the one to lean on another man for anything. He came along getting it on his own, so that was his mindset. When it all boiled down to it, it was a pride thing, and he was never one to compromise his morals, even for Yoshi.

"Fuck it," he said, flipping the phone open to call Yoshi; but he immediately closed it. No, a call wouldn't do in this case. He would make his apology face-to-face at the video shoot. Besides, it had been a while since he had prowled the jungle, and it would be good to link up with his old comrade Spooky. After placing a quick call to his young comrade Tech, Jah prepared to hit the streets.

"AND WHERE DO YOU THINK your hot ass is off to?" Reese asked her little sister, Sharon, who was admiring her ample rump in the living room mirror.

"Out," Sharon said flatly.

"Out where?"

"Damn, Reese, why you sweating me?" Sharon let out an aggravated breath.

"Sweating you? Sharon, you just got in from school and you're going right back out. Whatever happened to studying or homework?"

"I ain't have none," Sharon lied fluidly.

"Bullshit." Reese stood between Sharon and the mirror. "I used to run that same lie on Mommy so I could get back in the streets. Now, where are you off to in those tight-ass jeans?"

Sharon turned around and folded her arms defiantly. "Look, if you must know, my home girls are coming up from Brooklyn and we're gonna hang out with Karen and them from St. Nick. You happy now?"

Reese slit her eyes at the miniature version of herself. "You think you're slick, don't you? Y'all little hot bitches is going over to that fucking video shoot!"

"Reese—"

"Reese my ass." She grabbed Sharon by her arms roughly. Reese's eyes were wild with something that Sharon couldn't quite identify. "Ain't nothing coming out that camp but the devil. Little sister, y'all young girls see these cats with they jewels and whips and get too blind to see the fucking forest for the trees. Sharon, you think cause you picked up a little hip and thigh, you got the game figured out, but baby you still got some growing to do."

"I'm good." Sharon shook her off.

"I hear that hot shit. You trying to stomp wit the big dawgz in a size-two shoe." Reese laughed. "Sharon, your little ass is cruising for trouble. You ain't really ready for what the streets got to offer. You need to stay ya ass home once in a while."

Sharon glared at Reese. "For as much as you run the streets, I know you ain't trying to lecture me."

"Yeah, I run the streets, but I'm grown. You're a teenager who is trying to grow up too damn fast. I'm telling you Sharon, at the rate you're going you're gonna find yourself in a bad situation."

"Like you did?" Sharon shot back. "Reese, you can't tell me shit, because you do all the same shit I do. Every time I turn around your ass is somewhere getting it in wit ya crew, so where you think I got it from? The difference between me and you is, when I finally get pregnant I'm gonna know who my baby daddy is!"

Before Reese had a chance to stop herself she had slapped Sharon across her face. The younger girl flew backward, and if it weren't for the wall she would've landed flat on her ass. Rage flashed through Sharon's eyes and she was back on her feet in an instant. She took a step towards Reese, but common sense didn't let her go any further. Reese had a reputation for being nice with her hands and the look in her eyes told Sharon she was ready to pound her out for her statement. For, however she felt about her older sister, she knew that she couldn't win in a fist fight.

"I can't stand your ass!" Sharon screamed before storming off into her bedroom.

"I ain't too big on your ass either!" Reese called after her. She started to pursue her little sister and give her the ass whipping she had been holding for her, but the sound of Alexis crying brought her back to her senses. Reese went to the other side of the living room and lifted her daughter from the basinet where she had been sleeping.

Alexis represented everything that was good in Reese. She was a jovial child with her mother's smooth coco skin and God only knew whose eyes. In light of how she was conceived it took Reese a minute to be able to bond with the child. When she was born, Reese refused to touch her or feed her in the hospital. The doctor had told Reese's mother that she was suffering from postpartum depression, but that wasn't it at all. Every time she looked at the little girl she was reminded of how she had allowed Don B and his crew to violate her.

She had gone back to the room because she had feeling for a man, who in the end probably didn't even remember her name. Reese's eyes were on the prize, but she was actually feeling Don B and, based on the invitation, she thought he was feeling her too. But it was all a setup and her dumb ass walked right into it. He passed her around to his home boys, letting them smash her pussy out in succession. She even got down with a faceless female who was at the freak party. In the end, Don B never gave her a second look and his boys kicked dirt on her name all through the hood. It took a while for Reese to get over what had happened to her, but through counseling and the support of her mother and closest home girls, she was able to get through it.

As always, Billy was the backbone, going to prenatal appointments and being there for Reese, but it was in Yoshi that she found the strength and inspiration to overcome. Yoshi had been beaten and raped by the same circle of men that had run a train on Reese, and she had been left for dead in a gutter. Her body had been broken, but her spirit held fast and she made a full recovery. Reese figured that Yoshi's hell was harsher than her own, but if she could overcome, then so could Reese. Though it took some time, she was finally able to connect with her newborn daughter and appreciate her for the blessing that she was.

"What's good, Mommy." Reese held the little girl to her bosom. Before she could even situate Alexis, her phone rang. "Yeah," she answered with an attitude.

"Why you always gotta answer your phone like a hood rat? What if I had been somebody calling you about a job?" Billy started in.

"First of all, bitch, I pay this damn bill. Second of all, who the hell is gonna be calling me for a job at four in the damn afternoon?" Reese shot back. Both the girls bust out laughing. "What's up, Billy Jean?"

"Still over here with my team. You still coming through?" Billy asked.

Reese adjusted her grip on Alexis, "Yeah, I'm waiting for my mother to come through so she can sit with Alexis. I would've asked Sharon, but that little bitch is feeling herself."

"Y'all go at it like an old married couple," Billy said.

"Cause the little bitch think she grown. I be trying to tell ol' girl what time it is so she don't end up pregnant too fucking early, but the little bitch thinks she got it figured out. I had to slap the shit out of that lil ho a little while ago."

"No, y'all wasn't fighting in ya mama's house?" Billy disputed.

"You got that damn right. She came out her face all crazy, so I hit her wit the Iron Palm."

"Reese, you sick," Billy laughed. "So when is ya moms coming?"

Reese glanced at the wall clock. "Shit, she was supposed to be here already. I don't know where the fuck she at."

"Tell you what, why don't we just run the baby over to my mom's? I'm sure she wouldn't mind watching Alex," Billy offered.

"Nah, I ain't trying to impose on ya moms like that. She does enough for me and Alexis as it is."

"Reese, knock it off. You know that my mother loves that baby girl of yours. Besides, since I moved out I know she gets lonely being home alone. Tell you what, since I got the whip just stay there and I'll come through and scoop you. Come downstairs in like twenty minutes."

"A'ight, I'll see you in twenty."

Chapter 9

AFTER LEAVING MONIQUE TO THE LOCALS ON her stoop, Dena made her way to her building, where Nate, Spooky, and Shannon were passing a blunt around and gossiping like women. From the look on their faces, they were all high as kites.

"Y'all look higher than all outside." Dena stood in front of the trio.

"Please believe it," Shannon smirked. "I thought you was going to the movies or something?"

"Nah, I changed that plan." Dena lied. "I'm bout to throw something on and head uptown. The boy, Stacks Green, is shooting a video, so you know me and my girls gotta be on the scene." She flipped her hair.

Shannon shook his head. "Y'all chicks is off the hook. You gonna roll all the way uptown to stand around a video shoot?"

"Hell yeah. It's a nice day, so you know the block is gonna be packed. I'm trying to catch a balla!"

"You better watch that, Dena. You see what happened to the boy, Roots, for fucking with my lil sister."

"Yeah, you be thinking you somebody's daddy," she said playfully. "Let me hit that." Dena reached for the blunt.

"Man, you better get your little ass outta here with that." Shannon snatched the blunt out of her reach. "I ain't trying to have Mommy catch you out here smoking wit us, D."

"Shannon, stop acting like that, you know I puff," Dena protested.

"Yeah, but not wit me. You're still my little sister, recognize?"

"Hating ass," Dena pouted, and stormed into the building, switching harder than she had to for the benefit of the older men. Spooky snuck a glance at her onion, but Nate turned away. Shannon tended to be very sensitive when it came to his little sister.

"Your little sister is something else." Nate shook his head.

Shannon coughed and spat on the ground. "Her fucking ass thinks she grown. Talking about she trying to catch a balla. I'm gonna fuck around and kill Dena."

"You know she's right," Spooky spoke up.

"Fuck is you talking about?" Shannon glared at him.

"The video shoot. You know how many hos is gonna come out the woodwork trying to steal fifteen minutes of fame? I say we mount up and roll uptown."

"Dawg, I ain't really trying to roll uptown to gawk at no hos. Plus, my money funny cause these fucking fiends acting like they ain't getting high today," Nate said.

"Big bro, you know there's more than one way to snatch a dollar." Spooky flashed the butt of his gun. "Lets go see them monkey niggaz we been laying on in L.G."

WHEN DENA CAME INTO HER apartment she stepped on a doll head and almost busted her ass. She kicked the head and walked into the living room where several other toys were scattered around. Her twin niece and nephew were standing in front of the television watching videos. Sean mimicked along with the rapper, while Shauna sang the pop hook. They looked like a ghetto Sonny and Cher, dancing stiffly in front of the television. All Dena could do was shake her head.

"Y'all stay in front of the TV," she said, startling them.

"Hey, Auntie!" Shauna ran to Dena and jumped into her arms.

"What's going on, Mama?" Dena hoisted the five-year-old.

"We doing a video!" the little girl said excitedly.

"I'm doing the video and she's one of my video hoochies," Sean said defiantly.

"You better watch your mouth. Let your mother hear you talking like that and she's gonna beat your ass," Dena said, pointing her finger at him.

"She ain't even here," Shauna informed her.

Dena gave the little girl a serious look. "Nadine left y'all in here by yourselves?"

"Yep, she said she was going to the store to get us some sandwiches, but she been gone for a while."

"Don't worry about it, I'm gonna stay with y'all until she comes back." Dena placed her niece on the floor and headed towards her bedroom.

Unlocking the door, she slammed it shut behind her and tossed her purse on her queen-size bed. Nadine was always doing stupid shit. Dena knew damn well Nadine didn't just run to the store, because she had just come out of it, getting a loose cigarette. Knowing her sister, she was probably off at the weed spot or running her mouth around the corner. God forbid if something had happened to the twins in that house; Dena was surely going to jail for murdering Nadine.

Pushing her ignorant sister from her mind, she focused on a more pressing issue, Lazy. After pulling a no-show he had the nerve to be blowing her jack up. Dena was angry, hurt, and embarrassed by the stunt Lazy had pulled, and this time his sweet tongue and fantastic dick weren't going to get him out of it. If he wasn't going to act right, it would be nothing for her to find someone who would. "Fuck him," she said, walking over to her closet.

Dena had more clothes than she knew what to do with, but only enough closet space to hang some of them up. The rest of her stuff was stuffed into plastic bags or Rubbermaid containers. The apartment was crowded enough with her mother and siblings, but if Nadine kept popping out kids the house would soon be overrun. One more reason she needed to get a place of her own.

Picking out an outfit for the night was simple enough. Dena wanted to be fly, without looking like she was trying to get fly. There would be enough hood rats out in their Sunday best, so subtlety was better. After picking out the proper attire, she dipped in the bathroom for a quick shower. Just as she was stepping out to dry off the bathroom door burst open.

"Shit, I gotta pee," Nadine said, dropping her pants and plopping down on the toilet.

"Damn, you can't knock?" Dena shouted, covering herself with the towel.

"Girl, stop acting like I ain't seen your ass naked before. I used to change your nasty-ass Pampers. Oh, that nigga Lazy been calling here all afternoon. I thought you and Lazy was going to the movies?"

"Fuck him," Dena said, stepping out of the shower. "Niggaz ain't shit."

Nadine wiped herself and pulled her pants up. "You just figure that out? Shit, I could've told you the boy was loose and saved you the heartache. Street niggaz like Lazy ain't shit!"

"And who made you the authority?" Dena said heatedly.

"Them two no-good baby daddies of mine, that's who. They was both fine and promised the world, but at the end of the day I was just another hit—which is cool, cause I handles my business with or without a nigga."

Dena frowned at her. "Nadine, as much bullshit as you got in your life, I know you ain't coming down on me like you got all the answers?"

Nadine took a loose cigarette from her bra and lit it. "I might not have all the answers, but I sure as hell ain't got no delusions about some nigga rolling through here and sweeping me off my feet. What you should've done was went and got you one of them square niggaz that actually wanna do something other than run the streets and lay their dicks on the crap table. You need to listen to what I'm telling you, Dena, on the real."

"Nadine, you need to miss me with that. Every nigga you ever fucked with was either a drug dealer or a fucking bum, so you can't tell me nothing about my man!"

Dena tried to step past her sister but Nadine blocked her path. "What, you mad cause I'm giving you the lowdown on ya *lil* man? You better suck that shit up and take it for what it is, D. All these niggaz is the same at the end of the day. Dena, niggaz Lazy's age ain't bringing nothing to the table but a hyperactive dick and a bunch of drama. They roll from one pussy to the next, leaving broken hearts and unclaimed kids in their wake."

"Speaking of kids, why the hell did you leave the twins in here by themselves?" Dena asked, trying to change the subject. Nadine's words were striking a little too close to home for her.

"First of all, Bay was supposed to be up here with them, and I'ma kick his little ass when he decides to pop back up. And second of all, I just went to get some smoke from up the block. It's not like I dipped out and went to the club. As a matter of fact, why the fuck am I explaining myself to you about my kids'? You better check yourself and remember who the big sister is and who the little one is."

"Some fucking example you're setting." Dena stepped past her.

"Don't let your mouth write a check your ass can't cash!" Nadine screamed, but Dena had already slammed her bedroom door.

LAFAYETTE GARDENS WAS A HOUSING project in Brooklyn that was much like any other projects. It boasted neatly rowed buildings, manicured lawns, and brightly painted signs welcoming you. This was on the exterior. Within the confines of the projects, crime and poverty festered and the strong preyed on the weak. The unspoken law of the Gardens was that, if you weren't from L.G., you stayed out of L.G. Luckily, laws meant nothing to the three desperados sitting in the idling minivan.

"There that nigga go, right there," Shannon said from the driver's seat.

"Who? Son with the shine on?" Nate asked, picking a slender kid out of a group standing in front of the building closest to Classon Avenue.

"Yeah, them niggaz is shining real nice. They must've heard about the video shoot, too," Spooky said in a sinister tone. "I know a Russian uptown that'll give us a fair price for them chains. You think that's platinum or white gold?"

"Its about to be history," Shannon said, pulling a shotgun off the floor, which had the stock sawed off for stealth. "Nate, get ya old ass up front and keep the car running. Spook, you ready to mash on these niggaz?"

"All day, baby," Spooky said, before checking to make sure there was a bullet in the chamber of his P89. As silent as the grave, the two robbers slid out of the car and entered the projects.

"WHAT UP, WHAT UP?" RONNY said as he slapped the palms of his peoples who were assembled in front of the building. Dressed in a white Sean John sweat suit and a pair of white-on-white Airs, he looked more like a rapper than a criminal. Ronny was an up-and-coming ghetto star in Brooklyn, clocking decent paper selling weed and coke in the projects. He was better known for his skill with the ladies than his skills with a pistol, but the crew of wolves he hung around with balanced the scales.

"Ron, what da deal?" A soldier named Blick saluted him. Blick was a man of slight build with a quick temper. He was Ronny's right-hand man.

"You got these niggaz on they job?" Ronny asked Blick.

"You know that. Dooly is almost finished with the pack he's pumping across the way, and I told Rene to hit him with another one when he's finished. Mike is around here somewhere, too. He's gonna hold it down while we shoot up top."

"That's what I like to hear, kid. Yo, I ain't trying to be out there all night, son. We just gonna go check the scene and see if we can slide something, then we're back to the block, smell me?"

"I got you, Ron. I know how yo ass don't like to be off the block for too long," Blick teased him.

"Fuck the dumb shit, kid. I don't trust nobody to watch my paper but me. Speaking of paper, you got that on you?"

"Yeah." Blick patted the Gucci pouch that was secured to his waist. "Ron, you sure it's a good idea to be rolling with this dough on us like that?"

"Normally no; but I figure, since we're going uptown we might as well go see fam and them to get some more work. Don't trip though, I got that heat in the car in case a nigga wanna break fool."

"Yo, one of y'all know how to get to Bedford Ave?" Spooky asked, seeming to appear out of nowhere.

"You damn sure can't get there rolling through L.G., son," Blick said.

"My fault, money, a nigga just a little lost, that's all. Ain't no need to poke ya chest out," Spooky said, matching his tone.

"My dude, you must not know where the fuck you at." Ronny piped in.

"Oh, we know just where we at." Shannon appeared to the rear of them with the shotgun leveled. "Yeah, talk that tough shit now." He pointed the barrel at Blick, who was frozen with fear.

"Yo, my dude, be easy with that!" Ronny eyed the shotgun.

"Fuck that easy shit, you know what it is!" Spooky pressed the P89 to Ronny's forehead. "Come up off ya shine and that cake."

"Son, y'all think y'all can just roll in my projects and rob me? On some real shit—" Ronny didn't get another word out before Shannon slammed the butt of the shotgun into the back of his head. His afternoon erupted into a burst of stars and colors, and the pretty boy collapsed to the ground.

Pulling the slide back on the shotgun, Shannon pointed it directly at Ronny's face. "Nigga, you ain't no fucking gangsta. Run yo shit before I let you hold something."

Ronny could feel the blood leaking from the back of his head onto his sweatshirt. "A'ight, man, just chill," he said, while removing his chain and watch.

"You too, ya ugly muthafucka." Spooky pointed the gun at Blick.

"A'ight fam, you got this one." Piece by piece, Blick removed his jewelry. Though he was complying with the robbers he was also storing their faces into his memory bank. There was no way in the hell that he was gonna get robbed in his own hood and not strike back.

"What's in the pouch?" Shannon asked Blick, but still had his gun trained on Ronny, who was unscrewing his diamond earrings.

"Nothing, man, a few bags of smoke and my ID," Blick lied.

"Set it out," Shannon demanded. Blick just glared at him. "Boy, you ain't heard what I said?"

Blick cursed himself. If he let them take the pouch they'd be shot on the re-up. "Man, I can't let you take this."

"What?" Shannon pointed the shotgun at him. "Yo—" Shannon's words were cut off by a thunderous sound. Blick's thigh exploded, spraying Shannon and Ronny with blood. Spooky stood over both the men, holding a smoking gun.

"Nigga, this shit is nonnegotiable!" Spooky barked. He reached down and ripped the pouch from Blick's waist. After a quick glace inside, a broad smile spread across his lips. "Looks like we came up on some real ballers."

"Nigga, you shot me!" Blick shouted, as if Spooky didn't know what he had done.

"You'll live. Be glad I ain't split ya fucking cabbage." Spooky reached down and ripped the diamond earring from Blick's left ear, bloodying him further. "Good looking out, fellas," Spooky said, before jogging from the projects with Shannon on his heels, laughing hysterically.

Chapter 10

"THAT WAS SOME REAL CHICKEN-HEAD SHIT YOU pulled last night," Sugar said to Roxy, licking the edge of the blunt to seal it.

"That ho shouldn't have bucked. I can't believe that bitch was acting all crazy over a fucking T-shirt."

Sugar just looked at her. "Roxy, I ain't even about to go there with you on that one. You just make sure you hold your composure at the video shoot."

"Please, you acting like I don't know how to carry myself. I'm a fucking lady!" Roxy said, crossing her legs in a masculine way. "Damn, that reminds me. I gotta call Charlie and see if he got some of that piff." Roxy reached over and took the white cordless phone of its base.

"Roxy, what the fuck are you doing?" Sugar looked over at her.

"Sugar, I ain't gonna be on that long."

"I don't give a damn about how long you gonna be on, you know that's the Bat Phone. Convict calls only, ho!" Sugar had an extra phone line installed in her house just to receive calls from the various cats she dealt with that were locked up.

As ghetto as it sounded, there was a method to her madness. Sugar went above and beyond for her boos behind the wall. Everything from sending food packages to the occasional visit, she was on it. She reasoned that when her flavor of the month was back on the streets he'd remember his rider chick that went so hard for him, gladly reopening the money line. Sugar's mind was always on her chips.

"You is so fucking ghetto," Roxy said, getting up to get the other cordless.

"You don't like it, burn ya daytime minutes," Sugar shot back.

"You got a prepaid, too!"

"So what? Mine got a chirp," Sugar joked, and went back to lighting the blunt. "Yo, what's up with you and homey from last night— the cat with the suit?"

"Girl." Roxy flopped on the couch next to Sugar. "I did some research, and that boy is caked up. They call him Black Ice. He's supposed to be some kind of pimp or something."

Sugar gave her a suspicious look. "I know you ain't thinking about selling ya ass for that nigga?"

"Hell no, the only person I sell my ass for is me!" Roxy declared. "But I wouldn't mind seeing how deep his pockets go."

"You better be careful, Roxy. I know this chick that used to fuck wit one of them ol pretty niggaz. The last time I seen her she was washed up and strung out," Sugar said seriously.

"I got this, mama."

Roxy dialed a number. She spoke briefly to someone on the line, then hung up. "Ain't this about a bitch?"

"What's good?"

"I just spoke to Charlie, and his ass is uptown at the video shoot," Roxy told her.

Sugar took deep pulls of the blunt and said, "If the mountain can't come to Mohammad, please believe she can come to it. Did you bring ya fit?"

"You know that."

"Then let's get dressed and do what we do."

. . .

"TOOK Y'ALL LONG ENOUGH." SHARON greeted Dena and Mo as they got off the train on 125th and St. Nicholas. She had traded in her tennis skirt for a pair of skin-tight, faded jeans that were slashed just below the ass cheeks. Her fire-engine-red boots set off her red motorcycle jacket, making her look like one of Satan's angels. All the body stuffed into the fit, coupled with her flawless makeup, made Sharon look way older than she actually was.

"You're lucky we came, that hot-ass train almost finished my weave," Monique touched her hair. She was dressed in a tight-fitting black denim suit with leather lace-up sandals, balanced on three-inch heels.

Ignoring Mo's comment, Sharon turned her attention to Dena. "I see you, Big Time!" She smiled at her friend. "You on your real grown and sexy shit, huh?"

Dena just smiled. The faint brown highlights in her hair shone slightly under the fading sunlight as she brushed a strand of it away from her face. She was decked out in a pair of charcoal gray knickers and a black wool top that showed a little breast but kept it tasteful. A gold X.O. choker accented her slender neck, giving her a model's appeal. To cap off the fit, Dena had donned a pair of ankle boots with a heart-shaped buckle on the side. The heel was a little higher than Mo's, but Dena had the good sense to get taps placed on them for easier strutting.

"So, where we headed?" Mo asked, checking her makeup in her compact.

"Just a few blocks over in St. Nick projects, but I thought we'd make a quick pit stop." She held up a Dutch Master.

"You ain't even gotta ask twice," Mo readily said.

"What about the video?" Dena asked.

"D, they gonna be out there for hours. Where we're going to smoke at is a block over from the shoot," Sharon said.

"High-ass bitches." Dena walked in front of them like she knew where she was going.

"You better not let Lazy see you on Two-Fifth in that outfit, he might snatch ya ass up," Mo called after her.

"That nigga can clown if he want to, you know how we do it in the Stuy." Dena gave Mo a high five. "I ain't fucking wit son like that, never will you stand Dena mutha fuckin Jones up and think you ain't gotta pay the costs. I know I'm a bad bitch," Dena patted her chest for emphasis. "If Lazy can't see that, then that's on him."

"Spoken like a true G!" Sharon chimed in.

"I know that's right," Mo said, eyeing a group of young men that were passing them. The young men overlooked Mo and gawked at Dena and Sharon; but they paid them no mind.

"Knowing Lazy, I wouldn't be surprised to see him up here. You know he fuck wit Don B and them," Sharon added.

"Lazy is free to be wherever he wants, but he wasn't where he was supposed to be, so the rest of that shit is irrelevant," Dena said in a matter-of-fact tone. The conversation was left at that.

LAZY STEPPED OUT OF HIS building and gave his body a good stretch. He had been sleeping like a baby until his cell phone had woken him. His man Chiba had been pressing him about coming to the video shoot all week, but because he had plans with Dena he told him no. Seeing how Dena was looping his calls and he didn't feel like being around Michelle again so soon, he was free for the evening. It was time to hit the streets.

Chiba was sitting in front of Lazy's building behind the wheel of a silver Dodge Magnum, twisting a blunt. He was a slim Puerto Rican cat with cornrows that snaked down his back. A red headband bearing the Big Dawg log was slung half-cocked around his head. Most people didn't know it, but Chiba was his government name. His parents were notorious pot dealers who came up in the era of good weed and better highs.

"Sonny Chiba," Lazy gave him dap as he slid into the passenger seat.

Chiba passed Lazy the blunt and pulled the car into the street. "Lazy-Laze, what's popping, my nigga? You ready to hit the block?"

"Don't I look ready?" Lazy motioned towards his crisp jeans and black Averix. "Son, its gonna be a lotta pussy out there."

"And who gets more pussy than us?" Chiba grinned.

"Not a muthafuckin soul!" Lazy responded. It was sort of like their pretty boy credo.

"Yo, how'd you manage to shake Dena?" Chiba asked.

"Dawg, I fucked around and got caught up with Michelle and ended up losing track of time. Dena ain't even taking my calls," Lazy said sadly.

Chiba shook his head. "Dawg, you be playing ya self pulling them kinda moves. What do we always say?" Before Lazy got a chance to answer, Chiba continued. "The wife comes first. Man, a side bitch can always be put on the back burner, but we gotta make time for the wife."

"Nigga, I know the rules—shit, I helped invent them. Son, I was so stuck off that piff that I ain't know what time it was."

"More like stuck off Michelle. You showing all the signs, kid."

Lazy arched his brow. "Signs of what?"

"Signs that that old bitch got you open, son," Chiba said, without taking his eyes of the road.

"Chiba, you don't know what the fuck you talking about. I'm handling business," Lazy said defensively.

This time Chiba did look at Lazy. "Lazy, you've been my ace since junior high school, so you know I'm gonna always keep it funky wit you, right?"

"I wouldn't have it any other way."

"A'ight, so let me ask you a question: How you handling business when you spending more time wit ya jump-offs than wit ya wife?"

"Chiba, we run wit the same circle of bitches!" Lazy reasoned.

"But I ain't got no girl, yo. I can run up in every bitch from one end of Twelfth Street to the other, and ain't nobody got room to check me. You, on the other hand, got a main chick that you claiming."

"So what you telling me, to square up and stop fucking around on Dena?"

"Nah, I ain't said all that. You a grown-ass man, so whatever you do is on you. I'm just telling you to make ya next move ya best move and peep the writing on the wall."

"And what the fuck is that supposed to mean?" Lazy asked.

Chiba looked at him for a minute. He knew Lazy was a sensitive cat, but he was his dawg and therefore he could speak his mind. "Check it: Why you think Michelle go out of her way to please you and put up with the bullshit?"

"Cause I got the best cock game in Harlem," Lazy boasted.

"Fool, that title still belongs to me; but that's a different story. My dude, Michelle is a seasoned old bird with a plan within a plan. All she wanna do is trick ya stupid ass into getting her pregnant and trying to have you playing house, but you so blinded by the pussy and ya ego that you don't see it that way."

"Dawg, I'm on my job."

"Lazy, if you was on ya job then Dena wouldn't be looping ya calls," Chiba said, busting a left on 116th and Lenox. "Homey, you know I'm M.O.B. all day, everyday; but you got a good chick in Dena. All I'm telling you is not to fuck that up. Do ya dirt, but do it with some tact."

Lazy didn't respond to this, he just reclined back in the seat and kept puffing the blunt. Chiba and Lazy were only a year apart, but the boy was wise beyond his years. Lazy wanted to dispute his logic, but right was right. His shenanigans in the streets were seriously cutting into his time with Dena and he was glad his man had checked him on it, like a true friend. Michelle had some good pussy, but Dena was his heart. Until someone had pointed it out to him, he hadn't even realized he was neglecting her. It was a problem he made a mental note to rectify—as soon as she decided to pick up the damn phone.

"So what's up, you gonna sit there stressing over Dena all day, or shake out like we do?" Chiba asked, running through a street light just as it turned red.

Lazy gave him a solemn look. "I'm gonna get things right with my shorty . . . right after I see what's popping with these hos at the video shoot!" He bust out laughing.

Chapter 11

THE THREE GIRLS CONTINUED TO WALK UP ST. Nicholas Avenue taking in the sights. Dena loved Harlem not only for the action, but the feel of it. In her hood everything and everybody was tense. The young boys seemed to be prepared for battle at all times. It wasn't like Harlem didn't have its ghettos, but the tension level didn't seem to be so high. But, alien as the two boroughs were to each other, Dena wouldn't have traded Brooklyn for the world.

When Sharon finally slowed her pace they were standing in front of building 410, on 130th. It was a fairly decent-looking building with a great view of the park, but Dena didn't care too much for the looks the stragglers in front of the building were giving them.

"Who you know in here?" Dena asked, rolling her eyes at a young dude who was trying to get her attention.

"Girl, would you relax. My friend lives in this building. We can blow something down at his crib and then hit the video shoot," Sharon said, leading them into the building and onto the elevator. In a matter of seconds they were stepping off on the fourteenth floor and heading towards the apartment closest to the staircase. Sharon knocked, and after a few seconds the locks were undone and a man stood in the doorway, beaming at the three young ladies.

"What da deal, boo?" Sharon gave him a hug and kiss on the cheek. "These are my girls Dena and Mo from BK. Y'all, this is Sean."

Sean gave a light chuckle. "Rough-Sean, back in the days, but that's another story. How're you ladies doing?" Sean was a fairly handsome cat with peanut-butter skin and broad shoulders. His hair was cut low, but not low enough to where you couldn't see the waves rippling through the top of it. Lightly tapered sideburns ran the length of his jaw and connected with a budding goatee. "Come on in." He stepped back and allowed them to enter the apartment.

Sean's crib was decorated surprisingly nice for a dude. He had a plush white living room set, which rested on a smoke gray carpet. A plasma TV, tuned to *ESPN News,* was fastened to a wall he had bricked over when he moved into the spot, to give it more of a chic look. Along the shelves that were mounted on the wall were trophies of different shapes and sizes. Most of them were for football, but there was also a basketball award and two for baseball. Along the walls were pictures of him dressed in his high school football uniform, wearing a goofy smirk.

"Shit!" Dena cursed, looking at the blank screen on her cell phone.

"What's good, ma?" Mo asked.

"I was so busy rushing out the house that I forgot to charge my phone."

"If it's a local call you can use the house phone," Sean said, tossing her the cordless.

"I'm just checking my messages," she told him, punching in her number.

"You a balla, huh?" Mo asked Sean, admiring the picture.

Leaning against the wall he gave her a confident grin. "I used to play a lil bit."

"Sean won a D-2 national title last year," Sharon added proudly, taking one of the larger trophies off the shelf.

"You a college grad?" Dena asked.

"Not quite." He took the trophy from Sharon and placed it back on the shelf. "I got two more years before I get my bachelor's. You go to school?"

"I'm in my last year, but as soon as the fall hits I'm off to college," Dena told him.

Sean licked his lips, not in a seductive way, more like they were dry. But he was definitely transmitting something. "That's what's up. It's good to see a sister handling hers."

"What you got up in here to drink? A bitch is parched," Sharon cut in, not digging the way Sean was looking at Dena.

"Look at your lush ass." Sean playfully mushed her.

"Set it out, you know how I do!" Sharon told him before flopping on the couch and grabbing the remote, letting the other two girls know she and Sean had that kind of familiarity.

"Sharon, I better not get knocked for letting your young ass drink. If I do, I'm fucking you up for telling and fucking Be-Be up for bringing your young ass around." He cut a glance at Dena when he said this. "Y'all want something too?"

"Ain't you afraid of getting in trouble for serving alcohol to us minors?" Dena said slyly.

"You're gonna do it anyhow, so I'd rather it be up here where you're safe than out there where something could happen to you. Besides, you ain't that young," he said before disappearing into the kitchen. "Is Sex on the Street alright with y'all?" he called from the kitchen.

"I'm always for that," Mo mumbled, looking at a picture of Sean at his senior prom.

"What the hell is that?" Dena asked suspiciously.

"Just something me and my crew came up on. Its an original recipe," he said, milling about the refrigerator. He placed an ice-cold forty of St. Ides on the counter, beside a two-liter Hawaiian Punch. In old-school form, Sean turned the forty up and downed it just to the label, then replaced the beer with the Punch and swirled it around in the bottle. The finished product looked like red Alize, with a hit of bubbles at the top.

"Here we go," Sean said, coming out of the kitchen, balancing a tray with four full wine glasses on it. Sharon immediately began sipping hers, while Dena and Mo looked at the glasses suspiciously.

"There better not be no date rape in this." Dena smelled her glass.

"Ma, do I look like a nigga who gotta *take* the pussy? Come on, shorty, I wouldn't do that to the lil homey or her girls." He nodded towards Sharon, who looked upset at the statement.

"Yeah, I'm gonna remember that little homey shit." Sharon took a deep gulp of her drink.

Mo took a shy sip and nodded her head in approval. "It kinda tastes like a wine cooler."

"Told you so." Sean flopped on the couch between Dena and Mo. "Now, which one of y'all got the bud?"

For the next twenty minutes or so the quartet smoked weed and sipped the Sex. Dena had a good buzz, but Sharon looked like she was on the verge of being drunk, which was always a bad sign. She had one leg slung over the arm of the lounge chair and her eyes looked like they were trying to droop.

"You a'ight?" Dena asked her.

"I'm good, yo. That Sex on the Street be kicking my ass, though." Sharon slurred a bit.

"This shit is kinda strong. What did you say was in it?" Mo asked.

"I didn't," Sean said playfully.

Sharon suddenly sprung to her feet, scaring the hell out of everyone. "This shit got me feeling good!" she said, stretching so that her breasts were pressing against the fabric of her shirt. "Yo, Ima be up in the video like," she tried to bust a dance step, but mistimed it and stumbled, landing with her ass in Sean's lap and almost spilling the Sex onto Dena and Mo.

"Bitch, watch that!" Mo shouted.

"Damn, you drunk ass almost fucked up my outfit," Dena scolded her.

"Fuck y'all, ain't nobody drunk," Sharon shot back. She draped her arms around Sean's neck and gave him a seductive look. "Let me holla at you in the back for a minute," she tried to whisper, but everyone in the room heard her.

Sean's face turned a shade darker, but he tried not to look embarrassed. "Easy, ma," he said, while removing her hands. "You a little tipsy right now."

"Sean, stop acting like that." She was now trying to wrap her arms around his waist, but he resisted.

"Cut it out, Sharon." He removed her from his lap and stood up.

"Word, it's like that now?" she asked with hurt in her eyes and anger in her voice. "What, you acting brand-new cause these bitches is here? Sean, you know my head game is way good, so stop fronting."

"Sharon, that drink got you bugging right now," Sean said seriously. Sharon was blowing his cool in front of Dena and he was starting to get upset.

"Fuck you, nigga!" Sharon tossed the empty glass at him, but thankfully it didn't shatter.

"You acting like a real bird right now, shorty," Sean said, clearly irritated now.

"I got ya fucking shorty." Sharon hopped up like she was going to take a swing at him, but Mo grabbed her.

"Ain't gonna be none of that, Sharon, cause if he buck we all gotta buck," she said very seriously.

"Nah, I ain't even on it like that. Just get her drunk ass the fuck up outta here," Sean said, bending to pick up the glass. As soon as he was close enough, Sharon tired to kick him, but she ended up nicking Dena's leg.

Dena glared at her. "Now I know your ass is tripping."

"Come on, we out," Mo said, half steering, half dragging Sharon towards the door. Dena shook her head and fell in step behind her peoples.

"Yo, I'm sorry this shit happened," Sean said to Dena.

"Don't sweat it," she said casually.

"Maybe one day I could make it up to you?"

Dena gave him a seductive smile. "Nah." She glanced at Sharon and back to Sean. "I think I'm a little too old for you." With a playful wink, she was out the door.

Chapter 12

THE INSIDE OF THE CAMPER SMELLED LIKE A combination of body spray and pressed hair. Several of the more high-profile ladies to be featured in the video went about the task of getting themselves and their gear right for the shoot.

Yoshi sat at the vanity table across from the lead girl, Ayanna, carefully applying the finishing touches to her make up. Yoshi had successfully tuned her from a nice-looking, around-the-way chick to a certified diva, using a smooth coat of foundation and autumn colors where she knew the light would hit. Yoshi had always considered herself a fly bitch, so doing wardrobe and makeup came quite naturally to her.

"Yeah," Yoshi said, using her thumb to wipe a smudge from beneath her bottom lip. "These muthafuckas is gonna be on you, ma." She handed Ayanna a hand mirror.

"You did ya thing, Yoshi." Ayanna admired her face, and tugged at her Shirley Temple curls. "If these niggaz didn't know, they gonna know."

"Okay." Yoshi gave her a high five.

Ayanna got up and went to give her five-seven banana frame the once over in the mirror. She was wearing a black leather miniskirt and a black corset. Her China doll eyes seemed to sit perfectly in her angular face, brought to the forefront by a thin line of black mascara. The black leather pumps were a little snug on her feet, but it was a small price to pay for fashion. Like Yoshi, Ayanna was a young chick on the come up. She had graced the pages of magazines and calendars and was the talk of the town on the video scene. She was a young chick with an exotic look and one hell of a swagger.

"You killing em right now, but something's missing," Yoshi said, pacing around Ayanna. "Hold up, I got just the thing." Yoshi fumbled around in her case until she found what she was looking for. Rubbing a nice hunk of Vaseline in her palms, Yoshi began to smooth it over Ayanna's face and arms. When she was done she dipped one of her make-up brushes into a small jar of glitter and began flicking it on Ayanna. The flecks of gold clung to her, giving her skin a pixielike effect. For the finishing touch, Yoshi removed the gold slide necklace from around her neck and placed it on Ayanna.

Yoshi nodded. "Now you're ready."

"Damn, I thought you'd never get done. You ain't the only one that gotta get right for the camera," Peaches said, flopping her forty-eight-inch ass on the stool Ayanna had just vacated. She was a chocolate dime with hips like she was raised on nothing but corn bread and greens. Much like Ayanna, Peaches was on the come up in the entertainment business, but she represented the darker side of it. When someone said "down for whatever," they were probably talking about Peaches. The girls were bitter rivals.

"Yeah, some bitches need a head start," Ayanna said slyly.

Peaches faced Yoshi, who was just sitting back down to the vanity table, but addressed Ayanna: "Speaking of *head*, how did your private interview with Stacks work out?"

"Bitch, knock it off. I know you ain't trying to talk slick, wit all the dick you done sucked? Your head game is international. You throwing shade, when your ass is like forty, still trying to do videos. You ain't get the memo? It's a young bitch's world," Ayanna shot back, drawing laughter from the other four girls that were in the camper.

"Come on girl, dead that shit. I still got two more ladies to do after you and I don't wanna have to rush. You know I pride myself on quality," Yoshi said, trying to ease the tension so she could do what she had to do and kick back.

"I'm sorry, Yoshi, but you know how some of these bitches forget they place," Peaches said, in an attempt to taunt Ayanna further. Thankfully, she didn't bite. "So what you been up to, girl?" she asked Yoshi.

"Out here trying to get a dollar," Yoshi said, as she began to run the alcohol pad over Peaches's face. "How's the modeling thing going?"

"It's going, but not the way I want it to," Peaches told her. "These niggaz act like if you ain't trying to pose in a thong, they ain't fucking wit you."

"Who you got managing you?" Yoshi asked, evening out Peaches's makeup.

"Oh, my son's father and his cousin is handling that. His cousin used to work for Diddy, so you know he about his business."

"Peaches, a woman's worth is too precious to be measured by a man. Leaving a novice nigga in control of your destiny is like having a pimp. Remind me to give you the name and number of the agency I went through back in the days. My girl Laurie Gold will get you right."

"You used to model?" a caramel-colored girl asked from the loveseat.

Yoshi looked over at her. "Baby, I used to do some of everything, but now I'm just trying to make it through to tomorrow like everybody else."

"Yeah, I heard you was a beast on the streets," an older girl said from near the wardrobe. Yoshi remembered her face from the club scene, but couldn't place her name. "You used to headline at Shooter's, right?"

"That was a lifetime ago," Yoshi told her, moving from Peaches's eyes to her lips.

"I can't see it. You seem so . . . square," Ayanna said.

"You can't take everything you see for surface value."

The door to the camper swung open, drawing everyone's attention. "This shit is gonna be serious. Don B just rolled up." She was dark, with the look of a newscaster on a good story.

"Where them dollars at," Peaches sang.

Yoshi's face didn't show it, but a chill ran down her back. Every time she heard the name she got uneasy. Though Don B hadn't been a participant in the rape, they were his minions. To her, he represented the worst the streets had to offer, hidden behind a pair of blacked-out glasses.

"That nigga True looking like new money," the newscaster broadcasted.

"What's better than new money?"

"Long money!" Ayanna said. "Man, I'm about to hit the bricks and see who's out there. Time is money, bitches," Ayanna said, following the newscaster out of the camper.

Yoshi watched the young girls leave, feeling somewhere between amused and saddened. They reminded her of herself not so long ago. Yoshi tore through Harlem like she had papers on it. She was young, fine, skillful, and determined to manipulate her way to the top. Until the now-departed members of Bad Blood and Rel's grimy ass showed her how deep the rabbit hole goes. Just thinking of him made her want to vomit. Yoshi had never wished death on anyone, but she wasn't sorry that someone tossed him off a roof.

You have to really love someone in order to kill for them, and this is what had strengthened the bond between her and Jah. She was still pissed at him, but couldn't help but to laugh when she thought of him. How could someone so versed in the streets be such a novice at love? Jah had stood by her and constantly helped absorb the pain all through her recovery, but when it came to him opening up, he withdrew. She had tried to figure out the puzzle that made up the young man but was stumped. Yoshi considered herself an expert in reading men, but Jah's character was a puzzle she had yet to solve, and this is what often frustrated her most.

Yoshi was distracted by the beeping of her cell phone. "Hello?" she answered, without looking at the caller ID.

"What's good, skank?" Billy's familiar voice came through the phone.

"Takes one to know one," Yoshi shot back.

"What you doing?" Billy asked.

"Shit, working. Stacks Green is shooting his video uptown, so you know ya girl out there trying to get a check. Why don't you stop through, they got plenty of food and chronic. You know Stacks always feels like he gotta outstunt Don B, so it should be fun to watch."

"Damn, that sounds like what it is, but you know Reese ain't trying to come nowhere near Don B."

"My poor home girl is gonna fuck around and miss out on a lot, trying to hide from a nigga that's at every event. Yo, if it was me I'd have just stepped to the nigga by now."

"You and me both, but Reese don't wanna press it. She figures, as she's got Alex, she don't need no nigga; and truthfully, I agree with her. All a nigga can really do is bring you grief or a fucking disease."

Yoshi sucked her teeth. "Yeah, right, you don't be popping that shit when your ass be rushing home to watch *Girlfriends* with Marcus. His fake, tough ass watching a chick show is bananas."

"Leave my boo alone. I'll have you know that *Girlfriends* is an excellent show. Yo ass don't know nothing about upwardly mobile blacks," Billy said.

"And you do? Shit, ya man own a strip club," Yoshi pointed out.

"Baby, a check is a check," Billy told her.

"I know that's right."

"Anyhow, how long are you gonna be stuck over there trying to swat them country nigga's hands away from yo ass?" Billy asked.

Yoshi glanced at her watch. "I don't know. I've been through four wardrobe changes already, and these niggaz ain't even halfway through the shoot. I might be here for a minute, ma."

"You gotta do what you gotta do, Yoshi. Well, me and Reese is gonna go get something to eat and probably hit a bar up. It's been a while since I hung out with my girls."

"Cause you spend so much time on lockdown," Yoshi teased.

"Like Jah lets you run like you used to. Don't go there with me, Yoshi. Speaking of Jah, what's up with my little brother?"

"He's probably sulking around the house or playing that damn video game, fucking asshole."

"What's with all the hostility?"

"Nothin. That lil nigga just gets me tight. Stacks wanted him to do security this weekend and he acting all funny about the shit, like we don't need that bread. When I checked him on it he act like he was feeling in a way. I don't wanna have to filet that little thug-ass nigga, but damnit I will!"

"You need to calm down, Yoshi. You knew Jah was wild when you got with him, so don't go condemning him now," Billy said seriously. Yoshi was her girl, but over the course of Yoshi's recovery Jah had been a pillar. This is what earned her respect, and she was quick to defend him.

"Billy, if you only knew the half."

"Talk to ya girl," Billy urged her.

"A'ight, peep this . . ." Yoshi went on to give Billy the short version of the story. She ended with, "Yo, if the nigga don't wanna be around, he needs to just say so."

"Damn, that's crazy; but I don't think Jah meant it like that," Billy said.

"However the fuck he meant it, he said it. That was some hurtful shit, Billy, and to make it worse, he hasn't even called me today."

"Now that's whack, but the other shit I think you can work on. I know he should've called, but why don't you give him a ring instead?"

"Fuck that!" Yoshi spat.

"Yoshi, stop acting like that. You've got more experience with the opposite sex, so you know you understand the rules of engagement a little better than he does. Just call him."

There was a knock on the door, then a round-faced female PA wearing a headset poked her head into the camper. "Yoshi, they need you on set. One of Persia's tracks came out and they're ready to shoot."

Yoshi covered the phone. "I'll be right there. Billy, I gotta go, but I'll shout y'all later."

"Alright then, do what you gotta do, kid. Make sure you call me later. One."

Chapter 13

IT TOOK SOME DOING, BUT WITHIN A FEW HOURS the crew had the St. Nicholas projects looking like a BET soundstage. There were lights, trucks, high-tech equipment, and of course women. From far and wide they came. Black girls, White girls, Asians, you name it, they were out there. All came in search of their fifteen minutes of fame. As soon as the red Escalade bent the corner of 131st Street, blasting Don B's latest single off his sophomore album, all attention was turned to it. The Don was in the building.

Big Devil stepped from the driver's side, causing the car to rock. He was dressed in a black T-shirt with THE TRUTH etched across the front of it. Black sunglasses covered his eyes and looked like they were too tight around his massive head. Next out of the ride was his partner Remo. In contrast to Devil's dark skin, Remo was high yellow. Standing side by side they looked like human twin towers. The men were seasoned street vets and hired killers in the service of the Don.

Don B climbed from the rear of the car with a blunt pinched between his lips. In addition to his rottweiler medallion, he was sporting a colorful diamond chain that looked like someone had sprinkled Fruity Pebbles on it.

True was next, wearing a red bandana tied around his neck like a cowboy. A California Angels cap sat cocked on his head, looking like it would come off at the first strong wind that came through. Like Remo, he wore a black T-shirt with the title of his album scrawled across the front of it. With the twin towers at their heel, the two stars made their way across the street towards the projects.

Halfway across the street, Devil noticed a short light-skinned kid coming in their direction. He had a shifty glare about him and his hands were tucked a little too deep inside the pockets of his Yankee jacket. Before he could get close enough to do any real damage, Devil stepped in front of him.

"Sup, shorty?" Devil said to the kid.

"Chillin, my nigga," the kid said, trying to sidestep Devil.

"You know somebody over here or something?" Devil asked, blocking his path again.

"Fam," the kid said, as if Devil was becoming an annoyance. "Why is you acting like I'm a deranged fan or something when I'm just trying to go holla at my man?"

"Cause I don't know ya face, fam," Devil said in an icy tone.

"My dude." The kid went to take his hand out of his pocket and Devil went into action. He grabbed the kid by the arm and bent it behind his back. Though Devil had yet to apply any pressure, the kid yelled out, drawing True's attention.

"Yo, what you doing Devil?" True threw his hands in the air.

"My job, lil muthafucka!" Devil shot back.

"True, you know this nigga?" Don B asked in an unconcerned tone.

True looked at Don B as if he should know the man, too. "D, you mean to tell me you don't remember Wood?"

"Who?"

True shook his head. "Wood, nigga, little Hollywood. The fake John Singleton."

"Oh, fam wit the movies and shit?" Don B recalled. "True, I ain't really trying to fuck wit that nigga right now, we got business with Stacks."

"Come on, dawg, we can't just let Devil toss him up like that," True said.

Don B sighed heavily. "True, make this shit quick. Yo, Devil!" Don B called to the bodyguard. When he had Devil's attention he motioned for him to let Hollywood go.

"Told you, nigga," Hollywood said, before popping his collar and strutting over to where Don B and True were standing. "What it is, my niggaz?" Hollywood gave True a pound then jerked him in for a hug. He went to repeat it with Don B, but the scowl on the man's face changed his mind. "Right, right. So what's good fellas."

"Ain't nothing. Bout to roll over here to Stacks Green's video shoot," True told him.

"Oh word, that's what it is. I wasn't doing nothing anyway." When Hollywood tried to fall in step with them Don B stopped him.

"It's a closed set, homey. You're welcomed to stay around, though." Don B stepped off the curb, leaving True to deal with Hollywood.

"Yo, what's up wit ya man?" Hollywood asked True, once Don B was out of earshot. "Duke be acting like I did something to him, what's good with that?"

"Ain't about nothing," True lied. The truth of the matter was that Hollywood was a bullshit artist. He was one of those cats that had big dreams and no initiative. Every time you saw him he was popping shit about what he was into and how he had another surefire plan, but nothing ever panned out for Hollywood, because he gave a half-ass effort.

"Funny, cause it always seem like something," Hollywood said. "But fuck that shit, I hear you doing ya thing wit the music, True?"

"I ain't did nothing yet," True said modestly. "I killed a few mix tapes, but my album doesn't come out for another couple of weeks. That'll be the real test of fire."

"I hear that. Yo, y'all shot a video yet?"

"Not since the Bad Blood joint. I've just been writing and trying to jump on every mix tape out there."

"Nigga, that's what it is. But you know to come holla at me the next time you ready to shoot something, right?" Hollywood asked.

"I don't know, Wood. The record company usually chooses which directors we go with."

"Stop acting like that, True. You the biggest act on Don B's label, you know he'll listen to you. Check it: I got the high-eight joint at the crib right now. We can take that, shoot the video for the low. After we do that we can present it to Don B, to show him we know how to move." Hollywood was trying to sell game, but True wasn't buying.

"Wood, I can't speak for Don B, but I'll put it in the air," True said. He really just wanted Hollywood to go on about his business so he could go about his.

"That's what it is then. Yo, True, holla at ya man, we need to do something."

"A'ight," True said, moving to catch up with Don B.

"Big Dawg, kid!" Hollywood shouted at True's back.

"YO, WHY YOU WASTE YA time wit that kid?" Don B asked True while fishing around in his pocket for a light.

"You know Hollywood is from the block," True said.

"He could be from Mars, for all I give a fuck; the kid is a bullshit artist. Every time you turn around he's talking some upwardly mobile shit, but when its time for the follow-through he flakes. The nigga been like that for years."

"He a'ight. I mean, I know he's full of shit, but I don't dislike the cat."

"Then you ain't as smart as I thought you were. True, let me break something down to you about the nature of people. If a muthafucka ain't about what you about, then y'all ain't got nothing in common. If you come across a cat that ain't got no direction of his own but is all too willing to throw in his lot with your movement, then you don't need him."

"I don't agree with that, D. Some niggaz just feel ya movement so heavy that they can understand what you're trying to do, and they add to it," True tried to reason.

"Young'n, you're missing what I'm trying to tell you. Ain't nothing wrong with a nigga trying to strengthen your movement, but there should be and is always something gained from it. Every nigga should have a dream beyond riding the next muthafucka's coattail. If you ain't got no dreams, you ain't got no soul—and I don't want that kinda karma around me, dig?"

"Yeah, I dig," True said, trying to figure why Don B was so fucking paranoid about everybody. But paranoid as he was, Don B had always given True sound advice.

"Man," Don B continued, "with age comes wisdom, my nigga. You can't learn everything in a day or even a season for that matter, but pace ya self and listen to ya old head and you'll be alright. Now lets greet our adoring public."

THE INTERIOR OF THE CAR was filled with a combination of weed and cigarette smoke. So foggy in fact, that even through the tints, all you saw of the occupants were silhouettes. A young girl sat behind the wheel of the Honda nervously smoking a cigarette. Sha Boogie sat in the passenger seat wearing his trademark mean mug. A gnarled toothpick bobbed between his thick lips, while his eyes were glued on the cluster of people gathering across the street.

"Look at them muthafuckas, fronting like they some bosses or something," Charlie said, voicing what Sha was thinking.

"Them boys is shining something nice, fam. I say we ease up on these niggaz and pop off now," Spider said in his whispery voice. He was a wild young bandit who had gotten his name when he climbed four stories down the side of a project building to avoid being captured by the police.

"Man, you know this is Sha Boogie's call." Charlie gave him a stern look. Sha Boogie and True's beef went further back than Spider understood, and Sha hadn't made it a point to share that information with many. Besides his mother, only those closest to him understood why he hated True so much.

Sha Boogie glared and said nothing. He watched True scornfully. His shine, the quirky smile, everything about True made him furious.

True was living the life that every ghetto kid dreamt of, while Sha had to get by on his wits. Sha Boogie was living lick to lick, dealing with a mother who couldn't stand him, a dickhead parole officer, and a team that couldn't get right, while this little bastard was riding through Harlem like a boss pimp. It made Sha sick to his stomach, but he took some solace knowing the debt would be settled.

"Nah," Sha said in an easy tone. "Let him enjoy his fifteen minutes. We gonna lay up and wait for him to slip." With that, Sha relaxed in his seat but still kept his eyes locked on True.

IT ONLY TOOK A SECOND for one of the young ladies to recognize Don B and True and send the crowd into frenzy. In a matter of seconds they found themselves rushed by women and men in search of autographs, or trying to hand them demos. The towers went into action, forcing the crowd back, but Don B told them it was cool as long as they kept it orderly. True, who was trying to break the lock a young girl had on his arm, looked at Don B quizzically.

"Don't trip dawg, this is all a part of the life," Don B whispered into his ear. "Keep your distance from haters, but never make the fans feel like you're inaccessible. The more real you seem, the more the people will love you." He winked and continued the impromptu autograph signing.

"Y'all Harlem boys love to stunt," said a thin man wearing a platinum chain that looked like it weighed more than he did. The only thing keeping the crowd from mobbing him were the four serious looking cats surrounding him. They weren't as big as the towers, but their faces clearly said trouble.

"Soda, what it is?" Don B breached his protective circle and gave him a hug.

Soda was to Stacks Green what True was to Don B, a young cat with star potential. Back in the day, Soda's mother used to let Stacks stash guns and drugs in her house, as long as she was taken care of. One fateful night some cats robbed her house and shot her, making Soda an orphan. Though Soda's mother was a street chick and it was only karma coming back to her, Stacks felt responsible for her death, prompting him to take Soda in. Soda learned the game quickly and proved to be not only a top-notch earner, but a fierce MC. When Stacks started popping in the music industry he made sure that he kept Soda close to him, teaching the youngster yet another hustle.

Soda flashed his platinum grills. "Ain't nothing, brah, just trying to live. Who ya got wit ya?"

"This my nigga, True." Don B. pulled True into the circle. "True, this here is Soda. If things go right, y'all gonna be spending quite a bit of time together. I got both of y'all doing some shit on the boy Scatter Brain's next mix tape, so you might wanna get familiar with each other's styles."

"That's what's up," True said, not sure how he felt about teaming with a cat he didn't know.

"Yo, where that nigga Stacks at?" Don asked.

"Shit, he in the trailer burning that sticky," Soda told him.

"Y'all brought that country-ass shit up with you? You must be crazy, risking a charge for that fucking dirt," Don B teased him.

"Man, the Lone Star got some of the best green in the fucking country," Soda said, defending his state's weed game.

"Yeah, if you into crabgrass, nigga! You ain't ready for that Five-Six, son." Don B shot back.

"Well, don't talk about it nigga, light it up. Let's migrate to the trailer."

"After you, kid." Don B gave him a mock bow. The three young stars headed deeper into the projects with the six security guards trailing them.

Chapter 14

"MAN, FUCKING WIT YOU, WE GONNA MISS ALL the hos," Nate said to Spooky, while steering the minivan up Flushing Avenue.

"Come on, Nate, that shit wasn't my fault. Shannon is the one that had to change his clothes," Spooky protested.

"Because you splattered blood all over them!" Shannon interjected.

Spooky shrugged, "You shouldn't have been standing so close to the nigga when I shot him."

"That's my point. You didn't have to shoot him," Nate said. "Spook, you stay dancing with the devil and one day you're gonna get burnt."

Spooky looked at his older brother as if he had just called him a cock-sucking faggot. "Muthafucka, is you serious? What you think you do every time you hit the block with a package? Big bro, this is the jungle we live in, survival is the law of the land round here. Damnit, if the devil is gonna take me outta this hell, not only will I dance with him, but he can have my black-ass soul at half price!"

"Why don't you two niggaz stop beefing. We licked two drug dealers for their shine and they cake, where the fuck is the wrong in that?"

Nate cut his eyes at Shannon. "You just as twisted as this fool," he thumbed at Spooky.

"Birds of a feather eat together," Spooky shot back. Before he really got a chance to go in on his brother, his cell vibrated in his pocket. "Yeah?"

"Damn, I've been trying to call you for a minute," Jah said on the other end.

"My fault, my nigga, I was on one. What's good wit you though?"

"I'm on my way over to St. Nick to see Yoshi, she working on that nigga Stacks's video."

"Great minds think alike, cause we on our way over there, too," Spooky told him.

"You fucking wit them Brooklyn niggaz hard body, huh?"

"Hey man, some of us is still out here in the thick. How's that security thing coming along?"

"You got jokes, huh? I can't complain though. Ain't nothing like the hunt, but it makes my lady happy, ya know?"

"I can dig it, J. What's up wit Yoshi, anyhow?"

"Stressing, as usual."

"Fuck you do now?"

"Long story, but we'll jaw about it at the shoot," Jah told him.

"Fo sho. But yo, you got that sticky on you, cause we probably ain't gonna get a chance to stop?"

"You know that. Hurry the fuck up so we can get blazed!" Jah said, excited to see his friend.

"That's a bet, see you in a minute." Spooky ended the call.

"Who was that?" Shannon asked.

Spooky looked at him and said, "Another dedicated soldier."

STACKS GREEN WAS A MAN who bore a striking resemblance to a black-ass Buddha. His bulky frame rested in a burgundy barber chair that swiveled on a post that was bolted to the floor of the camper. A long diamond chain hung from his neck, while the pendant rested on his large gut. It was a beautiful, three-dimensional piece that was slightly larger than a bread saucer and shaped like the state of Texas. A diamond-studded S sat in the middle of the piece, and surrounding it were waves of bright green diamonds. Accented by a flooded watch and two gumdrop-size diamond earrings, Stacks Green was the poster boy for niggaz who had made it.

"You gonna pass that or what?" Cooter asked, nodding at the blunt between Stacks's chubby knuckles. At six-two, with coal black skin, and a missing tooth in the front, Cooter wasn't the prettiest thing to come out of the Lone Star State, but he was good to have with you in a fight.

"Man, we got like two ounces of smoke in this bitch, so why the fuck you clocking my choke? Man, you better twist you something and back the fuck up off this here," Stacks said in a lazy drawl.

"Nigga, I rolled the bitch and I can't hit it? Brah, that syrup got you tripping," Cooter laughed, plucking a cigar from the box on the counter.

Stacks jiggled the white foam cup he was holding before taking a sip. "Boy, I was raised on Texas tea. I used to mix that Dimetap wit my Kool-Aid, and Mama ain't Hip to it for a hot one. When she did she busted my ass wider than all outside!" Stacks laughed.

"Let me try some," a Puerto Rican girl, wearing a sequence halter, spoke up. She was supposed to be an extra in the video, but at that point and time she was providing entertainment for Stacks and his crew. She reached for Cooter's cup, only for him to snatch it away.

"Easy, baby, you ain't ready to get ya lean on," Cooter told her.

"I don't see what the big deal is; it's just cough medicine and a little Hennessy," she said, clearly not understanding what she was dealing with.

Cooter shot her a comical look. "Cough medicine? Stacks," he tapped his partner's leg, "you hear this square bitch? Shorty, this ain't just cough medicine. This is doctor prescribed, top of the line; kick a cold in its monkey-ass cough medicine!"

"Preach nigga!" Stacks called from the sideline.

"Pretty lady, this here is the drink of champions where I come from, and trust me when I say that the Hennessey in this cup is the least of your worries."

It seemed like everyone in the camper was laughing at her. Even the two other girls she had rolled in with were snickering. Normally, the Puerto Rican girl would've spazzed out for a nigga trying to play her in public, but Stacks and his crew were an exception to the rule. They could laugh all they wanted to now, but when it was all said and done, she'd see to it that they came up outta their pockets.

"What's the joke, I wanna laugh?" Don B said, following Soda into the camper.

"Don, what it is?" Stacks raised his bulk off the chair just enough to give Don B a pound. "You niggaz ready to lose ya money, or what?"

"I hear that hot shit." Don B invited himself to a seat, to the right of the Puerto Rican girl. She batted her eyes at him but he seemed not to notice. "I got some of the best players in the city riding for me, daddy. Y'all niggaz is gonna get scraped."

Stacks gave a friendly chuckle. "I hear you talking, cat, but them street niggaz you got on ya squad ain't got nothing for us. With my man Cooter running the point, y'all is sunk!"

"I see y'all bringing ringers into it?" True said, looking at Cooter. "Texas Tech, right?"

"I see you do your homework," Cooter smiled. Only a few people knew that Cooter had been a basketball phenomenon back in his day. He was an all-American point guard for Texas Tech university, but his hoop dreams were derailed when he went to jail on a gun charge. Since then he had given his heart and dreams over to the streets.

"All day," True replied.

"Dawg, I wouldn't give a fuck if you played for the Globetrotters, you gonna get ya ass cut," Don B insisted.

"We'll see," Cooter said, lighting the blunt he had rolled.

"So what the business is, D, I know you gonna show us some of that East Coast hospitality?" Stacks asked.

"You know that. We gonna drink good, smoke good, and taste some of the sweetest tenders New York has to offer. As a matter of fact, my man is having a locked door joint, and we're good for the VIP treatment."

"That's what I'm talking about," Cooter exhaled the smoke he had been holding in his lungs. "I just hope they some bad bitches, cause the last time we hit a strip club up here them hos was looking way rough."

"Nah, that ain't how the Ice Man rolls. He only deals in the best quality of bitches," Don B assured him.

"Ice? You talking about a kid named Black Ice?" Soda asked, reminding everyone that he was in the room.

"Yeah, you know him?" Don B asked.

"Nah, but I've seen him before. He came through All-Star weekend when they hosted it in H-town. The boy had them bitches in thongs riding up and down the strip on choppers. Stacks, you remember that nigga?"

"Yeah, yeah, the dark-skinned cat with the big chain!" Cooter cut in. "Stacks, remember Buck and them niggaz tried to roll him for his chain, God bless."

"Yeah, that light-skinned bitch he had with him put something hot in old Buck's ass," Stacks recalled.

"That sounds like Black Ice." Don B smiled. "Ya boy must've had it coming, cause Ice ain't the violent type. He deals in pussy."

"As long as them bitches don't start dumbing out," Soda said.

"Nah, we good money. Ice is a stand-up nigga, and his bitches is kept in check," Don B said.

There was a knock on the camper door and a man wearing a headset came into the trailer. The small blond almost coughed up a lung from all the smoke in the enclosed area. "Stacks," he coughed, "they're ready for you."

"Showtime," Stacks addressed the room as he hauled himself out of the chair.

Chapter **15**

"DAMN, I AIN'T NEVER SEEN THIS MANY MUTHA-fuckas in the projects!" Lazy said, making his way through the crowd.

"They know Dawg is in the house," Chiba said loud enough for a group of young girls standing off to the side to hear him. "Yo, you see Don B or any of them niggaz out here?"

"I can't see nothing through this damn crowd," Lazy said, craning his neck.

"What's up, stranger?" A voice called from somewhere behind Lazy. He turned around and didn't know whether to smile or slap himself in the forehead when he saw Becky. Becky was a short chick who had what looked like too much ass for her small frame. Lazy had met her at the weed spot and had been known to hit it a time or three. Becky was nice to look at, but as soon as she opened her mouth it was a turnoff. She was one of those girls that didn't have higher than an eighth-grade education but was always trying to front like she was scholarly. Becky was notorious for using big words out of context and sounding like a complete ass. Though she wasn't the sharpest knife in the drawer, she had some of the sweetest head in the hood.

"Sup, baby girl?" Lazy said, like he was actually happy to see her.

"You." She poked a finger in his chest. "I've been trying to get wit you for a minute, but you act like you can't return phone calls."

"Yo, ma, I lost that phone a minute ago, and since it's a burnout, there wasn't no way for me to call and get it disconnected," he lied.

"I hear that hot shit, Lazy. So what you doing over here, you turned out for the video shoot, too?"

"Nah, I just came through to check my nigga Don B."

"Oh, I heard Don B was out here, but I ain't seen him. You think you can get me an autograph?"

"Man, what we look like, some goddamn groupies? Get ya own fucking autograph," Chiba cut in.

"You better check ya boy." She was speaking to Lazy, but looking at Chiba.

"Dude is a grown-ass man," Lazy shrugged.

"Anyway." She draped her arms around Lazy. "When you gonna come see a bitch? My pussy misses this love bone." She grabbed his crotch.

"This love bone misses ya pussy too, ma. I'll call you and we can set something up," he said, trying to get rid of her. But, of course, Becky didn't take the hint.

"Tell you what, why don't we dip off right quick and I can suck you off in the staircase." She licked his ear playfully. "I'll even let you come in my mouth."

"Umm, I like the sound of that," Lazy said, remembering how good Becky's mouth felt.

"Yo, Laz," Chiba called.

"In a minute, homey."

"Lazy!" Chiba said with a little more urgency in his voice.

"Damn nigga, *what?*" Lazy turned around. As soon as he did all he could say was, "Fuck!"

"DAMN, WHAT WERE YOU EATING? It stinks to high hell," Monique said, standing off to the side, holding her nose.

"Fuck you," Sharon said, balancing against the wall with one hand and wiping slobber from her bottom lip with the other. They had gotten about twenty yards from Sean's building before she started throwing up.

"I don't know why you was trying to chug that shit like you built like that," Dena said, trying to keep Sharon's hair from falling into the line of vomit.

"I can hold my liquor, I just didn't eat before I started drinking," Sharon said between gags.

"I hope you don't get to the shoot and start playing ya self," Mo said, looking at the crowd of people across the street. "Look at all them muthafuckas."

"Mo, leave the girl alone. You act like you ain't never called earl," Dena said, handing Sharon a napkin.

"I'm good; I just need a minute to get myself together." Sharon said, wiping her forehead then her mouth.

"You think it's any famous people there yet?" Monique asked.

"I sure hope so, cause I need some things," Sharon said.

"Yo sack-chasing ass is fresh off tossing ya cookies, and you thinking about getting up in a nigga's face? Sharon, ya ass is too much."

"Dena, I know you ain't talking, with the way you was all pressed up on Sean."

Dena gave her a disbelieving look. "Wasn't nobody up on that child-molesting bastard but you!"

"Y'all bitches knock it off and lets get across the street before these Harlem skanks snatch all the good stock." Mo started across the street, with Dena and a wobbly Sharon behind her.

To the two girls from Brooklyn, the St. Nick was a marvel, with its sizeable turnout for the video shoot. Cars were double- and triple-parked along the outskirts of the projects. The police wrote tickets and tried to chase most of the illegally parked drivers off, but with little luck. Dena was just about to step off the curb when a pearl-white Escalade cut her off. The driver was a short man with a box-shaped head and very alert eyes. The man in the passenger seat was handsome, with chocolate-colored skin and dreamy eyes. There were three females lounging in the back, but none so much as gave Dena a second look. When the man leaned over to holla at her out of the passenger window, Dena saw the glint of diamonds.

"Baby, those feet is way too precious for you to be walking on em like that," Black Ice said through the partially opened window. "Can I offer you a ride somewhere?"

"I'm good," Dena said, stepping around the car and into the street.

"Sweetheart, you're colder than a December chill," Ice yelled out of the driver's side window.

"I've been called worse," she said over her shoulder.

"Sho ya right. But check it, when you decide to get off ya high horse, ask around about me. The name is Black Ice. See about me, love," Ice said, before tapping Shorty, who eased the car away from the curb.

"Girl are you crazy!" Sharon almost shouted at Dena. "That was Black Ice!"

"Black what?" Dena asked.

"Black Ice, bitch. Next to Don B, that's the most well-connected cat in Harlem. Ol' boy was trying to holla, and you blew him off? You've gotta be out of ya fucking mind."

"Well, excuse me for not being star-struck," Dena said with an edge to her voice.

"D, it ain't about being star-struck. We came out here to bag some ballers, and you blew off one of the biggest fishes in the pond."

"Shit, I'd fuck that slick-talking nigga," Mo added.

"Who wouldn't you fuck?" Dena teased her. Sharon was still ranting about how Dena had played herself, but Dena wasn't listening. She couldn't front the cat they called Ice was fine, and he was definitely sitting on paper, but if she bit the first time he threw the bait it would give him leverage, and she wasn't with that. Dena was a girl who liked things her way. She reasoned that Ice, like everyone else, was there for the video shoot, so she would see him again before the night was over.

"Oh, I know that ain't who the fuck I think it is," Mo said, looking at something across the street. Dena followed her eyes and immediately felt her face tighten. Lazy was posted up across the street with some big-booty chick draped all over him. The fact that he could stand her up, but make the time to mack at a video shoot, made Dena mad, but she tried not to show it.

"That nigga is playing his self. I say we go over there and set it on him and his bitch," Sharon said.

"I'm wit that." Mo began taking off her earrings.

"Nah, I got this," Dena said in a calm voice. Wearing a pleasant smile, she began making her way in Lazy's direction. His man Chiba spotted her and tried to warn Lazy, but he didn't seem to be catching on. By the time he noticed Dena, she was standing just a few feet away. He had a sick look on his face, but he had no idea how sick he was gonna be when Dena finished with him.

"What's good, ma?" Lazy asked, smiling as if he hadn't just gotten caught with his hand in the cookie jar.

"You tell me," Dena gave Becky the once-over and was not impressed.

Lazy tried to downplay it. "Becky, this is my girl Dena. Dena, this is Becky. I know her from the block."

"Oh, so now you just know me from the block?" Becky folded her arms and glared at Lazy, but he never took his eyes off Dena.

"Yo, why you ain't return none of my phone calls," he asked Dena.

"I was busy and apparently so were you." She rolled her eyes at Becky.

"Oh, nah, it ain't like that. Me and Chiba had to make a run and I lost track of time."

"Must've been one hell of a run," Dena said in a very dry tone.

"Baby, let me just rap with you for a minute." He reached for her but she jerked away.

"Nah, don't holla at me, holla at ya little friend."

"I told you it ain't like that, D," he pleaded, drawing a chuckle from Becky.

"What's funny?" Dena turned her glare to Becky.

"Life," Becky smirked like she had a secret and wasn't going to tell. "Lazy, we still gonna do that, or what?"

"Oh, I'm sorry. Did I interrupt your plans?" Dena asked sarcastically.

"Not really. What we had planned will only take five minutes or so, but you're his girl, so I ain't gotta tell you that," Becky said smugly.

"I smell an ass whipping on the horizon," Mo said from the side-lines.

"Becky, shut the fuck up. Dena, let me holla at you for a minute." Lazy poorly tried to hide the panic that was creeping into his voice.

"Nah, I think me and my girls are gonna spin the block and see who's out. Maybe Stacks and them will let us hang out for a while in their trailer."

"Dena, don't play with me," Lazy warned.

"The only one playing is you!"

"Lazy, I got things to do, so you come check me when your finished with your combine," Becky said.

"My what?" He was thrown off by the statement.

"Your combine, you know, mistress."

Dena had to laugh at that one. "The word is 'concubine,' you dumb bitch, and I think you're pointing the finger the wrong way."

"Bitch? I got ya bitch." Becky went to step up, but Lazy pushed her back.

"Dena, don't pay this crazy-ass girl no mind, just let me talk to you," Lazy pleaded.

"I'm done talking." She tried to step away, but Lazy gripped her roughly by the arm.

"Dena, don't walk away from me when I'm talking."

"Nigga, you better open ya fucking hand and let my girl's arm run out of it. I don't know how the fuck y'all do in Harlem, but we gets it popping in the Stuy!" Big Mo stepped up. Lazy thought about it for a minute and released Dena's arm.

"Lazy, you can keep ya little project bitch and make some project babies, for all I care, but I ain't got time for it. Me and my bitches is gonna go see where the real men are at." Lazy said something else, but Dena tuned him out and headed further into the projects.

Chapter **16**

JAH EASED ALONG THE EDGE OF THE PROJECTS, trying to draw as little attention to himself as possible. Though he wasn't still out laying niggaz to sleep, he had made countless enemies over the years. In fact, it was within the St. Nicholas projects that one of Yoshi's attackers and his crew had met their demise at Jah's hands. He had tracked Rel and his crew to their stronghold in the projects and murdered them in the most horrible fashion. The media talked about Slick getting his asshole shot out for weeks.

"Ashes to muthafuckin ashes," Jah said, flicking his cigarette to the ground. Lost in his own thoughts, he made his way towards 131st Street. Along the way he nodded to cats he knew and mad dogged the youngsters who were out trying to look hard. It amused Jah the way the young boys watched movies and tried to live them out in everyday life. Most of them didn't have the will or the balls to kill a man, and the few who did lacked the finesse to do it and get away with it.

Jah was about to enter the projects, when a familiar face caught his attention. Valerie was her name, if he recalled correctly. She still looked the same as she did last summer, with the exception of having lost almost ten pounds. Stress could do that to you. Her boyfriend had been a small-time dealer named Ralph, who ran with Rel's crew. It had been Ralph who led Slick and Rel to where Jah hung out and a gunfight followed that left young Crazy Eight dead. Ralph had managed to escape, but it was only temporary. On the night that he tried to leave town, Jah had cornered the young man and shot him in the face outside Valerie's apartment. The police tried to connect her to the murder but were never able to make the charges stick.

"Too many old memories here," Jah said, rounding the corner of 131st to enter the projects that way.

"Break yo self, nigga," a voice hissed behind Jah.

His body immediately went rigid, hands hanging loose at his sides. He thought about going for the gun he had holstered at his side, but doubted he would make it before he took one in the back. One thing was for sure though, he wasn't going down without a fight. At the exact moment he was about to spin he heard a familiar laughter. Turning slowly, his eyes fell upon Tech's smiling face.

"Nigga, I could've peeled yo shit!" Tech laughed, holding his 9 in plain view, like there weren't dozens of police out and about in the hood.

"That shit ain't fucking funny!" Jah snapped, snatching the gun from Tech.

"Come on, B, I was only playing. Why you getting so mad?" Tech asked, not really understanding why Jah was so uptight.

Jah was harsh with Tech, but he hadn't meant to be. In all the years Jah had been putting it down in the streets, he always prided himself on being on point. Had this been a year earlier, a youngster like Tech could've never snuck up on him like that. It just added to his already growing paranoia that being in a relationship was dulling his edge.

"Dawg, what the fuck took you so long to get here, anyway?" Jah handed him his pistol back.

"Man, this lil freak bitch came by Mom's house to break a nigga off, so you know I had to tap that pussy," Tech boasted.

"Horny-ass lil nigga." Jah mushed him playfully.

"Yo, kid, I peeped mad vics out there. These niggaz is shining and shit, like they don't know what it is. Yo, we can cake off on the real."

"Man, I ain't trying to stick nobody up out here. For one thing, its too many police rolling, and for another thing, my girl is working the shoot, how the fuck I'ma pull a lick out here?"

"You right, J, I wasn't thinking."

"You never are." Jah shook his head. "Come on, let's go in here and see if we can find Yoshi." He stepped into the projects and began picking his way through the crowd. It was amazing how people could don their Sunday best and spend all day trying to get their fifteen minutes of fame on someone's camera, but let there be a rally for something of note, and most cats found somewhere else to be. The logic of people sickened Jah sometimes, which is why he kept his circle so tight.

"Psst, hey, ma," Tech called to a trio of young ladies passing them. One he thought he had seen around before, but the other two were new faces. The big girl gave him a second look, but the other two didn't look his way. "Yo, stop acting like that; all a nigga want is a little conversation."

The big girl slowed her pace but didn't stop. "Shorty, see me in a few years." As an afterthought she added: "But tell ya man don't stray too far, ya heard?"

"Them some wild-ass girls," Jah laughed.

"Definitely not from Harlem," Tech added. "Yo, Jah, ain't that Yoshi?" Tech pointed to a cluster of people standing off to the side of the building closest to Eighth Avenue.

At first Jah couldn't see her through the crowd, but it only took a minute for his radar to kick in. There she was, his vision of perfection, hard at work, applying her craft. One of the girls appeared to be having a bad hair day, and Yoshi was carefully applying glue to the base of the track. She handled her business the same way Jah handled his, with tact and grace. Looking at her angelic face, he couldn't believe that he had said those horrible things to her earlier, and he intended to make it right.

"You wanna go holla at her?" Tech asked.

Jah thought on it for a minute. "Nah, looks like they're about to start shooting. So, let her handle her business first." Jah and Tech found perches on a nearby fence and watched intently.

"YOU HEAR THAT LIL NIGGA trying to talk slick?" Dena giggled.

"Hey ma, how tired is that shit?" Sharon added.

"I don't know, I think if shorty was a little older I might've let him eat my pussy," Mo laughed. "But the quiet nigga wit him could definitely get it."

"Who, Jah? Nah, he ain't ya speed Mo," Sharon told her.

"You know him?"

"I know of him. His brother had a baby with my sister's best friend, God bless. The looney nigga shot her, then killed himself in jail. The way I heard it all, them niggaz is crazy in that family."

"He looks too sweet to be dangerous," Mo said.

"Mo, this is my town, so I know the four-one-one on everybody. Now, I ain't never hung with the boy personally, but let my sister and them tell it, he's killed damn near as many muthafuckas as AIDS," Sharon said seriously.

"I ain't fucking wit him," Dena said.

A pale man shaped like a pencil, wearing a Starter cap with the brim creased way too deep, walked towards them at a brisk pace. He was speaking with a woman who looked to be on the verge of being plump, with red hair. Both of them wore nervous expressions.

"Judy, how the hell could you let this happen?" Starter Cap said to the redhead.

"Mark, it wasn't my fault, I was only doing what I was told. Sid said to make sure Stacks and his people had *whatever* they needed, and that's what I did. I didn't know she was going to drink the whole bottle."

"Fucking Gray Goose." Mark slapped himself in the forehead. "Judy, we're three hours behind schedule, and these girls and their fucking egos are driving me up the damn wall. I need a pretty face to put behind the wheel of that Cadillac like fucking yesterday."

"Mark, maybe we could just use one of the other girls?" Judy asked.

"You've gotta be kidding me? Ayanna and Peaches are the best eye candy we've got out here, and you know neither one of those cunts are gonna wanna compromise. Look, I don't give a fuck what you have to do; get me a girl to put behind the wheel of that fucking car in five minutes of get the fuck off my set!" Mark stormed away ranting to himself.

Judy looked around and saw the people looking at her who were trying to pretend they weren't. Mark had once again managed to make her feel like less than shit. It wasn't bad enough that he had made her suck him off to get the position as assistant director on the video, but he made her do most of the work and took all the credit. Judy wanted to fall down on the spot and cry, but she wasn't willing to give Mark the satisfaction. He was an asshole coke addict who couldn't keep his dick hard for a New York minute, but Mark Spellman was one of the most sought-after video directors on the coast.

"Fuck, I gotta get this done," Judy said, trying to compose herself. She quickly thumbed through the head shots of the girls she had in her portfolio and reluctantly had to agree with Mark. All the girls had body, but none of their faces were really camera-worthy. She scanned the crowd, hoping that God would be kind and send her a blessing, but all she saw were so-so looking females. She was just about to suck it up and turn in her radio when her eyes fell on the Brooklyn/Harlem trio. Judy suddenly had a brilliant idea.

"Excuse me." She motioned to the girls.

"Is this bitch talking to us?" Sharon asked.

"Ladies, hi." Judy walked over. "My name is Judy Goldberg and I'm one of the assistant directors on the video." The girls were all giving her suspicious stares. "Look." Judy dropped the phony smile. "I know you girls just saw me get my ass chewed out, so I'm gonna shoot straight with you. One of the girls got sick and we need a replacement for the video."

"Now you're speaking my language. Where y'all need me to stand?" Sharon stepped out and did her bad bitch strut.

Judy scrunched her nose a bit. "No offense sweetie, but we only need one girl, and I was kind of thinking of her." She pointed to Dena.

"Me? I don't know anything about acting," Dena resisted.

"Honey, you're not delivering an Oscar speech, all you're doing is sitting behind the wheel of the car and bobbing to the music. It'll take an hour or two tops, and I'll give you five hundred dollars in cash. But we only got about five minutes to get you dressed and on set, so it's now or never."

"I don't know . . . ," Dena began.

"Yes, she'll do it," Mo cut in. "Dean, you better quit playing and shine for that camera."

"Great. Come with me and we'll get you situated." Judy started to lead Dena away.

"What about us?" Sharon spoke up. Despite the look Mo was giving her, she continued. "How you just gonna leave us hanging, and we all rolled together. If she gets to be on set, we get to be there, too."

"Sorry, we just need one. Can somebody get me a twenty on Yoshi, I need a girl camera ready like yesterday!" Judy barked into her radio, ignoring Sharon. But hearing Yoshi's name gave Sharon a plan.

"Yo, how you not gonna let us on when my aunt Yoshi is working on the video?" Sharon said.

Judy just looked at her. She needed the girl dressed and in front of the camera by the time Stacks came out of his trailer, or heads would roll. Obviously, the young one was going to cause a problem, so Judy said fuck it. "Okay, but if you're not who you say you are I'm having you tossed off the set."

Chapter **17**

THE SUN WAS SLOWLY MAKING ITS DESCENT INTO the western horizon, but there was still enough natural light that you could appreciate the beauty of the day it had been. The heat was still a very relevant issue, but it didn't really bother Billy or Reese, who sat under the cool air conditioning of One Fish Two Fish.

"Damn, you act like you got a grudge against that." Reese nodded toward the snow crab leg that Billy was tearing into.

"I might as well have. For all the money they charge for these, they could at least cook them in beer. Ain't nothing like some beer and crushed red pepper to make ya crabs pop correctly," Billy said, dipping a piece of crabmeat into her melted butter.

"Told you we should've just hit the fish market and did it ourselves."

"Nah, cause then we'd have to clean all this shit up," Billy joked, motioning towards the pieces of shell scattered on the tablecloth. "But I don't mind, cause we don't get to hang much anymore."

"That's my fault, Billy, but you know I be crazy busy with Alex," Reese said.

"Reese, you ain't never gotta apologize to anybody for doing what you gotta do for yours. You know I love you either way, ma. We can't club forever."

"That's what I be trying to tell my little fast-ass sister. On the real, that girl is headed for trouble."

"Sharon's probably just feeling herself," Billy tried to reason.

"Billy, that little bitch is doing more than feeling herself. My mother thinks she's going through a stage, but I know different. The streets talk."

"I know she ain't on it like that?"

"Shit, why she ain't? Billy, I done heard some shit about that little freaky bitch in the streets that made me wanna go home and kill her. Of course she denies it all with the crying and extra shit to fool my moms, but I can see by the way she moves that Sharon ain't thinking like a little girl. We were that age once, remember?"

"Ain't no comparison, cause when you, Yoshi, and Rhonda was out here fucking like rabbits, I kept my pussy tight," Billy teased her. "Yo, I remember when Rhonda had Trev and Mongo up in her crib drinking and smoking together and shit, like they weren't both fucking her. Man, that girl was always dancing on the razor's edge."

"Yeah." Reese gave a halfhearted laugh. "Rhonda's ass was a trip."

"She was a pain in the ass sometimes, but I can't front like I don't miss my bitch. Not a day goes by when I don't think of her," Billy said.

Reese was silent for a minute, using her straw to stir the melting ice in her Sprite. When she looked up from the glass there was a very serious look in her eyes. "Billy, do you ever think about how life is gonna play out for you?"

"I mean, I *guess;* but I'm not sure I see what you're getting at?" Billy admitted.

"Life. How we live. Jesus, Billy, Rhonda had her bullshit about her, but she didn't deserve to go out the way she did. Is death and hardship the only thing this life has to offer us?"

Billy put her crab leg down to give Reese her undivided attention. "Reese, I agree with you about Rhonda not having to go out like that, but *that* end isn't for all of us. Rhonda played a dangerous game and it caught up with her. It came with the lifestyle. Reese, we already got two strikes against us because we're black and we're female, but I believe that life is really what you make it. Being born in the ghetto doesn't mean we have to stay there, ma. We can sit on our asses and apply our petty hustles to get by, or we can choose to take control of our own destinies."

Reese chuckled softly. "Billy, you always make things sound simple."

Billy shrugged. "Sometimes you gotta look at it in black-and-white for it to make sense. Long story short, you got a baby girl now, so it ain't about you no more. Alex is gonna need you on the way up; you just gotta make it your business to show her a better way than you were taught."

"That goes without saying. My baby girl is all I got," Reese said.

"And ya girls," Billy corrected her.

"True," Reese nodded. "It's just us against the world, fuck a nigga," she said scornfully. "I do what I gotta do for my daughter, but this load gets heavy sometime. You've got Marcus, so there's someone to help you shoulder it."

"Yeah, Marcus is a comfort, but I don't make myself dependent on him. I let him know from the gate that I *can* and *will* do for myself, and that's why he has to respect me. Reese." Billy placed her hand over Reese's. "Let me break something down to you, ma. Having a man in your life to help raise a baby is a blessing, true, but hardly a necessity in this day and age. You can be a mother and a father to your child and still give her all the love and affection she needs. Reese, I know you're down on yourself sometimes for the circumstances surrounding Alexis, but you gotta get over it. Stressing over some nigga that don't wanna be bothered ain't gonna do shit in helping you raise your daughter."

"I know, Billy. It just hurts sometimes, not having anyone to turn to," Reese said, barely above a whisper.

"Reese, for as long as my asshole points to the ground, you've got someone to turn to," Billy said. They both tried to remain serious, but couldn't help but laugh. "Now, I don't know about you, but I'm ready for a drink."

. . .

"YES, LORD, PUSSY AS FAR as the eye can see. What a beautiful sight!" Cooter said, ogling the scantily clad young ladies on the set.

"Just the way I like it," Stacks agreed. "One thing I gotta give y'all credit for is these fine-ass hos out here in Harlem, D."

"Come on, son, you know we only deal in quality," Don B said to Stacks, while listening to the caller on the other end of his cell phone.

Yoshi passed them, with three young girls on her heels. She waved hello to the group, but didn't bother to stop.

"Now, that's one lil bitch that I can't wait to bust out!" Stacks said, following her with his eyes.

"Yeah, Yoshi is a bad bitch, but her man is a beast. I ain't ready to go to the guns over no pussy," True said.

"Who, Jah? Man, that lil nigga can't possibly know what to do with all that," Cooter said.

"I used to think the same thing, but they've been rocking hard body since last summer, so he must be doing something right," Don B said.

"Man, that love shit don't mean nothing where Stacks Green is involved," Stacks said, speaking of himself in third person. "You throw enough bread at any bitch and she'll get down."

"Nah, not Yoshi. Shorty used to be on it, but since that shit that popped off she's been on some new shit—real square-like," True told him.

"Once a ho . . . ," Stacks began.

"Always a ho!" Cooter finished, giving his man dap.

"But yo, who them little bitches she got wit her?" Soda asked.

"One of them is a lil chicken-head bitch from round the way, but the other two I don't know," True said.

"Man, I wouldn't mind getting a taste of shorty in the gray shorts," Stacks said, enjoying the last glimpses of Dena's ass before she disappeared into the trailer with Yoshi.

"Who knows what's gonna go down before the day is over," Don B mused.

"Yo, Don!" a voice called from somewhere in the crowd. Don B swept his sunglass-covered eyes through the sea of faces and spotted Lazy and Chiba behind the security barricade.

"Yo, let my lil mans and them through!" Don B called over to security.

The beefy S.O.D. cop who was working the video shoot hesitated at first because he didn't know Don B, but if he was with the star then he must've had some sort of pull. Using a beefy arm to hold the crowd back, he allowed True and Chiba to pass the barricade.

"Punk-ass rent-a-cop," Lazy mumbled, stepping around the cop. "What it is, big homey?" He dapped Don B.

"Chilling, young'n. I see you over there making a pain in the ass out ya self," Don B joked.

"Man, fuck them pigs. They acting like a nigga was lying about being with Big Dawg. I thought I was gonna have to fuck son up."

"Chill, Laz, you know I can't have my star point guard out here getting into dumb shit; we got soldiers for that."

"So this is ya point guard?" Cooter gave Lazy a comical look.

"Starting point guard," Lazy corrected him.

"Yeah, this young Lazy," Don B introduced him. Stacks gave Lazy a pound, but Cooter just stared at him while Soda nodded. "My man is one of the hottest young boys to come out of Harlem. Ain't nobody fucking wit him."

"We'll see, come game day," Cooter said.

"Yo, what took you niggaz so long to get here?" True asked.

"This nigga was arguing with his broad," Chiba volunteered.

"Fuck you, Chiba!" Lazy spat. "You know I'm too cold to be out here arguing with a bitch. I was trying to straighten out a lil situation, that's all it was."

"Whatever, nigga. Dena looked like she was ready to black on ya ass when she saw you with Becky."

"See, that's why I ain't got no girl. A nigga out here getting too much money and love to be tied down with a broad nagging him and shit," Don B said. "I keep telling you, Laz, you gonna chase this paper or you gonna chase these bitches, you can't do both."

"Speaking of bitches, you see them fine mutha fuckas over there?" Cooter nodded behind Don B. The men turned around and saw three beauties coming their way, with a rail-thin man bringing up the rear.

"Ice Man!" Don B shouted affectionately.

"Don of all Harlem, how you be, my nigga?" Black Ice flashed his diamond smile. "You remember Wendy and Lisa—but the caramel filling is Cinnamon."

"So very sweet." Stacks eyeballed the ladies.

"I'm sorry, player, I didn't get your name," Black Ice addressed Stacks.

"Stacks Green, baby, cause that's all I do."

"A man after my own heart," Ice grinned. "Black Ice, homey; but if you spending for my goods, you can just call me Ice."

"Stacks, this is the cat I was telling you about," Don B reminded him.

"Yeah, the man with all the pretty ladies," Stacks said.

"The one and only," Ice tipped his white, fitted Yankee cap. "So, I hear that next to Big Dawg, the Green team is the next big thing?"

"We the only big thing, partner," Cooter said.

"Sho ya right," Ice said, looking at him like you would a butler who spoke out of turn.

"Stacks, we're ready for you," Judy said, walking up.

"A'ight, time to show these New Yorkers what stunting is all about." Stacks popped his collar and followed Judy to the set.

Chapter 18

"I DON'T BELIEVE YOUR LIL ASS," YOSHI SAID TO Sharon, while fixing Dena's hair.

"Yoshi, that white bitch was trying to stunt on me, so I had to pull her coat," Sharon reasoned.

"First of all, watch ya mouth, second of all, you don't come to my job clowning and dropping my name. You could've got me fired with that shit!"

"I'm sorry, Yoshi. Me and my girls just wanted to get up in here," Sharon hit her with the puppy-dog eyes.

Yoshi wanted to be upset, but she couldn't. Sharon and her crew reminded her a lot of what she and her girls were like back in the day. "Sharon, you need your ass kicked, and you can bet your last dollar that I'm telling Reese."

"Like she cares." Sharon folded her arms. "She's more concerned with finding a daddy for Alex than with what I'm doing."

Yoshi stopped doing Dena's hair and turned an angry gaze to Sharon. "Let me tell you something, for as long as your little ass is black I better not ever hear you say some off-the-wall shit like that about your sister or your niece. Reese has been through a lot, and instead of you acting like a damn brat you need to try and have some understanding.

A lesser bitch would've folded under the pressure, but your sister stepped to the plate and is taking care of business. Now, I don't care what y'all are arguing about this time, but what I do care is that y'all are sisters, and you better damn well remember it. Do you understand me?"

"Yes, Yoshi," Sharon said with her eyes cast to the ground. Of all Reese's friends, she had the most love and respect for Yoshi. She loved her because Yoshi was down-to-earth and easy to talk to, but she respected Yoshi because of what she had been through. Sharon knew that Yoshi had been through something that would've put most bitches on suicide watch, but Yoshi still managed to walk with her head high. She was a rider to the heart.

"Lets go, Yoshi!" one of the PAs called, knocking on the camper door.

"I'm coming, damn it!" Yoshi yelled, causing Dena to flinch. "Sorry, Dena, these muthafuckas be on my damn nerves." Yoshi shifted Dena's hair again, but still wasn't able to get the effect she was looking for. "Damn, this hair. If I had more time I could really hook you up, girl."

"Its cool, I think you did a good job," Dena said, admiring the slight curl Yoshi had applied to her hair.

"Nah, Yoshibelle don't do good; it's gotta be fire or nothing." Yoshi turned Dena's head from left to right trying to see what else she could do to spruce it up. She hated working under the gun, but the fact that Dena was a naturally pretty girl helped a great deal. She was still young, so she wasn't as stacked as some of the other girls, but she definitely had it going on. The camera would mostly be focused on her face, so it was important that everything was tight, but Dena's hair was killing her. She was sure that if she'd had ample time to get it together, Dena could be a killer. Sadly, time was a luxury they didn't have. Always good at improvising, Yoshi came up with something.

"Sharon, I need you to go tell Judy that we'll be ready in two seconds," Yoshi told her.

"Who's Judy? And why *I* gotta go tell her?"

"Judy is the white girl with the red hair and you have to go because I told you to, unless you think you're grown enough to whip my ass now."

"Nah, I ain't messing with you, cuzo," Sharon laughed.

"That's what I thought. Now go give Judy the message. Mo," she turned to the big girl who had been sitting quietly at a vanity table, "hand me that hat over there so I can get our girl right."

ALL DAY LONG THE PROJECTS had been buzzing with activity, but now it was strangely still. It was as if the noise had been sucked away and tucked in a box somewhere. A slow mist, totally out of place in the concrete jungle, rolled in and covered everything for up to a foot off the ground. Even the birds seemed still for a time, but the silence was abruptly ended when the heavy bass thudded through the mounted speaker towers.

The opening lines for Stacks's single, "Die for My Chain," tugged at the first cords of everyone's adrenaline. The beat was reminiscent of something Death Row would've put out in the nineties, but with a Crunk feel to it. Some hailed it as one of the hardest beats in the last ten years. Let Stacks tell it, Soda produced the track; but there were a few people who would've argued that. One story was that an up-and-coming producer named Cords had created it and struck a bargain to sell the beat for twenty thousand, but before the money changed hands Cords was found shot to death in his mother's car. No one ever proved Stacks's involvement, but the theory hung in the air.

A sour apple green Cadillac sedan DeVille lurched from the mist into the view of the camera. Stacks Green's massive frame sat perched atop the back seat of the car, with his Texas piece looking like the Bat Signal under the artificial lights. In a slow country drawl he began his verse, speeding up and becoming clearer as the beat changed. Young Soda was slouched in the seat beside him with a blunt dangling from his mouth. Much like True, the camera seemed to love him. Cooter sat in the passenger seat, bobbing to the beat with a scowl on his face.

Dena sat behind the wheel of the hog, looking almost ten years older than she actually was. Yoshi had done an immaculate job, applying just enough makeup for her to glow, but not enough to look painted. She was wearing a black leather jacket, accented by a black Apple Jack hat that only showed the ends of her loosely curled hair. With a cigar clenched between her perfect teeth, she looked every bit of a gangstress. Though focus was really on Ayanna, Dena didn't go unnoticed.

Chiba tapped Lazy. "Yo, ain't that ya wife?"

Lazy heard Chiba, but he didn't respond. He just stood there slack-jawed, wondering what he had missed. Dena was looking right, sitting behind the wheel of the Caddy, all dolled up for the camera. When the remote hydraulics kicked in, Dena bent and rocked in time with the car. There were several inquires circulating through the crowd about who the chick pushing the hog was. All Lazy could do was stare, as his boo claimed her fifteen minutes of fame.

When the car finally stopped bouncing, Stacks stepped over the back of it and hopped to the ground, surprisingly nimble for a man his size. With a combination of swift hand gestures Stacks blacked out on the track, occasionally raining spittle on himself. On cue, Don B and True walked into frame. Stacks gave True a pound while Don B got right up on the camera and dangled his Big Dawg chain. The police had a hell of a time holding the crowd back as the two Harlem heroes got their stunt on for the camera.

"Girl, you see the size of that nigga's chain?" Roxy tapped Sugar. A blonde China doll wig covered most of her face, but you could still see the sky blue feather dangling from her right ear. She was wearing a one-piece gold body suit with the matching thigh-high stilettos. The front of the suit was slit to the point just above where her pubic hairs would start, if she hadn't shaved.

"Shit, niggaz in the Stuy can see it, the way that muthafucka is shining," Sugar said. The denim mini she wore covered her ass but left little to the imagination.

"I wonder if it's real."

Sugar gave her a funny look. "Girl, of course it's real. I did my homework on them niggaz before we stepped out. You know I got the main line on everybody. Long story short, them niggaz getting cake."

"I can believe it," Roxy nodded. "So, you come up with a way to get close to these niggaz yet?"

"I ain't think that far ahead, but what nigga don't love pussy? Shit, who got a better shot than us?"

"Not a bitch out here!" Roxy said with conviction.

"That's what I'm talking about. I ain't sure yet, but by the time they break to shoot the final scene up this bitch, I'll have figured it out."

Chapter 19

FOR THE NEXT HOUR AND A HALF JAH WATCHED them perform the opening scenes of the video over and over, each time fascinating him more than the last. For someone who had never been out of the ghetto, the work that went into creating a video was simply amazing. As he watched Stacks Green strut through the projects like he owned it, kicking his verses, he felt a presence behind him. This time Jah wouldn't be caught off guard as he spun with his gun drawn.

"I surrender," Spooky said playfully, raising his hands in surrender.

"Big Spook," Jah said with a broad smile. "Boy, I see you still ain't got no sense of time. You'd probably be late to your own funeral."

"Bull shit. I wouldn't show to my funeral at all, cause ain't a nigga hard enough to kill me," Spooky boasted, hugging his comrade.

"If that's how you greet ya friends, I'd hate to see how you greet ya enemies," Shannon said from the sidelines.

Spooky introduced the newcomer. "Jah, this my nigga Shannon, from the Stuy. And I know you remember Big Nate."

"Big bro, what da deal?" Jah gave Nate a pound.

"Same shit, different day," Nate replied. "I see you still out here slinging iron."

"You know how it goes in the jungle, Nate, only the strong and the armed survive," Jah told him. "What took y'all so long to get up here?"

"Had a little mess to clean up," Spooky said casually. "I see you, Tech, what's good?" he asked the youngster.

"Trying to be like you when I grow up," Tech beamed.

"Nah, you don't wanna be like me. I'm barely old enough to drink and I feel like I'm pushing thirty."

"The life will do that to you," Nate added.

"So, what y'all doing over here in the cut, plotting on a vic?" Spooky asked.

"Nah, just taking in the show," Jah replied.

"The boy, Stacks, got skills for a country nigga," Shannon said.

"He a'ight." Jah cast a glance over his shoulder to where the video was being shot.

"I see them Big Dawg niggaz is still out here stunting." Spooky eyed Don B, who was bopping back and forth in front of the camera with a bottle of champagne in his hand.

"Them boys is shining something mean," Shannon said with a greasy look in his eye.

Spooky caught the look. "Nah, fam, they ain't for us. Don B and his team ain't nothing like them simple-ass niggaz in L.G. They jewels is heavy, but so is they muscle, and we don't need them kinda problems."

"Anybody can get got," Shannon said.

"They ain't for us," Spooky said in a tone that let him know it wasn't up for discussion.

"What's up wit all these fine-ass bitches out here? Jah, I know you and the boy Tech been out here macking all day," Nate said.

"I got at a few of them, but you know ya boy Jah gotta behave, unless he want Yoshi to run up in his shit," Tech said.

"Oh, ya girl is in the video?" Shannon asked, checking out the different chicks trying to figure out which one Jah was claiming, so he could peruse the rest.

"Nah, she works behind the scenes doing makeup and wardrobe," Jah replied.

"Yeah, sometimes a nigga forgets that Yoshi squared up. Where is she, anyway, so I can say what up?" Spooky asked.

"She round here somewhere." Jah looked around for her.

"Looks like they're about to break. Yo, lets get closer to the action, I wanna see who out here is holding." Spooky moved deeper into the crowd.

"This nigga is thirsty," Shannon said before following him, with Nate, Jah, and Tech creeping behind.

"GOD, I THOUGHT I WAS gonna faint when the cameras started rolling," Dena said excitedly, while fanning herself.

"Yo, my girl was on her gangsta shit for real!" Sharon said, mimicking the pose Dena struck behind the wheel of the Cadillac.

"Dena, I can't even front, you looked way natural in front of that camera. Maybe you found your calling," Mo said.

"I couldn't have done anything without Yoshi. Thank you so much." Dena gave Yoshi a warm hug.

"Girl, I didn't do anything but bring out what was already there," Yoshi said modestly.

"Group hug!" Cooter said, intruding on the girls' space.

"Cooter, get yo ass outta here." Yoshi swatted him away. Of Stacks's whole crew, she found him the most offensive.

"Yoshi, you know I got a secret crush on you." He winked.

"I don't care what you got, but you need to stay the fuck outta my space," she said seriously. Cooter looked like he was about to say something slick, but a stern look from Stacks kept him quiet.

"Sorry about that, Yoshi. You know Cooter don't know when to quit playing," Stacks said easily, stealing away some of the tension that was hanging in the air.

"Check ya boy, or do I need to?"

"Nah, I don't think that'll be necessary," Stacks said, trying to hide the amusement in his voice. He knew Cooter was an animal that could tear Yoshi's ass up, but telling her that wouldn't help the situation. "Look, we about to motivate back to the trailer and sip a lil something before we gotta dip to the next location. Y'all are welcomed to come."

"Nah, I think I'll pass," Yoshi said.

"Come on, Yoshi. I know you ain't too good to have a drink wit a nigga?" Stacks asked.

"Stacks, you know I ain't on it like that, but as soon as I get comfortable these people are gonna be calling me to dress the girls for the next scene."

Stacks gave her a look. "Baby, if that's the only thing stopping you, then you ain't got nothing to worry about. I'm the boss, remember?"

"I don't think so, Stacks."

Stacks moved closer to her and draped his arm around her. Though he didn't do it in a sexual way, Yoshi knew what was on his mind. "Baby, one drink ain't gonna kill you."

"Nah, but her boyfriend might," Jah said, scaring the hell out of everyone. "Am I interrupting something?" His voice wasn't threatening, but there was something dangerous lurking beneath the surface.

"Jah, what're you doing here, baby?" She shrugged Stacks's arm off and went to her man.

"I came through to talk to my girl, but if you're busy I can come back," he said to Yoshi, but he was looking at Stacks and his crew.

"Ain't nothing, playboy, we just out here jawing," Stacks told him. "Say, man, I've been trying to hit you on the Jack for a minute. What, you ain't fucking wit me no more?"

"Yeah, I'm fucking wit you, Stacks. A nigga just been busy, feel me?"

"Yeah, I know how it is, man, but the offer still stands if you want the paper. I'm gonna be here all week and can always use an extra gun."

"I'll get wit you on it."

"Jah, what's good, nigga?" True stepped up.

Jah's face softened a bit seeing True. "True, what it is?" He gave him a pound.

"Out here trying to eat, like everybody else. Yo, I ain't know you did security work?"

Jah shrugged. "I split a nigga's shit from time to time when the paper is right, you know how I do it."

"If I had known that, I'd have been fucked with you, kid. Devil and Remo is good, but them niggaz is way crazy," True joked.

"Crazy kept yo little ass outta the emergency room this long, T," Remo said, reminding everyone that he and Devil were shadowing them. Unlike True, he and Devil felt the heat coming from the young cats and positioned themselves accordingly.

"Fuck you, Remo," True said playfully. "But Jah, you need to come out and fuck wit us one night. Shit, the life might loosen you up a bit."

"Man, I be paying that muthafucka top dollar and he still act like it ain't enough bread," Stacks butted in.

Jah turned his cold eyes to him and said, "It ain't always about the paper, Stacks. For me to pop my gun I gotta truly believe in the cause."

Those last words brought down an uncomfortable silence. Stacks's lips were curled into a smile, but his eyes flashed menace. He was a king and used to being spoken to as such. Jah's face was neither pleasant nor aggressive. He stared at Stacks blankly, but his eyes never wavered. It was only a matter of time before the two trains reached the station prematurely and there was a wreck.

"Nigga, stop acting like we ain't damn near fam," Don B cut in, patting Jah on the back. He didn't miss the fact that Spooky tensed when he moved, but Jah remained completely at ease. "Jah, I remember the day when you and True got caught selling chopped-up aspirin on Convent," Don B reminded him.

True laughed. "Yo, that was some funny shit. Them big-head niggaz from up the block wanted to murk us, but Big Paul stepped in and deaded that." The moment True finished his sentence everyone stopped laughing. "Damn, my fault, Jah. I ain't mean to—"

"It's cool, man. We all had love for my brother," Jah said with conviction.

"Bless the dead," Don B said, pouring some of his champagne on the ground. "Check it though, Jah, you know the dawgz always had love for you, cause you one of the last stand-up niggaz in the hood.

You know how the Don do it, so refreshments will be served in the trailer. You and ya boys are more than welcome."

Jah nodded in respect. "I appreciate the offer, but let me mingle wit my peoples for a minute and see what's good."

"Nuff said," Don B gave him dap.

"Jah . . . ," Yoshi began.

"Let me get wit you for a minute." He took her by the arm and led her off to the side, leaving everyone else standing around quietly. It was young Soda who lightened the mood.

"Well, the last time I checked, we was about to get faded. Who's with me?" Soda asked.

"We wit it," Sharon spoke up.

THE CREW HAD GOTTEN ALL the shots they needed of the St. Nicholas projects and were packing up to move to the next location. It had been a hectic day, filled with ruined shots and improvising, but they managed to get the perfect shots for the video. Young ladies of different shapes and sizes were hand-picked by Soda and Cooter, while Don B and Stacks disappeared into the trailer. Bringing up the rear of the groupies were Roxy and Sugar. They had slipped behind the barricade and melted into the throng of women from the video. The way Sugar and Roxy were chatting it up with Peaches, it looked as though they were a part of the shoot. Unfortunately, the set security officer wasn't so easily duped.

"Hold up, where are y'all two going," the muscular black man in the too-tight T-shirt asked, as he stopped Sugar and Roxy at the door.

"Inside, where do you think?" Sugar tried to step past, but he blocked her path.

"I don't remember getting the nod about you two. Who sent you?"

"My man over there with the chain." She pointed at Cooter.

The man gave her a disbelieving look. "Yo, Cooter!" he called, getting the man's attention. "You know these two?"

Cooter squinted at them from across the park. "Man, if they legal let they asses in!"

The man gave Sugar and Roxy the once-over before stepping to the side to let them in. As Roxy passed, he grabbed her arm. "Ima see you later, ma." He patted her playfully on the ass and slammed the trailer door behind them.

A FEW YARDS AWAY, DENA was talking to a lanky black kid who claimed to have some type of connections. Like the five that had come before him, she took his card and tucked it into her purse. She was about to brush him off and catch up with her girls when Lazy and Chiba walked up.

"I need to holla at you," Lazy said, giving his back to the kid Dena had been talking to.

"Damn, ain't you got no manners?" Dena snaked her neck.

"Listen, man—," the kid began, but Chiba waved him silent.

"Dawg, this ain't ya concern, so I suggest you keep it moving," Chiba said seriously.

Though the kid was dressed the part, white T-shirt and baggy jeans, with a fitted cap, that was the extent of his thug nature. He knew the real thing when he saw it and really didn't want any part of the two Harlem teens. "A'ight," he nodded, trying not to sound too defeated. "Shorty, give me a shout when you get a minute," he slunk off under Lazy's murderous gaze.

"Yo, you outta bounds right now!" Dena said to Lazy.

"You out here talking to niggaz and playing video ho, and *I'm* outta bounds?" Lazy snapped. Before he even saw her move, Dena slapped him flush in the mouth, drawing stares from the crowd.

"Let me tell you something, Lance, I don't give a fuck how you talk to ya little sideline bitches, but for as long as your ass is black you better respect me."

"Is you fucking crazy? I should knock ya fucking head off!" Lazy went to rush her but True jumped in between them.

"Son, what is you doing?" He held Lazy back.

"Nah, shorty on some bullshit!" Lazy struggled against him, but the heavier True held firm.

"Homey, you the one on some bullshit now. Laze, it ain't none of my business what goes on between you and ya lady, but it is my business to make sure you don't play ya self and wind up in jail. Did you forget where the fuck you are?" True nodded to the police who were now watching with interest.

"You right, I'm bugging." Lazy took a deep breath. "Dena—"

"Lazy, miss me with whatever the fuck you're about to say, cause I don't wanna hear it. You've made a fool of me for the last time!" she shouted.

"Why don't you shut the fuck up and listen for a minute!" he shouted back.

"Nigga, you ain't got no papers on me, so I ain't gotta do a muthafuckin thing except stay the fly bitch that I am. Now, if you're finished embarrassing yourself and me, I'm going back to the trailer with my girls to get fucked up." She started towards Stacks's trailer.

"Dena!" he yelled after her.

"Kill ya self, nigga!" she said over her shoulder. Lazy moved to follow her, but Chiba grabbed him by the arm.

"Dawg, she hot right now. Let her cool off, then try talking to her," Chiba suggested.

Lazy stood there for a minute, just staring at Dena's back until she disappeared into the trailer. "I need to go for a walk."

"A'ight, why don't y'all niggaz gimme this walk to the store. I gotta get some more Dutch's," True said.

"Come on, man," Chiba steered Lazy towards the avenue.

DENA HAD AN EXTRA BOUNCE in her step, walking to the trailer on 131st, between the blocks. Inside, she felt like she could die every time she thought about Lazy and the lil bitch from the ave, but she refused to show him that. Being weak for a man was what had her ready to break down in the first place. She had an idea that Lazy was fucking around, but seeing it live and direct just did something to her. Then he had the nerve to try to act like she was the one with the attitude. "Wrong and strong," she mumbled.

There was a barrel-chested man wearing a tight T-shirt with the word SECURITY scrawled across it. He had a smooth chocolate face with a clean shaven head, putting one in the mind of Tyrese, if he were forty pounds heavier. When he saw Dena approach, the scowl on his face turned into a charismatic grin.

"How you doing?" he asked.

She shrugged. "Been better, but I'm here."

"I know that's right." He looked her up and down. "Yo, you did ya thing in the video, ma."

"Thank you, I was nervous as hell," she giggled.

"You'd never know it. I've worked on a lot of videos, and you played to the camera better than a lot of chicks I've seen."

"Maybe because I'm not a chick, I'm a lady," Dena told him.

He raised his hands in playful surrender. "My fault, ma. Didn't mean to offend."

"I'm not offended, sweetie, just telling you like it is," Dena said.

"Fo sho." He stepped to the side so she could enter. As Dena passed he touched her hand to get her attention. "Are you gonna be in the next scene at the 40/40?"

"I don't know yet. Why, you working that location too?" she asked.

"Oh, I'll be there, but I won't be working. Me and my business partner, Mark, are supposed to be meeting up for some drinks. You should come hang out with us if you're not doing anything."

"I'll think on it," she said with a slight smile.

The man handed her a gold business card. "Well, the name is Raheem and this is my contact info. Don't think on it too long though." He winked.

"Whatever," she said, stepping into the trailer with Raheem's eyes glued to her ass.

Chapter 20

"YO, THERE THAT NIGGA GO RIGHT THERE!"
Charlie said excitedly, as if Sha hadn't seen them already.

"He ain't got no security wit him. We need to move on his ass and smoke them pussies he walking wit!" Spider said anxiously. He was flicking the safety of his gun back and forth.

"Hold up, y'all ain't said nothing about killing!" Tina, who was behind the wheel, spoke up.

"Mind ya fucking business and keep the engine running, bitch," Spider snapped.

"The both of y'all shut the fuck up and stop acting like some damn clowns," Charlie quieted them. "Sha Boogie, what you trying to do?"

Sha Boogie just stared at Jah. He took slow puffs of his cigarette and expelled the smoke before answering Charlie's question. "Let's ride." With adrenaline pumping through them, the three men stepped from the car and made their way in True's direction.

"JAH, WHAT THE HELL IS your problem?" Yoshi asked, once they were out of earshot. Jah had led her out of the projects and over to the front of Gladys Hampton, on 131st Street and Eighth Avenue.

"I could ask you the same, walking up to find that nigga, Stacks, groping my shorty!" Jah shot back.

"First of all, you know how I feel about that 'shorty' shit, so please watch it. Second of all, wasn't nobody groping me. Them niggaz was going to get drunk and asked if I wanted to come."

"And you was on your way back with them to get ya lush on, right?" Jah asked angrily.

Yoshi took a step back and glared at Jah. "You must have a low fucking opinion of me, Jah. Unlike some of us, I don't let business and pleasure overlap or intermingle. I'm here to do a job, not get drunk with Stacks Green and the rest of them hillbilly-ass niggaz. First you kicking the bullshit this morning, now you popping up at my job acting a fool. Jah, what the hell is wrong with you today?"

The impulsive side of him roared for Jah to bark on her and let her know that there was still an animal lurking beneath the surface, but he resisted. Instead, he composed himself and spoke as calmly as he could. "Yoshi, I don't mean to zone out on you like that, but I know how shit goes on these video sets. These rap niggaz be in violation, and I don't know how I feel with you hanging around them all day."

"Jah, you know every time I do a video I get whoever's starring to give you first dibs on security so we can be on set together, but you're the one thumbing your nose at the jobs."

"Cause these pussy niggaz get under my skin. How many of these fake-ass thugs throw a little bread around and think they can have whatever they want? Come on, how many of these bitches have fucked Stacks or a member of his crew since they've been in town?"

"And what does that have to do with me?" Jah didn't answer, but the look on his face said a lot. "Oh, so you think I'm out there on some party-girl shit, huh? Baby, I told you that I hung that 'China' shit up when we got together. I can't change what happened in the past, but I can change my mind-set and the way I go about shit."

Jah opened and closed his hands, trying to get them to stop shaking. "I know," he said softly. "Its just that when I think of you maybe being with one of them other niggaz I just blank out."

Yoshi placed a hand against his cheek. Just feeling her skin against his quieted Jah's beast. "Jah, for as long as you're doing the right thing you don't have to picture me with anybody but you. You gotta learn to trust me like I trust you."

"I'm trying, ma, but—"

"But what? Jah, you know who I was when you got with me, like I knew who you were. I know at times it's a hard pill to swallow, but we agreed we'd try. The same way you worry about me out here chasing niggaz, I wonder if you're gonna come home at night. How many times have I sat up thinking I was gonna get that phone call telling me that you'd been killed out here? Trust is a two-way street."

Jah put his head down. "I'm sorry, Yoshi. Sorry for what happened earlier and sorry for being paranoid."

"Jah," she draped her arms around his neck, "lets not build our relationship on apologies. We just have to do better with understanding what makes the other tick," she kissed him tenderly on the lips. "Now, how bout I dip outta here early and we go home and have make up sex?"

"I dig the way that sounds. Let me just tell Tech and Spooky . . ." Jah's words suddenly trialed off and she could feel his heart quickening in his chest. When she went to ask him what's wrong, she found herself thrown to the ground. Dazed, Yoshi looked up to see Jah drawing his gun.

TRUE LED LAZY AND CHIBA through the crowd, occasionally stopping to sign an autograph or two. Lazy was a few paces behind him, talking to Chiba. Two young ladies had ran up on them and asked for autographs, not even realizing they weren't actually a part of the group. The attention from the ladies took the sting out of the way Dena played him, but he was still tight. They had managed to make it out to the avenue through the throng of young men and women trying to get a glimpse of True. The store directly across from the video shoot only had White Owls, causing the trio to have to venture further up and away from the shoot.

They had almost made it to 132nd Street when Chiba stopped

short. Noticing that he was talking to himself, Lazy turned around and saw three men wearing bandannas around their faces making hurried steps in their direction. By the time True even realized something was about to pop off, Chiba was already in motion. Yanking the small .25 from his pocket, he began firing wildly.

Charlie dove to the side, narrowly escaping one of the small bullets as it sparked off the ground. Sha Boogie returned fire with his 9, trying to lay True, who was now scrambling for cover. Spider noticed Jah standing off in the cut with his gun drawn and assumed he was an enemy. From a crouch, he fired two shots in Jah's direction. Jah easily avoided the bullets, but one came dangerously close to where Yoshi was crouched, distracting him. When he turned to shout for her to take cover, a bullet grazed his neck, throwing him off balance.

"Oh shit," Lazy screamed, as he crawled under a car. From his vantage point he could see True and Chiba banging out with the other gunmen in the middle of the street. Chiba tried to run up on the gunman closest to him to get a better shot, momentarily moving out of Lazy's line of vision. Lazy screamed for him to get down, but the sound of gunfire drowned out his frightened voice. Something heavy crashed into the car he had been hiding under, followed by Chiba's body hitting the ground a few feet away. Lazy looked into his best friend's eyes and watched in horror as the life slowly drained from them.

"Die, niggaz!" Spider roared, firing everywhere at once. He wasn't giving the trigger of his pistol a break, but his untrained arm hit more inanimate objects than targets. A flicker of movement caught his attention, causing him to turn and fire. There was a sound of a body hitting the ground behind one of the front pillars of the entrance to Gladys Hampton, but when Spider saw a female hand flop from behind it he knew that he had missed his target. He was about to move closer, but a wailing coming from somewhere near the lobby froze him in place.

JAH LAY AGAINST THE WALL of the Gladys Hampton lobby, breathing like he had just run a marathon. His eyes were fixed on Yoshi, who was laying on the ground bleeding from a hole Jah couldn't see, but he couldn't force himself to go to her. Seeing his lover down tipped the balance between madness and sanity in his mind and Jah howled. Instead of moving to check Yoshi, he stepped from behind the pillar with his weapon at the ready.

Spider saw Jah come into view, but there was something in the man's eyes that made him hesitate for a second. This was all the time Jah needed to put a bullet through his head, and dump three more in his chest as he passed him. Thinking about nothing but the kill, Jah started walking towards Sha and Charlie, popping shots. People screamed and ran for cover as bullets lit the corner of 131st and Eighth, but Jah kept firing.

Tina pulled to the curb and motioned for Sha to get in. Knowing when to bow out, he quickly did so. Charlie jumped out from behind a car and popped two shots at Jah. Jah acted like he hadn't even noticed as he turned and fired on Charlie. Charlie and Sha were just thugs shooting guns; Jah was a skilled killer. The first bullet exploded Charlie's shoulder, and he was saved from the second one when he fell behind the car. Before Jah could finish him, a car pulled up and Charlie's remaining comrades pulled him inside and peeled off. Jah continued to fire at the car until his clip and his soul were empty.

"JAH, GIMME THE HAMMER!" SPOOKY shook him.

Jah blinked and looked up at his friend as if he didn't understand what he was saying. At first he thought that the ordeal might've been a bad dream, but when he looked down and saw Yoshi laying unconscious in his arms he knew it was real. Her pulse was faint and she didn't respond when he shook her. Her clothes were so bloody that he didn't even know where to begin looking for the wound.

"You hear me talking to you, nigga? Gimmie the fucking strap before the bulls get here!" Spooky shook him roughly. Finally realizing what was going on, he handed Spooky the gun and watched him disappear around the corner.

"I'm sorry, baby," he sobbed over her, and then listened as the sounds of sirens closed in on him.

Chapter **21**

"I KEEP TELLING YOU, NIGGA, IF BALL'N WAS A sport, I'd be the fucking MVP!" Don B boasted, waving a bottle of champagne in the air, spilling a little on the group of girls who were hanging on his every word.

"Of the season, maybe, but it definitely goes to me in the playoffs," Stacks challenged, hoisting a bottle of Hennessy.

"Y'all niggaz is crazy!" Cooter laughed. "Yo, hurry ya ass up, Soda. I gotta take a leak." He banged on the bathroom door.

"In a minute!" Soda yelled back.

"That young boy is in there getting it in," Stacks laughed.

"I told y'all cats that I only deal in the finest quality of trim," Black Ice said from his seat in the lounge chair, minus one of his girls.

"I might have to see what that's about, if Soda's ass ever gets up out the pussy," Cooter said.

"All money down is a bet." Black Ice stroked Cinnamon's leg.

The door creaked open and Dena stepped in. The hungry glares she got from the men assembled made her feel like a piece of fresh meat tossed to a bunch of starving lions. She gave a brief glance around the room and spotted her girls crammed together on the couch with some of the others. Without looking anyone in the eyes, Dena made her way over to the couch.

"Ah, so we meet again," Black Ice said to her slyly. "It's a little cramped over there on the couch, but we got room for you over here." He patted the chair.

"I'm good," Dena said, sitting on the arm of the chair closest to Mo. Though she tried not to look over at Black Ice, she couldn't help it. He was fine as hell and looking like new money, decked out in shiny jewels. Though everything sensible within Dena told her Black Ice was no good, there was just something about him that she couldn't resist.

"So I hear you a big man in Texas?" Sharon asked Stacks in a flirtatious manor.

"Shorty, I'm almost three hundred pounds. I'm a big man wherever I go," he joked.

"Being big just means there's more of us to love," Mo added.

"I know that's right, lil mama." Stacks raised his bottle, to which Mo responded by raising her glass.

Soda came out of the bathroom looking like he had just been in a fight, with Lisa close behind him. Her lipstick was smeared and her clothes looked ruffled, but she still marched across the trailer like she was the queen of Sheba and plopped on Black Ice's lap. Whispering softly into his ear, she placed a small roll of bills into his jacket pocket. Dena peeped it all, but didn't say anything.

"Damn, Daddy, I hope you saved some for the rest of us," Roxy said to Soda.

"We country boys, ma. That means we go long and strong, feel me?" Cooter answered for him.

"That's probably cause you ain't never ran into a thoroughbred bitch from Brooklyn," Sugar added.

"I know that's right," Mo cosigned.

"I see the planet of Brooklyn is in here strong." Don B moved closer to Roxy. Draping his arm around her, he tipped his bottle and refilled her cup.

"If you don't know, ya might find out." Roxy hoisted her glass to toast Don B.

"So what's up, where the smoke at?" Sharon asked, sipping a plastic cup of straight Vodka. She was getting sauced up like she wasn't throwing up a few hours prior.

"You gets it in, huh?" Cooter said, giving her a seductive look.

"All day, every day." She matched his stare.

"Shorty, is you even old enough to be drinking and smoking and shit?" Stacks asked, lighting a blunt of Haze Don B had rolled for him.

"Hell yeah, I just turned eighteen the other day and a bitch is still celebrating," Sharon lied.

"Is that right?" Stacks was speaking to Sharon, but looking at Dena who just turned her head.

"Fuck it, let her hit the weed," Cooter said, disappearing into the bathroom. "Yo, it smells like straight ass in here!" he called out, causing everyone in the room to laugh. Soda just sat in the corner and blushed.

"Shorty, you don't talk much, do you?" Black Ice asked Dena.

"The name is Dena, not Shorty. And I talk when someone has something noteworthy to say."

Black Ice smiled. "Ms. Dena, everything that comes out of my mouth is noteworthy, you just gotta listen."

For the next few minutes the occupants of the trailer smoked weed and drank, with everyone catching a nice buzz. Black Ice was finally able to get through to Dena to the point of making small talk. For as brash as he seemed, the man was actually quite intelligent and articulate, which surprised her. When she asked him what he did he downplayed it as being in adult entertainment, but the look she got from the girl named Cinnamon made her doubt the sincerity of it. Dena was about to probe further into his profession when Raheem poked his head in the trailer.

"Yo, everybody stay put. Some shit just went down up the block," he told them, while still trying to listen to his squawking radio.

"What's going on?" Stacks asked.

"Somebody got shot. Is all ya peoples accounted for?" Raheem asked him.

"All my niggaz is here," Stacks looked around to double-check. "Don?"

Don B looked around and it dawned on him. "Oh shit, True and Lazy are out there." Don B bounded for the door, gun at the ready, but Raheem stopped him.

"Hold on, my man." He placed a hand against Don B's chest.

"Fuck that hold on shit, my lil brother might be hurt out there." Don B slapped his hand away. Though the years had been kind to Don B financially, he was still a hood nigga who would let it go at the drop of a hat. Raheem knew that trying to force him to do the right thing wouldn't work, so he tried reasoning.

"Don B, if you go charging out there with that pistol it ain't gonna help, cause the pigs is gonna slap them bracelets on you. My people are gonna make sure ya man gets back to you in one piece. Just let us do our job."

Don B continued to glare at Raheem through his shades. He had seen Raheem around the hood, so he knew he was a street cat, but he wasn't a Dawg and couldn't understand the bond they all shared. True was like family and there was no way he was going to trust his safety to an outsider.

"Remo, Devil, put them fucking drinks down and go wit this nigga and check on True. If y'all niggaz was on ya job, shit like this wouldn't happen," he barked.

Remo shot Don a murderous look, but Devil's hand on his shoulder cut off whatever he was about to say. Remo wasn't used to people speaking to him like that, even if he was on their payroll. He was a man first, and anybody that didn't respect that got dealt with accordingly. Devil, on the other hand, was more sensitive to the issue. He and Don B had a history spanning back to when his uncle Red was running the streets. Not only were they friends, but they hailed from the same set.

"Don," Devil addressed him. "I know you're upset right now, but you need to calm down. You pay me and Remo for a service, so let us handle it. Come on, Remo." Devil pulled him by the arm. Remo allowed Devil to lead him from the trailer, but made a note to himself to have a private conversation with the self-proclaimed Don when it was all said and done.

"Don, you my nigga; can't get no bigger, but you know ya boy hot and them people gonna wanna question everybody here," Black Ice said, motioning to his ladies that it was time to boogie.

"Do what you gotta do, Ice," Don snapped. The anger wasn't directed at Ice, so he didn't take it personal.

"My nigga." He draped his arm around Don B and leaned in to whisper to him. "Don, I'm sure True is okay, but on another note I'm gonna put some eyes on these Texas niggaz just to make sure our investment is protected, no disrespect to you, of course."

The mention of money brought Don B somewhat back to himself. "I feel you, Ice, that's why you'll always be my nigga."

"Its nothing. Yo, call my phone and let me know if the 40/40 is still the order of business. If not, we can take ya boys to Shooter's."

"That's a bet." Don B gave him a pound.

Black Ice stopped short of the door and turned to Dena and her crew. "I suspect the police will be asking around about ID in a minute. That offer for a ride still stands." He looked directly at Dena.

"We good," Sharon said, settling further into the chair, closer to where Soda was now sitting. He smelled like weed and pussy, but it didn't seem to bother her.

"Actually, I think we'll take you up on that." Dena grabbed Sharon by the hand.

"Shorty, the party ain't over just yet. We bout to shoot the next scene at the 40," Cooter protested.

"We'll catch you down there." Dena continued to the door, with Sharon still gripped firmly about the hand.

"Dena, why you tripping?" Sharon asked, trying to pull away.

"Bring ya ass on and be quiet," Dena continued. What she wasn't saying was that she was really saving them from embarrassment and Stacks from jail. If the police came through and found their underage asses drinking and getting high, all hell was going to break loose. The shoot-out would be nothing in the headlines compared to Stacks getting slapped with a child-endangerment case.

Seeing that the video scene was no longer popping, Sugar decided she and Roxy needed to be where the grass was greener. "You got room for two more?"

Chapter 22

JAH SAT IN THE DRAB WHITE ROOM LOST IN HIS own thoughts. The sound of the different machines and the whirling of the air conditioner made a strange rhythm in his head, giving him something to focus on other than his grief and feeling of utter failure. In the bed directly in front of him, Yoshi rested quietly. God had been merciful, as the bullet was able to be successfully removed from her collarbone. It would leave a nasty scar and there was always the possibility of nerve damage, but she would live, no thanks to him.

When the police arrived on the scene they found the streets riddled with bullets, a man dead on the curb and Jah clutching Yoshi's prone body. Initially, they had sought to arrest him until a cluster of bystanders gave them a fake story about what went down. Reluctantly, they let Jah go to attend Yoshi, but only after he agreed to come in for questioning later on.

Things had happened so fast that he didn't have time to think about it. One minute he saw men coming with guns, and instinct then took over from there. The next thing he knew he was caught in the middle of a war that had nothing to do with him. He had found out through the grapevine that the shooters were coming for True, and Jah drawing his hammer prematurely had made Yoshi a casualty. He wanted to cry every time he thought of it, but he had no tears left.

Jah placed Yoshi's limp hand between his and raised it to his face. Even smeared by blood and dirt, he could still smell the scent of her skin. He kissed the back of her hand and she stirred a bit, but the medication wouldn't let her open her eyes. Though the wound wasn't a fatal one, they had to give her a heavier dose of the anesthetic, because she had become frantic at one point during the surgery.

Death and Jah had walked hand in hand since he was a child, and the death of his mentor and closest kin was further evidence of that. Though he walked through the fire virtually untouched, those around him paid the penance. As he looked down at his own bloody clothes, flashes ran through his mind of all the times he found himself in that condition and when his would be the blood staining someone else's shirt. Jah's young soul had already racked up a good number of sins, so a few more wouldn't make much difference, he reasoned. True's beef or not, they had harmed his lady and had to pay.

"I'm sorry, ma." He stood up to leave. Yoshi's head flopped from side to side as if she was struggling to tell him something, but even if she could speak there would be no reasoning with Jah. When blood called, he answered.

OUTSIDE THE EMERGENCY ROOM THE police and hospital security did what they could to keep order. Though the rest of the video had been canceled for the day due to the shooting, there were quite a few hangers-on that weren't ready to let it go. There had been a procession of people on foot and in cars that followed the ambulance from St. Nick over the few short blocks to Lenox, all still trying to get at the Dawgz.

While Stacks and his people headed back to the hotel to get changed for the night, the members of Big Dawg headed to the hospital. Though his manager insisted that it wasn't a good idea, True insisted they come through to make sure Yoshi was good. Of them all, he was the closet to Yoshi through the bond he shared with Rhonda. He knew better than anyone else what she had endured, especially at the hands of his own comrades, so he felt obligated to help her along in the recovery. This is what prompted him to plug her with the wardrobe gig. To everyone's surprise, including True's, she was a natural at it.

The police had initially tried to make some of the members leave, as their presence was causing a situation, but True held fast, insisting that they were all family of the victim. A shoving match almost ensued between Big Dawg security and the police, but a young Black nurse had stepped in on their behalf. She was a chick from the hood that had been seen around young Lazy a few times. They agreed that the bodyguards could stay with True and Don B, but the rest of the entourage had to go.

"You know their faces from anywhere?" Don B asked True, who was leaning against the vending machine. Remo and Devil formed a protective barrier so that the two could speak in private.

"Nah, I ain't even get to get that good of a look at them," True said. "All I know is, me and the young boys was walking to the store, the next thing you know Chiba pops off. Don, they laid the young boy!" True said emotionally.

"I know it." Don B remembered the exploits of young Chiba. Of all the lil niggaz that ran around with Big Dawg, Chiba was one of the most solid, even more so than Lazy. Like Don and True, Chiba had been born in the streets.

"I hear one of em got laid out," Remo added.

"Yeah. The boy Spider. He's a little nigga from out of Brooklyn who ain't worth the sheet they used to cover his ass with," Devil said. "Any idea why some Brooklyn niggaz would want you clipped?" he asked True.

"Probably just haters," True said. "Fuck them niggaz, they can't see me."

"Still, I need to keep security on you at all times," Don B. insisted.

"Don, I can understand that shit when we out, but this is Harlem, baby—home!" True protested.

"Yo, you see what happened with Pain and them niggaz, and I ain't trying to let you go out like that. I don't know who I'm gonna put on you yet, but you're definitely getting a babysitter," Don B said, letting him know that his decision was final.

"Haters ain't gonna try to pop you with po-po lurking not even two blocks away. Nah, that shit is deeper than just hating," Don B said.

Billy and Reese came rushing into the emergency room entrance of Harlem hospital. In addition to their regular security, there were several police officers stationed around and outside the emergency room. Reese wondered if maybe there was someone famous getting treated at the hospital, too, but that thought died away to an icy ball in the pit of her stomach when she saw Don B and his minions huddled in the corner. If she'd had it her way, they'd have avoided them altogether, but of course Billy needed answers.

"Billy, what's good?" Don B nodded to her. He knew Billy from the hood, but they developed a somewhat personal relationship when she agreed to coach his team in the big game against Stacks's team. Though he would surely be clowned for his choice on game day, he was confident in her skills. Unlike some, he had seen Billy play, and the girl's play and her basketball IQ was off the chain.

"Nothing, just tying to find out what's good with my girl? Somebody tell me what happened?" When everyone seemed to be more interested in the floor than looking at her, Billy got aggressive. "Yo, you mean to tell me my girl got popped on a video shoot y'all niggaz was at and nobody gonna tell me what happened? Niggaz, that ain't Harlem, talk to me!"

"Billy, let me talk to you in private for a minute," Spooky spoke up. He had been so deep in the cut that Billy hadn't even noticed him in the waiting area. She agreed, but before following him outside she glared at all the members of Big Dawg in attendance. Reese just dipped her head and followed them out.

"Tell me something, Spooky," Billy demanded, clearly getting impatient.

"Look, near as I can figure, some cats came looking for the boy

True and Jah started popping. Yoshi was on the scene when it jumped and she got hit." He said matter-of-factly.

"What the fuck do you mean? Jah started popping with Yoshi standing there? Is he crazy or just stupid?" Billy fired back.

"Billy, don't shoot the messenger, a'ight? You know damn well Jah wouldn't put Yoshi in harm's way like that unless it was serious." He paused to let a cop pass who was returning from his cigarette break. "My guess is he seen the shooters coming and drew. When you've done as much dirt as that nigga, you don't know who might be coming for ya head."

"Where's Jah?" Reese asked.

"He's upstairs with Yoshi," Spooky told her.

"I need to go check on my girl. Come on Reese," Yoshi said, heading back into the waiting area. Just as they had crossed the room, Jah was stepping off the elevator. His clothes were a hot mess and there was blood dried to his skin, but the most disturbing thing about him was his tear-streaked cheeks. Jah was a man who didn't cry easily, and the few times when he allowed himself to, it usually went poorly for whomever was connected to it.

"Jah, what's going on?" Billy went to him. Though he tried to make his face pleasant there was something very disturbing in his eyes.

"She's sleeping," he said, just above a whisper. When he noticed the way Billy was looking at him he turned away. "I'm gonna go now, so y'all can have ya time with her."

"Jah, don't stray too far, cause I need to talk to you," Billy said.

Jah gave her a look that could've almost been mistaken for loving. "Billy, you know how much I respect ya, gangsta, but any talking I do from here on out will be done over smoking barrels." Ignoring her pleas for him to wait, Jah marched out to address the crew from Big Dawg.

DON B AND COMPANY WERE standing outside the emergency room smoking cigarettes and plotting. Spooky stood off to the side, talking on his cell and watching their movements. Though he didn't think the cats would intentionally put Jah or his wife in harm's way, it went without saying that the situation would get interesting. Jah was hardly one to let something like this slide, and he would need his crime partner at his side for whatever was going to come of it.

When Jah came out everyone got quiet. Spooky went to say something, but Jah totally ignored him and headed in the direction of Don B and his team. He looked like a serial killer, standing there in blood-stained clothes with a vacant look in his eyes. The streak of blood that had dried on his face didn't even seem to bother him. Devil and Remo went to block his path, but the look that Jah gave them gave the men pause. Though they didn't know Jah personally, they knew his type, and cats like that were unpredictable when dealing with grief. Sensing the mounting tension, Don B motioned for them to let Jah through.

"Yo, I'm sorry that—," Don B began.

Jah cut him off with a wave of his hand. "Dawg, ain't nothing you can say to ease what I feel right now. I'm gonna do some talking and y'all gonna do some listening."

Remo looked like he was thinking about flexing, so Spooky moved to stand directly beside his partner. With an icy look, he stared down the members of Big Dawg and their security without batting an eye. The look he gave them let each and every man know that he was more than willing to get down for his comrade.

"True," Jah addressed the youngster. "I need to know everything you know about them niggaz that came to hit you."

True tired to downplay it. "Yo, I don't know nothing about them. They was probably just some niggaz trying to make a name for themselves off me."

"That's bullshit and we both know it," Jah shut him down. "Ain't no niggaz, no matter how thirsty, gonna try to stick a muthafucka on a video shoot. Shit, not only was the NYPD on set, but there were hip-hop cops everywhere. Them boys had a personal stake on yo ass, and I think if you rack ya brain hard enough you'll think of a reason that a muthafucka wanted you dead; but until you do I'm gonna be ya fucking shadow."

"Shorty, me and my nigga handle security. We don't need some hot-under-the-collar, underqualified punk fucking up our rhythm," Remo said, stepping up.

Jah gave him a cold stare. "My dude, I'm nineteen years old and done dropped almost as many niggaz as years I been on earth. I think that makes me more than qualified. Furthermore, my girl got shot in this bullshit, so it's personal now. Y'all do what y'all do, but me and the boy True is gonna be joined at the hip until I taste some blood."

"You'll get to taste a lot of that, fucking wit us," Devil said threateningly.

"You'd be surprised how big my appetite is." Jah stared the older man down.

"Is there a problem over here?" a lanky cop, wearing a uniform that was a size too big, asked.

"Nah, we good," Don B told him. He waited until the cop returned to his post before addressing Jah. "Homey, I know you feeling in a way right now, but this is serious business we dealing with here. True is about to be a star, and we can't have niggaz around him just popping off from emotions. The stakes are too high."

"Don, don't nobody know how high the stakes is better than me," Jah told him. "How the fuck would you feel if ya lady got popped cause of some shit you ain't have nothing to do with? Nah, staying close to True is the only way I'm gonna get right with them niggaz. You can't deny me this, dawg."

Don B stared at Jah for a minute. To say that he felt Jah's pain would've been a lie, because Don B hadn't walked the same path Jah had. His girl raped, his brother committed suicide, and now this. The boy had been through a lot, and not even the Don could overlook his reasoning for wanting to get his hands dirty. But emotional cats sometimes made impulsive mistakes, which is why Don B was hesitant to put him on. The upside to it was that Jah was so vicious with it that a muthafucka couldn't get within twenty feet of True without catching something hot. In their situation, he would make the perfect guard dog. Another good thing was the fact that True and Jah were close in age and already had a history, so the young rapper would be comfortable with Jah at his side, as opposed to Remo or Devil. This solved both the problems of having someone reliable to watch over True as well as protecting Don B's interests.

"So be it," Don B. agreed. "Handle ya business with wifey, then come see me. You a part of the pack now, Jah."

"No disrespect, Don, but this wolf has already got a pack." Jah looked over at Spooky. "True, I'll see you in a minute." Jah headed out of the waiting area with Spooky backing out behind him.

IT WAS ALMOST ONE IN the morning when Michelle finally arrived back at her apartment. She was supposed to be working the three-to-eleven shift at the hospital, but the sudden arrival of the rappers and their entourage made of mess of that. They were loud, rude, and stunk of weed, so it was inevitable that the police would give them a hard time, especially when you had people outside pissing on hospital property instead of using one of the bathrooms. In all her days of working at Harlem Hospital, she had never seen the emergency room in such a circuslike state. The only reason she had even stuck her neck out and interceded on their part was because they were friends of Lazy's.

When Michelle stepped into her apartment she immediately froze. There was the distinct smell of cigarette smoke in the air, but she didn't smoke. Taking her mace from her purse, she made slow steps into the apartment. Her hand shook violently as she made her way towards the living room. From the hall she could hear the television blaring and the sound of a lighter flicking. Michelle jumped from behind the wall, prepared to blind whoever had broken into her home and almost shitted herself when she saw Lazy sitting in the dark in front of the television.

"Boy, you scared the hell out of me. What're you doing in here sitting in the dark?" she asked, flicking the light on. There was an empty bottle of Hennessey on the floor by his feet, and a half-drained forty-ounce bottle of beer. Lazy wore a grim expression on his face and his eyes looked like he'd been crying. "Baby, what's wrong?"

"He's gone?" Lazy whispered. His voice sounded raw and she could tell from the slight slur that he was piss drunk.

"What? Who's gone?" she asked, starting to get nervous. "Lazy, what's wrong?" She moved to stand in front of him. Without warning Lazy buried his face in her chest and sobbed.

From what she could make out, Lazy and his friend Chiba had been involved in the incident that led to the girl getting shot. When they brought the dead body in, it had never even occurred to Michelle to ask the identity. She knew Chiba, and though they didn't like each other, she wouldn't have wished death on the young boy. Her heart went out to Lazy and it was all she could do to keep from breaking down right along with him.

"It's gonna be okay, baby," she said, stroking the back of his head.

"My nigga gone, Michelle. They shot him right in front of me." Lazy sobbed hysterically. Even in his drunken state his hands rubbed absently up and down her body, as he liked to do when they were together.

Michelle felt his pain, but she also saw his condition as an opening to have her way with him. "Don't worry about it, baby," she kissed one tear streaked cheek then the other. "Your woman is here," she began trailing her tongue along his collarbone, drawing a low moan from the young man.

"Baby, it hurts so much," he half moaned, half cried.

"Hush, now. I'm gonna make all the pain go away." She slid down and undid his pants. Lazy's waterlogged eyes rolled back in his head as Michelle began to gently suck him off. She licked his balls, then made her way up to his shaft and thoroughly lubricated it with her spit so it would slide right in. Lazy protested a bit when she tried to mount him with no condom, but once she got him inside her it was all good. Michelle rode him in a slow rhythm, grinding just a little deeper when he hit her spot. Lazy was so drunk that she thought he would never cum, but just as she started to see spots from her own multiple orgasms she felt Lazy's body go rigid, just before warm fluid filled her womb. Panting, she leaned in, still with him inside her, and held Lazy while he slept.

Chapter **23**

THERE WASN'T MUCH ROOM TO LOUNGE IN THE Escalade, but for the most part they were comfortable. Shorty was at his usual post behind the wheel while Ice lounged in the passenger seat. Dena found herself wedged between Lisa and Cinnamon, with Roxy and Wendy against the doors. This left Mo, Sharon, and Sugar to occupy the rear row. They didn't look happy about it, but it was better than walking.

Wendy twisted up a blunt of some shit that smelled like scorched honey. Dena didn't usually smoke with people that she wasn't familiar with, but the weed smelled too good to pass on. As soon as she hit the weed and felt it tickle, her lungs she knew it was that sticky. After about four or five tokes she was starting to feel real good.

"Who wants candy?" Lisa sang, pulling a sandwich bag full of off-white powder from her purse. Dena had never tried it, but she knew cocaine when she saw it, or so she thought.

"Whooo-wee, you holding that brown!" Shorty said, looking through the rearview mirror.

"If the white don't get you right—," Lisa began.

"You can get down off the brown!" Cinnamon finished the cadence.

Lisa scooped a small amount of powder onto her pinky nail and inhaled. She was trying to hold back the sneeze that was building in her nose, but lost it, sprinkling the back of Ice's seat and neck. "Shit!"

"God damn, Lisa!" Ice yelled, wiping the back of his neck with his sleeve.

"I'm sorry, Daddy; you know this shit be up in a bitch's sinuses."

"Lisa, you are such a fucking pig," Cinnamon said, taking the Baggie from Lisa. She dipped her fingernail into the powder and started snorting it greedily.

"The both of you bitches ain't nothing but some hypes." Wendy shook her head. "Where the hell is y'all manners; did you see if the ladies wanted a bump?" Wendy motioned towards the other passengers.

"I'm good," Roxy said, smoking the blunt down to a clip.

"What about you, pretty lady?" Lisa draped her arm around Dena.

Dena stared at the Baggie that Cinnamon was now trying to hand to her. She felt like all eyes were on her, waiting to see what she was going to do. She glanced up to see Ice silently watching her in the rearview mirror. She wanted to impress him, but not enough to tamper with the foreign drug. "I'll pass," she said, pushing the Baggie away from her.

"Some people ain't ready for grown folks business," Lisa said, snatching the Baggie and dipping back into it.

Dena felt slighted, but didn't let it show on her face. She ignored Lisa and took the blunt when it came back around, but then she glanced up and saw the look of disappointment on Ice's face.

Somewhere along the line, the plans got changed, and instead of going to the 40/40 Club they ended up at a spot called Shooter's. Dena was a little bit leery about going to a strip club at first, but it actually wasn't that bad. It was tastefully decorated with modern furniture, and it had a beautiful glass horseshoe bar. Dena could tell that Black Ice was somebody important. From the bouncers to the bar staff, everyone showed him love. He took it all in stride, but kept glancing at Dena to see if she was impressed. Of course she was, but she would never tell him that.

Cinnamon and Lisa were clearly on another planet. Their eyelids were heavy, and occasionally Dena would catch them scratching like they had hives. Dena had heard that coke made people hyper, but they seemed to be the opposite. Cinnamon's legs almost gave out on her twice, and she even threw up just before they walked inside the club. Wendy rubbed her back while Lisa looked on laughing. Black Ice yanked Cinnamon upright by her arm and whispered something in her ear that seemed to sober her up a bit.

After procuring a table big enough to accommodate them all, Ice ordered four bottles of champagne and a liter of Hennessey. Before the waitress had sat the bottles down good, Sharon and Roxy were at it. It was obvious that the girls weren't used to quality drinking from the way they greedily gulped down the bubbly. Wendy was looking at them like trash, but Ice acted like he didn't notice.

Dena sipped her glass and watched Black Ice over the rim of it. At the video shoot he was cool, but he seemed out of place among the thugged-out rappers. Within the walls of Shooter's he seemed more at ease. This made Dena more curious about his character. At some point the girls she had come to know as Cinnamon and Lisa disappeared, leaving Ice, Shorty, Wendy, Dena's crew, and the two girls they brought with them from the video shoot. The champagne had loosened everyone up so much that you'd never know that most of them had only met hours prior.

"This spot is tight," Roxy said, looking around. From the way she was dressed, you couldn't tell if she was a patron or an employee.

"You've never been here?" Black Ice asked.

"Nope."

"I find that hard to believe," Sharon mumbled. Roxy flashed her a look, but didn't want to cut up in front of Ice.

Dena was sitting there taking in the scenery when she felt a presence looming over her. She turned around and looked up at the security guard from the video. He had traded in his T-shirt for a black thermal and a pair of blue denim jeans, cuffed over construction Timberlands. A nice but not gaudy cross hung from around his beefy neck.

"Hey." Dena smiled up at him. "Raheem, right?"

"Correct, Ms. Dena, how you doing?" He smiled back at her. His eyes briefly took in her company and came back to her. "I didn't know you did this spot."

"I don't, I just rolled in with some people." Dena motioned toward the table.

"Sup, Ice?" Raheem said to the man at the head of the table.

"You," Black Ice said, raising his glass. Though his face remained totally neutral, his eyes watched every move Raheem made around Dena. Ice was protective of his flock.

"You in here choosing?" Raheem asked sarcastically.

Black Ice sat his drink down and looked directly at Raheem. "Duke, the only thing I choose is what color diamonds go best with my outfit. I get chose, cousin. Can you dig that?"

Raheem smiled, but there was nothing genuine about it. "Yeah, I can dig that. So." He turned to Dena. "I didn't know you ran in the fast lane."

"Baby boy, I'm in here with some people drinking, so don't get it twisted." Dena snaked her neck.

"My fault." He raised his hands. "Yo, if you get a minute come see me by the bar and I'll comp you for some drinks."

"Oh, you got it like that, huh?" Dena asked.

"Yeah, I got a lil pull in the joint. This is me and my man's spot," Raheem boasted. "When you're ready, come see how the other half lives." He winked and walked away.

Ice didn't turn to watch as he passed, but he kept his eyes on him. "You sure you've never been here?" he asked Dena.

"Don't play ya self. I met son on the video shoot. He was security on Stacks's trailer," she reminded him.

A dancer wearing a purple thong and matching top strutted over to their table. Though her face bore some sort of tribal scars, she had a body straight out of a triple-X flick. Without waiting to be invited she grabbed an empty chair and pulled up to the table.

"Mr. Ice, what's going on?" Scar asked in a husky voice. She had lost most traces of her West African accent, but it still came out when she was making an attempt at being sexy.

"Moving and shaking like I do, Scar," Ice said pleasantly. The girl radiated sex appeal, but Black Ice was unmoved by her presence.

"Damn, Scar, you looking good as hell," Shorty said. He had a cigarette dangling from his mouth, but it wasn't lit. "When you gonna let me tap that pussy again."

Scar slipped her hand under the table and rubbed Shorty's crotch. "Shorty, you know you got too much dick for this old pussy. So, Ice." She turned back to him. "I see you've added some new flavors to your catalog." She let her eyes roll over the five new faces.

"Nah, baby, they don't know nothing bout this life here." He swept his hands through the air.

"The young ones, maybe, but these two—" she pointed at Roxy and Sugar "—they know something."

"What, you trying to call us hos, or some shit?" Sugar asked defensively.

Scar gave her a throaty laugh. "Didn't mean to offend, ma. All I'm saying is that you two are very pretty. You know, a girl could make a lot of money in this place."

"I can't see myself shaking my ass in front of a bunch of horny niggaz for dollars," Roxy said.

"Beats doing it for free." Scar gave her a wink. "Ice, I gotta go on soon, but I'll see you later."

"Without a doubt." Black Ice smiled. He watched Scar walk away, thinking how much money he could make with her on the team.

"She's a friendly one," Dena said, snapping him out of his daze.

"Yeah, Scar is good peoples," Black Ice said.

"I'll bet she's more than just good peoples," Dena teased.

"I wouldn't know."

"Yeah, right."

"That's the gospel." Black Ice raised his right hand. "Me and Scar are friends. Actually, its more of a business understanding."

"Speaking of business, what exactly do you do?" Dena asked. She glanced over at Wendy, who was smiling sheepishly.

Black Ice tried to keep his face serious, but there was a smile trying to creep onto his lips. "I told you, I'm into adult entertainment."

"Seems more like pimping to me," Monique said, letting Ice know she was hip to his bullshit.

"Sweet lady, there's no such things as pimps. And if so, I sure as hell don't fall into the category. What I actually do is manage girls in the business. You know, booking gigs, making sure they get to and from the locations? Pretty much anything that's needed of me to make sure they're good." It was a variation of the truth, but he didn't want to turn Dena off by giving it to her raw.

"How admirable of you," Dena said sarcastically.

Black Ice just shrugged. "I do what I do to get by."

"Looks like you're doing more than getting by." Sharon lifted the expensive pendant on his chain.

"I do a'ight." He gently removed her hand and slid a little closer to Dena. "So, tell me about yourself."

"Not much to tell, really. I'm just a chick from Brooklyn who isn't content to stay in Brooklyn. By hook or crook, I'm gonna live the good life one day."

"Ambition is a good thing." Black Ice raised his glass of Hennessey.

"Sitting on my ass ain't gonna get me out." Dena raised the glass of wine she had been sipping on.

Black Ice was about to follow her comment, but stopped when he caught sight of a familiar face across the room. "Dena, come over here with me right quick." He stood up and extended his hand.

"Boy, you must be crazy, I ain't going to no VIP with you!" she said defensively.

Black Ice laughed. "Girl, when I try to bed you, it won't be in a dive like this. I want to introduce you to the owner."

"A'ight." She got to her feet. "But if you try some funny shit, it's on!" she said, before allowing him to lead her across the room.

As they crossed the crowded club, Dena tried her best not to come in contact with any of the exposed flesh, but it was damn near impossible, with wall-to-wall naked women running around. Dena lived in a house with two other women, so it was nothing new to her, but seeing your sister or mother change clothes was nothing compared to the flesh parade at Shooter's. The girls seemed as comfortable with their nudity as she did fully dressed.

When Dena looked to the stage she had finally solved the mystery of where Cinnamon and Lisa had disappeared to. The women were onstage gyrating and licking each other, while bills of all denominations rained at their bare feet. It was simply amazing to her how out of control men got around the scantily clad women. Dena wasn't gay or even bicurious for that matter, but there was something about the show the women were putting on that wouldn't allow her to look away.

Lisa, who was the taller of the two, stood wide-legged in the middle of the stage, wearing nothing but a pink thong and clear heels. Her large, silicone-filled breasts bounced stiffly every time she moved. Kneeling in front of her was Wendy. A thin film of sweat covered her body, giving her an autumn-colored tint under the club lights. Her large ass rested on the heels of her feet, occasionally popping one cheek after the other to get the crowd going. With her tongue lolling from her mouth like a winded dog, she beckoned for Lisa to come closer. Resting one leg on Cinnamon's shoulder, Lisa enjoyed the oral sex performed on her while the crowd cheered them on.

"You enjoying the show?" Black Ice whispered into Dena's ear, startling her.

"That shit is so nasty." Dena turned her eyes away.

"Don't knock it til you try it."

"Sorry, strictly dickly," Dena checked him. Reflexively, her eyes cut back to the stage.

"Dena, the female body is a beautiful thing. There's nothing wrong with admiring it," Black Ice told her, as he stroked the back of a passing stripper. The girl stopped to see if he wanted a dance, but Black Ice tipped her a five and sent her on her way.

"If I wanted to admire a female body then I'd admire my own," Dena said.

"And quite a body it is," Ice traced a finger across her cheek. Dena felt chills when he touched her, but mustered the strength to pull away.

"Watch those hands," Dena told him.

"What's the mater, you don't like to feel good?" he asked.

"Who said it felt good?" she challenged.

"You did. Oh, you didn't say it out loud, but I saw the look in your eyes. Why you keep fighting what you and I both know is in ya heart, girl?" He reached out to touch her again. This time she wasn't so quick to pull away.

Black Ice's skin was almost as soft as hers. The overhead lights played tricks on his freshly polished nails as he brought his other hand up to caress her cheek. The band of his diamond pinky ring was cool against her skin, but his hands felt like warm silk. Dena stared into the depths of his brown eyes and found herself swallowed up in them. Her brain screamed for her to pull away, but her body wanted—no, needed—to be touched. When he leaned in closer to her face she could smell the sharp congnac floating through his perfectly bowed lips. He was going to kiss her in a room full of people, but Dena didn't give a shit, all she knew was that she wanted it. She closed her eyes in anticipation of his mouth, but instead felt nothing. When she opened her eyes he was staring at her with a smirk on his face.

"Lets go see my man." He took her by the hand.

Dena didn't know whether to be embarrassed, insulted, or turned on, but what she did know is that she would have to dip off to the bathroom soon to try and pat dry some of the moisture that had built between her legs.

Chapter 24

MARCUS SAT IN THE BACK OFFICE OF SHOOTER'S listening intently on his cell phone. Billy had just delivered the news about the shooting and sounded upset. Raheem had told him the story already, but he didn't know that Yoshi had been the victim. He felt bad for Yoshi, because whenever something bad could happen to her it did. He had first met her back when she was still dancing. Back in those days, he was the man at Shooter's but didn't have a stake in it. She had always gotten along well with him and his sister, Cat, and always carried herself like a cool-ass chick.

"How is she?" he asked sincerely.

"She's still doped up off whatever they gave her, but she's good. They wanna watch her overnight just to be sure; but if all goes well she can go home in the morning," Billy told him.

"You need me to drive you?"

"Nah, I'm sure my moms will let me use her car."

"You need to quit bullshitting and let me get you a car," he said.

"Marcus, like I told you before—"

"I know, I know, you make your own money, and all that fly shit," he said, cutting her off. "Making your own money is cool, but if you've got somebody in your corner that's willing to help you, then why not let them?"

"Marcus, you know how funny I am about that kind of thing. I'm just used to doing for myself, ya know?"

"Yes, and I applaud you for that, but everybody could use a hand up sometimes, Billy," he said. "Tell you what, why don't we go half on a car. We can go down to VA and get you something used from an auction. We'll make a weekend of it."

"As long as its not this weekend. You know I'm coaching that game Sunday," she reminded him.

"You're really going through with it, huh?" he asked, trying to hide the disappointment in his voice.

"Hell yeah, Don B is paying me a nice piece of change for a few hours of my time. Why you sound all like that about it?"

"Billy, you know how I feel about them niggaz," he said, as if she didn't already know. Marcus had witnessed firsthand the savagery their little clique was capable of, and he didn't like it. Cat and Yoshi worked the same clubs, so it could've easily been her. Though the offenders were dead and gone, he looked down on the crew as a whole.

"Baby, you know ya girl is good. They know I command respect," Billy said.

"Gangsta, gangsta," Marcus sang.

"Ain't about being a gangsta, it's about setting yourself apart from the rest. Now, getting back to my car . . ."

"You funny, Billy. Nah, but lets try and do it next weekend, though."

"You think Shooter will give you the time off?"

"I think the old man and Raheem can handle it," Marcus said louder than he had to.

"I got your old man, nigga!" Shooter grumbled from the love seat where he was watching the baseball game. The Red Sox were handing the Yankees their heads, and he was pissed about it. "You need to have ya monkey ass on the floor checking my trap, instead of sitting back here like you running some shit."

"Tell the old man I said hey," Billy giggled.

"I'll do that. But let me get to it before I have to fuck this cat up,"

Marcus said, tossing a balled up piece of paper at Shooter. "Keep me posted on Yoshi though."

"Alright, boo. Love you."

Marcus cut his eyes over to Shooter, who seemed to be fixed on the game, before answering. "Love you too, boo," he whispered before ending the call.

"If that wasn't the sweetest shit," Shooter said, with his eyes still fixed on the television. "You having gal troubles again?"

"Nah, me and Billy cool," Marcus said, coming around the desk and grabbing a folding chair, which he set next to the love seat and plopped down on. "Yoshi got shot."

"Jesus, Mary, and Joseph!" Shooter sat up and turned to Marcus. "Is she okay?"

"Yeah, took a slug to the collar, but she'll be okay."

Shooter laid back down on the love seat. "Man, that girl gets into more shit than a little bit."

"I know. Even when folks try to do right, wrong comes to them," Marcus said.

"Ain't that the truth? So how's Billy holding up?"

"You know that girl is a pillar. She ride or die for her team."

"Same as somebody else I know," Shooter chuckled. "I always liked that girl. She a lil on the hard side sometimes, but generally a good soul. I still don't know what she doing wit ya old gangsta ass," Shooter teased him.

Marcus laughed. "Sometimes opposites attract. I don't agree with some of her choices, but I love that girl, Shooter."

"You're acting like you're telling me something I don't know. Damn it, Jeter, stop swinging at every pitch!" He took a moment to yell at the television before turning back to Marcus. "So, what you gonna do, lil nigga, poke around her, checking shit you already know is straight, or you gonna make sure you're in the crib when ya lady gets home?"

"Right as always, Shooter." Marcus patted him on the shoulder.

"Don't I know it? I keep telling you, neglect that girl and you'll have a player like me tapping that pussy."

"Shooter, you're wrinkled-ass dick couldn't do nothing with my lady," Marcus said, laughing. Shooter tried to swat him with his cane, but Marcus was already slipping out the office door.

AS SOON AS MARCUS STEPPED out of the office, the heavy bass from the speakers clapped him on the cheeks like a long-lost grandmother. Beautiful women pranced back and forth advertising their wares, and the dudes were tossing cake. It was barely midnight and the club was already popping. Marcus first checked with the DJ, then made his way over to the bar area to make sure everything was good. As he was whispering into the bartender's ear he felt a tap on his shoulder. He turned and found himself staring at Black Ice and one of his new ladies. He and Black Ice weren't friends to speak of, but Ice brought him a lot of business. On the nights he busted out his stable or hosted one of his locked-door parties, the club raked in a pretty penny.

"Big Mark, what's up, man?" Black Ice gave him dap.

"Shit," Marcus shrugged, "trying to keep these niggaz in line and my paper right."

"Sho ya right, man. Say, I want to introduce you to a friend of mine." He pulled Dena over. "Marcus, this is Dena. Dena, this is Marcus, he owns the joint."

"Sup?" Marcus said pleasantly.

"Nice to meet you." She shook his hand. Though she tried to look calm, Marcus could tell she was uneasy by the way she tried to look everywhere but at the naked flesh in the room.

"Your first time?" Marcus motioned around him.

Dena blushed. "Yeah, I've never been to a strip club."

"Well, this isn't a strip club. Strip clubs are for hookers and drunks. This is a gentleman's club," Marcus corrected her.

"Well excuse me," Dena said.

"Its cool, people make the mistake between the two all the time. I've put a lot of work into establishing Shooter's as a place of leisure, and I take pride in it. You trying to get in the business?"

"Nah, she don't rock like that. She's a square," Black Ice answered for her. This surprised Marcus, because Ice wasn't known to associate with anything but whores, unless he was trying to break a new girl in, which Marcus suspected was the case with the pretty young thing at his side.

"I hear you talking," Marcus said, careful not to give away Ice's secret. Though he didn't agree with Ice's chosen profession, men like him helped keep the club running. "Ice, I got some things to take care of on the outside, but you know the lay of the land. If you need anything, just holla at Raheem."

"Nah, I can do on my own," Ice said with distaste.

Marcus shook his head. "Y'all two still carrying grudges?"

"Mark, you know I'm cool as a nigga on trial with no murder weapon, but ya boy takes his job too seriously. The nigga mad-dog all day long like he got issues, fronting muthafucka."

"I hear you Ice, but running security for this place takes a hard-nosed cat. I guess he's living out the part," Marcus shrugged.

Head of security, Dena thought to herself. And here this cat was fronting like he was the man. Dena didn't have a problem with him being a security guard, but he could've kept it one hundred with her. Lying was a big no-no in Dena's book. She might still try and tap his pocket, but his chances of getting the pussy had flown out the window.

"Well, let me roll out of here and handle my business," Marcus said, giving Black Ice a dap. "It was nice to meet you miss," he said before disappearing into the crowd.

"LOOK AT THAT BITCH," ROXY whispered to Sugar. For the past five minutes or so she had been shooting daggers at Dena and Black Ice while they mingled in the crowd, and it made her sick. "She hanging all over the nigga like that's her man, thirsty bitch."

"She beat you to the punch, Rox. Fuck that though, I see some niggaz in here that look like they holding, anyway." Sugar looked around. In the corner she spotted a short, light-skinned kid with his man in the corner, looking the role of Big Timers. They were sipping champagne out of the bottle and flashing a big wad of money. "Matter of fact, I think I see our next marks. You bout ready to go?"

"I've been ready," Roxy said, giving Dena and Ice one last grill.

"Excuse us." Sugar got up from the table, followed by Roxy.

Shorty gave them a disapproving look. "Y'all just gonna drink and run?"

"No disrespect, love, but it don't seem to be enough meat to go around," Sugar told him with a smile. "Maybe once the crowd thins out we can talk about a nightcap."

"That's a conversation I'll look forward to," Shorty said, watching the two girls depart.

HOLLYWOOD BOPPED UP TO THE front of Shooter's and busted his most serious gangsta lean. Trailing him was a kid from the hood, named Chris. Chris was a young boy who had yet to find his own way in the world, so he latched onto Hollywood. Unlike most cats in the hood, Chris actually bought into Hollywood's illusion. To him, Hollywood was the greatest thing since sliced bread.

"Yo, it's mad niggaz out here," Chris said, looking across the gathering of people in front of the club. "I hope it ain't more dudes than chicks."

Hollywood gave Chris the young-boy stare. "Man, do you think I'm gonna bring you to a spot that's not popping? Stop acting like a square. Come on." He led the way to the entrance. When the bouncer lifted the rope, Hollywood palmed a fifty-dollar bill and slapped it into his hand. "Good looking, my nigga. How we looking?"

"You know Shooter's don't boast nothing but wall-to-wall ass," the bouncer said, slipping the bill into his pocket. "Y'all go in there and get ya dicks wet off some of these big-butt bitches."

"That's a bet." Hollywood stepped inside, with an awestruck Chris behind him.

"Yo, did you slip that nigga a fifty?" Chris asked.

"Be easy, my dude. You know money come and go," he said, handing Chris a thousand-dollar stack from his pocket.

"Good looking, my nigga!" Chris said, excitedly thumbing through the bills. As he felt the strange texture he frowned at Hollywood. "Nigga, this ain't real, this is prop money!"

"I know. I swiped a box of it off the set yesterday," Hollywood whispered. "As long as we pay for our drinks with real money we're good, but these bitches is gonna be too busy trying to cake to check the authenticity of the dough."

"Hollywood, you sure are a smart dude," Chris said.

"That's why I'm the boss of Starving Entertainment." Hollywood popped his collar.

There were no more tables available, so they had to find a spot at the bar. Luckily for them, two stools opened up at the end, where a dancer had just lured a young dude away. Hollywood and Chris took the seats and immediately ordered two bottles of Moët. The two cats sipped champagne and tipped strippers with the fake bills, playing the role like they were getting it heavy. They were contemplating running a train on a thick, light-skinned chick, when two sexily dressed ladies approached.

"Is this a private party?" Roxy asked, making sure to push her breasts out.

"By invitation only, but consider yourselves invited," Hollywood said, offering his stool. Chris caught the hint and did the same. "Shorty, gimme two cups!" Hollywood shouted at the bartender.

"I see, y'all up in here doing the do?" Roxy moved closer to Holly-wood, who was thumbing through a mixed stack of real and prop bills.

"Nah, we just enjoying a night off. Running a production company takes up quite a bit of our time," Chris said.

"Oh, y'all in the business?" Sugar asked, seeing dollar signs.

"Yeah, I'm the CEO of Starving Entertainment, and my nigga Chris is the VP," Hollywood said, giving both the girls business cards that he had made using Print Shop.

Roxy leaned in to whisper to Sugar, "Looks like the night might not be a bust after all."

"Heeeyyy!" Sugar sang, lifting her glass.

Chapter 25

IT WAS JUST AFTER TWO IN THE MORNING, BUT you could still hear the loud thud of reggae music vibrating up and down Jefferson Avenue. Spooky had left Jah to handle his business and took up a perch on the rail steps of building 437. Also with him were Shannon and Yvette, who were passing a bottle of Hennessy back and forth.

"Shorty, you really trying to put the gangsta lean on that bottle," Spooky said, watching Yvette take a long drink.

"My motto is: Go hard or go home, Harlem," she told him.

"Vette, why you always calling me 'Harlem'?"

"Cause it sounds a hell of a lot better than 'Spooky.' I don't see why they call you that anyway, you ain't that scary."

"That's cause you ain't never been on my bad side." He winked at her. Spooky's attention was drawn by a white Escalade creeping down Jefferson. It looked familiar, but he couldn't remember where he had seen it. Shannon must've felt in a way too, because he retrieved his gun from the garbage can. When the car pulled to a stop directly in front of them Spooky stepped off the stoop so he wouldn't be trapped if trouble popped off.

"You know this nigga?" he asked Shannon. The windows

were tinted to the point where you couldn't see inside, but you could tell there were multiple occupants.

"Nah, but if they coming round here on some bullshit, they gonna know my four-four." He stood up with the cannon in plain sight. As the passenger door opened, both men stood at the ready to fight or flee, but it was only Dena returning from wherever she had just come from. Dena was visibly tipsy as she stepped from the back of the truck, but she managed to reach the curb without busting her ass.

It had been an eventful night for the high school senior and her clique. Black Ice had made sure that the champagne and weed flowed all night long. Normally, Dena didn't drink and smoke in excess, but this night was the exception to the rule. Regardless of what people hinted about him, Black Ice had proved to be a perfect gentlemen and fun as hell to hang out with. He kept Dena laughing with his quick wit all night long, and even coaxed her into getting a lap dance. Dena felt funny as hell about it, but the big-butt Puerto Rican girl handled her with great care.

When Cinnamon and Lisa rejoined their group they were heavy with cake. The men in the club had been pressing and throwing money at them up until the time they all rolled out of Shooter's. Dena was thoroughly impressed by the amount of money they made in such little time. The most surprising part was when they turned in their earnings to Ice. Dena wasn't so naïve as to not have figured out that Ice was some type of mack, but she was more focused on how she could use it to her advantage. She didn't think she had the nerve to shake her ass in front of a room full of people, but there were definitely advantages to hanging around Black Ice.

"Bitch, let me find out you twisted?" Mo said, getting out on the other side.

"Ain't nobody drunk. Quit hating," Dena said.

"You walking just like that lil hot-in-the-ass Sharon was when we dropped her off," Mo laughed. Before heading back to Brooklyn, they had dropped Sharon at 112th between Lenox and Fifth, near the Foster projects. Seeing that she was tipsy, Dena and Mo tried to convince her to get dropped off at home, but she wasn't trying to hear it. She supposedly had a jump-off in the block, and she assured them that he would get her home. She had been cock-blocking Dena the whole night with Ice, so she wasn't really sorry to see her go.

"Shit, what time is it?" Dena stretched.

"Time for little girls to be indoors," Ice said from the passenger side of the truck.

"First of all, I ain't no little girl. Second of all, if you wanna say something to me, you get out of the car and say it."

Black Ice laughed, and to the surprise of everyone in the car he stepped out. Cinnamon mumbled something under hear breath, but Wendy placed a firm hand on hers. Though Black Ice treated all of his ladies well, Cinnamon was new to the stable and didn't understand that there were two sides to every coin.

"You know, you don't give much for all that you ask of a nigga," Black Ice said smoothly.

"I don't give anything unless I deem the other party worthy," she said, moving to stand directly in front of him. They were nose to nose and the alcohol told Dena to take the initiative. Just as she leaned in to kiss him, Shannon's voice boomed out.

"Dena, what the fuck is you doing?" Shannon called from the stoop. He was shooting daggers at Black Ice. Shorty made to get out of the truck, but Ice waved him back.

"Is that yo nigga or something?" Black Ice asked, stealthily positioning his hand to draw the berretta tucked in the small of his back.

"Nah," Dena looked over her shoulder, then back to Black Ice. "Nah, that's just my brother tripping."

"Dena, I know you hear me talking to your lil ass?" Shannon took a step off the stoop. "If I gotta come over there you and ya lil boyfriend gonna be mad."

Black Ice gave Shannon a cold stare, but his eyes softened when Dena touched his chest. "Baby, I'm gonna let you go. But you got the number, so make ya next move ya best move." Black Ice gave her a pound and got back into the Escalade. As the truck pulled away, Shannon and Shorty locked eyes, both their glares silently threatening violence.

"Better get the fuck outta here!" Shannon called after the truck, which was halfway to Marcus Garvey Boulevard by then.

"What's up, Shannon?" Monique asked, trying to draw some of the tension away from Dena.

"Wondering where the fuck y'all coming from at his hour of the morning? Don't y'all got school or some shit?"

"Boy, you know we was shaking our asses up at the video shoot," Mo told him.

"Funny, I didn't see y'all up there," Shannon said.

"Cause we was VIP status, nucca," Dena said, doing a tipsy dance.

"I know y'all lil hot asses weren't fucking none of them country niggaz?" Shannon accused.

"Hardly," Mo said. "Dena was in the video. Shannon, you should've seen ya little sister doing it up for the camera."

"I don't give a fuck who you were doing it up for, y'all need to stay outta high-risk areas. Somebody got killed up that muthafucka."

"Word, I heard they was shooting, but I ain't know nobody got killed," Mo said surprised.

"Niggaz came through trying to get at True and ended up getting one of their own laid out," Spooky said, as if he'd heard it secondhand. Shannon was there, so he knew what role Jah played in the shooting, but it was none of anyone else's business.

"See, Dena, that's why I be telling you to slow ya fucking roll. You keep running round looking and you might not like what the fuck you find." He pointed his index finger in her face.

"Shannon, why you gotta act like an ass?" Dena slapped his hand away.

"Cause my lil sister is hopping outta some nigga's car at two in the morning. Who the fuck was that nigga, cause he sure don't look like Lazy?"

"A friend," Dena said.

"And what the fuck is that supposed to mean? Since when does a high school girl have friends who drive a sixty-thousand-dollar truck?"

"Shannon, he was just giving me a ride," Dena insisted.

"Shannon, cut her some slack," Yvette spoke up.

"Yvette, don't tell me how to check my sister!" Shannon yelled. "I refuse to have her wasting her life on the fucking stoop like the rest of these bitches." He hadn't directed the comment at Yvette, but it stung just the same.

"I'm going around the corner to the store," Yvette said, stepping off the stoop.

"Hold up, I'll walk with you." Spooky followed.

"Dena, Ima leave y'all to it. Call me in the morning for school." Mo waved good-bye and left the siblings to work out their differences.

"Dena, you need to check ya self. All this running around wild wit y'all girls shit ain't what's up." Shannon paced in front of the tiny stoop. "Yo, I know you be thinking ya ass is cute cause you got a little body and these niggaz be chasing you, but you have no idea what's waiting for you on these streets."

"Shannon, I can take care of myself," Dena said, as if she didn't really want to hear what Shannon was kicking.

"I'll bet that innocent girl that got shot felt the same way, but look at her now. D, your ass is so smart that you can be fucking stupid. You've got a golden opportunity and yet you're trying your best to fuck it up, to fit in with these low-life bitches. How many girls do you know on this block that's going off to college? Better question, how many of these broads have even graduated high school?"

"I'm good, I can hold mine out here." Dena sucked her teeth.

"You see, that's ya fucking problem. You think you know what life is about, but you really don't know shit outside of Jefferson Avenue. The world is a very big and a very cold place, little sister. You see me out here on these streets risking my life every fucking day just to get a dollar, to make sure we got the shit we need when Mommy can't come through. Shit, if it wasn't for me and Mommy, ain't no telling what the fuck would become of this family. Nadine sure as hell ain't got a clue, and I don't wanna see you walking a mile in that chick's shoes."

"I'm tired, I ain't got time for this shit." Dena tried to storm past him, but Shannon grabbed her arm.

"You got time for whatever the fuck I say you got time for. You ain't gotta listen, but you're sure as hell gonna respect me," Shannon snarled in her face. "Dena, before I let you throw ya life away on a slick-talking nigga, I'll put a hole in him. You better listen to what I'm telling you and stop trying to be so damn smart all the time. Do you understand?" The look in Shannon's eyes had her so terrified that all she could do was nod her head. "Good, now take ya ass upstairs so you can be on time for school."

Shannon stood on the stoop and watched his sister disappear into the building. Dena was just as hardheaded as Nadine, and that had gotten her nowhere. All he wanted Dena to do was recognize her potential and break the cycle that their family had been subject to. Thoughts of his sister's future distracted him from his immediate surroundings, which was a no-no for a man living life behind a gun. Shannon looked up just in time to see a green jeep barreling in his direction.

"BLOOD FIRE!" ROOTS SCREAMED, HANGING out the window with a beat-up Tech 9. With a sweep of his arm he sprayed the front of the building with bullets.

Shannon tossed himself over the railing and landed into a pile of overflowing trash just as the bullets ripped up the lobby door and first-floor window. Had the shooter not been so anxious, he could've cut Shannon down before he had a chance to react. It was a mistake that Shannon would make him pay for.

"Pussy boi, kill da man for Babylon come pon scene!" the driver barked at Roots.

"Don't tell me my business," Roots shot back. He turned to resume his assault and found himself looking down the barrel of Shannon's 44. Luckily for him, the driver peeped it, too, because he threw the car in reverse just before Shannon started popping. Windows were shot out and the front of the car started smoking, but no one got hit.

The jeep's tires squealed as it lurched backwards towards Throop. An oncoming car swerved and crashed into the gate of Ralphy's store to avoid hitting the jeep. Freedom seemed to be within their grasp, when the back window exploded. The driver turned around to see where the shot came from and took one in his mouth, leaving his brains on the window and steering wheel. With no driver the jeep swerved out of control and hit the light pole. Roots howled, feeling the bone in his arm snap on impact. Through his daze, Roots could see Spooky and Shannon closing in on the car from different directions.

"Shit," Roots said, trying to pull himself from the wrecked car. Before he could get out, Shannon kicked the door onto Root's wounded arm. The pain was so intense that all Roots could do was fall.

"You dirty little muthafucka." Shannon kicked him. "You roll through my block and try to wet me?" He gave him another kick. "In front of my building, where my family stay?" Shannon kept kicking Roots until the man stopped moving. He was about to put the four to him when Spooky stopped him.

"Not here," Spooky looked around to see who was watching. The entire block scattered when the shooting had started, but you could never be too careful. "Where'd you park the van?" Spooky asked, kicking the Tech away from Roots.

"Across the street, why?" Shannon asked, still wanting to shoot Roots.

Spooky smiled. "Cause we gonna take this bitch-ass nigga somewhere and make him suffer before he dies."

THE SOUND OF SHOTS COMING from in front of the building immediately sobered Dena up. She dropped to the floor and crawled to the room where the kids were sleeping. Thankfully they slept right through it. Normally, Dena would've just stayed until the danger passed, but her brother was still outside. Keeping as close to the ground as she could, she crawled over to the window and peeked out.

There was a man sitting on a car with its front end embedded into the gate of Ralphy's store. She looked up the block in time to see Yvette dip inside the next building like she had the devil on her heels. Across the street there was a jeep on the corner of Jefferson and Throop, smoking. Dena could see a man in the front, but she couldn't tell what condition he was in. She scanned the front of the building but saw no sign of her brother.

She was about to slip her clothes back on and go down to look for him when she saw his minivan come down Throop and stop on the opposite corner of the accident. He hopped out and knelt behind a car that was almost hidden by the shadow of the blooming tree. She almost didn't see Spooky crouched down over what looked like a man. After whispering something to Shannon, they dragged their parcel to the van and sped off.

"Talk about me," Dena mumbled, before heading back to her bedroom.

Chapter **26**

SHA BOOGIE LAY IN HIS BED STARING AT THE cracked ceiling. Next to his pillow lay a black 9 mm, chambered and ready for combat. Though it was doubtful that anyone would rush the house in some sort of retaliation attempt, it was better to be safe than sorry. He thought about smoking another cigarette, but all that would do was add to the bitter taste already in his mouth.

From the bottom of his nightstand drawer, Sha produced a tattered old photo. It was a picture of a man and a young boy who wore almost the same face, separated by about twenty years. It was all he had left of the murdered man who had impregnated his mother, and though Sha didn't know him well, he cherished the token.

The day had been a trying one. Spider was dead and Charlie was sidelined with a hole in his shoulder. Sha wanted to take him to the hospital, but Charlie had refused because he was running from a warrant. Instead, they had gotten an old street cat to patch the wound and prayed that it didn't get infected.

For only God knew how long, he had dreamt of popping True and watching him bleed out in the streets, and this day was supposed to be it; but of course, it didn't go down that way. They had made their move and fucked up. Now True knew someone was out for his head, taking away their biggest asset, which had been the element of surprise. A perfectly laid plan gone to ruin because of the stranger watching True's back. Sha Boogie wasn't sure who the man was, but if he was willing to kill for True then he would die with him.

Outside his window the sun was shining, which meant there was still work to be done. Whether his man was injured or not, Sha Boogie still had to handle his business. Grabbing his gray hoodie and the black gun, he left the bedroom, locking the door behind him.

When Sha Boogie got into the living room his mother was slumped on the couch, half asleep, with her mouth hanging open. Her hair was wrapped in a scarf, but nine times out of ten it wasn't done. A dingy yellow bathrobe was draped over her, with one bony shoulder sticking out from beneath. On the table was an ashtray that should've been dumped a long time ago, and a half-dozen empty beer cans. It was a sad sight, but one he was used to.

Sha's mother must've felt him looming over her, because her head popped up. A thin line of saliva dripped from her bottom lip and fell onto her lap before she had a chance to wipe her mouth with the back of her hand. Her eyes were sunken and had heavy bags under them from her nights of long partying and drug abuse. It hurt Sha to the core, because his mother wasn't even a shadow of the former fox she was hailed as. True had more to answer for than he could possibly imagine.

"What you doing creeping round my damn house like a burglar?" his mother slurred. She had come to a point where she had been drinking so long that even when she wasn't drunk, she sounded like it.

"Nothing, Ma, go back to sleep," he told her.

"How the hell am I supposed to sleep when my ribs are in my damn back, I'm hungry as hell and ain't no damn food in here." She pulled herself to her feet.

"Ma, I just bought some food in here the other day, what happened to it?" he asked, going to the refrigerator. Sure enough, it was empty.

"Me and Joe had some people over last night. You know niggaz love to eat," she said, like it was nothing.

"I'm a nigga that likes to eat from time to time, too." Sha slammed the refrigerator door.

"Don't be slamming shit in my house, Sha!" she teetered. "And watch how the fuck you talk to me, I'm still ya mama."

"Right," he said, brushing past her and going back into the living room.

"What's all the commotion?" Joe asked, slinking into the living room wearing a tank top and a pair of dingy boxers. He was a dude Sha's mother had met at an NA meeting. Joe spent the night a few months prior and hadn't left yet. Sha didn't particularly care for his drunken mother, but he hated Joe.

"Nothing but Sha's crazy ass acting like he got an attitude cause I asked him for some money. Shit, it ain't like I charge his funky ass rent," she said.

Joe loved an opportunity to sway Sha's mother further away from Sha, so he decided to instigate. "Shit, I moved out of my mother's house when I was sixteen years old." Joe lit a cigarette. Exhaling the smoke he looked at Sha Boogie. "If ya ask me, I think its about time you started kicking ya ma a few dollars from time to time."

"Well, ain't nobody asked you shit, so mind ya business," Sha warned him.

"You watch how you talk to my company; this is my motherfucking house!" Sha's mother barked. She went through the process of shaking several different beer cans until she found one with something left in it. After peeking inside to make sure there were no ashes in it she took a deep sip. "You gonna watch ya mouth Sha, or you're gonna find yourself on the fucking street."

"If you kick me out whose gonna buy forties for you and Joe?" Sha asked sarcastically.

"Hold on now, Sha, you know anytime I ever asked you for something it was a loan. To come round here talking like Joe don't make his own way," Joe said seriously.

Sha gave him a comical look. "Nigga please, most nights you can't even make ya own way to the bathroom without falling on your drunk ass."

"You better mind your tongue, Sha. I'm still a man," Joe said, like he was thinking about doing something.

"What-the-fuck-ever. Man, I don't even know why I'm talking to ya fucking ass," Sha fumed.

"What the hell did I tell you, Sha? Joe is here to see me, not you. You don't run shit up in here!" his mother yelled.

"Yo, every time I turn around you're defending some fucking drunk or crackhead over your own kid. This nigga ain't shit to hold onto!" Sha told her. During the heated word exchange between him and his mother, Joe rolled in from behind and sucker-punched him.

Sha Boogie turned to Joe with an animal fury in his eyes. Joe tried to throw his hands up but Sha didn't give him a chance as he moved in and started raining blows. He hit Joe in every exposed part of his body, trying to break everything he touched. Whenever Joe tried to slump to the ground, Sha Boogie grabbed him by the collar and picked him back up. At some point Joe managed to grab a beer bottle from the table and try to swing it at Sha. Sha blocked the bottle with one hand and came up holding his gun with the other. This gave Joe pause.

"Fuck is wrong with you," Sha placed the 9 to Joe's forehead. "Lowlife, drunk, crackhead muthafucka, I should kill you!"

"Please, man," Joe pleaded with tears in his eyes.

"Sha, you better get ya hands off him!" his mother shouted.

"Shut the fuck up!" Sha roared before turning back to Joe, who smelled as if he had pissed his pants. "Say something now, son. Come on, let me here you pop that fly shit," Sha pressed the gun further into Joe's skull. "I ain't got shit to live for but an old score, so try me if you want to, muthafucka, I'm ready to go!" Sha slammed Joe roughly against the wall and headed for the door.

"You get the hell out of my house, you black-hearted son of a bitch!" Sha's mother called after him. "You ain't gonna be shit, Sha. Just like ya snitching-ass father, you ain't shit!"

• • •

SUGAR WOKE UP WITH THE headache from hell. The inside of her mouth tasted like she had been tongue-kissing an ashtray, and she could've sworn her teeth had sprouted fur. Propping herself on her elbow she surveyed her surroundings. From the looks of the pale paint and the dime-store pictures on the wall, she knew she was in a motel room, but only the Lord knew where or how she got there. Her hand brushed against a lump that was wrapped in the sheets that she hadn't noticed before. It was roughly the size of a man, but Sugar had been so drunk the night before that she was almost afraid to look.

Peeling back the rough blanket, she saw that there was a light-skinned kid laying next to her. He was snoring his ass off, with his mouth draped open and a tart trail of slobber running from his mouth to the pillow. Suddenly, pieces of the night before came flooding back to her.

The light-skinned kid was one of the dudes she and Roxy had met at Shooter's. At first they seemed way cool, but the kid who called himself Hollywood couldn't stop taking about himself or his delusions of being the next Don B. Hollywood and Chris played the roll of true ballers, making sure the ladies' glasses never ran empty. After leaving the club, they smoked four blunts in Hollywood's van on the way to a local diner. Seeing the wads of money the young boys were flashing affected the decision of whether to fuck them or not. A no-brainer. This is what landed them at the Holland Motor Inn in Jersey City.

Back at the motel, Sugar had given young Chris a run for his money, making him cum in less than ten minutes, while Roxy handled hers with Hollywood. She wanted to nominate her girl for an Oscar, the way she snarled and hollered like he was killing the pussy. Sugar would later find out that this was far from the truth. When their soldiers were able to stand back at attention they decided to switch off. Sugar sucked Hollywood's dick like it was a rib bone, letting him spray nut in her face. When he tried to doze off she slapped him back to alertness and rode him almost until the sun came up. From what she recalled, he didn't have much of a stroke—but he licked her ass cleaner than a wet wipe.

"Sop it like a biscuit," she mused, thinking back to the multiple orgasms she had in Hollywood's mouth. Careful not to disturb him, Sugar slipped from the twin bed. Just across the room, in the other bed, Roxy was knocked out. She was naked as the day she was born with her arm hanging off the side. Chris was sound asleep with his head resting on her ass.

Sugar located Hollywood's pants lying in a heap on the floor at the foot of the bed. As quietly as she could, she picked them up and went through the pockets until she found his money. She had a little difficulty at first, but was finally able to yank the large knot from his pocket. Her lips parted into a wide grin at the site of the cake, but the grin faded as she began thumbing through the bills. To be sure she wasn't bugging, she took the money over to the window and held it to the light.

"Dirty muthafucka," she said, realizing it was funny money. All except about two hundred and fifty dollars were fakes. Sugar continued her search but came up empty, which infuriated her. The thought of her ditching Black Ice and his crew for the two con artists made her want to cut them both in their sleep, but Sugar had an even better plan.

"Roxy," she whispered, shaking her friend. "Roxy, get yo ass up."

"Huh?" Roxy looked around, sleepy-eyed. Her wig now sat at a funny angle on her head.

"Get ya shit. We outta here."

"Sugar, you bugging. Checkout ain't till twelve, and I'm trying to go shopping when these niggaz wake up," Roxy told her, and tried to roll back over, only to have Sugar shake her again.

"Ain't much we can buy with this," Sugar slapped one of the phony bills in Roxy's hand. It took Roxy a second to understand what Sugar was trying to say, but as soon as she felt the bills she knew what time it was.

"Dirty muthafuckas," Roxy hissed, about to bop the sleeping Chris in his head, but Sugar grabbed her arm.

"No need for that. I've got something much crueler in mind. Come on," Roxy said, plucking her clothes off the floor. In less than five minutes both the girls were dressed and on their way out the door.

"How we gonna get back to Brooklyn?" Roxy asked, still holding her stiletto boots in her hand.

Roxy stopped short and held up Hollywood's van keys. "Oh, we good. But them two fronting muthafuckas will be hitchhiking all the way back to wherever the fuck they're from."

SHARON TRIED TO IGNORE THE sun's rays as they shone through the bedroom window. There was no shade on the window, so the best she could do to avoid the light was pull the blanket over her head. This helped to protect her from the annoying light, but it was useless at that point because her rest had already been broken.

"Shit," she mumbled, trying to remember the pleasant dream she was having. To her left her latest conquest, Scooter, was still fast asleep.

Scooter was a cat from Foster that had been getting money in Harlem for years. He was a little older than her sister Reese, but had a thing for young flesh. Sharon used to swoon every time he came through on his motorcycle with Yoshi, or some other model-looking chick on the back, in something tight. She often imagined what she would look like with her ass cocked up on the back of his bike, but it wasn't until recently that the dreams of a little girl would come to fruition.

Sharon was supposed to have just been going to the store for her mother, but when she saw Scooter and his team ride up on their bikes it was a wrap. That first night he had wined her, dined her, and fucked the lining out of her little pussy. Since then, they had had an on-again, off-again secret romance. Scooter said that it was important that they keep their affair a secret, because he didn't want his enemies targeting his loved ones; but the truth of the matter was that the man was married, with five kids.

Leaning over, she let her breasts brush his chest, while her lips met his. "You awake?" her hand trailed down his stomach and touched his rock-hard penis.

"I am now," he grumbled. His breath smelled like a shit sandwich, but Sharon knew Scooter had deep pockets, so she endured. "Yeah." He placed his hand over hers and pressed it down harder against his dick. "That's that wake-up dick." He rolled on top of her.

Sharon placed her hand behind his head and pulled him down into a deep kiss. Wrapping one leg behind his back, she beckoned him. Scooter's throbbing penis slid up and down against her soaked pussy, with the head almost slipping in a time or two. With animal lust, Scooter started sliding himself in her, but Sharon placed a hand against his chest.

"You got a condom on?" she asked, nicking his bottom lip with her teeth.

"Don't worry about it, baby, I won't cum in you," he whispered, sliding in deeper. Waves of pleasure rode through Sharon, as good common sense flew out the window for a morning of mind-blowing sex.

RONNY STOOD IN THE DOORWAY of the small kitchen watching the stove like a hawk. The cocaine in the bottom of it was now a sickly colored goop, on what was starting to resemble a cookie. The potency of the coke was so weak that he had lost a good amount of it during the cooking process, and now he found himself several grams shorter than when he started. It was a tough pill to swallow, but it was the best he could come up with, considering the dent the robbers had put in his pockets.

"Man, watching that pot ain't gonna make that shit cook no quicker," Blick said, coming from the bedroom, leaning heavily on a cane. Though the doctors were able to remove the high-caliber shotgun slug from his leg, it had caused muscle damage and he would most likely walk with a limp for the rest of his life.

"Son, I feel like a bird, even trying to make something out of this weak shit." Ronny lifted the pot and swished the water around a bit. "I wish to God I knew where them bitch-ass niggaz was from, so I could pop off!"

"Well, I might be able to arrange that." Blick lowered himself into the chair. "You know, the world we live in is entirely too small."

"What's popping?" Ronny asked, setting the pot on the table.

"I just got off the phone with my cousin, Dee-Dee."

"Who, the swollen-ass broad from Myrtle Ave?" Ronny joked.

"Fuck you, man, she got a gland problem. Anyhow, it seems like her sister, Shakira, got into it with a bitch off Jefferson over some dude named Shannon."

"And what does that have to do with me?" Ronny asked, trying to figure how he could best break the cookie down to get his money back.

"She described him to see if I knew who the nigga was, and guess what?" Blick smirked.

"What nigga?" Ronny finally tired of Blick's riddle.

"She described that same Napoleon nigga that jacked us!"

"You lying. How you know it's the same dude?" Ronny asked excitedly.

"I don't know for sure." Blick picked his .38 up off the table and checked the chamber. "But we're gonna find out real soon!"

Chapter 27

"YO, I HEARD IT WAS POPPING OUT HERE LAST night," Mousy said, licking the ends of the Dutch to seal it. "I woke up in the middle of the night to use the bathroom and I seen police had this whole shit taped off."

"My moms was coming in from work and she said that she heard from crackhead Bill that they was out there shooting in front of 437. The boy Roots was supposed to have got murked. Quiet as it was kept, I heard it was Shannon and that nigga from Harlem he be with," a girl named Stephanie added.

"With them trigger-happy niggaz, I wouldn't be surprised. Yvette, you was out here with them niggaz last night, so I know you got the scoop?" Mousy asked anxiously.

Yvette just shrugged. "Shit, we smoked like two blunts, then I broke out and Shannon went upstairs," she lied. Yvette had been coming from the store with Spooky when they heard the gunshots. Before she even got a grasp of what was going on, Spooky was blasting away. That boy carried himself like a real thug nigga, which only made Yvette more fascinated with him.

"Ah, shit," Mousy said, nodding down the block. Shakira was headed in their direction with three hard-faced chicks that weren't from the block. She was dressed in Timberland boots and sweat pants, with a scarf tied on her head, so it obviously wasn't a social call.

"Mouse, if these bitches try to get stupid, be ready to grab my hammer out the garbage can," Yvette said, stepping off the stoop.

"All day," Mousy assured her.

"Yeah, there that bitch go right there!" Shakira pointed at Yvette, trying to amp herself up.

"I see that last ass whipping ain't taught you nothing about that word," Yvette said.

"We gonna see who gets their ass whipped this time," Shakira bounced in place. She was acting like she wanted it, but knew better than to get within arm's length of Yvette.

"Yo, I hear you cut my little sister?" This came from a rough-looking chick who had to weigh at least two hundred pounds, easy.

"She came at me with a bottle and I did what I had to do," Yvette said, making sure to keep all four of the girls in her line of vision.

"Well, we ain't really feeling that shit, so something gotta be done about it," Big girl said, slipping on a pair of gardening gloves.

"I'm down for whatever," Yvette said defiantly. The girl out-weighed her by quite a bit, but she refused to back down.

"I say we carve this bitch up right now." This came from a skinny girl wearing a ponytail. Something shiny glinted in her hand. "Yeah, we gonna tear ya lil cute ass up." The skinny girl moved in Yvette's direction, but a clicking sound stopped her in her tracks.

Mousy stepped up to stand beside Yvette, holding the nickel-plated .25. "You bitches must be crazy coming up this end of Jefferson wit that bullshit. Shakira, you got ya ass beat, so take it like a real bitch and bounce."

"Nah, ain't nobody going nowhere," Big Girl said. She was acting like the gun didn't mean anything, but she wasn't stupid enough to try and move on the armed girl. "Look, give my sister the one-deep and lets settle this."

"Bet," Yvette said, taking a fighting stance.

Shakira had hoped they could just catch Yvette slipping and

stomp her out, but it didn't go down like that. She had been called out and would have to answer the challenge.

DENA WAS AWAKENED BY A loud commotion coming from under her bedroom window. Her head was still spinning from the night before, so she really didn't feel like the antics of Jefferson Avenue that morning. She sucked her teeth and rolled out of bed, shuffling over to her window to see what was going on.

On the ground below Shakira and Yvette were reenacting *The Clash of the Titans*, while the stoop rats cheered them on. Shakira was obviously the more powerful puncher, but Yvette was a much more skilled boxer. For every punch Shakira threw, Yvette threw two, connecting with most of them. Shakira tried rushing Yvette, only to catch a quick uppercut to the jaw.

Shakira grabbed a hand full of Yvette's hair, and the pain that shot through Yvette's skull seemed to graze her brain. But it only made her angrier. While Shakira shook her like a rag doll, Yvette went to work on her face with a series of combinations. Finally, not being able to take any more punishment, Shakira went down to one knee, exposing herself to the flurry of punches Yvette was throwing. It was then that the other girls tried to jump in. They had all become a mass of bodies and flying fists, until Mousy licked a shot in the air and scattered them in all directions.

"Just another day on the block," Dena mused, moving away from the window. When she checked the time on her digital clock she was surprised to see it was after eleven-thirty. Apparently she had slept through the alarm, and nobody thought enough of her education to wake her up. Being that school was now out of the question, she decided to get an early jump on her weekend.

The first thing she did was charge her cell. The battery had been dead since the previous afternoon, and she could only imagine how many messages she had. She had several from Lazy, singing some sad-ass song about he was sorry that he stood her up for the movie date.

"You're sorry, alright. A sorry fucking excuse for a man," Dena said out loud. There was a message from Mo that had come sometime that morning, with her cursing Dena out about having her standing in front of her window shouting her name for over a half hour. She said that she was off to school and would catch up with her later. "There goes my cut partner for the day."

Of course there was another message from Lazy, this one coming shortly after Mo's. He sounded upset as he went on about how he wanted to make sure she was good, because of the gunplay at the video shoot. His voice was still rambling on as she hit the delete button without listening to the whole message. There was also a more recent message, that had come sometime after their little argument. He was going through some spiel about wanting to check on her because of the shooting at the video shoot, but Dena didn't want to hear it, so she deleted it before listening to the whole thing.

The oddest message was the one from Sean: "Hi, this is Sean."

This nigga has got big balls, Dena thought to herself. Not only was it creeping her out that he had tracked her number down, but he was fucking her friend and had the nerve to try and holla at her, like he was built like that. Sean was handsome and seemed cool enough, but she couldn't get over the fact that he was fucking Sharon's little ass. Sharon had the body of a grown woman, but it didn't change the fact that she was still a little girl. He lost major points for this in Dena's book.

Tossing the phone on the bed to continue charging, Dena picked out an outfit for the day. As she was going through the process of switching purses she came across a number scribbled on a matchbook from Shooter's. Just thinking about the night they had brought a smile to Dena's face. Black Ice was so very different than the guys she was used to dealing with. Though only a few years older than her, he had a wisdom about him that most men didn't come into until they cracked thirty. Yes, Ice was definitely worth looking into, so she decided to forgo her normal week-long wait-out and give him a call.

· · ·

BLACK ICE LOUNGED ON THE peach-colored love seat in the living room of his duplex, wearing nothing but a blue silk robe and a pair of flip-flops. Normally, he would've still been sleeping from the night before, but Dena's call had caused him to start his day a little earlier than usual. Cradling the cell to his ear he smiled like the Chesshire cat.

"Yeah, that sounds like a plan," he said in a sexy voice. "Tell you what, I got some business to take care of in the city, so why don't I pick you up in a couple of hours and you can ride shotgun? We can finish that conversation we were having last night." Dena said something that caused him to laugh. "A'ight, that's a bet," Ice said before ending the call. No sooner than he closed the phone than Cinnamon was in his mix.

"Who was that, ya new little girlfriend?" she asked sarcastically, staring at him from the living room entrance. Her hair was wrapped around her head and pinned, with only a sheer robe covering her nude body.

Black Ice cast his sleepy eyes up at her. "When you start paying my phone bill you can ask me about who's on my line. What you doing up so early, anyway?"

"Well, I thought I could crack on you for a little dick this morning, before the rest of the world consumes your precious time." Cinnamon walked over to the couch and sat on Ice's lap. "You think I can get a little bit of that love bone before you run off to see your high school sweetheart?"

Black Ice smiled at her lovingly just before he shoved her off his lap and onto the floor. "Bitch, if you trying to be funny, I sure as hell ain't laughing."

Cinnamon's eyes flashed hurt, but her words were sharp and cruel. "Oh, so you got some new young pussy lined up, so mine ain't good enough for you. I guess once we cross the eighteen-year-old mark our shit ain't tight enough for Black Ice no more. You must be suffering from that R. Kelly syndrome."

"Cinnamon, you better quit while you're ahead," he warned her.

"What, you don't like me talking about ya new little pet, Ice?"

Cinnamon barked, getting off the floor. She stood in front of Black Ice, who was glaring up at her from his spot on the couch.

"What's going on?" Wendy asked, coming into the room. She had heard the commotion through the walls of her bedroom, where she was counting the last of the money that had to be dropped off to Don B.

"This bitch is trying her damnest to get her head split," Ice told Wendy.

"Cinnamon, why don't you calm down." Wendy placed her hand on the girl's shoulder, only to have it knocked away.

"Fuck calming down, Wendy, I wanna know what that bitch has got over Ice?" Cinnamon asked, with tears in her eyes. "Is she prettier? Is her pussy fresher?"

"Cinnamon, you know how it goes. Ice is trying to bring a new baby home for us to raise." Wendy tried to sooth her.

"That's just it: *I* used to be the baby," Cinnamon sobbed. "Ice, when I first came up here from Arkansas, you laid the world at my feet and treated me like royalty, but since you broke me in it ain't the same. I don't see that fire in your eyes when you look at me. What happed to that? Ain't I special no more?"

Black Ice leaned back on the sofa and gave her an emotionless stare. Cinnamon searched his eyes for something to hold on to, but there was only emptiness. "See, pampering ya ass is what has misconstrued your perception of me and what the fuck I'm about. All of my ladies get treated like queens because they go out and hustle hard for they man, but ain't no emotional attachments. A sporting nigga with a tender heart for a broad ain't got no place in this game, and may God Almighty strip him of all his bitches and pass them my way. I am a grade-A, muthafucking mack, not some goddamn wet nurse for overly emotional bitches. In case you missed it, we ain't playing house, we playing cop and blow; so if you can't dig the shit I'm kicking to you, then pack the shit you had on ya raggedy ass when I found you and don't let the door hit you in the ass on the way out."

"Is that all I am to you, Ice, just another source of income?" Cinnamon asked, with tears streaming down her cheeks.

"Ho money is sho money," was his reply.

They say that there is power in words, and Cinnamon knew this to be true, as the force of Black Ice's words hit her like physical blows. She knew when she hooked up with Ice that he was about pimping, but he treated her better than her own mother had. Sure, she danced and turned an occasional trick, but it was by choice. Black Ice never forced her to ho, only opened her up to the earning potential in it; and Cinnamon's naïve ass bought into it, thinking she was going hard for her man. At the end of the day she was just a means to an end, and this is what hurt her the most.

Black Ice was about to get up and head to the shower, when he heard what sounded like a cat being dragged over a barbed wire fence. He turned around just in time to catch a glimpse of Cinnamon rushing him at top speed. She had a look of madness in her eyes and a brass lamp in her hand. Cinnamon swung the lamp at Ice's head with everything she had. At the last second, he moved to the side, letting her momentum carry her past him. Grabbing her by the back of her wrapped hair, Ice shoved, and sent her flying over the couch.

With a low growl erupting from his chest, Ice bounded over the couch and landed on top of Cinnamon. Locking his forearm under her chin he pinned her to the floor and raised his right hand to finish her off. Cinnamon braced for the blow, but thankfully it never fell. She looked up at Ice, who had a confused expression on his face as he stared at his raised fist. Throughout his career as a pimp, Black Ice had always prided himself on the fact that he didn't beat his women. If you could break a woman's mind, you didn't have to do anything to her body, which was a code he lived by; but now found himself about to smash out one of his own. Had living amongst savages for so long begun to wither away the gentlemen in him that had made him such a successful mack?

Regaining his composure, he got off Cinnamon and stepped around the couch to where Wendy was standing with a shocked expression on her face. "Wendy," he began in a very calm tone, "there's been a change in plans. Leave the money in the case and I'll take it to Don B myself. I got another job for you. I want you to get this bitch cleaned up and out of my pad. She's welcomed to take whatever belongs to her, but whatever was bought by my money does not cross this threshold."

"Ice, baby, I'm sorry," Cinnamon crawled over to him. She had taunted Ice to get him to notice her, but the childish stunt had blown up in her face. "Daddy, don't kick ya little freak bitch to the curb." She tugged at the bottom of his robe.

"You ain't no bitch of mine," he said with ice in his voice. "I need solid whores at my call, not little girls who throw tantrums. Scram, bitch." He yanked the robe from her hands.

"Ice, the girl didn't mean it," Wendy spoke up. She knew what Cinnamon was going through, because she had been there before, so Wendy more than anyone else understood her pain. She was a young girl in love with a man who was incapable of loving anything but a dollar.

Ice pointed a bony finger at Wendy. "I already had one bitch question me today, and I'll be damned if it happens twice. Now, if you don't like what I'm putting down, you can pack ya shit and bounce with her. We clear on that?"

"Yes, Daddy," she said, just above a whisper. Wendy felt bad for Cinnamon, but not bad enough to jeopardize her standing in the stable. Compared to the last man she had, who forced her to turn tricks in the streets, Ice was a godsend who treated her well. She would be damned if she would go back to sucking dick in staircases because some young girl couldn't control her mouth.

Chapter 28

AS SURE AS TRUE'S ASS WAS BLACK, JAH WAS WAIT-
ing for him when he stepped out of his building. He didn't
even know the man knew where he laid his head, but Jah
had proven to be full of surprises. He looked every bit of a
South African mercenary, wearing black fatigues and a
scowl. Just beneath the thin black jacket True could see the
butts of two guns strapped to either side of Jah's hips.

"What's good?" Jah gave True dap. "You ready to hit the
turf?"

"Yeah, man. We got a busy day ahead of us, so try to
keep up," True joked.

"Don't worry, you couldn't lose me if you tried," Jah
said seriously. True let it rock and led the way down the
block to where his car was parked. It wasn't quite hot
enough to bust out the roadster, so True jumped behind the
wheel of a silver GS300. It was the only kind of Lexus he
would drive. No sooner than they had pulled out into traffic, Jah was at it with the questions.

"Any word on them cats that tried to get at you?" Jah
asked, trying to adjust himself so the twin 9s wouldn't bite
into his sides.

"Not a peep," True admitted. "The Don put some feelers

out to members of the set in Brooklyn to see if we can get a line on the other two, but so far nothing has panned out. A nigga can't even get his shine on without a muthafucka hating. But its all good though, them niggaz know not to try me. We'll probably never see them again."

Jah gave him a funny look. "You don't even believe that shit. True, them boys might not have been professionals, but they had hell of heart to do it like they did. Nah, it was definitely a hit, but for it to go down in such a public place, there must've been some heavy cake on the table, or a personal grudge."

"And what makes you so sure of that?" True asked.

"Cause I'm a killer, and those are the only two things that would make me jump out the window like that. Now, can you think of anyone you might've pissed off recently?"

"Jah, I'm young and bout to be filthy fucking rich. I piss people off just by waking up in the morning." True wasn't boasting but making a point. Being young and on the come up could be detrimental to your health in the hood. Instead of people around you wishing you well, they wanted to come for your head. Hate is a muthafucka.

"Say, whatever happened with them niggaz that killed Pain and them last summer?"

"Them Spanish niggaz? Locked up, last I heard. Police caught them for that and some mo shit. It's a good thing, too, because Don B was about to send the wolves for them."

Jah glanced over at him, then turned back to the road. "Don B is a regular Robin Hood, huh? Real down-for-a-nigga type."

True looked over at Jah, unsure if he was trying to be funny. "You might call it that. Don B is a nigga who, when he made it, didn't forget the hood. You know how many niggaz he's pulled off the streets when he started Big Dawg? Fuck, without him I'd have never been able to get my shit popping. Shit, he paid for the production of my entire album, kid. I love that nigga."

"So, he stands to make more money off you alive than dead?" Jah asked.

True slammed on the breaks of the car and gave Jah his undivided attention. "Let me tell you something, Jah, we've known each other for a long time, so the respect is there, but I ain't really feeling what you're getting at."

"True, first of all, get us the fuck out of the middle of the street before the police come. Did you forget I'm dirty?" Jah lifted his jacket. "Second of all, I'm not getting at anything; I'm exploring all avenues on this shit. How many niggaz you know got murdered by someone close to them on some jealous shit?"

"It ain't like that with me and the Don. That's my man, and he would never do me dirty," True said, defending Don B with vigor.

"True, Paul and Larry Love knew each other all their lives; but did that stop Larry from crossing my brother? The point I'm trying to make is that, as far as your life is concerned, you can't take no chances." With that being said, Jah let the conversation drop.

The two men drove in silence through Harlem, looking out at the streets that had spawned them both. True glanced over at Jah in his black fatigues and then at himself, dressed in a Sean John sweat suit and heavy jewels. Everyone claims to be a product of the streets so there's somewhere to place the blame, but True didn't believe in that. He believed that it was the heart of the man that determined which path he would walk. It could've easily been Jah behind the wheel and True behind the gun, but their hearts craved two different things. Jah gave himself over to the dark side, while True chose the spotlight.

Before Jah knew it, they were pulling up at the park at 145th and Lenox. After parking the car, he and True hopped out and made their way inside the park, with Jah's eyes constantly on alert for danger. True led the way over to the courts, with Jah a few paces behind him.

For the most part, there were mostly neighborhood cats shooting around, but there was also a sprinkling of kids who decided to cut school and brush up on their games. Off near the far hoop, Don B stood amongst a cluster of his minions. He was dressed in a white T-shirt, blue jeans, and a California Angels fitted cap. The young boys around him listened intently as the Don spoke.

"Yo, y'all niggaz gotta make sure y'all bring ya A game on Sunday, cause these down-south niggaz is bringing theirs," he said in his gruff voice. "That's my word, y'all better not let these muthafuckas come in our house and leave with a W."

"Fuck them niggaz, we gonna smash on Stacks's team," Goose said from his position against the fence. He was a six-nine monster that was slowly making a name for himself on the street-ball circuit.

"You better do more than smash. I want these niggaz violated!" Don B mashed his fist into his hand for emphasis. "Its more on the line here than just money and bragging rights, we gotta win this one for the boy, Chiba!"

"Word," one boy agreed.

"For Big Chiba," another boy chimed in.

Lazy added to the chant, but his mind was elsewhere. So many things were going on in his life that he didn't know where to begin, as far as straightening them out went. Dena, who was supposed to be his better half, was playing herself. He could understand her being upset about seeing him with Becky, but there wasn't anything going on between them, at least not recently. Then she gets her fifteen minutes of fame in Stacks's video and starts acting like her shit didn't stink—and flaunting the fact that she was keeping close company with the hustlers. Lazy knew that Dena wasn't as materialistic as most of the girls in the hood, but she had expensive tastes, tastes that sometimes were too pricey for him to accommodate. For all he knew, she could've gone back to that trailer and given the whole squad head just to spite him. The visual made him cringe. He had been calling her back to back, but she didn't take his calls or return them. He thought she would've at least called back to give her condolences for Chiba, but she was off having too much fun to care about a young nigga dying in the hood.

Chiba had been his right-hand man since forever, and now he was gone over some bullshit that didn't have anything to do with them. He had seen dead bodies before, but never someone he knew, someone so much like himself. In a sense, looking at Chiba's lifeless body had been looking at himself. Would he ever make it out of the concrete jungle, or would some Harlem gutter serve as his final resting place?

"A'ight," Don B's voice boomed out, "y'all niggaz hit the baseball diamond and start ya laps. Lazy, I need to holla at you for a minute." The rest of the team dispersed, leaving Lazy and Don B standing under the rim. "What's good wit you, kid?"

"I'm good," Lazy said, dribbling a basketball.

The look Don B gave him clearly said that he saw through the lie. "Listen, fam, I know you hurting over Chiba—we all are—but being down on ya self ain't gonna bring him back."

"I know, Don, but every time I close my eyes I see him. Yo, when they tore my nigga up, I was close enough to smell his breath. Man . . . forget it, you wouldn't understand."

"And why wouldn't I?" Don B asked, taking the ball away from him. "Lazy, you think you're the first one to lose a homey? I lose people close to me every day, cause that's just how fucked-up the world is; but the blessing is that we're still here to carry the memories of our fallen comrades. My uncle used to always tell me that tragedy comes into our lives for two reasons: so we can learn and become stronger from it. It's okay to mourn your man, Laze, but walking in the shadow of death only brings his icy touch closer to us, smell me?"

"Yeah, I feel you, but that don't change how I feel, Don," Lazy countered. "These niggaz came into Harlem, where we're supposed to be untouchable, and shot my best friend. The worse part was that I couldn't do shit about it but hide under a car. Man, if I had a gat I would've—"

"You would've what?" Don B cut him off. "You'd have tried to pull that thang, an ended up lying next to ya man or waiting on a trial date. Let me tell you something about guns and the character of people: Just because you got a hammer doesn't make you a killer, just another nigga with a gun, and that's one of the biggest problems affecting American society today. There are too many guns on the streets and not enough niggaz with enough common sense to know what to do with them. When you kill somebody you can't take it back, Lazy. Now, for as much as I know, you would've loved to have been able to blast for ya man, but think about what you would've had to sacrifice in the process. Don't no D-1 college want a nigga with charges, dawg."

"Yo, Don!" True called, interrupting their conversation. "What's good?" True gave him dap.

"Ain't nothing, just over here kicking it with the boy, Lazy," Don B said. "Jah, what up? You on ya toes out here?"

"I don't know no other way to be," Jah said.

"That kid is too fucking serious," Don B snickered.

"Lazy, what it do?" True addressed Lazy. "You a'ight?"

"Yeah, I'm cool," Lazy said halfheartedly.

"How many points you gonna drop on them niggaz Sunday?" True asked, trying to lighten the mood.

"Fifty," Lazy said, sinking a jump shot.

"That's what I'm talking about." Don B patted him on the back. "Now, go do ya laps with the rest of the team." Lazy nodded and headed off to the baseball diamond. "That boy has got potential like a muthafucka!"

"How's his head? I know he stressing over what happened to Chiba," True said.

"Yeah, the boy is down about it, but his head will be right come game time. I got too much riding on this to let emotions fuck it up," Don B said coldly. Jah gave him a look but didn't say anything.

"So, everything still popping for Sunday?" True asked.

"Oh, yeah, a lil bloodshed ain't gonna come between the Don and his chips. Them young boys is ready. Oh, I got a line on them kids who tried to hit you!" Don B suddenly remembered.

"Well, don't keep an asshole in suspense," Jah stepped closer to listen.

"Well, like we already knew, the cat you dropped was named Spider. He's a low-life nigga from Brooklyn who until recently was just doing renegade shit. Word has it that a few weeks ago he started hanging around with two badasses named Sha Boogie and Charlie Rock."

"Those names mean anything to you, True?" Jah asked.

True thought hard on it. He thought he had heard the name before, but for the life of him couldn't remember where. "Nah, I don't think so."

"So, what kind of niggaz are we dealing with?" Jah turned back to Don B.

"Well, we still don't know too much about them, but from what I heard, Sha Boogie is the biggest threat out of them all. He ain't got no real soldiers behind him, but is quick to pop off. I got Devil and Remo out in BK now, getting at fam and them to see what else they can come up with. Until then, True, you just keep a low profile."

"Don, I ain't wit this hiding shit. I'm ready to ride into Brooklyn and see about these niggaz!" True said heatedly.

"True, calm yo ass down," Don B told him. "Ain't no way I'm gonna let you run off into the lion's den with an album about to drop."

"So, what? I'm gonna spend the rest of my life looking over my shoulder?"

"I doubt that, True," Jah said, watching an Escalade that was creeping to a stop outside the park fence. "If this Sha Boogie is the kind of nigga I think he is, he's gonna move on you again sooner than later."

Chapter **29**

THE MORNING SUN FELT GOOD AGAINST YOSHI'S face. The heavy doses of medication she had been pumped full of still had her feeling like she had just woken up, but it was a small price to pay if it numbed the intense burning in her neck. Touching the heavily packed bandage, she thanked her God for the thousandth time to be alive.

"Yoshi, if you keep picking at it, it'll never heal correctly," Billy said. Like the true friend she was, she had been there to pick Yoshi up and had been looking after her ever since. For all Billy's nagging, she was the one person Yoshi could depend on, no matter what the situation, unlike a certain person who came to mind.

"It's gonna scar anyhow, so what does it matter," Yoshi said.

"Yes, but scars fade or can be removed," Billy pointed out. From the look on Yoshi's face, she could tell something was wrong. "Okay, spill it."

Yoshi was about to try and pass it off like it was nothing, but she knew Billy would keep pushing until she came clean. "I don't know. I guess it's this whole hospital thing." She absently rubbed her arm. "I guess it's just got me a little rattled."

"Yoshi, you just got shot. I'd think something was wrong if you didn't feel some type of way about it."

"That's not what I meant. I mean, yeah, I was scared shitless that I was gonna die, but I mean, the whole experience of being laid up in the hospital. It made me think of . . . well, you know." She didn't have to say it for Billy to know that she was referring to the rape.

Billy stopped walking and turned to face Yoshi. Tears glinted in her friend's eyes, but none fell. "Sweetie, you've been through a ton of shit over the past year, so there's gonna be some residue. The important thing is that you keep fighting and doing the right thing with your life."

"A lot of fucking good that's doing me." Yoshi pointed at the bandage. "For all the good I'm trying to do with my life, I feel like my karma is still fucking me for some reason."

"You can't say that, Yosh. I mean, look at where you were last year, as opposed to where you are now. You've got your job, your health, and a man that loves you to the moon."

"I'm so sure," Yoshi said sarcastically.

"What, you don't think Jah loves you?" Billy asked.

"Nah, I'm not saying that. I know he loves me, or at least I think I do; but I can't help but feel that he committed to me so quickly out of guilt more than anything else," Yoshi confessed. It was something that had been on her mind for a while, but it was the first time she had said it out loud to anyone but herself.

"I can't buy into that. That boy worships the ground you walk on. Before you, Jah was running around here wilding, no purpose, no bounds."

"I know, and that's part of what I'm talking about. Before me and Jah got together he didn't have a care in the world, with the exception of dying too young, but that was the life he chose and he was happy with it. Then you have old victimized me changing the game in the ninth with my bullshit." Yoshi rubbed her hands over her arms like she was chilly, though the temperature was in the mideighties. "Sometimes I think I can actually see the life draining from his eyes while he's sitting at home playing babysitter. The streets call to that boy so strong, but he sits up in the house with me, making sure I'm good. That shit is crazy!"

"That ain't crazy, baby, that's love." Billy placed a hand on her arm. "Yeah, we all know how Jah's psycho ass was out here rocking and it was only a matter of time before the police or one of these crazy niggaz slowed him down, but you stepped in and helped him change that. Baby girl, you gave a man who felt like he had nothing to live for something to die for."

"But all I did was complicate things for him, Billy. Jah is a young man who should be enjoying his life, not playing nurse to a bitch suffering from a mean case of hard luck."

"Yoshi, can't nobody make Jah's strong-willed ass do nothing he don't wanna do. He tends to you that way because he cares."

"Why, even before the rape I was damaged goods. Ain't no secret about how many niggaz done had their turn at this pussy," Yoshi said heatedly.

"See, now you talking some other shit," Billy said, obviously not feeling Yoshi's line of thought at that moment.

Yoshi's eyes took on a far-off look, and when she spoke, she did so with great effort. "You know, when I lay in that bed, lumped up with my pussy ripped to hell, all I could think was *why?* What had I done to piss God off so much that something like that was allowed to happen to me?"

"Yoshi—"

"No, let me finish. I ran through the list of sins that I had committed throughout my life and figured it was a no-brainer. What good could come to a woman who lives her life as a whore and a liar? I figured that if I could just manage to do the right thing, maybe my luck would turn around, and for a time it seemed like it would. I manage to land a good nigga, a high-profile job, and through the grace of God, none of those dirty muthafuckas gave me the package. So, if I'm doing all these things right, why the fuck do I keep getting thrown the curveballs?"

Billy took Yoshi by the uninjured shoulder and turned her so that they were facing each other. "My mother always told me that God worked in very strange ways, but never to doubt his intentions or purpose for us. Yeah, you've got some heavy shit going on in ya life, but you know what? You're still here. Rhonda's kid's gotta grow up with no mother, and Paul's talent died with him in that prison shower, but that doesn't have to be us. Yoshi, can't you see that we're blessed? Girl, I know it might not look that way now, but trust and believe, it will get greater later."

"Sometimes it just feels like I'm carrying the weight of the world on my shoulders," Yoshi whispered.

"Then let your friends and that crazy-ass man of yours help you with that burden. Yoshibelle, at the end of the day all we got is each other," Billy said with conviction.

The tears that had been forming in Yoshi's eyes slid down her cheeks one at a time. The bright sun made them look like diamonds rolling from her face, dripping onto the blouse that Billy had loaned her to come home in. Her face seemed to be caught between stages, like she didn't know whether to cry or rage. Not being able to hold it off any longer, Yoshi collapsed in Billy's arms and had a long-overdue cry.

CHARLIE ROCK SAT ON AN old milk crate in front of the bodega on the corner of Sterling and Ralph avenues. His left arm was in a sling, but his right was still free to grab the gat stashed under the tire of a parked car if trouble popped. The codeine pills he had managed to score from his grandmother's house had him feeling like Neil Armstrong, but he was coherent enough to spot One-Time if they tried to roll. It wasn't the smartest thing in the world, him being out in the element with a gaping hole in his shoulder, but he had to eat, and the pound of Cali dirt he had in the crib wasn't gonna sell itself.

"What you working wit?" a skinny kid wearing a pair of jeans that were too sizes too small said as he rolled up on Charlie.

"Tens and twenties," Charlie replied, looking up and down the block for police.

"A'ight, let me get a dime," the kid said.

Charlie dipped his hand inside of the sling holding his arm up and pulled out a dime sack of weed, which he slapped in the kid's palm like he was giving him a pound. The kid took the bag and made hurried steps down the block. As he was leaving, Charlie couldn't help but to look at his tight-ass jeans and wonder what the hell the world was coming to.

A burgundy minivan came coasting down Ralph, honking its horn. As a rule, Charlie never walked up to strange cars. He moved himself into a position where he could fight or flee, depending on what the situation called for, and strained his eyes to see who was in the minivan. It was then that Roxy got out of the passenger's side.

"Roxy, why the fuck y'all rolling on the block like that, knowing a nigga out here trying to stay low?"

"Stop acting like the feds taking pictures, you ain't that high on the food chain, nigga," Roxy teased him. "Yo, how you gonna leave a bitch assed out yesterday, I thought you was gonna be at the shoot?"

"My fault, something came up, so we never even made it uptown," he lied.

"Damn, kid, what happened to ya arm?" Sugar said, stepping onto the curb. She had a cigarette dangling from her mouth that bobbed when she spoke.

"Oh, this ain't nothing." He brushed it off. "So what y'all doing up this early, looking like y'all coming in from the track?" He motioned towards the club clothes they were still wearing from the previous evening.

"Long story," Roxy told him. "So what's up? Can we get high?"

"Y'all spending or reaching?" He looked at the girls suspiciously.

"Yeah, we spending, but a bitch need a lookout," Sugar said.

"What you need?" Charlie sat up on the crate.

Sugar sifted through her purse like she didn't already know exactly how much money was in there. "Let us get the five for forty-five, son?"

"Must've been a good night, huh?" Charlie asked, digging into his sling.

"Not really, we thought we caught these niggaz slipping, but they was faking," Roxy said.

"Shit, I wish y'all would've caught some donkeys, cause a nigga out here on thirsty."

"I'm surprised you and that nigga, Sha Boogie, wasn't out creeping, cause there was damn sure some ballas out there," Sugar said.

"Charlie," someone called from behind Roxy. Charlie craned his neck and saw little Sheeka making her way towards him. Of all the people he could've bumped into, he didn't want to see her. Still, she was Spider's little sister, so he acted like he wasn't disturbed by her presence.

"Sup?"

"Charlie, you seen Spider?" she asked, with a worried expression on her face.

"Nah, not since some time yesterday," Charlie lied.

"Well, I thought he was with Tina, but she said she dropped him off with you and Sha Boogie last night."

Charlie hoped that no one had seen his eye jump when Sheeka said it. "That was like yesterday afternoon. The nigga said he was going to see some chick out in C.I., and that was the last we saw of him."

Sheeka stared at him for a minute as if she was trying to weigh the truth in his words. "A'ight, well if you see him tell him to bring his ass home, somebody wants to see him. Plus, my moms is pissed cause he stayed out all night without calling."

"I'll tell him," Charlie said, fishing around in his pocket with his good hand, looking for a cigarette.

Sheeka turned like she was going to leave, but stopped short. She looked Charlie directly in the eye and asked, "What happened to your arm?"

Charlie's heart began to beat faster, making it feel like the blood was draining from his face. "You know how we on it," he told her.

"Yeah, y'all wild as hell with it," Sheeka laughed, but there was something sinister about it. "Alright then. Tell Spider to come to the crib. Bo is home and he wants to see his little brother." Not missing the sickened look that came over Charlie's face, Sheeka went back across the street towards her building.

"Yo, was that one of Killer-Bo's sisters?" Roxy asked.

"Yeah," Charlie said in a very flat voice. His mouth was suddenly very dry and he found it hard to swallow. What everyone assembled on that corner and ten blocks squared knew was the legend of Killer-Bo.

Killer-Bo was a throwback to old-school Brooklyn, where senseless murder and robbery were the norm. Killer-Bo was never some big drug dealer or notorious crime boss, but he was recognized throughout the five boroughs as a certified headache. Killer-Bo had been arrested for damn near every crime from murder to rape and still hadn't learned his lesson. He was a nigga who was content to die in the streets as long as his name carried on. Bo was brutal and untrustworthy, but aside from all that, he loved his sisters and baby brother, Spider.

"What did she want?" Sha Boogie startled them. No one had heard or seen him approach.

"Ain't nothing. She was looking for Spider," Charlie said nervously. "Yo, you knew Killer-Bo was home?"

"Should I have known?" Sha asked, as if he really didn't give a fuck. "Sup, ladies," he said, addressing Sugar and Roxy.

"Ain't shit," Roxy told him. "We was about to puff, what's good?"

"I'm wit it, but I ain't trying to stand out here and smoke," Sha told her.

"We don't have to, we got the whip right here." Sugar pointed to the van.

Sha looked at it and the girls suspiciously. "Where did y'all get this shit from?"

"It's a long story. Just bring ya ass on in." Sugar grabbed him by the arm and led Sha to the van. Charlie grabbed his gun from under the car and jumped in the van behind them.

ON THE OTHER SIDE OF town, Shannon's minivan was parked several blocks away from an abandoned building that they were in the process of climbing the steps to. Spooky played the lookout, while Shannon worked the lock on the rotted wooden door. No matter how many times he did it, it was never a simple task. After gaining entry, they hiked up to the third floor of the building. Most of the steps were rotted out or missing, but the two men had been inside the building so many times that they could've navigated the stairs in the dark.

From the end of the third floor hallway came two very distinct sounds, a muffled cry and the scampering of rodents. The whole building was lousy with them, but for some reason the majority seemed to be focused on the room Spooky and Shannon were approaching. Spooky stopped outside the door and picked up a fire extinguisher that was propped against the wall.

"You ready?" Spooky asked Shannon.

"Man, let's just get this shit over with. You know I hate fucking rodents of any sort," Shannon said, placing his hand on the doorknob and bracing his shoulder against the door. With a grunt he shoved the door open and Spooky slipped inside.

The room had once probably been a bedroom, judging by the peeling, violently streaked wallpaper. Rats of all sizes were moving throughout the room like singles at a bar, most seemingly oblivious to Spooky and Shannon's presence. A large cluster of rats were gathered in the middle of the room with their beady eyes fixed on Roots's limp and naked body. His hands were cuffed above his head and looped over a rusty pipe. He was too high up to plant his feet on the floor and possibly free himself, but he wasn't too high up that the rats couldn't nip at him throughout the night.

Spooky and Shannon had brought the dread here right after the botched hit. They beat him something awful, but let him live to see another day, if the condition he was in could still be considered living. Instead of just leaving him chained up, Spooky thought it would be funny if they rubbed sticky Apple Butter on him before they left, to see what would happen. His legs, feet and even genitals bore the nicks and scratches the rats had left trying to eat the sweet spread off him.

Spooky sprayed the fire extinguisher at the rats, clearing a path for Shannon and himself. One of the rats scuttled across Shannon's foot and he had to fight against the urge to pull out his gun and start shooting. Once the last of the rats had been cleared away, the two men moved in on Roots.

Shannon slapped him viciously across the face, snapping Roots's eyes open. "Wa fe do, star?" Shannon taunted him. "Did you sleep well?" Roots responded by trying to scream through the gag, any hopes he had of escaping had probably fled with the all-night buffet.

"Damn, they fucked you up," Spooky said, crouching to examine the rat bites. The thought of what Roots's ass had probably endured during the course of the night was sad, but Spooky got a kick out of it.

Shannon grabbed Roots by the jaw and squeezed as hard as he could. Something slick dripped from Roots's mouth, over the gag, and onto Shannon's hand, but he didn't seem to notice. "You picked the wrong muthafucka to try and kill." Roots mumbled something, but they couldn't understand him through the gag. "My fault," Shannon said, ripping the gag from his mouth.

"Muthafucka, you think this shit scare me. Me from the yard, pussy boy!" Roots spit blood into Shannon's face.

Shannon wiped the blood from his face and looked at his stained hand. He cocked back to hit Roots, but suddenly he had a better idea. From the corner he retrieved a piece of wood with a rusty nail lodged in the end of it, and he hefted it, tested the weight.

"So, you wanna spit on niggaz, huh?" Shannon asked, before smashing the wood into Roots's ass as hard as he could. Roots opened his mouth to scream, but Shannon smashed the wood into his gut, knocking the wind out of him. Slowly, he made his way around Roots, tearing him up with the piece of wood while Spooky smoked a cigarette and laughed like he was watching *Def Comedy Jam*. He had just about beaten Roots into unconsciousness when Spooky stopped him.

"I told you, we want the nigga to suffer before he dies," Spooky told him. Shannon looked on, confused, while Spooky rummaged around in an abandoned tool box that sat in the corner. When he came back over to Roots he was holding a small can of lighter fluid.

"Fuck is you gonna do with that?" Shannon instinctively backed up.

"Bout to show you how to make a nigga suffer," Spooky said and began dousing Roots with the fluid. The tough-guy persona Roots was wearing faded when he realized what Spooky meant to do.

Unfortunately, his pleas fell on deaf ears, as Spooky tossed the smoldering cigarette butt at Roots, igniting him.

Never had Shannon, in all his years of life, heard a man scream the way Roots did that day. The fire seemed to flare everywhere at once, as Roots struggled hopelessly against the handcuffs. The sound of Roots's crackling flesh reminded Shannon of hearing fried bacon on Sunday mornings. As soon as the smell hit him, he immediately ran off to vomit, while Spooky watched intently. When Roots stopped moving Spooky decided he had seen enough. Before turning to leave, he took another cigarette from the pack and lit it on Roots's flaming body.

Chapter **30**

DENA CAME WALKING DOWN THE STEPS OF HER
building like she was strutting the catwalk in Milan. She
had blown out her hair and let it fall straight down around
her face and shoulders. A green tunic was slung across her
chest, with a gold belt across her flat stomach. Tight denim
Capris hugged her hips and thighs, stopping just above a
pair of gold strap-up sandals.

"Oh-oh, I see you, boo!" Yvette shouted when she saw
her. "You must got a date, or something like that?" She had
traded in her pajama pants and slippers for jeans and
sneakers. They had chased Shakira and her skank-ass crew
off the block, but if they came back Yvette wanted to be
ready.

"Something like that," Dena said, pushing her hair out
of her face. "What the hell was y'all doing out here scrap-
ping so early in the damn morning?"

"Bitches came through like it was something sweet, so
we had to teach em," Yvette said, giving Mousy a pound.

"On the real, D, you need to tell Shannon to check that
lil bitch before she finds herself in a bad way," Mousy said.
She, too, had traded in her normal stoop attire for jeans
and sneakers. In addition to Yvette's .25, which was stashed

in the trash can, Mousy had a hatchet inside her dingy denim Guess bag.

"Shit, y'all see him more than I do, tell him yourself," Dena said.

"Damn, look at that pretty muthafucka," Mousy said, looking towards the corner of the block. The white Escalade took its time rolling down the block, blasting Don B's hood anthem, "Everything is Food." When the truck finally pulled to a stop in front of 437, Black Ice rolled down the window and stared at Dena from behind black Gucci shades.

"Well, its been real," Dena smiled at them and stepped off the stoop.

"Damn, you rolling like that?" Mousy asked, with a bit of jealously in her voice.

"I see you, Dena-D. Yo, see if that muthafucka got a brother!" Yvette shouted at her back.

"DAMN, IF YOU WERE AN ice cream cone I'd lick you," Black Ice said, admiring Dena's outfit as she hopped in the car.

"Well, I ain't made from no dairy products, but if you play ya cards right you might get a taste," Dena teased. "So, where's your entourage?" She asked, noticing that Ice was alone.

"I gave everybody the day off so I could kick it with you," he said, pulling away from the curb. He didn't miss the look that Yvette was giving him, and he silently wondered how she would look cleaned up and how much bread a thick chick like her could check in. Ice's mind was always on paper.

"Wow, I feel special," Dena said, adjusting her seat.

"You should. I ain't had a day off in almost five years," he said seriously. "So, you free for the rest of the day, or do I have a time limit?"

"I'm all yours."

Black Ice looked at her. "Better watch what you say, cause there's a lot of power in words."

"Is that right?"

"Sure as my ass is black," he chuckled.

"So, where we off too?" Dena asked, changing the radio station without invitation. It irked Black Ice, but he didn't let it show.

"Gotta hit Harlem for a minute to take care of something, then we can start our date. I got something special lined up for your pretty ass; but don't ask, cause it's a surprise."

"I like surprises," Dena smiled.

Black Ice licked his lips. "Baby, I'm full of them."

Instead of going the most direct route, which would've taken them up Atlantic Avenue, Black Ice came back around to Throop and went up Putnam. Black Ice claimed to have been born and bred in Harlem, but he seemed to know Brooklyn pretty well. Once they hit the bridge, it was a straight shot up the FDR to Harlem.

Just being uptown made Dena think about Lazy and how things had been going between them lately. They had had their ups ad downs in the past, but the last few days had been really stressful. A part of her felt like she was violating by rolling through Harlem with Ice, but Lazy didn't seem to have any qualms about who he sported on his arm. Seeing him out in plain view with the chick Becky made Dena feel disrespected. Sure, Harlem was his domain, and she knew he had a wayward bitch or two, but Dena felt like when she was on the scene it was supposed to be strictly about her, whether he was expecting her or not. And to top it off, he was trying to stunt for his boys like he could bark on her in public. She quickly shut that down and reminded him who the fuck she was.

The truth of the matter was that she really did love Lazy, but they had considerably different views on the life. All she wanted him to do was love and respect her like she respected him, but he was constantly fucking up. If it wasn't something going on with him and another chick, he was putting his boys and the block before their relationship. Dena was growing tired of the senseless arguments they were getting into, and frankly didn't know how much longer she could, or would, put up with it.

Getting off on the 135th Street exit, Ice steered the car east and hung a left on Lenox Avenue. As they sat at a red light in front of

Harlem Hospital, Dena thought she saw the girl Yoshi outside talking to someone, but the light changed before she could make a positive ID. Ice continued north on Lenox until they arrived at a large park. As soon as Dena saw Don B and True watching the Big Dawg basketball squad run around the baseball diamonds, she got a very sick feeling in the pit of her stomach.

"BLACK ICE, WHAT IT IS?" Don B walked up on the car followed by True and Jah. "I didn't expect to see you, where's Wendy?"

"Change of plans," Black Ice said, giving Don B a pound. "Young True, what it do?" he nodded at the young rapper. "You got a new member of the group?" He looked at Jah.

"Nah, he ain't no rapper. This is my man, Jah," True told him. Jah nodded in greeting, then went back to watching the block.

"So, that the squad?" Black Ice motioned towards the eight young men running around the diamond.

"Yeah, those is my young pups. Eight of the meanest young niggaz from the hood that are gonna bring the glory back to Harlem," Don B boasted. "Matter of fact, let me introduce you to my secret weapon. Yo, Lazy!" Don B called over to the diamond.

Dena couldn't believe how rotten her luck was. Of all the places Black Ice could've brought her, they had to come to the same park where the Dawgz practiced. Watching Lazy jog across the park, she felt her heart sink a little more, the closer he got. Dena wished she was Barbara Eden so she could blink and disappear, but it was the real world, not television, so she had to face the music.

"What's good, D?" Lazy said, sounding a little winded. He saw Black Ice behind the wheel, but couldn't make out the face of the passenger because she was leaning too far back in her seat.

"Lazy, this my nigga Ice," Don introduced him.

"Sup man?" Lazy reached into the car to give Ice a pound, but stopped midreach when he saw Dena in the passenger's side. "What the fuck are you dong in here, Dena?" Lazy asked heatedly.

"Hello to you, too," Dena said, trying to keep her cool.

"Oh, now I see why you ain't return my phone calls, cause you running around with a damn pimp!"

Black Ice leaned over and stared Lazy down. "Little nigga, you better watch ya mouth around grown folks," Ice warned.

Ignoring the threat, Lazy focused on Dena. "Get yo ass out of the truck!" he barked, trying to yank the door open.

"Man, you better un-ass my fucking door," Black Ice said angrily.

"Mind ya fucking business before you get knocked out!" Lazy shouted. "Dena, I said get out of the car now!"

"I see you one of those hardheaded niggaz," Black Ice said. He grabbed his .45 from the holster that was hitched to the driver's side door and made to step out, when Dena's hand on his arm stopped him.

"Don't," she said softly. Black Ice's face was still a mask of anger, but he sat back in the seat.

"Don, you better check this little nigga before I let him hold something," Black Ice said, placing the gun on his lap.

"My fault, Ice," Don B apologized, which was rare for him, but he needed that twenty-five thousand and wasn't about to let Lazy fuck it up. "Yo, what's wrong with you kid?" he asked Lazy.

"Dena, I ain't gonna ask you again," Lazy said, ignoring Don B.

"Hold the fuck on, I'm coming," she said, opening the car door. Before her feet hit the ground completely, Lazy had her by the arm and was dragging her back towards the park. "What the fuck is ya problem?" Dena snapped, trying to keep her balance.

"Do you know how long I've been trying to get hold of you?"

"I've been busy," she said in a very uninterested tone.

"So I see," he glanced over at Ice, who was speaking with Don B but watching them closely. "My best friend is dead and gone and you're too busy running with your new clique to even return my phone calls."

"Oh, my God, Chiba?!" Dena knew the man and was actually quite fond of him, when he wasn't off doing dirty with Lazy.

"Don't act all concerned now. I left you a message, but I guess you and your new boyfriend were having to much fun to check it," Lazy said.

"Lazy, Ice is not my boyfriend. We're just cool," Dena said, trying to downplay it.

"You sure got a lot of high-profile friends lately. I don't even wanna know where the sudden popularity came from," Lazy said scornfully.

Dena snaked her neck. "And what the fuck is that supposed to mean?"

"Dena, I ain't new to this. Yesterday it was Stacks, today it's the nigga in the fly ride. What the fuck is really good with you?"

"Lazy, this is the second time in the last two days that you've all but called me a whore," Dena said, trying to keep the hurt out of her voice.

He looked at her coldly and said, "If it walks like a duck . . ."

The sound of her hand connecting with his face rang out through the quiet morning. Dena was about to curse Lazy out, but to her surprise, he slapped her right back. Though he hadn't meant to hit her so hard, the blow knocked her on her ass. When he went to help her up, Dena was on him like a wild animal. She kicked, punched, and scratched at Lazy until Jah grabbed her about the waist and dragged her away.

"Get the fuck off me!" Dena snarled.

"Shorty, chill. I'm just trying to help," Jah told her, just missing a backward kick she directed at his nuts.

"Lazy, what the fuck is wrong with you? You can't be beating on no bitch in the street!" Don B roared. A blur of motion whizzed passed him and before he had a chance to do anything, Black Ice had materialized in front of Lazy.

The young man tried to take a fighting stance, but Black Ice was a much more skilled fighter. He caught Lazy with an overhand right and followed up with a left to the lip. Blood shot from Lazy's mouth as he crashed to the ground. The other members of the Big Dawg basketball team rushed in to help Lazy, but Black Ice's .45 stopped them short.

"Is all you lil niggaz crazy?" Ice swept the crowd with the gun. "The next muthafucka to buck is gonna catch something hot!"

"Ice, chill," Don B tried to defuse the situation.

"Don, I come up here to do business and this is how it goes down?" Ice wasn't aiming the gun at him, but the look in his eyes wasn't a friendly one.

"Ice, that's word to mine; you know I'd never let you get caught in a cross. The little nigga lost his friend and apparently his girl," he glanced at Dena, "in less than twenty-four hours, so he ain't thinking straight."

"I got something to straighten his ass out," Black Ice said to Lazy, who was still sitting on the floor in a daze.

"On everything I love, I'm gonna check son, but don't pop the lil nigga over some words Ice, you a bigger man than that." Don B tried to stroke his ego.

"I am, ain't I." Ice's face softened, but he didn't put his gun away. "The bread is in the back seat, D."

"A'ight," Don B nodded to True, who retrieved the case containing the twenty-five large. "Ice, I hope this doesn't sour any future dealings?"

"Don, you know the bullshit don't matter where a dollar is concerned, but you better teach these young boys some fucking etiquette." Ice looked over at Lazy.

"Get off!" Dena broke loose from Jah and went to Lazy. "Are you okay?"

"Bitch, get away from me." Lazy kicked out at her angrily.

"Lazy, I didn't mean for this to happen," she said, with tears filling her eyes. "I swear—"

"Fuck you, ho bitch. You think ya whack-ass pussy is the only one out here. I got a hundred bitches waiting to take ya place."

"Lazy, why you talking to me like that?" she cried.

"That's how I talk to all sluts. Why don't you and your new pimp boyfriend go downtown and see how many STDs y'all can pick up!"

The words cut Dena to the core of her soul. In her seventeen and a half years on earth she had never had a man talk to her like that. It hurt even worse coming from someone who was supposed to love her. At that moment, a little piece of what she had felt for Lazy died, and there was no coming back from death. She knew he was speaking out of hurt and anger, but it was obvious that things would never be the same between them again.

"You about done here?" Black Ice asked, draping his arm around Dena, but keeping his eyes on Lazy in case the man still had some frog in him.

She looked to Lazy to protest, but he remained silent, only staring at her murderously. "Yeah, I'm done," she said sadly. Before she got into the truck she looked back at Lazy for signs that it all must've been a bad dream, but the hateful look in his eyes said it was very real.

Chapter 31

"SHORTY IS WILD FOR THE NIGHT," JAH SAID, AS the Escalade pulled off.

"On the real, I thought she was gonna stretch your lil ass out," True teased Lazy.

"Fuck you, man, that shit ain't funny!" Lazy spat.

"True, don't make it worse," Don B scolded the youngster. "Yo, that was some real chicken-head shit you pulled, Lazy. Ice could've smoked ya little stupid ass."

"That nigga a pimp, not a killer," Lazy argued.

"Don't judge a book by its cover. I've known Black Ice for a long time, and he might not be the hardest nigga out, but if you back him into a corner you'll find ya self short."

"Fuck that, he shouldn't have been out here trying to sport my lady," Lazy said. "You come between a man and his woman and you get what ya hand calls for."

"Not for nothing, I didn't see him put a gun to her head to get her in the car," Jah volunteered.

"And who the fuck are you again?" Lazy flexed on Jah.

"Easy, man," Don B stepped in between them, knowing full well that, whereas Ice might've just given the youngster an ass whipping, Jah would murder him—and that would be bad for business. "Lazy, you're a good dude, but you acting real out of order right now. I told you from the gate about playing cat and mouse with these hos. Now, if shorty would rather live in the fast lane with Ice, let her. In a minute you're gonna be a national superstar, and you'll have more hos than you know what to do with."

"I hear you talking, D. and I'm cool. I just need some time to get my head together behind this shit."

"You gotta get ya head right, son," Don B broke his train of thought. "You're gonna be my floor general, and I need you to be on point; so, I don't know what you gotta do, but you gotta get shorty outta ya system and run my team."

"The Don is right, Lazy. Bitches come a dime a dozen," True said.

Lazy just glared at the men. It was easy for a man who had never known love to suggest that it be written off like a lost bet. Not one member of this so-called support system could've understood just what type of hell he was going through. Sure, Lazy was a class-A bastard and womanizer, but Dena was the one woman who managed to claim his heart. Those other girls were time fillers, but at the end of the day it was Dena with whom he saw himself enjoying his success.

Though she had never come at him like a sack chaser, Lazy knew Dena was a high-maintenance chick, so he did what he could to make sure she felt appreciated. He didn't have Stacks's or Black Ice's kind of cake just yet, but he was never stingy with the ends he did hustle up. He never thought that when it was all said and done it would come down to a dollar.

Jah was about to get at Lazy about coming at his sideways, but his cell phone postponed the conversation. "Speak on it," Jah answered.

"Jah, it's Billy," she said on the other end.

"What's popping? How's my girl?"

"She's a little shaken up, but she's good. Listen, I'm bout to drop her off at the crib, but I can't stay."

"That's cool, tell her I'll be by there in a few hours, cause I'm on the job right now."

"So you decided to take the gig with Stacks?"

"Nah, I'm covering True," he said.

"True? What's that all about?" Billy asked, guessing she already knew the answer. When Jah didn't answer that confirmed it. "You're going after those boys, aren't you?"

"Billy, they popped my boo," he tried to justify it.

"Boy, ain't there been enough bloodshed already?"

"Billy, just listen—"

"No, you listen for a minute," she cut him off. "Jah, I understand the nature of who you are, so it's no surprise that you're out there *hunting*, as you like to call it, but you've got a woman at home that needs you."

"I know Billy. I'm just trying to make sure that something like this never happens again."

"Jah, only God can dictate what will and won't happen. For as long as there are ignorant niggaz running around with guns, there will always be innocent people getting shot. All you can really do about it is keep you and yours out of harm's way and be there for each other. Tend to ya lady, Jah."

"What about True?" Jah asked, looking over at True, who was speaking with Lazy and Don B.

"True will be fine for a few hours, Jah. Get home to ya lady before I come to wherever y'all are at and drag you back, and none of y'all want that!"

"A'ight, you got that," Jah laughed.

"I thought I would. I left some Spanish food in the fridge for y'all, cause I know ya ass can't cook, and I don't want my girl overexerting herself."

"Bet. I'll be there in a sec." Jah ended the call. As usual, Billy was right. Jah had gotten caught up in the thrill of the hunt and almost lost sight of what was really important. Yoshi had almost been killed, and he had been so consumed with revenge that he hadn't really been there for her. It was a mistake that he intended to rectify.

"Jah, everything good?" True asked, dribbling a basketball.

Jah thought about it for a minute. "Nah, I gotta go check on Yoshi."

"Yo, first Lazy's tweaking over his shorty, now you're dipping off to tend yours? Is this the game, or an episode of *Ricki Lake*?" Don B huffed. Jah just glared at him.

"It's cool, D," True spoke up. "Jah, do what you gotta do. Call me in a few hours so we can link up. I'll be good until then." Unlike Don B, True knew how it felt to lose someone you cared about. Though Rhonda wasn't his girl, it still hurt like hell when she was killed. Jah had gotten a second and even third chance with Yoshi, and he wasn't going to keep him from his heart's desire.

FOR A LONG TIME DENA and Black Ice sat in the car, both lost in their own thoughts. The fight with Lazy weighed heavy on her mind. They had had plenty of arguments, but they never got physical. She understood that he was grieving for his friend, but that still didn't give him the right to put his hands on her.

At first she had been angry with Ice for putting the beats on Lazy like that, but after the way he had carried it, he deserved it. She never took the pretty boy as one to come to the rescue of a damsel in distress, but Ice had surprised her yet again. She was used to Shannon coming to her defense, but never another guy. It both flattered and intrigued her.

"Penny for your thoughts," Ice offered.

"Nothing, I'll be okay," she said flatly.

"Look, if you want me to take you home, its cool?"

"Did I ask you to take me home?" she snapped. She hadn't meant to, but she was still feeling the rush from getting into it with Lazy.

Black Ice slowed the truck and looked at Dena. "Baby girl, I know you're uptight over what happened with ya peoples, but all that hostility you sending my way is uncalled for. Now, I ain't been in the way of being talked down to by anybody, woman or man, so give me the same respect I give you."

His sternness surprised Dena because he had always been so laid back, but he was right. "I'm sorry, I guess I'm just running off emotions right now."

"You wanna talk about it?" he asked sincerely.

Dena shrugged. "There's really nothing to talk about. Lazy is my . . . well, *was* my boyfriend. We had a falling out."

"So I saw."

"Nah, this has been going on before we even met. He thinks that he can run around with anything sporting a pussy, and I'm supposed to sit back and take it."

"At that age a nigga'z hormones are in overdrive. You know how young guys are, Dena."

"I'm not concerned about young guys, Ice, I'm concerned about the guys that are supposed to be with me. If I'm with a dude and we have an open relationship that's one thing, but if we're supposed to be committed, then I expect him to act like it."

"So, you've never stepped out on Lazy?" Black Ice asked, catching her by surprise.

"Well . . . yeah, but only after he did it to me."

"So you knew he was cheating, but stayed with him; now you're leaving him for it?" Ice asked, pretending to be confused.

"No, I mean . . . I don't know what I mean." She folded her arms and flopped back in the seat.

"Dena," Ice began, steering the truck north up Harlem River Drive. "Men are closer to animals than women. Whereas women use logic, we move off base instinct. It's like, if you see a guy you like, you ain't just gonna jump out the window and act on it; but a dude ain't gonna rest until he gets that pussy. Men think with their dicks, not their heads."

"Does the same hold true for you, Black Ice?" Dena asked.

"I ain't no man, baby. I'm a freak of nature," he said playfully.

Dena was so wrapped up in the conversation that she hadn't even noticed they were going to New Jersey until she saw the signs for the turnpike. "Why we going to Jersey?" she asked, now quite suspicious.

"We ain't going to New Jersey, we're going to Philly," he said, before falling in line with the southbound traffic.

For a girl who had never been out of the city, the short ride down the turnpike was fascinating. Before taking the trip with Ice she'd never realized how big New Jersey was. They passed towns she'd never heard of and still hadn't left the Garden State. Everything seemed so much fresher and greener outside the iron walls of her city.

When they finally hit Philly, she found herself in awe of what looked like a miniature version of New York, with a more classic feel.

Black Ice first took Dena through the mall where they did a little shopping. Dena picked out some dynamite outfits for herself and even picked up something for Mo. Other than a Stacy Adam's hat, Ice didn't buy anything for himself. He seemed to just be enjoying watching Dena shop, which suited her just fine. When they left the mall, Ice took Dena to a cute little spot called Ms. Tootsie's. Technically, it wasn't even the right day for the spot to be opened for business, but after a well-placed phone call they opened their doors for Ice and his guest.

"I take it you come here a lot?" Dena asked, checking out the décor.

"Only when I'm in town," he replied, pulling her chair out for her.

"And how often might that be?" she prodded.

"As often as necessary," he said, before calling the waitress over. Ms. Tootsie's didn't serve alcohol, but they managed to scrounge up a bottle of Pinot for the Ice Man. Black Ice excused himself from the table to use the bathroom, which he had been doing throughout the day. Dena chalked it up to all the vitamin water he had consumed on the way down, even joking that he had a weak bladder. When he returned, his movements seemed more sluggish and there was a sleepy look in his eyes. Something was out of place, but Dena didn't dwell on it.

Black Ice and Dena sipped wine and made small talk under the dim lights of Ms. Tootsie's. A few times during the conversation Ice's words trailed off midsentence, but he recovered gracefully. They compared notes on each other's lives and gazed passionately into each other's eyes until the food came. Ice had liver and onions with white rice and gravy, which he just picked at, while Dena selected steak and mashed potatoes. Dena didn't even know they made steaks as big as the Porterhouse in front of her. It was safe to say that Black Ice had her thoroughly impressed.

They both left the restaurant feeling like stuffed pigs. Black Ice was telling Dena about the history of the city, but she only half-listened. When Ice realized he was talking to himself he called her on it.

"You still thinking about homey?" He touched her arm.

"Nah, Lazy is yesterday's news," she assured him. "I'm just thinking about our little road trip."

"What, you didn't have a good time?"

"No, that's not it at all. I actually had a great time. It's not every day that a man whisks you off to another city for dinner."

"It could be," he said seriously. "A nigga could see himself spending some heavy time with you, Dena."

"Ice, you got too many hos on your plate as it is," she told him.

"Who, Wendy and them? Nah, its more of a business relationship than anything."

"And your business is flesh peddling, right?" She finally put it out there.

Black Ice gave her a comical look. "Dena, I haven't pedaled anything since I fell off my bike in the seventh grade. I'm a manager for adult entertainers," he told her. She gave him a disbelieving look, so he explained: "What I do is all about supply and demand. See, sex does and always will sell. I don't put a gun to those girls' heads and make them climb on them poles; they do it because they want to. Hell, the majority of them were in the life when I found em, all I did was show them how to manage their money."

"By pocketing it?" There was no malice in her tone, but a dire curiosity.

"Dena, you got me fucked up," he began. "You think that I put these girls on the street and take their money so I can live, right? I don't just drop them off and pick them up; I clothe them, feed them, and keep a roof over their heads. Lisa is enrolled in medical school off my dime, so it's a two-way street. Black Ice and his ladies aren't just people, we're a business. Them girls you see on my arm got ownership in barbershops, Laundromats, and a whole slew of other shit, so the money ain't all going in my pocket."

"I didn't mean to offend you," she said, feeling like she was out of bounds.

"I ain't offended, Dena, just telling you what it is. It's easy to confuse what I do with pimping, but that ain't the case. All I do is give hope to the hopeless."

Black Ice said he wasn't offended, but his body language said otherwise. What he said made sense to Dena. She knew countless girls who were running the streets lawless and ended up broke with worn-out pussies. All his girls stayed fly and they seemed pleased as punch with his treatment of them.

"So, where to now?" she asked, trying to lighten the mood.

"I don't know, I thought you might wanna get back to the city?" Ice said.

"Nah, I'm not really in a rush. I thought maybe we could hang out a little while longer. I know you know some hot spots in Philly?"

A wicked smile crept across his lips. "I think I know a place."

Chapter 32

JAH LAID IN THEIR KING-SIZE BED, BASKING IN THE glow of the mind-blowing sex they had just had, with his lady resting peacefully on his chest. He brushed a strand of hair from her face and admired how beautiful she was, and how that beauty was almost stolen from him.

When he saw the men with the guns, instincts took over. He didn't think about himself or anyone else on the block, all he knew was that there was danger and Yoshi had to be protected at all costs. Without thinking, he engaged the enemy—and his girl had gotten shot because of his impulsiveness. She was lucky this time, but what would happen if there was a next time? Would Yoshi catch a fatal shot? Would he be gunned down? The thought of being away from her made him frantic.

"What's wrong?" she asked in a sleepy voice.

"Huh, nothing, baby," he lied. "Go back to sleep."

"Jah, don't lie to me. Your heart is beating out of your chest, so I know something has got you rattled." She tried to sit up, but winced in pain when she tried to put weight on her injured arm.

"Yoshi, you shouldn't be moving around like that." He tried to help her up.

"Jah, cut it out. I'm shot, not paralyzed." She swatted him away. "Besides, you weren't saying that when you had my ass cocked in the air," she teased him.

Jah smiled. "You know how I like it, ma."

"Yep, face down, ass up!" she giggled. "But for real, what's bothering you?"

Jah hesitated before speaking. "I don't know, I was just thinking about what happened."

"Jah, I know you didn't put me in harm's way on purpose. You saw some niggaz with guns and did what you felt you had to do."

"That's just the thing, Yoshi, I didn't have to do anything," he told her. "Them boys were coming for True and I put my nose where it didn't belong, and you almost died because of it."

"Jah, I didn't almost die, I got shot in the arm," she pointed out.

"Yeah, but what about the next time?" he asked emotionally. "Baby, it's just an arm this time; but what happens the next time I fly off the handle? I'm supposed to protect you, not get you caught in cross-fires." He sat up and turned his back to her so she wouldn't see the moisture that was building in his eyes.

"Jah," Yoshi placed a warm hand on his back. "You're a young man that's had a very hard life. All you know is the law of the jungle, so you act accordingly. Yeah, it was dumb of you to bang out with those cats, but what would've happened if they were coming for you and you didn't react?" She slid around and straddled his lap, facing him. Though she had seen him get emotional before, this was the first time he looked like he was gonna cry.

"Baby." She stroked his cheek. "I can't lie and say that I don't want you to outgrow this thug-ass exterior of yours, but at the same time, this is the person that I fell in love with. When I was down you were my rider. You've done things that another man would've never dreamed of, to see that I was safe."

"I only did what I felt I had to, ma," he said.

"And I love you for that, Jah. But on the flip side of things, we both agreed to do things differently when we got together. I stopped stripping and you hung up your pistol—that was the deal. I know you can't effect change overnight, but I want to help you try, if you're willing?"

"Yoshi, I'd move heaven and earth for you," he said sincerely.

"And so you have." She kissed him gently on the lips. "Now, I want you to do one more thing for me."

"What?" he asked suspiciously. Yoshi whispered in his ear, bringing a smile to his grim face. "Now, that I can do," he said, leaning back in anticipation of round two.

DENA LAY ON THE PLUSH bed of the Hyatt hotel, located near Philadelphia's airport, waiting for Black Ice to come out of the bathroom. Rose petals decorated the bed sheet and floor surrounding the bed. On the nightstand sat a half-empty bottle of champagne, and pinched between her fingers was a blunt of Cali cush. She took light tokes of the sweet-smelling blunt and watched the yellowish clouds waft to the ceiling. She was so high that it was almost as interesting as watching one of her favorite shows.

Coming to the hotel was supposed to be a spontaneous move, but when they arrived, the room had already been prepped. Ice obviously had it up his sleeve from the gate, but she wasn't mad at him. She wanted it just as much as he did, if not more.

Black Ice came out of the bathroom with a white towel wrapped around his waist. Standing there under the dim lights, he looked like a chocolate god, with his rippled stomach and bulging chest. Her eyes traveled down the length of his body and came to rest on another bulge. Never taking his eyes off her, Ice crawled onto the bed and hovered over her.

"Ice, it's been a while since—," she began, but a finger over her lips quieted her.

"Lets not ruin this with words, baby," he whispered. Black Ice placed soft kisses on her lips and chin, making Dena shudder. Lazy was a great kisser, but Ice had it down to a science. He seemed to know just where to kiss her to get a reaction, as if he had studied the art, which he had. From her chin, he worked his way down her neck and chest. Taking great care, he ran his tongue around one nipple and then the other. Once the nipples were fully erect, he made his way south to her love cave.

Dena had her pussy eaten before, but mostly by guys closer to her age. Ice lapped at her clit, using just the tip of his tongue, until it puffed out. He then stuck his tongue deeper inside her. Ice's tongue felt like a hot spear as it explored the walls of her pussy. Just as she was about to get into it, he stopped.

"Where're you going?" she asked, as he scooted off the bed.

"Just setting the mood, baby," Ice said, fishing around in his pocket. He produced a small piece of tin foil and returned to the bed.

"Is that coke?" she asked, looking on curiously as he unfolded it.

Ice gave her that charming laugh. "Nah, baby, this ain't coke." He dipped one finger into the powder and held it out for her to examine. "This here is a ticket to on the Love Boat." He ran the powder over his gums.

"I don't know how you can do that shit," she said.

"Dena, we come from two different worlds, so there's a lot of shit I do that you wouldn't understand," he said, this time taking a snort. As the powder entered his system his eyes took on a dreamy look.

"What's that supposed to mean?"

Ice took a minute to clear his sinuses. "What it means is that you're a square," he said flatly.

"Ice, I know you ain't bring me all the way down to Philly to try and play me?" she snapped.

"Calm down, sweet lady. I didn't mean no disrespect by the statement." He stroked her cheek to soothe her. "Dena, all I'm saying is that I'm a street nigga and prone to do street shit. The world I come from is about flash and cash, while the world you come from is about going to school for sixteen to twenty years so you can work for another twenty and retire with half pay. Now, ain't nothing wrong with being a square—that's part of what attracted me to you in the first place: your purity. Personally, I think we need more women like you in the world. Beauty and intelligence is a rare thing." He kissed her forehead.

"So, because I want to be something in life means I ain't good enough for you?" she asked, trying to hide the hurt.

"On the contrary, Ms. Jones, you're too good for me." Ice let his eyes water up for effect. "Dena, I care for you so much, but I know that we can never be together the way I want, because of the fact that we're from two different worlds. All I'd do is bring you down."

"Ice, don't talk like that," she said, taking his face in her hands. "I feel you too, baby. I want us to be together," she said seriously.

"We can't." He snatched his face away. It took every last bit of his self-control to keep from laughing. "You don't know anything about the world I come from, and it'd be wrong of me to bring you into it." With that statement he let a lone tear run down his face.

Seeing him like that made him seem more like a real person than a superstar. In her mind, she saw her and Ice as some sort of power couple, with him dominating in the streets and she in the boardroom. It was at that moment of vulnerability and need that Dena decided that Ice was the man whom her soul called to.

"Then let me in," she whispered.

"What?"

"Let me in," she repeated. "Ice, let me be there for you. Let me into your world."

"Dena—," he began, but this time it was her finger that silenced him.

"Let's not ruin it with words." She traced the line of his jaw with her fingers. "Make me feel good." She looked down at the heroin.

Black Ice looked at her with sorrowful eyes, but his wicked brain was praising his pimp god. When he'd first decided to recruit her, he thought it would take a minute to crack the tough young girl from Bed-Stuy, but at the end she was like so many others: a young girl who just wanted to be loved. It was almost sad that his black heart was incapable of the emotion, because, had things been different, he could've seen himself wifing her. But that was the life of a square nigga who believed in that kind of thing. Black Ice was forged in the fires and battle-tested on the streets. There was nothing that could override the code that had been instilled in him since birth, not even what was left of his cold-ass heart. He was forged in the fires of mack-ing and hoing, so the logic of a square could never make sense to him. After he traced a line through the powder, he ran his stained finger over her lips and whispered, "Baby, only if you want to."

She licked the heroin greedily off his finger. "I want to."

Grinning wickedly, Black Ice moved on to the next phase of the turnout.

FIVE MINUTES AFTER TAKING HER first snort of heroin, Dena threw up the meal they had just consumed as well as parts of a bacon, egg, and cheese bagel she'd had for breakfast. If it weren't for Black Ice swiftly placing the hotel wastebasket beneath her, she'd have ru-ined the green carpet.

Dena tried to lift her head and found that the room was spinning. She tried to focus on something, anything, to stop the whirlwind that was now her senses, but she couldn't. The sick feeling, eventually faded, giving way to what felt like a dream. Out of nowhere her eye-lids began to droop and there was nothing she could do to stop them. It was as if she was nodding off, but couldn't quite cross the finish line to sleep.

"How do you feel?" Black Ice asked her. He was speaking nor-mally, but to Dena, his voice sounded distorted.

"I don't know." She tried to shake her head to clear it, but couldn't seem to do it. "What's happening to me?" She stared around the room as if she was trying to figure out the where it had come from.

"You're on the Love Boat, baby." He ran his leg up her exposed thigh, sending chills through her.

She moaned under his touch. "Daddy, I've never felt like this before."

"Don't worry baby, it gets better." He slid off the bed. When Ice came back to the bed he was holding the bucket that the champagne had been cooling in.

"And what do you plan to do with that?" she asked, with a dopey grin on her face.

He smiled. "You'll see."

Ice popped two ice cubes in his mouth and slid up the length of Dena's body. Just the feel of his skin against hers made her moist, but it was nothing compared to what she was about to experience. With the ice in his mouth, he went back to work on Dena's breasts. At first the cold was uncomfortable, but she got used to it and even started enjoying it. Again he retraced his steps down her stomach to her vagina. Using his tongue, he slipped the first ice cube in, drawing a yelp from Dena. She tried to pull his head back, but he swatted her hands and plunged the cube deeper.

The best way to describe what Dena was feeling was like an out-of-body experience. Waves of pleasure swept through her body and carried her to a place of flowers and pink clouds. From the tips of her toes to the top of her head, everything was tingling. Through her blissful haze, Dena could see Ice unwrapping the towel from around his waist. When his horse dick flopped out from between his legs Dena wanted to scream "Sweet Jesus!" None of the boys in her school were hung like that. Ice lowered himself for penetration, but Dena stopped him.

"No glove, no love." She placed a hand against his chest.

Ice ran his hand under the pillow and produced a box of magnum condoms, which he held up for her to examine. "I wouldn't have it any other way."

Dena was putty to be molded in the hands of the experienced man. Even with the condom on, Ice had an extremely hard time penetrating her. She hissed like an alley cat as he tried over and over to dip into her warm, until he finally hit pay dirt. He fucked her on her back and stomach, and then flipped her into several positions that she had never even seen, let alone tried. Ice had been with hundreds of women in his young life, but Dena's pussy went into the top ten. When it was all said and done, Ice had cum so hard that the condom almost came off inside her. Ice rolled over on his back to catch his breath while Dena lay there trembling.

"That was fucking amazing!" Dena said, squeezing her thighs together. Even though he wasn't inside her anymore, Dena was still cumming. Her mind was racing so fast that the thoughts ceased to make sense to her. Dena rolled over to face Ice and saw that tears were twinkling in the corners of his eyes. She thought that Ice was crying because of the beautiful sex they'd had, but he was actually thinking about how much money he could make with her and her sweet pussy in his stable. Dena snuggled against his sweaty chest and drifted off to sleep to dream of the life she and Ice could have together.

SHA BOOGIE AND CHARLIE ROCK had spent the last few hours bullshitting with Roxy and Sugar. They smoked weed and cruised Brooklyn in the minivan just killing time. Charlie had told Sha what Tina said to Sheeka about them being the last ones to see Spider, and Sha didn't like it one bit. When the police finally identified the body it would surely lead back to them, thanks to Tina's big mouth. Sha still had too much to do to worry about fighting a charge, and he reasoned that something had to be done.

After making up an excuse about having a matter to take care of, Sha Boogie got Sugar to drop him and Charlie off on Tina's block. The girls wanted to hang some more, but neither of them were talking about fucking, so Sha reasoned it wasn't worth it. When the girls had pulled off, the two men made hurried steps towards Tina's building and planned their next move.

"You think she's home?" Charlie asked.

"She's gotta be. The girl ain't ventured from the block since the shooting," Sha told him, fumbling around with the keypad on Tina's lobby door.

"So, what you think we should do?" Charlie asked, looking around to make sure nobody was watching.

"We're just gonna go up and talk to her," Sha said, continuing to punch in a series of different combinations on the keypad.

"Then why are we breaking into the building instead of ringing the bell?"

The door beeped and popped open. "Sometimes you ask too many questions," Sha said, stepping into the lobby. The two men hiked the few flights of stairs to Tina's floor, where Sha put his ear to the door and listened.

"She in there?" Charlie asked nervously. He didn't really like the look in Sha's eyes, because he knew the man was prone to do irrational shit.

"Yeah, I can hear her on the phone," Sha said, fishing a key out of his wallet.

"Where did you get that?"

"I stole it out of her purse and had a copy made. Call it insurance," Sha said, with his ear still pressed to the door. When he heard her hang up the phone he quietly slipped the key into the door and undid the lock.

Tina had her back to them, doing the dishes, so she never even knew they'd slipped into her house. The phone rang, causing her to turn in their direction. When she saw Sha and Charlie she dropped the plate she had been washing, shattering it.

"What the hell are y'all doing in my house!" she shrieked.

"Calm down. We knocked but you didn't hear us over the water. The door was open so we came in," Sha lied. "You know, you can't be leaving your door unlocked in a neighborhood like this, T." Though Sha hadn't done anything threatening, there was something about him that made Tina uneasy.

"Ben probably left it open. He just ran downstairs to the store. He should be back any minute," Tina lied.

"Word, we just seen Ben on Bedford like twenty minutes ago," Sha said, inviting himself to a seat at the kitchen table.

"He must've been on his way here. Now, what y'all want?" She addressed Charlie, knowing she had the best chance of reasoning with him.

"Tina, you tell anybody what happened uptown?" Charlie came out and asked.

"Hell nah, I ain't spoke to nobody since it happened," she lied.

"So you didn't see Sheeka?" Sha Boogie asked from the table, where he was playing with an elastic key chain. From the look on Tina's face, he knew that he'd hit a sore spot.

"Oh, I forgot I bumped into her the other day. She just asked if I'd seen Spider and I told her I hadn't seen him since the day before."

"You wouldn't lie to us, would you?" Charlie asked, moving closer to her, causing her to back up.

"Look, what y'all do is your business and ain't got nothing to do with me. I could care less if—" Her words were cut off as Sha Boogie looped the key chain around her neck. Tina tried to grab for the elastic that was now cutting off her wind, but Sha had all his weight leaned back, digging it further into her throat. Though Tina fought with everything she had, in the end she was no match for Sha's strength. Even after her body went limp, Sha continued to pull on the cord. When he was satisfied, he let her drop to the floor.

"Man, you said we was coming to talk to her!" Charlie said, looking nervously at Tina's lifeless body.

"Charlie, calm ya ass down," Sha said, stuffing the length of elastic into his pocket. "This bitch was gonna leave a trail of bread crumbs right to our doors for the police to follow. She had to go."

"This is bad business, Sha," Charlie said, as if he was about to have a breakdown. Faster than his eyes could follow, Sha was nose to nose with him.

"No, what's bad business is doing life on a fucking murder charge, dummy. Now come the fuck on. We've got some people to see at Club Envy tonight." Sha headed for the door.

Charlie stood motionless over Tina's dead body, unable to turn his eyes away. Tina had been a cool chick from the neighborhood who was just trying to help Sha settle a personal score. As with most things, Sha discarded her when she'd outlived her usefulness. It made Charlie give some serious thought as to what his future might hold.

"Come the fuck on!" Sha called from the door. Charlie Rock took a minute to make the sign of the cross before leaving Tina's body for someone to find.

Chapter 33

JAH WAS AWAKENED BY THE LOUD RINGING OF HIS cell phone. Day had given way to night, so he had to fumble around in the dark to find it. When he looked at the caller ID he didn't recognize the number, so he answered with attitude. "Yeah?"

"Rise and shine, playboy," True said on the other end. "Man, I've been trying to call you for the last two hours, where you been?"

"I had some shit to take care of," he said, looking over to make sure the phone hadn't waked Yoshi. "What's good?"

"Get ya shit and lets roll. We're heading down to Envy."

"Envy? What the fuck is going on down there?" Jah asked.

"Stacks is doing a show at Envy tonight and the Don says we need to be there."

Jah sighed. He and Yoshi had been going at it off and on for the better part of the day, and he really didn't feel like going out. Still, he had made a commitment to True, and as a man of his word, he had to honor it. "A'ight, gimme a few ticks and I'll meet you on the block."

"No need. We're parked in front of your building. Just get dressed and lets roll," True told him.

"A'ight," Jah said, peeking out his window. Sure enough

there was a red Bentley double-parked downstairs. "I'll see you in a minute." He ended the call.

"Who was that?" Yoshi asked, startling him.

"Nobody, ma." Jah got up and went to the closet to select an outfit.

"Nobody has got you getting out of bed with me, so they must be somebody. Let's not start this half-truth shit, Jah."

Jah sighed. "It was True."

"Jah, I know you ain't still gunning for them kids from the video shoot? We just talked about this."

"Calm down, Yoshi, I know what we talked about. I took a contract with Big Dawg to guard True, so I gotta honor it."

Yoshi sat up and clicked on the bedside lamp. Even with a scarf tied around her head and no makeup, she was still beautiful. "Jah, True is hot as a firecracker right now. Can't you pass on this? I'm sure it won't be a problem."

"Baby, you know I can't do that. You were the main one talking about how I should stop thumbing my nose at checks." He kissed her on the forehead. "Besides, what kind of nigga would I be if I left him out to dry? True has gotten himself into some serious shit, and those steroid-pumped niggaz on Don B's payroll ain't gonna keep him alive." Jah made it out to be like he was just honoring a contract, but it went deeper than that. He just couldn't seem to get past the fact that Sha Boogie and his crew had violated. Regardless of what anyone said, they would pay for it.

"Okay, supper nigga, but whose gonna keep you alive?" Yoshi asked seriously.

Jah took his twin 9s from the dresser. "These bitches right here. Look." He placed the guns back. "As soon as Stacks leaves town and some of the heat dies down I'll pass the contract off to somebody else. Stop worrying," he told her, before disappearing into the bathroom.

Yoshi tossed a pillow at the bathroom door and only succeeded in aggravating her injury. She understood Jah wanting to be a man of his word, but she knew firsthand what could happen to people who ran in Don B's circle. They said that everyone was only separated by six degrees, and she knew it to be true from the six deaths associated with the Big Dawg camp. Pain, Lex, Jay, Rhonda, Paul, and Chiba—all of them had dealings with Big Dawg in one way or another, and they had all met with horrible ends. She didn't want that for Jah, but knew that running in Don B's circle made it a very real possibility.

Jah came out of the bathroom and began dressing. For the night he selected a black button-up shirt, with black Akademik jeans and an Atlanta Falcons fitted hat. From the closet he pulled out the lock box containing his .380 and dropped the small gun in his pocket. When he turned around to tell Yoshi he was leaving, he found her glaring at him.

"What, you just gonna be mad all night?" he asked, flopping down on the bed next to her.

"Nah, I ain't mad Jah," she told him.

"Look, I know you're not feeling this whole situation, but everything is gonna be cool. As a matter of fact, why don't I call you when I'm finished at Envy, and you can get all sexy for me, so we can get back to business." He ran his hand up her exposed thigh, but she was unresponsive.

"It's cool, Jah. Handle ya business, I'm cool," she said, and picked up the copy of *Gutter* she had been reading from the nightstand. She thoroughly enjoyed the prequel, *Gangsta,* and had waited five long years to see how the story had played out.

"A'ight, I'm out." He slid from the bed and headed for the door. Before he left the bedroom he stopped short and turned back to Yoshi. "I love you, ma."

"I love you too, baby," she said sincerely. Feeling a little better about the situation, Jah bounced. As soon as he was out the front door, Yoshi picked up the phone and dialed Billy.

WILLAMINA JEFFERSON FOUND HERSELF IN a very awkward predicament. She was stretched out on a king-size bed, ass-naked, with her hands cuffed to the post above her head. Pacing the bed was a man in a leather mask who was also nude, only from the waist up.

He had a well-built physique and skin the color of melted chocolate. In his hand he held a cat-o'-nine-tails, which he impatiently slapped against his palm.

"So, are you going to tell me where the drugs are?" he asked in a heavy Spanish accent.

"I told you, I don't know anything about any drugs," she said frantically.

"Still not talking, eh? Well, I have ways of making you talk." He laughed sinisterly, moving away from the bed. She couldn't see what he was doing, but she knew from the devilish chuckle he was up to no good. When the masked man turned back around he was holding a squeezable water bottle containing a brown substance. "Still not talking?"

"I don't know anything," she insisted.

"Very well then." The masked man moved around the bed to stand over Billy, shaking the bottle of strange liquid. The terrified look in her eyes only succeeded in exciting him more. Uncapping the bottle, he slowly began squirting the liquid on her naked body. Billy squirmed as the liquid coated her breasts and stomach, splashing over to the sheets. The masked man tossed the bottle and climbed on the bed straddling her.

"Please don't," she pleaded, struggling under his weight.

Leaning in to whisper, he said, "Begging won't help you, sweetie—but it turns me on." Starting with her neck, the masked man began making circular motions with his tongue. His firm hands gripped her ass, pulling her body closer. Billy's head lolled back in ecstasy, while her arms tried to fight the masked man off. In the end her defenses gave way, and she allowed herself to be a victim. Just as she was about to get into her groove, her cell blared, ruining the moment. She would've ignored it, but hearing Mary's vocals on "Runaway Love" told her it was important, because only an important person had that ring tone. She tried to reach for the cell, which was on the nightstand, but the cuffs reminded her of her situation.

"Baby, grab my phone," Billy panted.

The masked man stopped his licking session. "What? Are you fucking serious?" Marcus asked, losing his accent and the mask. "I was just about to start my interrogation!"

"I know, baby, and we can get right back to it, but I need to take this call, cause she wouldn't have called me this late if something wasn't wrong," she explained.

"Man," Marcus whined, climbing off Billy. He grabbed her phone off the nightstand and tossed it onto her stomach.

"And how do you propose I answer it?" She jerked the chains a bit. Marcus sucked his teeth and held the phone to her ear. "What, bitch? You fucking my groove up right now." Billy answered. Marcus used his right hand to hold the phone to her ear and his left to play with her erect nipples. Billy gave him a fuck face and tried to focus on the phone call.

"Well, hello to you, too, slut," Yoshi teased.

"Yoshi, you got me at a real bad time, so if it ain't life or death, give me the details tomorrow," Billy said, using her legs to pull at Marcus.

"How you feel about clubbing tonight?" Yoshi asked, now going through her closet to find an outfit.

"Bitch, you called to ask me about the gitty?" Billy asked, rolling over onto her side so Marcus had a better angle at her pussy. Keeping his eyes locked with hers, he slipped between her legs and kissed her inner thigh.

Yoshi listened in for a minute before asking, "Billy, you on the phone fucking?"

"No, but I'd like to be," Billy said, biting the sheet, as Marcus nibbled at her ass cheeks. "Yoshi, I ain't fucking wit you."

Yoshi changed her tactic. "Billy, you know I wouldn't have called if I really ain't wanna go. Stacks Green is performing at Envy tonight."

Billy managed to roll over on her stomach and cocked her delicious ass in the air. Marcus shoved damn near his whole face inside her pussy and went for what he knew. "Yoshi, I could give less than a fuck about Stacks Green, Stacks Blue, or Stacks muthafucking Purple. What I wanna know is, does this have anything to do with Jah and True?"

"Yes and no," Yoshi said.

"Shit, nigga, watch that." Billy swatted at Marcus after he bit her clit a little too hard. "Yoshi, I got too much on my plate right now to be dealing with riddles, but since you my bitch, I'm gonna do you this courtesy." Billy had to pause for a minute, as Marcus's dick slid into her moist pussy. "Meet me at the crib in like an hour and we'll talk about it." Billy tossed the phone onto the floor and gave her man her undivided attention.

Chapter 34

JAH STEPPED OUT OF HIS BUILDING WITH A MA-
jor chip on his shoulder. He was high, tired, and thirsty for
another romp with his boo, but duty called. When he
stepped out of the building he noticed Devil leaning against
the car, smoking a cigarette. His movements were neutral
but his eyes attempted to be threatening. Jah maintained
eye contact with him until he was tucked inside the back of
the Bentley.

"What it is, soldier?" Don B gave Jah a dap as he settled
into the seat. "You handled ya business and all that, fam?"

"I'm good," Jah said, giving True, who was sitting to his
right, a pound.

"That's good to know," Don B continued. "We keeping
it local, so tonight should be easy. Stacks and them is doing
they thing at the spot, and we gonna shake through there
and shine, simple as that."

"Yo, y'all niggaz is on some real *Mission Impossible* shit
right now," True said, licking the ends of the blunt to seal it.
"Who the fuck is gonna try to hit me in a crowded-ass club,
with all the security and shit?"

"They tried to get you at the video shoot, and that was
in Harlem, under police surveillance," Jah reminded him.

"You really think these niggaz wouldn't try to take ya head in a dark club?"

True thought on it for a minute, but had to agree with Jah. The shooters from the video had been brazen and reckless, so they'd surely have no qualms about popping off at a crowded nightclub.

"Yeah, that reminds me," Don B spoke up. "We can't take the hammers up in there, so I hope you can get down with the hands as well as you get down with a pistol?" he asked Jah.

"I'm good," Jah said, immediately planning a new strategy. He had expected their celebrity status to make them exempt from security checks, so his guns played out in every possible scenario; but Jah was by no means a novice at boxing. He had made a rep as a knockout artist before one as a shooter.

"In case you run into a situation." Devil handed Jah a retractable baton. "Hit the button and it extends. That's the best we can do for the venue."

Jah examined the baton, testing the weight and extension time. Though the rod was very slim, it was sturdy, and that's what was important. It didn't have the range of a gun, but in the close quarters of the club he wouldn't need it. He could split a nigga's shit and keep it moving with little hassle. Satisfied, he said, "I can make do with this."

The ride was a short one, with plenty of blunts and booze to go around. From the moment the Bentley pulled up, all eyes were on them. Chicks rushed over, trying to get pictures on their camera phone with the rapper. True posed modestly and signed autographs while Don B put his best Hollywood moves on for the camera. Remo, Devil, and Jah hung back, checking the crowd.

It didn't take long for club security to lift the rope and usher the entourage inside. The manager came down personally to show them to the area where Stacks and his people were already lounging. Getting through the crowd seemed to be a task in itself. Don B got love from the ballas, but the young girls that recognized True went crazy. Girls were coming at him left and right, in the hopes of getting chosen for the night. A few even came at Jah just for being with True. The girls didn't give a damn who was on the scene, as long as they were seen with them.

Tucked in a far corner were Stacks and his crew. They were waving bottles in the air and slapping the asses of two girls who had come over to serve as entertainment. Forming a massive wall around them were the bodyguards from the video shoot. The beefy black dudes were on constant alert, seemingly oblivious to the freak show taking place behind them. Spotting Don B and his men, Soda waved them over.

"What's good, my dude?" Hollywood cut across their paths. Don B glared at him and kept walking, while True slowed, with Jah right beside him.

"What's popping? You look like you just lost ya best friend." True said.

Hollywood sucked his teeth. "Man, I ain't tell you how my van got jacked last night?"

"Say word?"

"Word to mine. Me and this nigga Chris hooked up with these Brooklyn bitches last night at Shooter's on some stunting shit. We knew they was dirtbag bitches from what they had on, but we trying to fuck, so that's even better. So peep, we take the hos out to the joint in Jersey and do the switch up and all that fly shit, but when we wake up the next afternoon these hos was gone with my van!"

"Yo, that's the wildest shit!" True said. "So, how did y'all get home?"

"That's the worst part. They took our fucking bread, so we couldn't even jump on the bus and come across the bridge. My nigga, we had to take a cab back uptown, then dip out on the nigga."

True couldn't hold it anymore and bust out laughing. He hadn't meant to, but the look on Hollywood's face was priceless. He had been doing stupid shit to people for years, and now found himself a victim of his own karma.

"Damn, kid, that's a heavy pill," True said, trying to compose himself. "I hope you catch up with the bitches." He tapped Jah, letting him know he was ready to roll. He'd made it two steps before Hollywood was back in his ear.

"I'm saying, though, why don't you come on over to the bar and let me buy you a drink?" Hollywood asked, hoping to get a chance to shine with the young star. "I got this concept I wanna run by you, anyway."

"Not right now, Hollywood. I gotta go get wit my peoples." True tried to be nice about it, but Hollywood wouldn't let it go.

"Yo, why you acting like we ain't play summer league together, son? You too big for niggaz now?" Hollywood accused, drawing a small crowd. He was a little tipsy and feeling himself.

"Hollywood, you know I ain't on it like that, so kill the bullshit," True said, anger creeping into his voice.

"My man, that bullshit is why you rap niggaz can't go back to the hood when you blow up, cause y'all stunt when you get a lil paper."

True ran his hand across his face, trying to calm himself. "Hollywood, right now that drink got you talking real crazy."

"Nigga, I'm a grown man, I can hold my liquor. Stop trying to play me, word up." Hollywood moved a little closer. He had a look in his eye that said he was weighing his chances, so True forced him into action.

The punch was so quick that the only reason people knew it was thrown was because Hollywood was backpedaling across the dance floor. Young Chris came through the crowd wielding a Corona bottle, only to have Devil take him off his feet with a fierce right. He hit Chris so hard that you could almost see his cheek cave in. Hollywood had finally composed himself enough to come back at True, but found himself at Jah's mercy. He rained lightning-quick blows all over Hollywood's face and head. The fight was finally broken up when security came and dragged Hollywood and Chris to the exit.

ROXY AND SUGAR HAD JUST stepped out of the cab when the doors to the club came flying open. Security was tussling with a short, light-skin kid and his man, trying to get them out. Roxy thought she recognized one of them, but wasn't sure. As the ball of arms and bodies got closer to the club, Roxy's eyes lit up and a broad smile crossed her face.

"What you smiling at?" Sugar asked, trying to move away from the fight.

"Look." Roxy nodded at the short kid who was being handled by the back of his shirt.

Sugar's eyes lit up with recognition. "Oh, shit! That's shorty and them from the motel!" she screamed, before doubling over with laughter.

Hollywood heard the familiar laugh and turned his attention to the two girls. As soon as he saw Roxy and Sugar his anger doubled. He tried to rush the girls, but security had a firm grip on him. In trying to jerk free he had managed to rip his brother's three-hundred-dollar shirt. When he refused to stop struggling, the security guard body slammed him on the concrete. The slam hurt, but not as much as Sugar's laughter as she and Roxy sauntered into the club.

SHA BOOGIE WAS DRESSED IN a pair of crisp blue jeans and fresh white Airs. He had a Makaveli button up shirt on under a black blazer. On the brim of his nose sat a pair of wire frames. He looked nothing like the street cat who had tried to murder the young rapper in Harlem a day prior. With a nervous Charlie on his heels, he made his way inside the club.

"Damn, look at all these bitches," Charlie said, trying to take his mind off Tina's dead body.

"We ain't here for that," Sha reminded him.

"Damn, why don't you lighten up, that lil nigga ain't going nowhere," Charlie told him. Sha Boogie's obsession with True was starting to make him uneasy. He was determined to keep coming until the man was dead or he was, and Charlie's beef with True didn't go deep enough to where he was ready to die. As soon as it was over with, he was gonna cut Sha Boogie loose.

Though it was still kind of early, the inside of the club was packed with people. Sha knew that if the rappers were in attendance they wouldn't be hard to spot. It was as simple as looking for the largest cluster of people. Sure enough, the Don and all his men were gathered in the corner. Security was tight, but it didn't matter to Sha. He hadn't come to kill; he'd only come to observe.

Chapter 35

AFTER RIDING AROUND FOR ALMOST AN HOUR, Billy finally broke down and agreed to put the car in a parking garage. Instead of parking at the one around the corner from the club, Billy decided to drive up a block further, because there was a two-dollar difference in the price. Reese was tight because she had to walk all the way to the club in needle-thin heels.

"I don't know why you didn't just park closer," Reese said, fighting with the cute but uncomfortable shoes.

"Because these cats are cheaper," Billy said, fixing her studded belt. She was dressed in a pair of skin-tight gray jeans with a matching jeans jacket. Her hair was braided up into a Mohawk, showcasing her pretty face.

"Y'all need to come on, by the time we get there the bar is gonna be closed." Yoshi walked ahead of them. She was wearing a pair of painted-on leather pants, with a five-inch boot heel. Her hair hung down around her face with a lazy curl, bringing out her Latin features.

"I don't know why you're in such a rush. You better hope Jah doesn't knock you upside the head for popping up on him," Billy yelled after her.

"He needs to, so I can say that my night was interesting.

I still can't believe I let y'all talk me into this," Reese said. It had taken quite a bit of coaxing to get her to come out with them. Reese hadn't changed her clubbing ways, but she refused to be anywhere where she might see Don B. The only reason she agreed to come was because Yoshi had run a guilt trip on her about not hanging out together anymore.

"You ain't the only one who needs to have a worthwhile night. You know how much drama this private eye bitch caused in my house with this?" Billy thumbed at Yoshi. "Marcus had my ass speaking in tongues, and she ringing the damn phone. That nigga was beyond pissed when I told him I was going out."

"How'd you manage to shake loose?" Reese asked.

Billy smiled devilishly. "I sucked him off until he fell asleep, and then I broke out."

"You nasty little skank!" Yoshi squealed.

"If that ain't the fucking pot!" Billy swung at her playfully.

"Fuck that, I'm happy she's getting it on the regular. I remember we used to think she took penis off the menu," Reese admitted.

"Baby, I've had the best of both worlds, but ain't nothing like planet dick!" Billy gave Yoshi a high five.

"Amen to that," Yoshi agreed. "I appreciate y'all coming out with me, though."

"We knew if we didn't come, your crazy ass would try to go at it alone and get shot again," Billy joked.

"Bitch, that ain't funny. I could've died," Yoshi shot back.

"And be away from Jah? I don't think so, Yoshibelle. If you and that nigga don't make the cutest couple." Billy pinched Yoshi's thigh.

"You and your boo are worse than us, wit ya wine-drinking asses!" Yoshi laughed.

"Don't hate me cause I'm cultured," Billy did a fake model walk. She and Yoshi found it hilarious, but Reese wasn't laughing with them. Yoshi and Billy had been blessed to find love hiding right under their noses, but Reese was still the odd woman out. For all she'd been through, you would think she deserved a little happiness; but outside of Alex she had yet to find it.

. . .

ALMOST A HALF HOUR AFTER the incident had gone down, Stacks Green was still laughing about the fight. "Yo, shorty got it in on ol' boy!" he bellowed.

"You see the lil nigga move? Man, he looked like a lil-ass Tasmanian devil on that mutha!" Cooter added.

"You know Harlem don't breed nothing but official niggaz, Stacks. And if you don't know, you'll see on the court!" Don B boasted.

"You sure is in a rush to loose ya bread, Don. Them young boys you got might be good, but they ain't got nothing on my goon squad," Stacks told him.

"Stacks, I seen ya boys get down in St. Louis, remember? Y'all barely beat them east side boys," Don B reminded him. The boys from East St. Louis had given Stacks's team a hard run, but ended up losing by eight points.

"Yeah, that was a good team, but it ain't the team y'all will be playing. I did a lil rebuilding in the off-season," Stacks said coolly. Don B had anticipated playing the team he had already scouted, but Stacks's revamping of the lineup was something he hadn't expected.

"Its all good. We take all comers," Don B said confidently. In his mind he was wondering if his high school point guard and cast of street stars would be enough for the Texas ballers. He had fifty thousand reasons why they had better be.

Jah half-listened to the men babble, because he was too busy scanning the room for haters. As his eyes roamed the bar he had to do a double take. The man was hunched over the bar with his back to Jah, but he knew the curve of the back. He no longer had braids, but it didn't matter. Jah knew him, and he knew his crimes. Larry Love would be forever burned into Jah's mind as the enemy. So much fury burned through Jah that his hands began to shake, drawing a curious glance from True.

"You good?" True asked him.

"Yeah, I just need to throw some water on my face," Jah said, getting up.

"Damn! You drunk that quick?" Cooter asked, pouring himself another shot of Patrón. Jah just ignored him and kept walking.

SHA BOOGIE SAT ALONE AT the bar, sipping a glass of vodka and cranberry juice. Charlie was mingling in the crowd, supposedly checking for weak spots in their security. Sha knew that getting shot had taken some of the fight out of Charlie Rock, and it was cool. For what Sha needed to do, it was best that he did it alone. Using the mirror behind the bar, Sha Boogie continued to watch True.

There was some sort of running joke going on among the men, because Stacks kept laughing. Sha peeped the bottles of expensive champagne and the ladies flocking to them, which only increased his hate and resentment towards True. The young gunner who had killed Spider sat off to the side watching everything at once. Sha Boogie had to give it to him, though the towers were efficient bodyguards, the young boy was meticulous with work. Sha respected, if not admired, his style, and almost felt bad about having to kill him.

The shooter looked in Sha's direction and for a moment he thought he was spotted. Sha cursed and slouched down a bit more when he saw the shooter whisper something to True and start toward the bar. Sha Boogie wasn't armed, but with Big Dawg's celebrity status he figured the shooter might be. A confrontation was something he really didn't want. Still, if he came for it he would get it, Sha reasoned, sliding an abandoned Corona bottle closer to him.

JAH MOVED ACROSS THE ROOM with such grace that he hardly touched the mingling partygoers. His eyes were so fixed on Larry Love that everything and everyone in the room was drowned out. Larry Love had been like family at one point, but his greed had made him an outcast. Paul trusted Larry like a brother, only to be rewarded with betrayal and death. Marlene was a lawyer, and therefore protected from Jah's wrath to an extent, but Larry was a product of the streets and therefore subject to their laws.

There were many nights that Jah laid awake thinking of his brother. Paul had made some mistakes in his life, but he wasn't like the rest of them. He actually wanted to do right and take care of his responsibilities; but, like so many others, he became a victim of hood shit. Rhonda had subjected him to three years of hell over nothing, and the two people he trusted most were fucking behind his back. Paul's heart cracked under the pressure, but Jah's only got harder. On Jah's list of unclaimed souls that had to be pushed from the world, Larry's name was still number one.

Larry was perched on the bar stool, kicking it with a young lady and oblivious to death hovering just an arm's length away. Jah knew it was him from the moment he spotted him, but he had to get up on him to feel it . . . to make it real. He loomed just behind the man, not approaching the bar, but hovering close by. Jah was unarmed, and though he could surely kill the man with just the baton, there would be no escape. Larry was a piece of shit, but hardly worth going to prison for. Jah eased away from Larry, in the direction of the bathrooms, and contemplated how he would kill him.

Jah bumped through the crowd going over different torture methods he and Spooky had used over the years, trying to decide which one was best suited for Larry Love. A commotion that was brewing to his right caused him to turn. When he saw who was in the center of it his eyes narrowed to slits. Clutching the baton at his side he made his way in the direction of the crowd.

SHA BOOGIE BREATHED A SIGH of relief when the shooter walked right past him. He had initially thought he'd been spotted and that the shooter was coming over to get it popping, but he had someone else in his sights. He watched as the young man moved in on a heavyset cat at the end of the bar. He expected there to be some kind of confrontation, but the shooter just stared at the man for a minute and left. It was obvious from the look on the shooter's face that he had some kind of issue with the man, but Sha wasn't sure exactly what.

The shooter came within three feet of Sha but didn't even acknowledge him. He moved through the crowd with an angry look on his face, mumbling to himself. Halfway across the room he stopped short and changed direction. Sha watched as he walked up on a man and three girls who had just come into the spot.

"THIS SHIT IS A SWEATBOX," Reese said, wiping her forehead with a folded napkin.

"What do you expect when you stuff three hundred people in a room big enough to fit one hundred? You know niggaz draw heat," Billy joked. A dude wearing a fake diamond in his ear rolled up on Billy, licking his lips. He started to say something to her, but the look on her face choked back any game he had thought about spitting.

"What'd you do to that boy?" Reese asked her.

"Its not about what I did *to* him, its about what I'd never do *with* him." Billy looked around the room to see who was in the party. Of course, Don B and his team were over in the corner making the most noise, but it was who she saw sitting at the bar that made her heart skip. "Oh, shit!"

"What's wrong?" Reese asked, trying to see what Billy was looking at.

"Over at the end of the bar," Billy motioned.

Reese didn't see him at first, but her second sweep of the bar spotted him. "I don't fucking believe it."

"What?" Yoshi came over. When her eyes saw what theirs did, her mouth dropped open. "Larry? That nigga has got nerve showing his face back in town. He better hope Jah doesn't see him."

"I think he just did," Billy nodded at Jah, who was making his way in Larry's direction.

"He's gonna kill him!" Yoshi started trying to make her way through the thick crowd. She saw Jah moving silently towards Larry Love with murder flashing in his eyes. She knew if she didn't get to him in time, Jah was going to do something very impulsive and get himself into trouble. Between the swell of people and the different hands trying to grope or get her attention, she was getting nowhere fast. A heavy dude, clearly tipsy, bumped into her injured arm, sending fire shooting up through her body. The pain in her arm was intense, but nothing compared to what Larry Love was about to feel.

She had almost reached her destination, when a firm pair of hands grabbed her from behind. Yoshi turned around in flip mode and found herself looking at a dude from the block she knew, named Red. Red had been one of Yoshi's sponsors when she was running the streets and they had had some memorable times together.

"China, what's good?" he called her by her stage name.

"Not much, Red, I'm kind of in a rush," she said, trying to keep it moving, but he pulled her back.

"Hold on, I ain't seen you in months and you ain't got time for a nigga?"

"Its not that, Red, I'm just trying to catch up with someone," she told him.

"Oh, you got a new flavor of the month, huh?" he asked, sounding offended.

"I don't get down like that no more, Red, I'm in here with my man."

"Your man?" he looked at her quizzically. "Ain't no one nigga never been enough for you, ma. Come on over to the bar and let me buy you a quick drink," he insisted.

"Red—"

"My dude, I don't know if you understand English, or you're just pushy as hell, but my girl just told you she's in here with her man," Billy cut in.

"Do I know you?" Red asked Billy, clearly not feeling her cock blocking.

"No, but you might know me," a male voice called over the music. Everyone's breath caught in their chests when they saw Jah standing behind Red and Yoshi.

"Jah, what's good?" Red extended his hand in greeting. Jah just looked at it. Red was a little older than Jah, they knew some of the same people on the streets. Jah had a reputation as being a goon that you didn't want to cross.

"Hey, baby." Yoshi kissed Jah, but he was unresponsive, keeping his eyes on Red.

"What're you doing here?" Jah asked coldly.

"I came down to surprise you. I know we didn't get to finish our night properly, so I thought I'd come down and grab a drink with you right quick." She slipped her arm around his waist to try and drain off some of the tension.

"I'll just bet," Jah said, talking to Yoshi but staring at Red. The man fidgeted nervously under Jah's gaze.

"Oh, this is ya man?" Red asked, finally catching on. "No disrespect, my dude, but I used to know China, so I was trying to buy her a drink for old time's sake."

Hearing the name China, he knew exactly how Red knew Yoshi and wasn't pleased with it. "Well, for as much as I appreciate you trying to buy my girl a drink, it ain't necessary, son."

"My fault." Red raised his hands. "See you around, China." He winked before moving back across the dance floor to where his team was standing around.

"You shouldn't be here," Jah said, turning to Yoshi.

"Damn, don't sound so thrilled to see me," she said, sounding offended.

Jah pulled her close and kissed her on the forehead. "You know I'm always happy to see you, but I'm working."

"I know, sweetie and I ain't trying to be in your hair, that's why I brought them with me." She motioned towards Billy and Reese. Until she pointed them out he hadn't even noticed they were there.

"What's good, y'all?" Jah greeted them. He kept his face pleasant, but his eyes kept flashing over to Larry Love.

"Baby, not here." Yoshi touched his hand. From the pleading look in her eyes he knew she had spotted Larry, too.

"Maybe not here, but somewhere," he assured here. Yoshi wanted to argue further, but she knew that that was a confrontation that she couldn't deny Jah.

"Anyway, we're gonna shake out and have some drinks, but when you get a minute, come throw one back with us, okay?" She placed a hand on his chest.

"I'll do that, ma." He raised her hand to his lips and kissed it. "Let me get back over here to True and them niggaz, but I'll have my eye on you, too." He pinched her.

"I sure hope so," Yoshi told him, as she went to join her girls. Knowing Jah was watching, she threw it as hard as she could, giving him something to think about for later on.

Jah stood there wearing a goofy grin until she was out of site— and then made tracks for the bathroom. Once inside, he locked himself in a stall and hopped on his cell phone. "Yo, Tech, wake ya ass up. I need you to do something for me."

"SAY, MAN, I KNOW YOU ain't trying to tap that? Shorty is locked up tighter than Fort Knox," Cooter joked, as Jah walked back over.

"Show some respect to my man's girl," True said.

Cooter looked from Jah to True disbelievingly. "You're shitting me? Hot damn, young boy, there may be some hope for you after all!" Cooter slapped Jah on his back and laughed hysterically. Jah didn't find the joke so amusing.

"Guess that's why she ain't wanna give you no rhythm?" Soda teased Stacks. He was borderline drunk and his humor was very ill-timed.

"Soda, why don't you shut ya stupid ass up," Stacks ordered, hoping that Jah didn't take offense. He knew that Yoshi was Jah's girl, but that hadn't stopped him from pressing her. He tried everything from gifts to money, but she still wasn't moved. Whatever hold Jah had over Yoshi, it was a secure one.

"So, y'all had any luck tracking them boys down that tried to blast on the young'n?" Stacks asked, trying to change the subject.

"Yeah, we got some names, but still no location," Don B admitted.

"Man, they lucky this ain't Houston. Let a muthafucka try to kill Soda, and it'd have been at least a hundred niggaz trying to bring me they heads. You better tighten ya ship, Don," Stacks taunted him.

"New York is a big city, Stacks," Don B said in a neutral tone.

"Houston might not be as big a city as New York, but trust and believe that whole muthafucka belongs to me," Stacks said in a matter-of-fact tone. He and Don B locked eyes. Though there was no threat coming from either man, both crews tensed. The tension lingered for what seemed like forever, but was broken up by a loud thumping sound.

"Ain't this about a bitch!" Cooter said, looking down at Soda, who had fallen clean off his chair.

"Put me in coach, I can still play," Soda slurred. He was laying flat on his back, looking like he was trying to make snow angels.

"That muthafucka is done," Don B patted Stacks on the back.

"Sho is," he agreed.

Chapter **36**

IT WAS ALMOST SATURDAY MORNING WHEN DENA got back to Jefferson Avenue. She had awakened from the comalike sleep Ice had put her into and found that her muscles were wracked with cramps. She thought that she was going to keel over and die, but of course Ice was there for her. He explained to her that it was a side effect of the Love Boat and that, as she got used to it, the cramps would fade—which was a lie, but she bought into it because someone who loved her the way Ice proclaimed to love her so much would never put her in harm's way. With this in mind, she snorted some more Love Boat with Black Ice.

When she stepped out of the truck her legs felt like spaghetti. Black Ice had made love to her in as many ways as possible and she took it like a champ, he even taught her to properly deep-throat a man. Around the forth or fifth round, they had ran through the magnums as well as the condoms they were able to scrounge up from the front desk, so they didn't even bother with one. She wasn't worried about catching anything, because Ice looked to be the picture of perfect health.

Black Ice had sexed her all afternoon, through the evening, and going into the next morning, and she loved every nasty-ass minute of it. It was safe to say that he had awakened the woman trapped inside the little girl.

"I wanna thank you for a wonderful time." Dena came around to the driver's side. "I've never had this much fun in my life!"

"Come on, cutie, shit like this should go on in ya life regularly." He touched her cheek. "Fucking with the Ice Man has its privileges."

"I'm trying to see about that," she told him.

"That's what I'm trying to tell you, baby. Dena, I'm feeling ya style in a major way, and I can see somebody like you on my arm when I step out. But I only deal with the most qualified ladies. Ladies that I know will go hard for their man, feel me?"

"Oh, I feel you!" she assured him. "Ice, I'm tired of dealing with loser-ass niggaz. For once I wanna be on the winning team."

"Ask and you shall receive, sweet princess." He winked at her. "Check it, though." He placed a small piece of tinfoil in her hand. "Take this in case them nasty cramps come back. You should be good, but I'd hate to think of my new lady being uncomfortable."

"Always thinking of me, huh?" She stuffed the foil in her purse.

"Even when I'm trying not to. Dena, I'm gonna open you up to a whole new world. Fucking with the Ice Man, there's going to be nothing but the best for you," he proclaimed. "Go on and get some rest and I'll get with you this afternoon." Ice put the truck in gear and peeled off. Dena almost got her foot ran over when she leaned in to kiss him good night. After the things he had done to her body, she could let him slide on the kiss.

Dena turned around to walk into her building and herd someone shouting her name. Her body stiffened, hoping it was a bad dream. She knew that voice could only belong to one person, and when she turned around it was confirmed. Her mother, standing there with a scarf on a jacket over her pajamas, looking mad as hell.

"Ma, what you doing out here on the stoop?" Dena asked.

"What am I doing on the stoop? The better question is what the hell you are doing climbing out of some nigga's car in the wee hours like a common whore," her mother snapped.

"Ain't nobody hoing, ma. That was Sharon's uncle dropping me off. I just came from her house," Dena said.

Her mother squinted her eyes. "If you'll lie, you'll steal. Sharon called here twice looking for you. She said she couldn't reach you on the cell and neither could I. What's good with that?"

Dena had completely forgotten she had cut her cell phone off when she and Ice were having sex. "Look, if you must know, I was out on a date," Dena huffed.

"Date? With who? I know Lance ain't got no truck. And where did all that stuff come from?" She motioned towards the shopping bags Dena was carrying.

"It wasn't Lance," Dena said, walking toward the building. Dena's mother grabbed her arm with a force she didn't know her mother possessed, and spun her around.

"Little heifer, I ain't Nadine or Shannon, so don't try me wit that walking away shit, you hear me?" her mother snarled.

"Yes, Mommy," Dena said sheepishly.

"I don't know what the hell has gotten into you lately, Dena. You're running around with these gangsta-ass niggaz and fast-ass girls like Sharon and Monique. What happen to the nice schoolgirls you used to run around with, like Rachel?"

"Rachel got pregnant and moved to Atlanta," Dena informed her.

"That's beside the point. I don't like the looks of some of these characters you run around with, and that's the skinny of it," she said, as if she was going to have the last word. But of course, Dena couldn't let it rest.

"There's a lot of stuff I don't like, but you don't hear me complaining about it," Dena mumbled, making her way into the building.

"What did you just say?" Her mother stopped short.

"Nothing." Dena kept walking.

"Nah-uh, you're Buster Badass, so say what you gotta say."

Dena faced her mother and took a deep breath. "Alright then. Look, Ma, you come down on me about any- and everything under the sun, but you let Nadine and Shannon run wild. How fair do you think that is to me?"

"First of all, I was a much younger mother when I had Nadine, and because I gave her freedom, look how she turned out. I love my daughter, but I wish her and her bad-ass kids would move the hell out of my house. And Shannon, he was outta my hands since day one. The boy has got way too much of his father in him. You, on the other hand, I had a plan for. Why do you think I bust my ass working two jobs to make sure you didn't want for nothing?"

"Some plan! Locking me down in the house?" Dena said sarcastically.

"You need to be glad I locked you ass down; or maybe you wanna be like them lil derelict bitches on the stoop?"

"At least they're not prisoners in their own homes," Dena shot back.

"Dena, you can pop that fly shit until the cows come home, but I'm the boss around this muthafucka. When you go off to college and are out on your own, then you can talk some shit. Until then you dance to my music."

"Well, maybe I need to speed things up a bit," Dena stormed up the stairs. On the way up she bumped into Shannon. He tried to say something to her, but she brushed past him and kept going into the apartment.

"And where the hell are you going?" his mother barked.

"Dag, I'm just going to the store. What's your problem?" Shannon asked. They were all good before she bumped into Dena.

"My problem is the crazy-ass hours of the night you choose to run the streets. Ain't nothing but killers and crackheads running round this time of night. Which category do you fall into?"

"I sure as hell ain't no crackhead," he chuckled.

His mother pointed her finger in his face. "Don't play with me Shannon. And why is it that every time I turn around your name is associated with some street shit."

"Ma, what are you talking about?" Shannon asked, genuinely not knowing what his mother was talking about. He had been involved in so much shit that she could've meant anything.

"Little Bunchy from over Tompkins way said she heard you was out here shooting the other night," his mother accused.

"Bunchy is lying. I wasn't even on the block last night. Ma, how you gonna listen to a crackhead?"

"Crackhead or not, that's the word on the streets. I'm telling you now, the police better not come round my damn house looking for you again. The last time they broke my new china cabinet looking for some damn drugs."

"Nah, the police ain't got no reason to come around here looking for me," he said. Making a mental note to himself to slap the shit out of Bunchy when he saw her.

"They damn well better not. And since you're supposedly going to the store, bring me back a cold Pepsi. I forgot to get it when I went out."

Shannon wasn't stupid, he knew this was her way of getting him to come right back. She was going through something, so he wasn't gonna give her a hard time about it. The streets would be there the following night. "Okay, Mommy," he said, continuing down the stairs.

DENA WENT DIRECTLY INTO HER room and slammed the door. Her mother had her so mad that she wanted to cry, fight, and a whole list of other things, but all she could do was stew on it. She was almost eighteen years old and her mother was still treating her like the little girl who went to the store for dollars. If a man as worldly as Black Ice could recognize her as a grown woman, why couldn't her own mother? Dena felt like she was going to have a nervous breakdown, and she needed to get out of the house.

She took out her cell and punched in Ice's number. When he picked up she asked, "Are you still in the area?"

SHANNON TOOK HIS TIME COMING back from the store. He had a Dutch Master tucked behind his ear and a Red Stripe in a bag. He planned to smoke a blunt and drink a beer before he went upstairs, but when he saw the familiar white Escalade bend the corner he suspected that his plan would be altered.

Shannon bent the corner in time to see Dena coming down the steps of the building, carrying some stuff in shopping bags. She gave a careful glance around before scurrying to the truck. He called her name, and he knew she heard him, because she looked in his direction, but she continued to the truck. Shannon dropped his beer and broke into a run, but by the time he made it to his building the truck was already at the corner of Jefferson and Marcus Garvey.

WHEN LARRY LOVE LEFT ENVY he wasn't feeling any pain. On his arm he had a tall brown-skinned honey by the name of Roxy. She had been with another girl, who Larry tried to convince to come along, but she wasn't into the group sex thing, so they parted ways, leaving Larry with the shapelier of the two. Shorty had a mean body, but wasn't the sharpest knife in the drawer. All she did was talk, but Larry had something she could stick in her mouth to shut her up.

Larry and a drunken Roxy staggered to the curb and tried to hail a cab. It took them a good minute, but they finally managed to catch a driver who was just coming out and needed to make that bread. Larry told the driver where to take them and settled back to enjoy the kisses Roxy was planting on his neck.

TECH WAITED FOR THE YELLOW cab to pull out into traffic before he motioned to his driver to follow. The Senegalese Harlem cab driver had gotten a bad vibe from the young man when he picked him up, but he paid for the three hours hold time in advance, so he took the fare. He didn't know what the young man had planned for the drunk couple, but he knew from the look in his eyes it was nothing nice.

Chapter **37**

SHANNON SAT ON THE STOOP OF HIS BUILDING sipping a forty and smoking a blunt. Though it was barely nine in the morning, he had a lot of shit on his mind. Dena had taken off after having words with their mother and no one had seen or heard from her since. He called her cell at least fifty times, but she wasn't picking up or returning his calls. None of her friends had heard from her either, and everyone was beginning to worry.

His mother was beyond stressed over her missing baby girl. Shannon tried to assure her that Dena was just acting out, but it didn't do much in the way of easing her mind. All his wolves were on the streets searching for the mysterious white Escalade, but so far nothing had come of it. One thing was for sure, when Shannon finally tracked down the well-dressed owner of the truck, fists and lead were going to fly.

"Hey, Shannon." Mo walked up. She was wearing a pair of skin-tight jeans and a tank top.

"Sup, Mo? You hear anything yet?" he asked.

"Not yet. I tried calling her when you told me she broke out, but she ain't hit me back."

"Yo, who was that nigga pushing the truck y'all was in last night? Cause that's who she left with."

Mo shrugged her meaty shoulder. "Other than the fact that his name is Ice and he's some kind of pimp or some shit, we don't know much about him. We just met the cat at the video shoot."

"Of all the niggaz to hook up with, my crazy-ass sister chose a pimp!" Shannon spat on the ground. "Mo, I'm gonna body that nigga when I catch him."

"Shannon, calm down. Dena's a smart girl, so I know she's never jump out the window and do something stupid." Mo tried to calm him.

"Well, what do you call that dumb shit she did last night? My mother is on the verge of a nervous breakdown fucking with her."

A black Honda Accord pulled to a stop next to the fire hydrant in front of the building. The music was blasting so loud that it was a wonder that the slim Black kid behind the wheel could hear himself think. As if on cue, Nadine came strutting out of the building. She was wearing a short skirt and one of Shannon's Nautica rugbys.

"Still no word from Princess Dena?" she asked, coming down the steps of the building.

"Nah," Shannon said flatly. He really wasn't in the mood for Nadine or her bullshit.

"Well, call me when and if the little hussy shows up," Nadine said, walking towards the car.

"Nadine, where are you going and where are your kids?" he asked.

"They upstairs with Mommy," she said.

"Nadine, you know she's stressing over Dena, so why would you leave your bad-ass kids with her adding on to it?"

"First of all, my kids ain't bad, they're mischievous. Second of all, I'm just running over to Marcy to get some smoke. I won't be gone more than twenty minutes."

Shannon looked at her as if she couldn't be serious. "Nadine, you are so full of shit."

"What?" she asked, as if she didn't know what he was talking about.

"What is, you need to show some fucking consideration. We're going through a family crisis and you can't even sit still for a minute until it gets worked out," he accused.

Nadine sucked her teeth. "Look, ain't none of my kids named

Dena, and my daddy's name damn sure wasn't Shannon. Dena is a big girl. If she needs us she'll call."

"Nadine, whether Dena needs or not has yet to be determined, but what about Mommy?"

"What about her?"

"Did it ever occur to you that she might need us?" he asked.

"Man, I ain't beat for this shit. I'm trying to go get some smoke." She started walking away, but Shannon's next words stopped her in her tracks.

"Youz about a selfish bitch."

"What did you call me?" She turned around.

"I called you a selfish bitch. Your seventeen-year-old sister absconded with a fucking pimp and you don't care. Your mother is damn near a basket case over it and you don't care. All you care about is running the streets and getting your stank-ass pussy worked on. That's how you ended up with all them kids in the first fucking place."

"Nigga, you better watch your mouth and show some respect!" she snapped in his face.

Shannon looked at her quizzically. "Respect? Bitch, you can't be serious. How the fuck can I respect somebody that ain't about shit but getting high and getting tossed up?" Nadine tried to slap him in the face, but he caught her by the wrist in midswing. The ferocious look in his eyes told her that she had gone too far. "You must think I'm one of these bitch-ass niggaz you be out here tricking with."

The kid in the Honda stepped out. "Yo, everything cool?"

Shannon turned his murderous gaze to the kid. "My dude, if you know like I know, you better get yo ass back in ya whip and mind ya fucking business."

"Shannon, you better get your damn hands off me, before it's be some shit!" she warned.

"Nadine, miss me with ya empty-ass threats, because you already know what time it is with me. You run around the damn house, plopping kids out left and right, and got the nerve to look down your nose at everybody else, and frankly, I'm sick of it." He applied more pressure, causing her to wince.

"Shannon, please let her go," Mo pleaded. She had seen him angry before, but never like this and never towards a member of his own family. Mo and Shannon were cool, but if he started beating on Nadine out there, she seriously doubted if there would be anything to stop him. As luck would have it, his rage found a new target.

"Man, you better take your hands off her." The kid grabbed Shannon by the arm.

Shannon blinked as if he was just realizing what he was doing. There was a look of sorrow in his eyes—but that was quickly replaced by madness, as his eyes landed on the stranger. All of the rage that Shannon had been keeping bottled up inside him rushed to the surface and spilled over. With a guttural roar he finally snapped.

The kid's eyes got as wide as saucers, hearing such a sound coming from a man instead of an animal. Before he could even mount a defense, Shannon slammed a fist into his mouth with the force of a jackhammer. The kid tried to sag, but a follow-up punch to the gut kept him on his feet. Shannon rained rights and lefts to every exposed part of the kid's body. He even took a page out of Mike Tyson's book and bit a chunk of the kid's ear off. When the kid finally hit the ground, Shannon began viciously stomping him in the face. Had it not been for his mother shouting his name, he'd have surely killed the young man.

"Shannon, what in God's name is you doing?" she asked, with a horrified look on her face.

It took a minute for the beast to subside and Shannon's sanity to come back to him. On the ground beneath him, the kid lay motionless and his face had swelled to the size of a pumpkin. Shannon's shirt was ruined and his mouth and knuckles were smeared with blood.

"Shannon, have you lost your damn mind? You could've killed that boy!" his mother shouted. Shannon heard her, but was too mad to respond.

"Get away from him, you bastard!" Nadine screamed, kneeling beside the unconscious young man. If Shannon understood her, he showed no signs of it.

"Come take a walk with me," Mo said, taking him by the arm. His face still wore a confused expression, but he allowed her to steer him up the block.

"You ain't shit, Shannon. I fucking hate you!" Nadine shouted at his back. "You hear me, you murdering piece of shit. I hate you!"

"DAMN, YOU SEE THE WAY he put the beats on that muthafucka?" Blick asked from the passenger seat of Ronny's Dodge Magnum. "So, what you think, dawg?"

Ronny hesitated for a minute, watching the girl try to revive the young man. He looked at the .380 on his lap and said, "We're gonna need a bigger gun."

Chapter **38**

THE AFTERNOON SUN SHONE THROUGH THE
large picture window and tickled Dena's sleeping face, stir-
ring her from the most wonderful dream. For a minute she
almost thought that she was back in her tenement apartment on Jefferson Avenue, but feeling the soft, feather-top
mattress beneath her, she knew she couldn't be. Dena rolled
over, still wrapped in the satin comforter, and searched for
Ice, but she was alone. In the space he had vacated there was
a long-stemmed white rose. Inhaling the sweet fragrance,
she looked forward to the first day of her new life.

When Dena tried to sit up, her stomach was rocked
with cramps and she felt a slight twinge of what felt like the
flu. The cramps weren't as bad as the ones she'd had in
Philly, but they hurt like hell. Fighting off the nausea, she
reached for her purse to retrieve the package Black Ice had
given her. Her hands shook so badly that she almost spilled
the heroin while trying to unwrap it.

For a good minute she just stared at it. In the back of her
mind she could hear her mother preaching to her about the
ills of drug use and its ability to ruin lives, but Black Ice's
life seemed more together than most. A part of her wanted
to flush the drugs, but the cramps were kicking her ass. She

promised herself that once she got in good with Ice she would stray from the heroin and try to get him to do the same. Once the heroin worked its way into her system she felt a little better and decided to explore her new surroundings.

Black Ice's bedroom was very impressive, with authentic cherry wood furniture and a bed big enough to sleep four people comfortably. The fur carpet felt good beneath her bare feet as she plodded to the bathroom, which she found to be just as marvelous as the bedroom. The bathroom was cream, trimmed with gold plating. The sink, bathtub—even the towels and cloths were of gold-dyed cotton. On the edge of the sink she found a folded towel and a brand-new toothbrush, which she helped herself to.

After taking a quick shower and brushing her teeth, Dena decided to check her cell messages. She had turned it off the night before so that she and Ice wouldn't be disturbed. The last thing she needed was her mother or Shannon blowing her jack up and ruining her groove. Sure enough, her voice mailbox was full. There was a call from Mo, who she had forgotten all about, but the rest were from Shannon and her mother. They had the nerve to sound concerned. If they were really concerned about her they'd have treated her more like a woman than an incompetent little girl, she reasoned. She would let them stew on it for a minute before she called back, but as soon as she got a chance she was going to call Mo and tell her of her good fortune.

The distinct smell of bacon frying reminded Dena she hadn't eaten since Ms. Tootsie's. Slipping on a blue satin robe that she found hanging in the bathroom, Dena headed out to investigate. As she descended the stairs towards the smell she could hear feminine voices coming from the kitchen. Dena came around the corner to find Wendy and Lisa chatting away about something. She was taken aback a bit, because she knew that they worked for, or with, Ice depending on who you asked, but it never occurred to her that they might live there, too. When they noticed her standing there the conversation came to an end.

"Well, good morning," Lisa said pleasantly. She was wearing a white terry cloth robe that was partially open, showing off her breasts. Dena had trouble looking at her and not thinking about the show she and Cinnamon had put on at the club.

"Hi," Dena said sheepishly. Without even thinking about it, she clutched the neckline of her robe to make sure none of her body was exposed.

Lisa, picking up on Dena's discomfort, decided to have a little fun. "Don't just stand there looking shy, come on and have a seat." She patted her lap.

"Lisa, leave that girl alone," Wendy said, flipping a pancake. "Come on in and take a seat at the counter." Wendy nodded to the empty stool on the other side of Lisa. "Dena, right?"

"Yeah," Dena said, ignoring the hungry look Lisa was giving her.

"Pay Lisa's ass no mind, she's just giving you a hard time," Wendy assured her. "Are you hungry?"

"Starved," Dena admitted.

"Good." Wendy slid the now-browned pancake onto the plate with some bacon and two fried eggs. "I hope you ain't on a no-pork kick, cause we eat a lot of it around here."

"The pig ain't never did nothing to me." Dena admired the restaurant-worthy spread in front of her.

"Not yet." Lisa snatched a piece of bacon from Dena's plate. "But stick around for a while." This got her an angry look from Wendy.

"Ice should be back in a few hours, but he says that we should help you get situated while he's gone," Wendy said, trying to change the subject.

"Where is he?" Dena asked, dipping her pancake into some of the syrup that had run off.

Wendy hesitated as if she was thinking about how to answer. "He had to take care of some business."

"You know Ice makes sure the business is straight," Lisa said. From her tone of voice, Dena couldn't tell if she was being sincere of sarcastic.

"So, do all of you guys live here . . . ? I mean, together?" Dena asked curiously. This got a slight chuckle out of Wendy.

"Not all of us, only a few. Me and Lisa stay here and there's one more girl who you'll meet later."

"You mean Cinnamon?" Dena asked. This seemed to strike a sore spot with Lisa, who got up and went to smoke a cigarette by the window. For a minute Dena thought she had done something to offend her.

"No, she's not with us anymore," Wendy said. Dena looked like she wanted to question it further, so Wendy tried to put her mind at ease. "It's a long story that you don't need to concern yourself with. Now, hurry and finish your breakfast. We've got a long day ahead of us, ma."

"Where're we going?"

"First to the Dominicans to see what we can do about that hair." Wendy brushed a loose strand from Dena's face.

"What's wrong with my hair?" Dena asked.

"Nothing. It just needs a little life, that's all. From there, we're getting manicures and pedicures. Consider it a girl's day out."

"I like the sound of that." Dena smiled at the idea of being pampered for the day. "But what's the occasion?"

"Ice is throwing a party tonight and he wants you to look extra special on his arm," Wendy said. Dena was looking at her suspiciously.

Lisa flopped down on the stool beside her. "Don't look so grim, girl. It's your coming-out party."

"Coming-out?"

BLACK ICE LEANED AGAINST THE white Escalade, trying to keep from fidgeting too much. He had just flicked one cigarette away and was about to light another one. He always got like that when he lost money. In the past twenty-four hours he had parted company with thirty thousand dollars. Twenty-five to Don B, and five to the judicial system to post bond for one of his latest cops. The girl hadn't been with him more than a month and she was already costing more than she was bringing in, definitely a sign that she wouldn't be a part of the team long. After what seemed like a lifetime, Shorty finally came bouncing down the courthouse steps with Lexi in tow.

Lexi was twenty-one years old with the face of a schoolgirl and the body of an African queen. She had come to New York from Chicago in search of fame and fortune, but instead found Black Ice. At five-five, with a mean walk and a killer smile, Ice had plans to make her his next break-out star; but, as with a lot of the young girls he had come in contact with lately, she couldn't let go of her old life.

Lexi was a notorious drunk, and more often than not her heavy drinking got her into the trouble, which is what landed her in jail to begin with. She and another whore, who's name Ice couldn't recall, had gotten into an altercation over a trick in a bar. Ice always preached tact to his ladies, but Lexi was young and bull-headed. The girl slapped her, so Lexi cracked her over her head with a beer bottle, requiring the girl to get a dozen stitches in her head. The standing charge was felony assault, but Ice was trying to get it down to a misdemeanor, which would require more money. In a short time, Lexi had dug herself a heavy debt, which Ice fully intended to collect on.

"Man, you think y'all took long enough?" Ice asked, when the two of them reached the car.

"Dawg, you know how the system is," Shorty said.

"No the hell I don't, cause I ain't never spent a day behind the wall."

"Lucky son of a bitch." Shorty laughed.

"Hi, Daddy," Lexi said, trying to sound like she wasn't on his shit list. Her hair was all over the place and she smelled like the bullpens.

"Bitch, don't you 'hi, Daddy' me. What did I tell you about fucking up my groove?" Ice snapped.

"Ice, it wasn't my fault. That bitch threw the first punch," Lexi tried to explain.

"Lexi, she threw a punch and you clubbed the bitch over the head with a bottle. You're lucky you didn't kill her!"

"I'm sorry," she whispered.

"You sure are. One of the sorriest, drunkest bitches I've ever had the misfortune of coming across. I teach you girls to be ladies and you wanna carry ya self like common, fucking trash? Get yo simple-minded ass in the car before I kill you!" He grabbed her by the back of the neck and shoved her into the back of the truck. Lexi barely had a chance to get her legs into the car before Ice slammed the door and hopped in on the passenger side, with Shorty behind the wheel.

"So, what's up with the lil bitch you've been kicking around with?" Shorty asked Ice, once they were out in traffic.

"Who, Dena? She's at the crib right now getting to know her new family. I got Wendy and Lisa getting her all pretty for tonight so I can introduce the bitch to the world properly." Black Ice smiled.

"You picked up another girl?" Lexi asked from the backseat.

"Lexi, you ain't one of my favorite muthafuckas right now, so my advice to you is clam the hell up," Ice told her sternly.

"You know you cost me five hundred bucks," Shorty told him.

"For what?" Ice asked.

"Because I bet Wendy that you couldn't pull her."

Black Ice just shook his head. "Shorty, me and you been hanging around for damn near as long as I've been alive, and you keep forgetting the cardinal rule."

"And what would that be?"

"Always bet on Black, my nigga."

Chapter **39**

IN THE LAST SEVERAL YEARS THERE'S BEEN A growing number of magazines claiming to cater to the inner city and the people that inhabited it, but one stood out above the rest. *Dream* magazine was founded in 2003 by a former drug dealer named Tito, as a means of not only cleaning up some of the wealth he had amassed over the years, but of giving back to the communities he had helped destroy. Not only did it give a voice to the streets, but it provided jobs for men and women who were fresh out of jail, to help them stay off the streets. Within a year of printing its first issue, *Dream* landed major distribution and was now available in every U.S. city, as well as several overseas. A year earlier, its founder Tito was murdered over an old beef, but the magazine continued to flourish, carrying on his legacy.

Unique Lane had been an intern when the magazine first started, but through hard work and a good nose for a story, she managed to work her way up from contributing writer to eventually becoming editor-in-chief. Along with Tito's daughter, Maria, she ran the magazine, but that day found her revising her old role as reporter for a very special story. She was getting a one-on-one interview with Harlem's latest rising star, True.

"What's going on, Don?" Unique greeted him warmly as she entered the lounge area of the Big Dawg studio. She was wearing a black blouse and a pair of gray slacks that hugged her shapely bottom just the right way.

"Unique, what's good?" He hugged her. "Damn, I ain't seen you in a minute. Where you been hiding girl?" Don B and Unique had a history dating back to the beginning of his career. Back then he was an up-and-coming rapper, while she was a reporter on her grind. The chemistry between them was apparent, but she wasn't the type to mix business with pleasure. Though the romance went nowhere, they kept in contact over the years and traded an occasional favor.

"Running *Dream* keeps me pretty busy," she told him.

"I heard you're moving up in the world, that's why I was so surprised when I heard you were coming to conduct the interview. What happened to Nails?" he asked, referring to the gentleman who normally hit the streets for the magazine.

"Nails is good, but I had to come do this one myself. The buzz on True in the streets is retarded!"

"You know the Don has always known how to pick em," he bragged. "Come on," he motioned for her to follow, "True is in the booth."

As soon as Don B opened the door to the studio a cloud of smoke washed over them. The haze lingering in the air was so thick that Unique got dizzy. She smoked weed from time to time, but not of the grade Don B and his crew smoked. The usual goons were in attendance, minus the deceased Pain, Lex, and Jay, but there was a young man sitting off in the corner with whom Unique wasn't familiar. He had the face of a boy barely in his teens, but cold, menacing eyes that ran over her. Behind the glass was the man she had come to see, True.

Don B hit a button on the console, cutting the music off. "Yo, somebody is here to see you," he said into the intercom. True nodded and removed his headphones.

The last time she had seen True in person he was a thug-ass teenager running behind Don B, but the man emerging from the sound booth was all grown up. His face was still as youthful as she remembered it, but there was a wizened look in his eyes that hadn't been there before. True wiped his sweaty face with his tank top, exposing his rippled stomach. Something stirred low in Unique, but she maintained her professional demeanor.

"Yo, kid, you remember Unique, right?" Don B, nodded to the dark-skinned young woman.

True stared at her for a minute until a light of recognition went off in his head. "Oh, from *Dream?* What's up, ma?" He hugged her. True's shirt was damp and uncomfortable against her skin, but she pretended not to mind.

"Chilling," she said. "Thanks for agreeing to sit down with me."

"You know Big Dawg and *Dream* is like family. Stop that."

"So you wanna do this right here?" she asked, taking out her recorder.

"We can do it wherever you want." He flashed a near-perfect smile.

"I'll be damned if you don't sound like somebody I know." She looked over at Don B, who was grinning. "Okay." She hit the button on her recorder. "Let's get started."

JAH SAT IN THE CUT while the girl Don B had introduced as Unique conducted her interview. He had expected it to be pretty much the same as most interviews with rappers that he'd read up on, full of bling and bravado, but True was surprisingly interesting to listen to. He articulated himself well and was very passionate about his craft. The most interesting part of the interview was when he spoke of his mother.

As the story went, she was a hustler from Harlem, much like her boy. True's mother had gone to prison on a drug charge off the word of a snitch, and was killed shortly after by one of the guards. When asked what became of the man who turned state's evidence on his mother, he claimed not to know, but there was something in his eyes that made Jah wonder how true that was.

"Okay, I've got just a few more questions, then we can wrap it up," Unique said, glancing at her watch. "Now, I don't put much stock into rumors, so I decided to go to the source. I hear that you were in a shootout the other day. You wanna talk about that?"

"Man, True wasn't in no shootout," Don B answered for him.

"So the report about there being a shooting at Stacks Green's video shoot are untrue?"

"Man, it wasn't like that. I happened to be walking with a cat who had a problem with some other dudes and ended up getting caught in the crossfire. That shit ain't have nothing to do with me," True lied.

"Well, like I said earlier, I don't put much stock in rumors, but some people are saying it was a hit and not a robbery."

True shrugged. "I couldn't tell you what it was about, cause it wasn't my situation." He said it nicely, but it was clear that he didn't want to talk about it.

She nodded, but the look on her face clearly said she didn't believe him. "A'ight, well, thanks for taking the time out for me, True." She stood to leave.

"No problem, ma. Thanks for letting me speak my piece." His face softened.

"Yo, Unique, you better e-mail me a copy of the interview before it goes to print." Don B hugged her.

"Don, you know I'd never print anything without letting you proof it first." She headed for the door.

"You better not," he called after her. As soon as Unique was out of the room, True started speaking.

"What the fuck was that shit all about? How did she even know what went down?"

"The streets talk, baby, and Unique has always had her ear to the streets," Don B said.

True frowned. "I don't like having my business out there like that, son."

Don B looked at him. "True, let me explain something to you. When you decided to get in the music game, your private life flew out the window. Every time you do or say something it becomes public knowledge. Get used to it."

"Whatever, Don. I still don't like it," True said.

Don B removed his shades and stared directly into True's eyes. "It ain't for you to like, it's for you to accept in pursuit of that fucking paper." He stood up and walked back over to the console. "You better get your shit together, True."

True glared at Don B but said nothing. Back when becoming rappers was just a dream for the kids from Harlem, it was about fun and self-expression, but the larger they got the more Don B became obsessed with paper. There was someone trying to murder the young rapper for something that he had no clue about, and all Don B cared about was album sales.

Jah sat off in the cut, silently watching the exchange between Don B and True. True was his charge, but his eyes were fixed on Don B. The older head couldn't seem to grasp True's anxiety over his situation, but Jah fully understood the mind-set of someone put in the position of prey. Being a hunter for many years, he had to familiarize himself with their thinking. He was resentful of how seemingly unmoved Don B was by the plight of his protégé, and wondered how he would react if the shoe was on the other foot. Though True wasn't as close to Jah as, say, Spooky or Tech, he still recognized him as a good nigga in a bad situation, which is what Don B seemed to be missing in his quest for number-one stunter status.

Jah had once credited Don B as being an official street nigga at one time, but as with most people, the money had changed him. If it had been one of Jah's close comrades who had been marked for death, stopping the murderer would've been first priority; but Don B was more concerned with it interfering with his pockets. Suddenly he felt sickened by the sight of the man and needed to be away, before he let his personal dislike of rappers complicate what he was trying to do.

"I'm bout to roll. I got something to take care of." Jah stood to leave.

"Son, what we paying you for, if you gonna keep dipping off?" Don B asked angrily.

Jah glared at Don B. He started to bomb on him, but held it. "Homey, my daddy died years ago, and I ain't real good with people coming at me like a kid. Remo and Devil are on the entrance and you got at least another half dozen able-bodied niggaz running around this bitch. I got a move to make, but I ain't going too far for too long. True," he turned to the youngster, "you gonna be here for a minute?"

"Yeah, for at least another couple of hours trying to finish this song," True said, scribbling on a notepad. "Go handle yours and we'll pick you up later for the locked door, I'm a'ight."

"A'ight, if that changes then hit me on the cell." Jah held up his phone. "Now, with the Don's permission," he said sarcastically.

"Whatever, man," Don B grumbled.

Jah stared at him for a moment longer before moving towards the door. Aside from wanting the men dead for what they did to Yoshi, Jah wanted True to live through the ordeal and see his dreams come to fruition. They were from two different spectrums of the game, but cut from the same cloth. It wasn't every day that a real nigga made it out of the hell they called the hood. Don B was proving to be another case. If the shooters showed up again, Jah would protect True to the best of his ability, but if it came down to a choice between he and the Don on the slab, he might just have to turn the other way.

MICHELLE SAT ON THE EDGE of her bathtub smoking a cigarette, which was something she normally didn't do, but she had a bad case of the jitters. She had fucked and sucked Lazy into a coma, so he was fast asleep in the other room—which was a blessing, because she needed privacy for what she was up to.

Ever since she had met the young boy she knew he had to be hers. There wasn't a doubt in her mind that Lazy was going to go on to become a successful athlete and maybe even go to the league one day, and she refused to take a backseat to his high school sweetheart. When he took that ride, she had every intention on taking it with him. In Lazy she saw someone that she could mold in the image of her ideal man, but it was proving to be a bit more difficult than she had expected. For as much love and material affection as she showed him, his was still a heart divided. Michelle would lie awake many nights, trying to figure out what a seventeen-year-old girl had over her. She was financially secure, had her own crib, and a plan of what she wanted to do with her life, but it didn't seem to be enough to move him. He was young and still quite wild, which made him reluctant to commit. But there were ways around that.

With a trembling hand, she reached for the little white strip on the sink and checked it. Two lines, just like the first. She could count on one hand how many times she and Lazy had had unprotected sex, so they should've been okay, had it not been for the fact that she poked holes in the condoms from time to time. It was grimy, but she couldn't wait forever for Lazy to decide he wanted to square up with her. She had to speed things up. Girls like Michelle were one of the main reasons why it was important for young men to carry their own condoms, instead of completely trusting the ones their jump-offs provided. Michelle wanted to shout for joy, but she had to hold her composure so as to seem sincere when she dropped the bomb.

She forced tears to well in her eyes before heading into the bedroom to confront Lazy. He was lying on his back with one leg slung over the edge of the bed. She knelt by the bed and shook him as roughly as she could until he stirred.

"Huh?" he looked at her with sleep-heavy eyes. He immediately knew something was wrong when he saw the crocodile tears streaming down her cheeks. "Michelle, what's wrong?"

"Lance, we need to talk," she said, placing the strip in his hand.

Chapter **40**

"AIN'T Y'ALL GOT NOTHING BETTER TO DO THEN play this stoop?" Yvette asked playfully, as she walked up. Shannon, Nate, and Spooky were passing a blunt around.

"You got nerve for as much as you be out here sacking!" Shannon shot back.

Yvette dug into the pocket of her sweatpants and pulled out a wad of money, which she flashed in Shannon's face. "These bitches sack, I *stack,* muthafucka!"

"Well, let ya boy hold something?" Nate asked.

"You better go snatch a purse," she joked.

"Baby girl, that's a lot of bread for you to be running around with on your person," Spooky said.

"I ain't worrying about it, cause I know you wouldn't let anything happen to me, Harlem," she said flirtatiously.

"I got ya back, ma," he said, and winked.

"Let me find out," Shannon said, looking at them suspiciously.

"Let you find out what?" Yvette asked defensively.

"That you let that nigga hit it before me."

Yvette sucked her teeth. "Shannon, ain't nobody hitting nothing, especially not your ass. I'd fuck around and have to fight every bitch on the block," she joked. Though she downplayed it, she and Spooky shared a secret. Not only had he hit it, but he had been hitting it for the past few weeks.

Ever since Spooky had started coming around there had been some sexual tension. On a drunk night when everyone else had turned in, she called him on it. They had snuck off to the roof of her building, where she and Spooky engaged in a bout of some gangster-ass sex. Spooky pounded her out so severely that her pussy was sore for days afterward—but that didn't deter her for going back for more. Though it was obvious that they felt each other deeply, they decided to keep it a secret, as neither wanted their business in the streets.

"Man, that nigga Spooky wouldn't know what to do with all that ass." Shannon slapped Yvette playfully on the ass.

"You better watch ya fucking hands!" She hit him with a sharp jab to the chest. Shannon and Yvette horsed around on the stoop, while Nate and Spooky laughed. None of them ever saw the car pull up or the men get out, but they all felt the aftermath.

The report from the shotgun sounded like thunder on the clear afternoon. Yvette took a burst to the back, sending her flying into Spooky's arms. There was a terrified look in her eyes, as she coughed blood into his face. She pleaded something, but Spooky couldn't make out the words. For the first, time in his life, Spooky froze in battle, but Shannon didn't.

Leaping off the stoop with his .44 in hand, Shannon opened fire on the men. There were at least five of them, so there was no shortage of targets. Shannon managed to drop one of them, but the others returned fire, forcing him back. The shortest of the men, who Shannon recognized as the cat Spooky had shot, leveled a Tech-9 and sprayed the front of the building. Spooky leapt behind the gate where the trash was stored, while Shannon managed to take cover behind a car, but Nate wasn't so lucky. He tried to run into the lobby but was too slow. Bullets ripped up his legs and back, eventually splitting his skull and dropping him. Spooky watched from his vantage point, as his brother's body tumbled down the stairs and rolled onto the curb.

"Muthafucka!" Spooky jumped out, letting off with his Glock. Blick took one to the chest, dropping him. A stray shot whizzed passed his ear, drawing his attention to the young man firing from behind a car with a 9. He had been firing so frantically that the gun ended up jamming on him, which spelled his undoing. Spooky hit him twice in the chest and kept pumping rounds into the man, even after he was down.

Not wanting to be left out of the action, young Dooly went in with his .380. He let off four rounds, but didn't manage to hit anyone. Thinking he was living out a movie, he tried to rush the car he had seen Shannon duck behind and found himself staring down the barrel of a long-nosed .44. Grinning wickedly, Shannon shot the young man flush in the face.

When Ronny put their little rider mission together, he had expected them to have the advantage because of how deep they were, but he hadn't expected to come to a head-on collision with two wild dogs. Deciding that a good run was better than a bad stand, he bolted.

Spooky tried to drop the man, but the bullet missed Ronny and shattered the window that Ralphy had just replaced. Ronny had almost made it across Throop, when a car turned the corner and slammed into him. He rolled over the length of the car before bouncing off the hood and hitting the ground. Ronny made one last attempt to escape, but his now-broken leg wouldn't support his weight.

Spooky stood motionless in front of 437 Jefferson Avenue staring at the two bodies of his loved ones. Nate was facedown on the sidewalk, while Yvette was propped on the steps where he had left her. Her beautiful face was frozen into the same horrified expression it had taken on when the shotgun slug hit her. Nate played the game, so he knew the threat of death was everpresent. But Yvette was innocent. It was just a sad case of being in the wrong place at the wrong time. Feeling moisture on his cheek, Spooky initially thought he was bleeding, but when he touched his finger to the spot the liquid was clear.

"We gotta dip, Spook!" Shannon yelled, hearing the sirens getting closer. Spooky ignored him, instead picking up Blick's abandoned Tech-9 and walking into the street. "What the fuck are you doing? Nigga, we gotta bounce!"

Spooky walked casually over to Blick, who was still squirming and put one in his skull. Oblivious to the approaching police and the crowd of people who saw him, he continued across the street to where Ronny was trying to crawl to safety. Spooky raised the gun and shot Ronny in his good leg, which stopped his crawling.

"Spooky!" Shannon called again, but got no answer. It was obvious that his friend was someplace else at the moment and wouldn't be returning any time soon. Spooky was his man, but Shannon didn't look forward to going to jail for him. He called his name one last time, and when Spooky still didn't answer, Shannon took off running towards Marcus Garvey.

Ronny saw the blank look on Spooky's face and knew that he was in a world of trouble. Knowing he couldn't shoot his way out of the situation, Ronny tried a different approach to save his life. He tossed his gun into the street and raised his hands in surrender.

"Chill man, I ain't even armed!" Ronny pleaded. Spooky looked down at him with almost-sane eyes, and for a minute Ronny thought he might actually live through the ordeal, but when Spooky raised the Tech-9 Ronny knew the game was over.

"Like I give a fuck," Spooky snickered, cutting loose with a barrage from the automatic. Ronny's body flapped on the ground like a wounded fish before eventually going still. To be sure that he was dead, Spooky placed the Glock in Ronny's mouth and pulled the trigger twice. Killing the men wouldn't bring his brother or Yvette back, but he'd sleep better that night knowing that the gunmen's families would be grieving right along with him.

Out of nowhere, several police cars converged on Spooky, who was still kneeling over Ronny holding a smoking gun. Even if he wanted to run, he couldn't, because they had him boxed in. Seeing the curtain about to fall on the last act of his street run, Spooky stood up to meet his end with dignity.

"Drop the fucking guns!" a pale officer with red hair barked. His, as well as several of his fellow officer's guns, were aimed at Spooky, all ready to blast.

Spooky took a deep breath and lowered his guns to his sides—but didn't put them down. Looking around at the carnage he had helped to create, he felt a bit of sadness in his heart and what had become of his life, and the legacy he would pass on to his seed. Nobody wakes up and says they want to be a killer, stick-up kid, or dope boy, but they play the hands they are dealt—as Spooky had done all his life, and as his son would probably do with his, unless someone showed him better. It was a bitter pill, but he had to swallow it. He knew the rules of the game before he played, and if he had it to do all over again, he wouldn't change a thing.

"Son, nobody else has to get hurt. Put the guns down and let us take you in. Better in cuffs than a bag, so let's do the right thing." This was from a Black officer who sounded strangely sincere.

Spooky looked at the officer and nodded sadly—before a grin spread across his face. "You can't be fucking serious," he laughed, then hit the Black officer full in the chest and face with a burst from the Tech-9.

He had managed to kill three of the officers and wound four more before going down in a blaze of gunfire. Nobody knew for sure how many shots were fired, but when the smoke cleared Spooky had more holes in his body than a noodle strainer. Jason "Spooky" Benjamin died alone and in the gutter on the corner of Jefferson and Throop at the hands of the NYPD, ten minutes after his older brother, Nate. And so ended the chapter of the Benjamin brothers, whose only real crime was being born into the life.

MO SAT IN THE EMERGENCY room of St. Vincent's hospital, impatiently looking at her watch. She had already been there for three hours and the staff was still moving as slow as molasses. Just another example of how the city treated you when you didn't have the proper insurance.

Several hours prior, she had gotten a frantic call from her girl Sharon, stating that she needed her and Dena to get to Fourteenth Street and Tenth Avenue immediately because it was about to go down. Apparently, the wife of some old nigga she was fucking with had found out about them and wasn't too happy about it. She and a few of her girlfriends had tracked them down at the Liberty Inn and started lunching, threatening to kill her and him if they came out. Not wanting her sister to find out what she was up to, she called her girls to come get her back.

Mo had tried to call Dena, but she still wasn't taking any calls, which was starting to concern her. With Dena or not, Mo couldn't let her girl go out like that, so she snatched her Rambo knife and headed into Manhattan. When she got there, the scene in front of the Liberty looked like something out of a movie. There were police everywhere and the man's wife was in handcuffs. Apparently, Sharon tried to slip out of the Inn and got caught up. The girl had beaten the hell out of her and scratched her face pretty bad. She even managed to bite a small chunk out of Sharon's shoulder as the police were trying to break it up. Mo and Dena had warned her about tampering with other people's men, especially the married ones, but her hot ass didn't listen. Now Mo had to sit in the crowded-ass emergency room waiting for the doctors to finish treating Sharon.

Mo's cell phone rang, breaking her train of thought. The security guard shot Mo a nasty look, motioning towards the NO CELL PHONE sign, but Mo ignored him and answered anyhow. "Yeah?" she answered in a stink tone.

"What's popping, hussy?" Dena capped on the other end.

"Dena? Girl, where the hell have you been? Shannon and your moms are worried sick about you."

"I'll bet. I ain't stunting that shit. I spent the night with Ice," Dena said proudly.

"That pimp-ass nigga from the other night? Dena, I know you must've fell and bumped ya damn head," Mo accused.

"Bitch, cut it out, Ice ain't no damn pimp, he's a manager. And furthermore, he's been treating me like royalty ever since I've been with him. Shit, I'm uptown with Wendy and Lisa right now getting my wig tightened up. Ice wants me to look good on his arm tonight at the party. Mo, this nigga is balling with a capital B!" Dena went on to tell Mo about the last two days she'd spent with Ice and how he'd tricked off a good amount of his dough on her. She expected her friend to be happy for her, but Mo was unmoved.

"Dena, I don't know about that nigga. Ice is cool and all, but I ain't under no illusions about what time it is with Mr. Black Ice."

Dena sucked her teeth. "Mo, why you hating cause I finally found an official nigga?"

"Dena, I could never hate on my girl, but I'm trying to tell you to be careful."

"Trust that ya girl got this. Anyway, what're you doing tonight?" Dena asked.

"From the looks of this shit, I'll probably be sitting up in this fucking, nasty-ass emergency room."

"Emergency room? Is everything okay?" Dena asked, concerned about her friend.

"Yeah, but Sharon's ass is in some shit as usual." She went on to tell Dena about Sharon's run-in with Scooter's wife, and the two girls shared a laugh.

"That girl is always in some shit," Dena said.

"Tell me about it. I hope this ass-whipping will finally slow her ass down."

"I doubt it. You know how Sharon is. But check it: Since you're already in Manhattan, why don't you come through tonight? I know it's gonna be some heavyweight niggaz up in there, cause that's all Ice fucks with," Dena boasted.

"I don't think so, girl. As soon as I get finished with this dizzy ho, I'm heading back to BK. I got a nine-inch piece of meat on hold for me that I can't wait to taste!"

"Nasty ass," Dena laughed. "A'ight, but if you change ya mind, hit my phone and I'll make sure you're good at the door. I'll talk to you later, Mo." Dena was about to end the call, but Mo stopped her.

"D, you make sure you're careful around them Harlem niggaz. I got a bad feeling about this whole situation."

"Mo, I told you I got this," Dena said, clearly not wanting to be lectured anymore. "I gotta go cause I'm next under the dryer, but if I don't see you tonight I'll call you in the morning."

"Make sure you do, D," Mo said, and ended the call. She was glad to hear that her friend was alright, but didn't know how she felt about the situation. Dena could say what she wanted about Black Ice, but Mo saw right through his slick-talking persona. For as sweet as his words were, she knew he had a poisonous tongue. Mo couldn't fault Dena for milking him, but hooking up with the man was an accident waiting to happen. And since Dena was grown and would have to see the light on her own, all Mo could do was be there for her when it happened.

A few minutes after Mo hung up with Dena, Sharon came out of the back. Aside from a few scratches on her face and a bruise under her eye, Sharon was good. But Mo could see the bandage they had applied to her shoulder peeking out from her neckline.

"I can't stand fucking hospitals!" Sharon said with a major attitude.

"How'd it go?" Mo asked.

"They had me back there all this fucking time to take some blood and give me a prescription for antibiotics."

"What? They think the bitch gave you rabies or something?" Mo joked.

"I don't fucking know, they claim the shit is routine when dealing with bites or scratches. I swear to God, when I see that bitch uptown it's on!"

"Sharon, you need to leave that shit alone," Mo told her.

"Fuck you mean, I need to leave it alone? You see what that bitch did to my face?" Sharon pointed to her scratches.

"Well, you *were* fucking her man," Mo pointed out.

"That's beside the point. If her old-ass pussy wasn't so trash he wouldn't keep coming back for this young shot. She ain't nothing but a hating-ass bitch."

"Whatever," Mo said. "Oh, I spoke to Dena."

"Ms. Prissy finally poked her head out? Where the fuck she been?"

"Catting around with that nigga Ice."

"That is one lucky bitch," Sharon said scornfully. "If she hadn't been all up his ass, I could've bagged him."

"Sharon, he's a pimp. Why the fuck would you want him?" Mo asked, not really understanding Sharon or Dena's thinking.

Sharon looked at her as if the answer to the question should've been obvious. "Mo, I wouldn't give a fuck if a nigga sold pussy or vacuums for a living, as long as he had long enough dough to keep me fly, I'm good." With that, Sharon left the emergency room.

Chapter **41**

THE MOMENT THE SUN DIPPED BEHIND THE
horizon Jah's eyes snapped open. An eerie feeling crept over
him that he couldn't quite explain. After leaving the studio
he came home to spend some time with Yoshi before he had
to get ready for the locked-door party. Though he had been
sleeping for almost five hours, he still felt drained.

Sliding off the bed as carefully as he could so as not to
wake Yoshi, Jah went into the bathroom and took a five-
minute shower before he began the process of selecting an
outfit to wear for the night. Jah had never been big on fashion, so it wasn't like he had a very wide selection of things
to choose from. Most of the stuff on his side of the closet
consisted of hoodies and jeans, but Yoshi had picked him
up a few pieces that were suitable for the occasion. Jah selected a pair of black jeans and an oversize black button-up
shirt that he'd never gotten a chance to exchange. It was a
good thing that he hadn't, because nothing short of a
hoodie would've concealed the thin bulletproof vest he
would be wearing.

As he was slipping into his pants his cell phone started
vibrating. Slipping back into the bathroom, he answered it.
"Yo?"

"You about ready to roll?" True asked on the other end.

"I will be, in a hot minute."

"That's what's up. We're meeting Stacks and his crew on 125th and Broadway in the McDonald's parking lot so we can roll through the spot mad thick."

"True, you think it's a good idea to have a mass meeting in the parking lot, with a nigga trying to kill you?" Jah asked. His strategy was to have True keep a low profile, but it was proving to be a near-impossible task.

"Man, its gonna be like twenty of us out there, so I doubt if a nigga is gonna be stupid enough to try something. Besides, I got the Terminator watching my back," True joked.

"Youz a funny nigga," Jah said in a flat tone.

"Nah, but on the real, I appreciate you holding me down like this, fam. Don B and them niggaz don't really understand what I'm going through. They want me to run around town with two big-ass body-guards, like I'm soft or some shit. That kind of thing can make a nigga look bad."

"Don't worry about it, True. Look, y'all niggaz just call me when you're close and I'll meet you downstairs."

"A'ight, my nigga. One." True ended the call.

Jah flipped his phone closed and eased it back into his pocket. When he came out of the bathroom, Yoshi was sitting up on the bed looking at him.

"Who was you on the phone with, Jah?" she asked suspiciously.

"That nigga, True. I took it in the bathroom so I wouldn't wake you," he told her, beginning the task of slipping into the bulletproof vest.

"Since when did you start wearing that?"

"Since I started running around with a bunch of knuckleheads who don't know how to stay out of trouble."

"Which club are you guys hitting tonight, so me and my girls can crash?" she said playfully.

"I don't think y'all will be crashing this one. It ain't exactly a club," Jah said.

"Well, if y'all ain't doing the club what's with the button-up?"

Jah stared at her for a minute as if he didn't know how to answer. Several decent lies raced through his mind, but in the end he decided to be honest. "Black Ice is having a locked-door tonight."

All the humor suddenly drained from Yoshi's eyes. She had been on the circuit for a good number of years, so she knew just what a locked-door was and the things that went on. Whereas, at a strip club there were certain rules and etiquette that were followed, a locked-door wasn't the same. Within the walls of the roving orgies, anything went, and she knew this for a fact from having attended several of them in the past.

"I don't know about this, Jah," she said.

"What you mean, you don't know? What is there to know? I'm supposed to be guarding True, so that's what I'm gonna do," he told her.

"Jah, I know what goes on at these kinds of things. There's gonna be a bunch of nasty pussy bitches throwing their stinking asses in your face!" she said heatedly.

"Yoshi, you know a nigga ain't moved by no flesh but yours. I'll be too busy watching True to even look at another bitch."

"Tell me anything." Yoshi was laying on her stomach, looking away from Jah.

Jah stopped fumbling with the buckles of his gun holster and went to the bed. Gently, he ran his hand over Yoshi's back. "Baby, you know me better than that. When I gave my heart to you, I meant it. Trust me when I say, if I hadn't committed to doing this job, then I wouldn't be going. Besides, you're the one that told me that doing security for rappers was easy money."

She turned to face him. "Yes, *rappers* being the key word. Most of the guys you've worked with are playing the role, but Don B and True are living it out. They're gangsters, and anything could happen to you fucking with them."

"So, I guess ya man Stacks is a boy scout?" Jah asked sarcastically.

"Jah, you and I both know that's not the same thing. Stacks is a bastard, too, but he isn't local. You'd be on him for two to three days tops before he was back on a plane to Texas. Any enemies you make with guarding True could be long-term."

Jah sighed heavily. "Yoshi, how long I been in the streets? I can handle myself in any situation, boo. I'm the hardest nigga out. I can't be killed!" he playfully boasted.

"Yeah, that shit is funny now, but how funny will it be when I get that phone call in the middle of the night?"

"Yoshi, that ain't gonna be me," he said seriously.

"Jah, nobody ever thinks it's gonna happen to them until they're on that gurney fighting for their lives," she said emotionally. "I've seen this shit play out time and time again, where the good nigga catches the bullet and the piece of shit it was meant for skates without a scratch. I don't think I could take it."

Yoshi rolled over to face him. He leaned in so close that their foreheads were touching. "Do you love me?"

"Of course I do," she said.

"Then that's all I need to bring me home," he said, and kissed her gently on the lips. "I'll be fine, ma." He headed to the door. Before exiting the bedroom he turned back to Yoshi. "I love you, baby."

"I love you too," she whispered to the closing bedroom door. The moment Jah left a cold chill swept through the bedroom. She knew that Jah was a street soldier and could handle himself, but a sense of dread filled her. She knew nothing positive could come from hanging with Don B and True, but Jah insisted on keeping his word. Sometimes she hated that he was like that, but it didn't change anything. Yoshi clicked on the television and settled in to wait up for Jah to come home.

"I'M TELLING YOU NOW, MARCUS, if yo ass go in there acting like you ain't got no sense, it's on and popping!" Billy warned him. Her arms were folded firmly against her chest, which she tended to do when she was heated.

"Billy, why you acting like that, ma?" he asked, slipping his diamond chain over his head. He knew damn well why she was acting like that, but he asked the question just to irritate her. Seeing her uptight reminded him of when he was courting her. Billy made him move heaven and earth for her affection, but at the end of the day it was well worth it.

"Don't play with me, Marcus, you know damn well why I'm acting like this. I don't want none of them stinking-ass hos all up on my piece!"

"Billy, I'm around pussy damn near every night of the week, and if I ain't strayed yet, I ain't gonna stray." He pulled her close to him. She tried to push him away, but he held her tight. "Baby, I'd rather go blind than look at a woman other than you." He kissed her.

"And you sure would, cause I'd cut your damn eyes out of your head." She nicked his bottom lip. "And you better not be in there tipping them hos."

"Billy, it ain't even that type of party. I'm rolling with Shooter to check out some new girls for the club."

"Oh, and that's supposed to make me feel secure. That old-ass man is hornier than the damn kids I coach."

"That Viagra is a muthafucka!" Marcus laughed. "But on the real, I'm gonna behave myself." He kissed her once more and then broke their embrace. Shooter and Raheem were downstairs waiting for him, so he had to go.

"You better, nigga! I love you, Marcus." She patted him playfully on the ass as he passed.

"I love you too, Willamina," he snickered, and closed the door behind him.

"Asshole!"

Chapter 42

WITH THE DARKNESS SWEEPING OVER THE ROT-
ten Apple like the shadow of death over Egypt, the children
of the night began to stir. The normally quiet block of
128th Street, between Fifth and Lenox avenues, was abuzz
with activity. Luxury cars slow-coasted down the block in a
futile attempt to find parking, or to see who was at the set.
Nobody wanted to miss out on Ice's party.

For the auspicious occasion, Black Ice had rented out an
entire brownstone, including the lower levels, which would
be used for the real entertainment. Ice had spared no expense making sure the house was jam-packed with ladies.
From the exotic island of St. Lucia to the slums of Charlotte, N.C., Ice made sure they came in droves. Fifty-three
of the finest hos he could scrape up, all ready to do business.

As expected, the rappers made a grand entrance. Led by
Don B's signature red Bentley, a caravan of at least five luxury cars made their way down the block. Men hung from
sun roofs, and out windows, popping shit and throwing up
gang signs. Cooter wanted to let off some rounds in the air
from an AK47 he had bought from some big head Dominicans off Broadway, but Soda convinced him it was a bad

idea. Instead, he resorted to shouting obscenities and spraying champagne all over parked cars. To say that these cats were ignorant would've been an understatement.

As the two crews filed out of the cars and made their way towards the brownstone entrance, the crowd went crazy. Even with the aid of Stacks's security team, Remo and Devil had trouble holding off the throngs of people trying to get autographs or integrate themselves into the crowd to gain quicker entry into the club. It was amazing to Jah to see grown-ass men acting like starstruck groupies. While security did crowd control, Jah's eyes continuously swept the crowd for hostile faces.

"Big Bear, what it is?" Don B greeted the hulking bouncer who stood vigil outside the front door of the brownstone.

"Ain't nothing, Don. Trying to get a meal ticket." He let him pass without a search, as he did with most of their crew. It was only when he got to Jah that he stopped him. "Oh, hell nah," Bear said, placing a hand against Jah's chest.

"Bear, what's popping? You ain't happy to see me?" Jah smiled at him.

"Happy to see you? Lil nigga, I should bust ya shit for getting me fired!" A year earlier Bear had made the mistake of allowing Jah into a club he was working while armed. Jah promised not to cause trouble, but of course he did. The young man had caused a stampede inside the club and escaped with Yoshi through a side entrance before Bear could catch up with him. Since Bear was at the door, the club owners fired him and threatened to bring him up on criminal charges if he came within one hundred feet of the spot.

"Man, that wasn't my fault. Them niggaz was tripping," Jah tried to explain.

"It ain't never your fault, Jah," Bear scolded. "Up the strap, cause I know you holding." Bear extended his hand.

"Come on, man, I'm on the job," Jah told him.

"And I'm Britney Spears," Bear said sarcastically. "I ain't letting ya monkey ass in with no hammer."

"He's with us, Bear," True told the bouncer.

Bear was waiting for True to say it was a joke, but True wasn't smiling. "You serious?" He looked from Jah to True.

"As a heart attack. He's my personal security," True informed him.

Bear hesitated. "A'ight, you got that. But I'm telling you now," Bear pointed his finger at Jah, "if you start any shit tonight I'm gonna kick ya ass personally."

"Whatever, nigga," Jah taunted him before slipping behind True into the brownstone.

The air inside the brownstone was muggy and stale. It smelled like cigarette smoke and musty pussy, but the vibe was crazy. Ballers from all over were staggering around chasing naked women and drinking like it was the last supper. Never in Jah's young life had he seen as many women in one place at one time, and he seriously hoped that all the sweet pussy wouldn't distract him from the task at hand.

Inside the club they were greeted by Wendy, who was dressed in a yellow thong-and-bra set under a see-through teddy. She escorted the rappers and their thick entourage to the third floor, which was reserved for VIPs, and seated them at a large table in the back, where there were complimentary bottles of champagne already chilling. Though the action on the third floor wasn't as intense as on the lower levels, it was still packed with females.

Soda was the first to grab a bottle and start chugging. "This is what I'm talking about. A nigga gone get his double L on in this bitch," Soda said, slapping a dark-skinned honey on the ass as she walked by.

"What's double L?" True asked him.

"Leaned and laid!" Soda roared, turning the bottle upside down.

LAZY STOOD OUTSIDE THE BROWNSTONE, mad at himself for not being on time. He knew that Don B and the gang had set the meet time at eleven thirty, but he had been so caught up in his bullshit with Michelle that time had passed him by. He still wasn't quite sure how he had managed to get himself caught up.

When Michelle had broken the news to him he was totally numb.

A *baby?* Oh hell nah, that was something he definitely wasn't ready for. He was just a kid himself. He tried to explain to Michelle that she should get an abortion because a baby would only complicate things, but she hit him with some shit about how it went against her religion as a Catholic. That was laughable, because he had never seen her go to church since he'd known her. Still, he couldn't force her into it. He'd contemplated the idea of beating her into a miscarriage but didn't have the heart for it. She literally had him by the balls. For as much game as Lazy thought he had, Michelle apparently had a bit more.

In light of the bullshit he was going through, he found himself missing Dena. She might not have had her own pad or job to speak of, but at least he knew that she was with him for who he was and not who he would become, like Michelle. Seeing Dena with another dude had driven him batty and he'd said some very hurtful things that he couldn't take back. He tried calling her to apologize, but she wouldn't pick up the phone. He'd thought about popping up at her house, but couldn't be sure what she had told Shannon, and Lazy didn't want a problem with him. He would just have to hope that their paths crossed in the street, so he could tell her how sorry he was and pray that they could work it out.

After almost twenty minutes of waiting, Lazy had finally made it to the front of the line. Slipping into his young star persona, he bopped to the front of the line, where the bouncer was looking at him with suspicious eyes. "What's good, my dude?"

Bear looked down at him and grumbled, "Fifty bucks and valid ID."

Lazy looked at him as if he couldn't be serious. "Son, I'm here with the Don."

Bear glared at him. "Is that right?"

"Yeah, that's right. This is big Lazy, star point guard for the Dawgz," Lazy boasted loud enough for everyone to hear. When he saw Bear's face soften he thought he had pulled it off.

"Excuse me, Mr. Big Lazy from Dawg. How could I not recognize a star of your caliber? Of course you're here with Don B," Bear said sarcastically. "Say, who else is here with Don B?" He addressed the line. Almost all at once, everyone claimed allegiance to Big Dawg. Bear glared back down at Lazy. "Lil nigga, you and everybody else in this muthafucka is claiming to be somebody. Either cough up that fifty cash or get off the line."

Lazy was about to black out on the bouncer when he was roughly shoved aside from behind. He spun around and found himself staring into the cold eyes of a man who was barely five feet tall. The man glared up at Lazy, who bit back the sharp words he was about to fire off and allowed him to pass. Trailing him were two more girls and the cat Lazy had gotten into it with at the park. The real kick in the ass was who the well-dressed man had on his arm.

"Dena?" Lazy whispered.

As sure as his ass was black, Dena strolled casually on the arm of Black Ice, moving towards the entrance of the brownstone. The stones in her ears looked like two flashlights, catching faint rays from the pale moon. She was dressed in a black evening gown with a diamond collar, and stiletto heels, which she walked on as easily as if they were sneakers. Her beautiful face was flawlessly made up and Shirley Temple curls danced all over her head. Lazy couldn't believe that this was the same teenage girl he had shared so many good times with, because at that moment she was looking like a grown-ass woman.

"What's up, D?" Lazy beamed at her. He could hardly contain himself, being so close to his one true love.

When she turned her eyes on him there was sleepiness to them, as if she had way too much to smoke. "Do I know you?" Dena asked, looking at him like he was a piece of shit.

"Word, you gonna play me to the left like that?" he asked, with hurt filling his voice.

"Baby, who is this lil nigga you're talking to?" Black Ice draped his arm around her. Just to make Lazy tight, he started kissing her cheek.

"Just some square-ass nigga that I thought I knew," she said scornfully.

Lazy's body began to tremble with rage. "Dena, how you gonna play like you don't know ya man? This nigga you wit don't know your heart like I do!"

"Young buck, you better calm down before you find ya self missing," Shorty warned him.

Lazy ignored him. "So that's how it is, huh? You gonna play me for some fake-ass pimp?" Lazy wanted to cry, but there were too many people watching.

"Son, call me what you want, but the reality of it is that I'm probably the realest nigga your simpleminded ass will ever lay eyes on. Come on, baby." Ice pulled Dena along. "If he ain't talking about cake then it ain't worth listening to."

"I know that's right, Daddy," she followed her new man into the club.

Lazy was left standing in front of the brownstone feeling like a meatball, with Dena and Ice's mocking laughter echoing in his ears.

Chapter **43**

IT WAS SAFE TO SAY THAT DENA WASN'T FEELING much pain that night. During the entire ride down in the limo Ice had rented, they snorted heroin and drank high-end liquor. It seemed like the more Dena danced with the devil the more comfortable she got with it, which seemed to please Ice. Lisa had even warmed up to her and started treating her like family, instead of some square-ass outsider. Though the white girl was still a little too wild for her taste, it made Dena feel good to be accepted.

When Dena entered the brownstone she was totally unprepared for what she was about to see. There was nudity everywhere she turned. Girls were running around in their birthday suits performing the most lewd acts while men chased them and showered them with money. They even stepped over a couple that couldn't make it to one of the VIP rooms and were fucking on the staircase. A fat cat wearing heavy jewelry and clutching a fistful of money tried to entice Dena into giving him a lap dance, but Ice marked his territory by pulling her closer.

"These niggaz is off the chain," Dena said distastefully, looking back at the fat cat, who was still watching her hungrily.

"What do you expect in a house of sin?" Ice rubbed her back. "These niggaz is all in here to blow their cake and their loads, so it's only natural that when the baddest bitch on two legs walks in the joint everyone wants a piece of her."

"Well, ain't nobody getting a piece of this but the Ice Man," she told him.

"Loosen up, baby, ain't nothing wrong with showing a lil flesh," Lisa said, flashing her breasts at a man who was passing. He was so stunned that he tripped over the sexing couple and fell on his face.

The happy little group was shown upstairs to the third-floor VIP section, where they were seated behind a velvet rope. For nearly a half hour Black Ice received people who wanted to either wish him well or offer to buy him a drink. The way they catered to him, you'd have thought he was the president. Dena proudly snuggled next to her man, drawing a nasty stare from the girl who had been introduced as Lexi. She had been shooting Dena nasty looks all night, but knew better than to cut up in front of Black Ice.

After a few drinks Lisa and Lexi went to get changed, leaving Dena, Ice, and Shorty sitting at the table alone. They drank, snorted more heroin, and talked shit, having the time of their lives. The mood was light and jovial, but that changed when Marcus and Raheem escorted an older man that Dena had never seen before over to the table.

"My man, Shooter," Ice stood up and embraced the older man. "How's it going?"

"Long and strong as when I was twenty-five," Shooter joked. "And who is this fine young thang in the midst of you sorry muthafuckas." He let his eyes roll over Dena.

"This is my new lady, Dena. Dena, this is an old and dear friend, Shooter."

"Pleased to meet you," Dena extended her hand.

"The pleasure is all mine," Shooter said, kissing the back of Dena's hand. "So tell me, what would it take for an old man like me to occupy a bit of your time, Ms. Dena?"

"More bread than you're holding onto, Jack!" Shorty bust out laughing.

Shooter slanted his eyes at Shorty. "Little nigga, I don't care how dangerous you think you is these days, old Shooter will still kick ya ass like it was 1985!" he said in a good-natured tone. Back in the days, Shooter used to run with Shorty's father when they were both breaking into the mack game. He had watched him go from a young man who was curious about the game to one of the most dangerous men in New York City.

"Sup, Dena?" Raheem asked, looking at her slyly. "I see you're still slumming."

"You know what, I'm getting a little tired of your mouth, fam." Shorty stood up. He was more than a foot shorter than Raheem, but it didn't deter him one bit.

"You clowns knock that shit off. I'm in here to get chose, and if y'all fuck that up cause of this street bullshit I'm gonna kick the both of your asses!" Shooter warned. Shorty returned to his seat, but kept his eyes locked on Raheem.

"I see you've got a packed house tonight, Ice," Marcus said, changing the subject.

"You know I don't do nothing half-ass," Black Ice boasted. "We got every flavor under the sun, all ripe for the plucking, if the bread is correct."

"Even this one?" Raheem nodded at Dena.

"Nigga, don't play yaself. This pussy ain't for sale," she shot back. She had initially thought Raheem to be a cool nigga, but he was proving to be more of an asshole than anything.

"Not yet," Raheem mumbled.

"Nah, cat daddy. Dena is special," Ice told Raheem, snuggling Dena against him. He knew the man was trying to get a rise out of him, but he refused to step out of his character in front of Shooter or his girls.

"Well, I'm gonna move around a bit and see what you're working with, Ice. If all goes well, we can place most of these bitches, can you dig it?" Shooter said.

"Sho nuff can," Ice responded. "Y'all go on and have a good time and everything, except the women are on the house."

"That's a bet," Shooter shook Ice's hand and led his small entourage back through the crowd. Raheem stopped short and gave Shorty a hard look before falling in step behind Shooter and Marcus.

"Ice, that nigga is asking for it." Shorty slammed his fists on the table, scaring Dena.

"Yeah, you're right about that, Shorty. Raheem is out of pocket." Ice scratched his chin in thought. "You know what, go on and give him a dose."

"Bet!" Shorty hopped up eagerly, but Ice grabbed him by the arm.

"Nigga, not now. Shooter is probably gonna cut out early; and when he does, I want you to split that nigga's shit," Ice said wickedly.

DENA SAT AT THEIR TABLE, tossing back glasses of champagne, fuming. For a good portion of her night she found herself fending off advances from men trying to pay her for sex, and it was starting to piss her off. What made her more uptight was the fact that Ice seemed oblivious to it. He continued to laugh and drink with the different guests while Dena was damn near molested. When she had finally tired of being groped, she decided to step up to Ice.

He was standing on the other side of the room where Don B and his team were seated, with Lexi at his side. She had traded her street clothes for a thong and some clear heels. The small purse she wore slung over her shoulder was damn near bursting with dollars. With an ass ripe enough to sit a drink on it, Lexi drew more than her fair share of attention.

"Can I talk to you for a minute?" She tapped Ice interrupting a conversation he was having with Stacks Green and Don B. They seemed to be bartering about something, but Dena wasn't really sure what. Knowing those three, it could be just about anything.

"Give me a minute, baby," he said, brushing her off. He was currently trying to gas Stacks Green to spend some cake on Lexi. He knew that she had the stamina to do his whole crew and still come back for more, so Ice was trying to capitalize on it before the bitch got too drunk to perform.

"I need to talk to you now!" she demanded. This drew stares and snickers from the men assembled at the table.

Black Ice's face remained unmoved, but there was a fire building in his belly. One of the most important aspects of the game he played was appearances. It was crucial for him to appear to be in control at all times, especially at a venue such as the locked-door. If word got back that his hos were back talking or trying to give him orders, he'd be ruined in the game—and he couldn't have that.

"Damn, where you been hiding that one?" Soda asked, openly admiring Dena. He tried to touch her ass, but she slapped his hand away.

"Excuse you? What do I look like, one of these ho bitches?" she snapped.

"You really don't wanna hear the answer to that," Cooter snickered.

"Fuck you, too, you country muthafucka!"

"Damn, I like a bitch with some fire. How much, honey?" Stacks asked, pulling out a brick of money.

"More than your fat ass could come up with!" she barked. A look of rage crossed Stacks's face as he tried to raise up from the seat; but Cooter held him back. Seeing the situation about to turn ugly, Black Ice stepped in.

"Hold on, playboy. No need to get hostile," Ice said pleasantly.

"Man, I thought you was a mack, but how you macking and ain't got no control over your bitch?" Stacks accused.

"Man, don't never mistake my game from not being together. Ol' girl is new, but I'll straighten this whole mess out," Ice told him.

"Had it been me, you'd have probably broke your foot off in my ass," Lexi said slyly, while sipping her fourth glass of Hennessey.

"And I still might if you don't mind ya fucking business," Ice said coldly before turning back to Stacks. "Look, y'all have a bottle on the house while I go straighten this shit out." He grabbed Dena by the arm and dragged her back to his table.

"Ice—," she began.

"Bitch, don't you say another fucking word," he hissed. "Now, I don't know what the fuck your problem is, but you better damn well fix it."

"My problem is that you ain't making these niggaz respect your lady. Muthafuckas keep grabbing on me and shit." The drinks had her feeling herself.

"Are you fucking blind? Every bitch in here is getting felt up, and you're the only muthafucka complaining, coming out ya mouth like some square-ass bitch."

"I'm complaining because I didn't come here for that, Ice," she told him.

"Then what did you come here for, to look good on my arm and say you've been with the Ice Man? Dena, look around you." He motioned to the various girls trying to hustle up a buck. "Some of these girls in here are gonna turn tricks until their pussies feel like they're gonna fall out they assess, all so we can live a step above the rest. You looking down on hos, but you ain't looking down on ho money. How the fuck does that sound to you?"

"Ice, I just ain't used to niggaz coming at me like I'd sell my body for money."

"Dena, did I ask you to fuck any of these niggaz? See, that's where you got it fucked up. Sure, a lot of these niggaz is in here paying for a shot of honey, but a lot of them just wanna talk some shit and maybe feel a little ass, but your prissy ass is too good for a lil chitchat, huh? I don't need no prima donna on my team, I need bitches that's about a dollar. You know what, I think I'm gonna have Shorty run you back to ya mama's house, cause you clearly ain't built for the fast lane."

At the threat of being cast out of heaven Dena began to panic. "Ice, I'm sorry, Daddy. This shit is just so overwhelming." She flopped in the seat. "I just need a little time to get used to it. I'll be okay."

Ice knew he had her right where he wanted her. He knew that there was gonna be fellas hitting on Dena, but he hadn't expected them to come on so strong out of the gate. Dena was green to the game and had to be broken in gradually, but the plan had changed. He saw the money-making potential in her that night and formed a deliciously evil plan in his mind.

Ice sighed heavily. "It's cool, baby." He sat next to her. "I didn't mean to snap at you. There's just a lot going on right now and I'm under a tremendous amount of pressure."

"I know, baby, and I don't mean to add on to it." She stroked his face. "I just thought for a minute that you were gonna toss me to the dogs like some tramp."

Ice pulled her close to him and nestled his face in her hair. "I'd never toss away such a precious jewel. You just gotta understand the hearts of men in this game. My daddy used to always tell me never to let an opportunity pass you by, because you never know when or if another one is gonna come along. I'd never ask you to do anything you didn't wanna do, Dena, but I need all my ladies reading from the same page. If a nigga comes up on you and wants to spend a little paper for some conversation, let him. Do you think you can do that?"

Dena hesitated. "I don't know, but I'll try."

"That's my girl." He kissed her on the cheek. "Shorty," he called to his man, who had been watching the exchange, trying not to laugh. "Go to the bar and see if you can scare up one of them Blue Diamonds for my girl."

"I'm on it," Shorty said, knowing how the story was going to play out. It was rare for Ice to resort to outright trickery, but when he did it always got results.

"MAN, THAT BITCH BARKED ON you, Stacks," Don B teased him.

"Fuck that bitch; hers ain't the only pussy floating around this joint," Stacks spat.

"I know that's right, big time," Lexi lowered her big ass into Stacks's lap and began grinding on him. "Don't stunt that uptight bitch, she probably don't know what to do with her little pussy anyway."

"And I suppose you do?" True asked.

"Lil fella, not only do I know how to work my pussy, but I got a shot of head that's so retarded that you would think you was in the pussy."

"I need to see what that's about," Stacks rubbed her leg.

"All money down is a bet," Lexi said looking around the room. Before she had a chance to press her pitch, Black Ice came back over.

"Stacks, I wanna take this time to apologize about that lil scene a minute ago. My girl is new, so she was a lil nervous," Ice said.

"Its all good, cause I think ya girl Lexi got what I need right here," Stacks replied.

"Indeed. Lexi is a mean bitch, on a mean team, but what say we sweeten the pot?" Black Ice leaned in. "How much is it worth to you to have both these fine hos show you the time of your life?"

Stacks looked over at Dena, who was getting drunk with Shorty, and back to Lexi on his lap. "Shit, I'd spend a good piece of change with you, homey."

Black Ice rubbed his hands together greedily, thinking how he was going to charge Stacks a king's ransom for a taste of Dena's sweet candy. "A'ight, give me about an hour and then I'm gonna show you Texas niggaz how juicy the Apple is."

Chapter 44

JAH SAT IN THE CORNER WATCHING EVERYONE watch the rappers. Though being around them repulsed him, at times he had to admit that they knew how to party. Being behind the gun more often than not didn't allow him much time for fun, and sometimes he missed it. His reflecting was disturbed when his cell phone vibrated. Looking at the number on the caller ID screen, he knew it was a call that he had to take in private. Excusing himself from the table, he dashed to the bathroom and flipped the phone open.

"Tell me something good."

"Yeah, I think you gonna like this," Tech said on the other end. "I've been laying on this nigga since last night and he ain't strayed too far, so I'm guessing this is where he stay at."

"Is he home now?" Jah asked excitedly.

"I'm looking at his fat ass right now," he said, watching his mark stroll up the street, busy with a scratch-off. He had no idea how closely the shadow of death followed him, but he would learn soon enough. "You want me to bust his brain?" Tech asked, praying Jah would gave him the green light. The mark had never done anything to him personally, but he wanted to kill him just off the strength that he had gone out like a faggot.

"Nah, I'm bout to jump in a cab, so I should be there in like twenty minutes. I wanna see the life drain from his muthafucking eyes when I peel his shit," Jah told him. "Sit tight and I'll be right there." He ended the call. Jah was so excited that he had to compose himself before going back out to join the group. He had waited over a year for this moment, and Larry Love's number was finally about to be called. When he arrived back at the table, Cooter and Soda were arguing over who had second dibs on Black Ice's new cop. For as hostile as they were, you would've thought shorty had a golden pussy.

"True, I'll be back in about a half," Jah whispered in his ear.

"You leaving?" True asked.

"Nah, I got a little jump off down on the second floor that said she wanted to suck my dick from the back, so you know I gotta see what that's about," Jah lied.

"You might wanna stick around, kid. These niggaz is scheming on running a train on shorty over there." He nodded towards Dena.

Jah looked over at the young girl who was clearly high out of her mind off of something more than weed. She was laughing at everything and couldn't seem to sit still. The way Don B hungrily watched her, Jah knew the man had something sinister up his sleeve, and he just hoped the girl didn't end up like Reese, with a trick baby. He sometimes wished Reese had been his sister so he could've had a reason to take revenge on the man.

"You a'ight?" True asked, noticing the change in Jah's facial expression.

"Yeah, man. I just ain't wit that train shit," Jah told him.

"Me either. All that balls-swinging shit ain't my cup of tea. I don't wanna see nothing but pussy when I'm going in on a bitch."

"I know that's right." Jah gave him dap. "But let me go ahead and get wit this bitch before somebody else snatch her up."

"Handle. You're my nigga!" True called after the departing man.

"BITCH, WHERE THE HELL HAVE you been? I ain't seen your ass since you slid the other night. I was beginning to think home boy had snatched yo ass," Sugar said, cradling the phone between her ear and her shoulder. Her hands were covered in flour from the chicken she was frying for Sha Boogie and Charlie, who had come by with liquor and weed.

"Damn, you're worse than my mama. And for your information, he did snatch my ass. My ass, my hair, and some of everything else!" Roxy squealed. "Girl, let me tell you that the saying about fat niggaz having lil dicks is not true for everybody."

"Youz about a dick-thirsty bitch," Sugar said.

"Takes one to know one."

"But fuck the dumb shit, is the nigga holding?" Sugar asked.

"He tricked a few dollars, but his crib ain't all that. I did see some credit cards in his wallet though, when he went to the bathroom."

"We can do some serious shopping with those on the Internet," Sugar said. Credit fraud was another one of her talents.

"That's what I'm talking about. I ain't snatched em yet, but please believe I'll have them shits before I leave here," Roxy assured her.

"So, when you coming back to BK?" Sugar asked.

"Probably tomorrow afternoon. I'm trying to get him to take me shopping on Fordham when the stores open."

"Bitch, don't bullshit around with that fat muthafucka all day. Don't forget we gotta hit that barbecue tomorrow."

"I ain't forget. I'm gonna throw on something real slutty and press that nigga Stacks. Its time to take the gloves off."

"Amen to that!" Sugar agreed. "Maybe we can convince Sha Boogie and Charlie to rob his ass."

"I don't see why not. Them niggaz is crazy as hell anyway." Roxy paused when she heard a key jiggling in the front door. "Bitch, I gotta go cause that nigga is back from the store. I'll call you in the morning." Roxy hung up before waiting for Sugar to respond. When Larry came into the bedroom she acted like she was just waking up.

"Damn, yo ass is still sleeping?" he asked, placing a plastic bag on the floor.

"Yeah," she stretched, "you put it on a bitch."

"They don't call me Larry Love for nothing." He began fumbling around in the bag. He pulled out a fifth of Hennessey and a box of magnum condoms. "You think you're up for another round?"

"SHA, HOW LONG WE GONNA play cat and mouse with this nigga?" Charlie asked, putting flame to the end of a blunt.

"We play till I say the game is over. What, you getting scared or something?" Sha snapped.

"Hell nah, you know we ride together. I'm just saying, we need to bump this nigga off before we miss the chance. Its bad enough them niggaz is always crew-thick, but that lil nigga he running with is starting to give me the creeps."

"Man, fuck that nigga, he ain't hard." Sha put his cigarette out in the ashtray. "You should've seen that nigga all uptight over his bitch in the club."

"That was a bad lil bitch. I think she used to dance at Shooter's," Charlie said and tried to remember.

"Clown-ass nigga trying to turn a ho into a housewife," Sha Boogie laughed. "Maybe we'll run up on her ass, too, when her man is dead."

"If we ever get around to killing anybody," Charlie said. He didn't mean anything by it, but he could see that Sha Boogie was offended by the statement. "Sha, I ain't mean nothing by it. I just wanna get this shit over with so we can get back to business. I really ain't trying to chase True all summer."

Sha Boogie gave Charlie a disgusted look, but deep down he knew his partner was right. The hit had taken months to plan, but the execution wasn't going exactly how he had expected. After the botched hit he decided to have a little fun and make True sweat, but the time for games was over. True had to die and the debt had to be settled.

"Fuck it, Charlie Rock. We gonna push over to that locked-door joint in Harlem and end this shit once and for all. Let's go twist these niggaz caps back." Sha pushed away from the table.

"Where the fuck is y'all niggaz going, and I done fried all this chicken?" Sugar came into the living room holding a bowl full of fried chicken.

"Something came up and we gotta bounce," Charlie Rock told her.

"Fuck you mean, something came up? Y'all niggaz come through my house, have me cook and shit, and you breaking out? That's some real bullshit."

"Listen," Charlie Rock pulled her to the side, "it's five bags of weed and twenty cash for your trouble, but if you know like I know, you'll leave this situation alone," Seeing the frightened look in his eyes, Sugar decided to take his advice and she didn't say another word until they were out of her apartment.

THE RIDE FROM HARLEM TO the Concourse was a short one, so Jah had enough time to do what he had to do. When he hopped out of the cab on 156th Street Tech was on the corner waiting for him. Tech was his usual smiley self, but Jah's face was grim and hard.

"Jah, what it do?" Tech gave him dap.

"It dies, my nigga," Jah said, continuing past him. The two bandits made their way to the building where Larry Love was held up, with murder on their minds. There was a group of young men sitting on the stoop, and they gave the two men a wide berth. The young street punks knew death when they saw it.

Thanks to the recon done by Tech over the last twenty-four hours, not only did Jah know which building Larry lived in, but the apartment as well. Moving as silently as they could, they jogged the four flights of stairs and positioned themselves outside Larry's door.

"He alone?" Jah asked, checking the clips of his twin 9s.

Tech shrugged. "He was when I seen him last."

"Then lets get it popping," Jah said, just before kicking the apartment door off the hinges.

THE SEX DIDN'T LAST AS long as the first few times, but Larry got his nut off. Whether Roxy did or not was irrelevant. While Roxy was in the bathroom cleaning herself up, Larry reflected on how easy it was to dupe her. He had made the girl think that he was holding, not knowing he was ass-popped and all the credit cards in his wallet were canceled. He would continue the façade until she was gone, and he hoped she didn't have to go into her purse for anything, because she was going to be mad as hell when she found out that he'd swiped her money and Medicaid card. Roxy thought she was slick, but nobody was slicker than Larry Love.

Larry smiled at his own cunning, but the smile faded when the door to his studio apartment came crashing in. Larry tried to reach for the .22 he kept in the drawer by the side of the bed, but the shorter of the gunmen was on him before he could get to it. There was something about the dark-skinned teenager that was familiar to Larry, but he couldn't place it; but he knew exactly who the second shooter was and what he had come to do. Not being able to control it, he pissed himself.

Jah took his time coming into the room with a pistol dangling in each hand. He had waited so long for this moment that it almost didn't seem real. The look on Larry Love's face was one of pure terror, which only made Jah's dick hard. Larry made a quick movement and Jah thought he might be going for a weapon, but to his surprise the big man bolted for the window. Larry hurled himself at the flimsy glass, and though it shattered, the frame kept him from making an exit. All he succeeded in doing was cutting himself up something awful.

"Now that was dumb," Tech laughed at the bleeding man.

"Damn, Larry, that ain't the reception I expected from my long lost *brother*," Jah said icily.

"Jah, Jah, Jah . . . wait a minute, man," Larry stuttered. "Before you do something stupid, you need to know that my next-door neighbor is a cop."

"Good, then it shouldn't take the meat wagon long to come collect what's left of you," Jah kicked him in the face, knocking his head into the wall. Larry was dazed but didn't pass out.

"Oh, your ass is gonna get it!" Tech said, while doing the cabbage patch over Larry. His little warped ass was getting a kick out of Larry's situation. He stopped mid-dance and sniffed Larry. "Nigga, did you piss yaself? Jah, this nigga pissed on his self!"

"Tech, shut the fuck up," Jah snapped.

"Dawg, lets talk about this," Larry pleaded through his bloody lips.

Jah placed his guns back in the holsters and crouched down so that he and Larry were eye to eye. "What we got to talk about? How you and that skank bitch Marlene crossed my brother?" He slapped Larry viciously across the face. With rage adding strength to his slim arms, Jah grabbed Larry by the throat and lifted him to his feet. "Paul was a good dude, Larry. He didn't deserve to go out like that!"

"You don't think I know that? I live with the guilt of what happened to him every day, so ain't shit you can do to me that's worse than what I'm already going through!" Larry shouted. He really felt bad for what had happened to Paul, but it was mostly theatrics for Jah's benefit.

"Larry, a piece of shit like you couldn't begin to even grasp the fundamentals of guilt," Jah said, reaching down to retrieve a piece of the broken window glass. "But you will know pain."

ROXY PRESSED THE PALMS OF her hands against her ears as tight as she could, but she still couldn't seem to block out Larry's screams. After a bout of so-so sex she had gone into the bathroom to take a shower and shortly after heard a loud crashing. She was about to come out and check on Larry, thinking maybe he had fallen, but then she heard the voices. From what it sounded like, Mr. Larry Love had written a check his ass couldn't cash.

She paced the tiny bathroom trying to figure out her next move, but kept coming up blank. She thought about trying the window, but it was barred. "Shit," she mumbled. She was caught between a rock and a hard place, ass-naked. The only way out was through the front door.

FIFTEEN MINUTES AFTER JAH AND Tech had run up on Larry Love in his crib, he looked like a totally different person. His eyes were almost both nearly sealed from the beating by Jah and Tech, while his body sported well over a hundred paper-thin cuts. At several points they thought he was going to pass out from the blood he'd lost, but tough-ass Larry Love was still breathing, though it was very ragged.

"This nigga look like a muthafucking pack of chopped meat," Tech half laughed, half wheezed. He had attacked Larry with more vigor than Jah, and with almost as much brutality. Though he hadn't done anything to Tech physically, psychologically he fucked him up. In Tech's young eyes, Jah was like a ghetto Superman. He was the closest Tech had ever been to a legend in the streets, and the young boy wanted to mold himself in Jah's image. When the events spawning his brother's death came to pass, something in Jah changed. Tech wouldn't have gone as far as to call it depression, but it was something akin to that. What Jah was going through dispelled his idea of there being such a thing as the hardest nigga out. Everyone was vulnerable to something, which fucked with his head about his own morality. All this he blamed on Larry Love.

Blood soaked into the cheap carpet and stained the walls of the studio apartment. Larry Love was stretched out in the middle of the living room, shaking and speaking in tongues. It must have been a muthafucka to be laying there helpless, knowing you were about to check out, but it was his karma that had brought him to that point.

"P . . . please," Larry begged, coughing blood as he spoke.

Jah leaned in so that his lips were brushing against Larry's ear and whispered, "I don't bargain with the dead." In a sudden thrust, he plunged the piece of window glass through Larry's nuts. Tech turned away as Jah shoved the glass deeper into Larry's groin. With a grunt he dragged the glass from Larry's groin to his chest. When the glass hit Larry's breastbone, the piece of glass snapped off inside him. Only when the con artist known as Larry Love sighed his last breath did Jah step back to admire his handiwork.

Suddenly the bathroom door burst open and someone came darting out, catching Jah and Tech by surprise. Before Jah could even clear his gun from the holster, Tech had taken aim. Two loud shots rang off and what appeared to be a woman dropped in the hallway.

"I thought you said he was alone?" Jah barked, kneeling beside Roxy. She was breathing shallowly, but Tech had hit her with a .40 cal, and there wasn't no coming back from that. "Damn, you stupid!" Jah yelled, feeling the woman's pulse slowly stop.

Tech shrugged as if he had just broken a glass instead of killing an innocent woman. "I didn't know he was still here with the bitch from the club."

Jah rolled Roxy over onto her back. Roxy's face was peaceful, as if she had just dozed off, but the exit holes in her chest said that she wouldn't be waking up from that nap. He glared at Tech, ready to bark, but he couldn't blame anyone but himself. He had brought a teenage boy to do man's work, and the price was the life of the girl.

The two bandits manage to escape without incident, but Jah stopped at a pay phone two blocks further up to call 911. Though they wouldn't make it in time to save her life, she wouldn't have to lie around rotting until someone found her.

Chapter 45

THE SWEET-TASTING DRINK THAT HAD BEEN IN-troduced to her as a Blue Diamond tasted like a cross be-tween blueberry Kool Aid and Tums, but it had succeeded in getting her completely twisted. The combination of alco-hol and heroin had her feeling like her nerve receptors were in overdrive. Every time Black Ice touched her, even casu-ally, she thought she was going to cream her panties.

"You okay, baby?" Ice stroked her cheek, almost causing her to faint from sheer pleasure.

"Yeah, I'm just a lil twisted." She ran her hands along the sides of her face. "That Blue Diamond was strong as hell."

"Its Ice's very own recipe," Shorty snickered. He had mixed the drink for her, so he knew what it had in it. A Blue Diamond was a mixture of Hpnotiq, club soda, sugar, and ecstasy pills. One of these could make a woman feel more promiscuous than normal, and Dena had already downed three. She would've downed a forth, but Ice cut her off, fearing she would overdose.

Dena giggled like a schoolgirl at what she'd taken to be a joke. Slipping her hand under the table, she began to mas-sage Ice's dick. "Daddy, when we get out of here I want you to fuck me in every hole," she whispered in his ear.

Black Ice smiled at knowing the drug had completely kicked in. "Why wait?" He stroked her crotch under the table. He could feel that Dena had completely soaked through her panties. Black Ice took Dena by the arm and helped her to the feet. Had it not been for his strong hands holding her up, she'd have fallen back down.

"Dena, are you okay?" Wendy asked, not knowing what Ice was up to.

"Yeah, girl, I'm good," Dena slurred. Her lids were so heavy it was a wonder she could see anything.

"Damn, Ice, that girl is fried!" Lisa exclaimed.

"Yes, our lil fresh fish is finally coming out of her shell," he said slyly. Ice leaned down to whisper into Shorty's ear. "Go find that bitch Lexi and send her in the back. Then go see Stacks and tell that fat muthafucka to have my money right when I get back." After giving Shorty his instructions, Black Ice led Dena towards the bedrooms.

Black Ice had barely closed the bedroom door before Dena was on him. She was kissing his face and touching him everywhere she could get her hands at one time. Ice had to restrain her to keep the girl from ripping his silk shirt.

"Take it easy, baby," he said, tossing her on the bed. The room was only illuminated by the street light shining through the window, but he could see her squirming, with her eyes rolling back in her head.

Dena rolled around on the bed like she couldn't sit still if she wanted to. "Oh, I need you inside me, Ice." She hiked her skirt and began playing with herself.

Black Ice stood at the foot of the bed and pulled his dick out. Glaring down at Dena, he began stroking himself. "You want some dick, do ya?" he teased. "Then beg for it. Beg Daddy for this love bone!"

"Please," she pawed at him, "Daddy, come put this fire out."

"Suck it, like a good bitch!" he ordered, and Dena all too happily complied.

She took Ice in her mouth and began to suck him like a Rocket Pop on a summer day. Dena dug her nails into Ice's ass cheeks through his slacks, forcing him further down her throat. He was thoroughly surprised when she took all of him without gagging. Suddenly there was a third set of hands added to the mix.

With one hand, Lexi juggled Ice's balls, while stroking Dena's cheek with the other. With some effort, Lexi was able to pry Dena's mouth off Ice's wood and began kissing her. Dena resisted at first, but it felt so natural that she eventually just went with the flow. Lexi forced Dena back onto the bed and mounted her. In slow deliberate motions, she began grinding her naked pussy against Dena's panties. Dena could feel the beautiful heat, but the fabric seemed to be denying her some of the sensation, so she ripped them off and tossed them behind her.

Ice watched from the doorway as the two girls kissed passionately and grinded against each other. The scene was so hot that he had to stop himself from joining in. But Ice believed in business before pleasure. Smiling like a proud father, he slipped from the bedroom and rejoined the party.

"WHAT'S GOOD, HOMEY?" STACKS ASKED eagerly as Ice walked back over to their table.

"Everything is right as rain," Ice said proudly. "The bitch is all primed and ready for you in the back, man." Stacks almost knocked his chair over trying to get to the bedroom, but Ice stopped him short. "Now, there's the little matter of my bread."

"How much?" Stacks asked hungrily. Paying for pussy wasn't a problem for him, because that was the only way he got laid before he started getting money. Besides, he had been smitten with Dena ever since he had seen her at the video shoot.

"A grand for Dena and five hundred for Lexi." Ice said flatly.

"Shit, you want a thousand dollars for that pussy?" Cooter spoke up as though it was his money on the table.

Black Ice turned a cold stare to him. "Man, all my bitches pull top dollar, and that lil freak back there ain't never been touched."

"Sweet pussy!" Don B raised his bottle. He and everyone else at the table was drunk as hell. "Stacks, go ahead and break that bitch in so I can get a taste."

Stacks hurriedly pulled out his bankroll and peeled off fifteen one-hundred-dollar bills, which he slapped in Ice's palm. "We good?" Ice had watched him count the money out, but took a minute to do it again to build on Stacks's already mounting lust. "Do ya thing, player." Ice patted Stacks on the back.

"You niggaz hold down the fort and I'll be back in a minute," Stacks told his crew as he waddled towards the bedroom. His hands shook nervously as he fumbled with the door to the bedroom. When he pushed the door open and saw the freak show that was going on, a lone tear rolled down his cheek. This was going to be his most memorable trip to New York yet.

LEXI PICKED HER HEAD UP from between Dena's thighs when she heard the door creak open. When she saw Stacks Green's bulky frame slide into the room a broad smile spread across her face. She had been jealous of Dena since Ice had copped her and was glad the high-maintenance chick was finally about to get busted out. She stopped eating Dena's pussy and positioned her to return the favor. Dena was so gone that she didn't even complain, she just did as she was told.

Dena had never been with a woman before, but under the sway of the drug she took to it like a fish to water. With her ass cocked in the air she proceeded to lap at Lexi's pussy. When Lexi came in her mouth it was like a sweet cream that Dena wanted more of, so she plunged her tongue deeper. Dena felt a large pair of hands grip her waist, but when she tried to lift her head to see what was going on, Lexi pulled it back down into her pussy. She could feel fingers being inserted into her and it sent shockwaves of pleasure through her body. She pushed back against the fingers, shoving them deeper into her box.

Stacks's dick got hard as a rock when he saw how wet his fingers were. Dena's ass looked like a sweet apple, hiked in the air. Him being the freak nigga he was, he couldn't avoid burying his face in her pussy. Dena came so hard that it dripped down Stacks's chin and onto the bedsheet below. Her cum tasted bitter, yet sweet at the same time, as he lapped at her pussy, and worked his tongue up to her asshole. Dena hissed like a cat, and if she could've she would've shoved his whole head inside her pussy. He was glad that his boys weren't inside, because they would've surely clowned him for it.

When Stacks finally raised up to slip inside Dena, the head of his dick was already swollen and dripping. He went through the motions of fumbling with the condom, but seeing Dena's beautiful dripping pussy he knew he had to taste it raw for the first time. Aiming it with his thumb, he slipped his short, fat cock inside Dena. With a squishing sound he plunged as deep inside Dena's box as his belly would allow, and sure enough it felt like a summer day. Stacks had intended to only get a stroke or two off before putting the condom on, but before he knew it he had already cum. If Dena knew that he had come inside her she showed no signs of it, as she continued to eat Lexi's pussy.

After all the money he had spent, Stacks would be damned if all he got was one nut. Pulling his wet dick out of Dena, he moved around the side of the bed to stand over Lexi. Being a seasoned ho, Lexi already knew what he wanted and proceeded to suck Stacks's dick. Looking behind Dena, she could see the door creak open again she could see Don B slip into the room for his chance at glory. Had Lexi not had Stacks's dick in her throat, she would've laughed at what she knew was about to go down.

BLACK ICE SAT AT HIS table with his man Shorty and his ladies, sipping champagne like it was all good. He carefully watched the line starting to form at the bedroom door and did the math in his head about how much money he would make off Dena by the end of the night. Yes, he had indeed picked a winner.

"Damn, Lexi's ass is getting it in back there," Wendy said, watching the crowd.

"Shit, Lexi might get the best supporting actress, but lil Dena is the star," Lisa informed her.

"Dena? Ice, you left that poor girl back there?" Wendy asked heatedly.

"Poor my ass, she was begging for a cock the last time I saw her," Ice said.

"Nah, don't break her in like that," Wendy stood up to go rescue Dena, but Ice's steel grip clamped on her wrist.

"Bitch, where do you think you're going?" he asked in a chilly tone.

"Ice, you and I both know that girl ain't in her right frame of mind. Now, I'm all for the game of pimping and hoing, but not like that. It ain't right!" Wendy told him.

"Bitch, who is you to tell me what the fuck is right? I'm the Ice Man!" He snatched her back down into the seat. "Now, that lil ho is earning me twice as much paper as yo old, emotional ass brought in tonight, so I say she can take dick till she passes the fuck out. If you don't like the way I do thangs, then you can hit the high road like that bitch Cinnamon."

Wendy looked at him with tears in her eyes. She wasn't crying because of what he said, she was crying because of what he'd done. Once upon a time, she had been Dena, and the end result was her not being able to have children anymore. The men who Ice had let run up in her had damaged her physically and psychologically.

"You're a real fucking asshole, Ice!" She jerked away from him and stormed off.

"You want me to go get her?" Shorty asked.

"Nah," Ice said over the rim of his champagne flute. "Let the bitch roll. If she wanna bounce I got a replacement for her," he said, watching a girl who didn't look to be more than sixteen or seventeen, shyly giving a man a lap dance in the corner. "You've got more pressing business to attend to." Ice motioned towards Raheem, who was leaving the spot alone.

Shorty nodded his head. He gave Raheem about a thirty-second head start before getting up to follow him.

Chapter **46**

JAH WAS GONE LONGER THAN HE HAD INTENDED to. After sending Larry Love to the after-life, he had to change his shirt because the one he had on was bloody. He couldn't go home to Yoshi like that, so they had stopped by Tech's crib to get a replacement. The shirt was a little snugger against the vest than Jah would've liked, but it would do. After leaving Tech's house Jah went back to the brownstone.

When he got back there seemed to be twice as many girls there than when he left, if that was possible. Picking his way through the crowd, he literally bumped into the short cat that he always saw with the pimp, Ice. Shorty bounced off Jah without giving a second look. His eyes were fixed on someone or something near the exit. It wasn't Jah's business, so he kept it moving.

It took him almost ten minutes to make it to the third floor and another ten to get back to his table. Soda and True were getting lap dances from two young ladies, while Don B and Stacks were sitting in the corner wearing sleepy grins, but there was no sign of Cooter.

"That must've been one hell of a nut," True said as Jah sat back down.

"I had a little situation I had to take care of right quick," Jah told him.

"A situation that needed you to change clothes?" Don B asked suspiciously. "You know what, fam, I don't even wanna know. As long as you don't bring no heat on our heads, I'm good."

"Damn, that was a good shot," Cooter said, flopping back into his seat. "Stacks, you wasn't lying about that pussy. Shorty sho nuff got that good!"

"My nigga, I think she was so high she couldn't tell my dick from yours," Stacks said.

"Man, high or not, a bitch can tell the difference between a snake and a worm," Cooter teased him.

Don B and Stacks kicked jokes back and forth about how good the young whore's pussy was, and how, though she was high, she loved every minute of it. Jah's mind whirled back to how his own woman had been taken advantage of in a similar, yet more brutal, manner. He wondered if her attackers had told roundtable stories about Yoshi before they died, and it made him furious. Before he even realized he was moving, his hand was on the butt of his gun. Thankfully, he was able to get himself under control before he did something stupid. At that moment he made up his mind that when he caught True's stalker it would be the last job he took from a rapper.

RAHEEM WAS ROARING DRUNK WHEN he left the locked-door, but that didn't stop him from staggering down the block to his car in an attempt to drive himself home. Shooter and Marcus had left a few hours beforehand, but Raheem decided to stay so he could run up the tab Ice opened for them. He made sure to order the best of everything on the man's dime.

As he stumbled east on 128th he cursed the parking situation in New York City. He had to leave his car all the way on Park Avenue. As he crossed Madison, an eerie feeling crept over him, like he was being watched. Raheem looked around but didn't see anybody but a crackhead shambling down the other side of the street. Shrugging it off, he continued to his car. Thankfully, he found the Camry just as he'd left it, sitting under a broken streetlight. When he opened the passenger side door to put his jacket in, something looped over his head and tightened about his neck. Raheem struggled, but there was too much weight on his back.

"Talk that shit now," Shorty whispered into his ear. His legs were wrapped around Raheem's waist, while his hands pulled as tightly as they could on the length of cord. Shorty looked like a deranged midget as he choked Raheem out.

Raheem spun around like a man on fire, trying to shake Shorty, but the man's grip was too strong. Raheem felt his legs trying to buckle on him because of lack of oxygen to his brain. When he went down to one knee, Shorty planted his feet firmly on the ground and pulled with all his might. There was a faint popping sound and Raheem fell over, dead.

Shorty panted heavily from the rush of what he'd just done. There was something so satisfying about killing someone you hated that Shorty felt like he'd just busted a nut. He grabbed Raheem under his limp arms and dragged him to the back of his car. After making sure no one was watching, he stuffed the dead man inside and slammed the trunk shut. After a few days the car would most likely be towed, but by the time anyone found the body in the trunk it wouldn't be his problem anymore. It'd be on the ticket-thirsty NYPD.

AFTER THE LAST TRICK LEFT Lexi breathed a sigh of relief. Her pussy throbbed and her jaws felt like they were about to fall off their hinges. She had taken multiple dicks in a night before, but never this many.

On the bed, Dena lay on her stomach sound asleep. Compared to how she looked when she came in, you could hardly recognize her. Her hair was everywhere and stuck together in certain areas with left-over semen. Her honey brown ass was bruised and discolored from being slapped and pounded against for the last two hours. There were still traces of blood on the bed from when Don B hit Dena in the ass.

After seeing the size of his cock, Lexi half admired Dena for letting him go there. *Not that she was sober enough to do anything about it,* Lexi mused.

"Let's go, fresh fish!" Lexi slapped Dena playfully on the ass. When Dena didn't respond Lexi slapped her a bit harder. "Bitch get off your ass, its time to punch out for the night." There was still no response. Nervously, Lexi rolled Dena onto her back and saw that she had thrown up at some point. She shook Dena as hard as she could, but the girl remained still.

"Oh, shit!" Lexi grabbed her stuff and bolted into the other room to get Black Ice.

FROM THE WAY ICE AND his minions were darting nervously in and out of the bedroom, Jah knew something was wrong. Lexi was in the corner crying while Ice chain-smoked cigarettes. He whispered something to the short man, who had only recently come back from wherever he was, and disappeared back into the room. With his curiosity getting the best of him, Jah went to investigate.

Creeping along the wall, he tried to get a peak inside the room, but the door was shut. The short brown-skinned girl had her back to him, trying to console Lexi. When the tall white girl came out of the bedroom, also in tears, Jah got a glimpse of what had everyone so uptight. The girl Don B and his people had gang-banged lay on the bed, not moving. From where he stood, Jah could see blood on the sheet, but didn't know where it was coming from. He didn't know if she was alive or dead, but the expression on Black Ice's face made him think the latter. Having seen enough, he made hurried steps back to the table.

"Yo, I think its time for us to boogie," Jah told True.

"Son, its only like three o'clock," True protested.

"Jah, sit ya ass down and get a drink," Don B tried to coax him.

"Man, if we don't get the fuck outta here the only thing we'll be drinking is watery-ass Kool Aid in the bullpens." Jah recounted to the group what he had seen in the other room, which was all the prodding they needed to do as he told them. They almost caused a stampede getting out of the joint. For, as ignorant as Stacks and his crew were, they all knew that being at the scene of a murder, with guns no less, wouldn't be good for any of them.

"Say, baby, what's the big rush? You guys ain't enjoying ya selves?" Black Ice asked, coming out of the bedroom.

"It was a blast, but we gotta dip, my nigga," Don B told him, slapping Ice five and continuing on his way.

Dumfounded, Black Ice watched the men leaving. A minute ago they were spending bread and getting twisted, but now they were running out like all the bitches in the joint were burning. Ice didn't know exactly what had gotten into them, but the look the boy called Jah was giving him meant that they knew something they weren't telling.

Ice shrugged it off as nothing. If they wanted to bounce, then that was on them, they had already blown a few grand with Ice on the bitches, so they had served their purposes for the night. Now Ice was free to focus on a bigger problem, which was what to do with Dena.

NORMALLY, MICHELLE WOULD'VE BEEN OPPOSED to working the night shift on a Saturday, because that was usually her hangout night, but this particular Saturday night she needed something to focus on other than her anger at Lazy. When she'd broken the news to Lazy about her being pregnant he'd been less than pleased.

Until that night, she thought that Lazy was the man for her and that he had forsaken all others for her. But he came at her like a common street nigga. "Old and worn-out pussy" was a phrase that he kept throwing around in reference to her. In the end, there was a lot of furniture breaking, harsh words, and drama, which resulted in Lazy storming out of the apartment in a rage. Lazy was really showing signs of his age, but it was Michelle's own fault for not treating him like what he was, a piece of young dick.

Michelle noticed something odd going on over in a far corner of the emergency room. There were two girls, one white and one black, sitting another young lady on a chair. At first, Michelle took it as them bringing a drunken girlfriend in for treatment, but when the black and the white girl hightailed it out of the emergency room, Michelle knew something was up. Placing her clipboard on the counter, she walked over to investigate.

As she drew closer to the girl something about her was familiar. It wasn't until she got right up on the girl that it dawned on Michelle where she had seen her before, and that was in a picture she had seen in Lazy's wallet. This was her rival, Dena. The girl was unresponsive, and there were traces of dried blood on her legs. Regardless of her personal feelings towards Dena, she was a nurse first, and the young girl needed help.

"I need a doctor over here!" Michelle called out, while checking Dena for vital signs.

Chapter **47**

MO ALMOST JUMPED OUT OF HER SKIN WHEN
the phone rang. The young boy she had been with sexed her
for over two hours before finally calling it quits. She had
only been home for about twenty minutes and was too tired
to talk to anyone. Looking at her digital clock, she saw that
it was almost five in the morning, and nothing good ever
came from a five a.m. call, so she decided not to answer. Before she dropped off to sleep she thought of Dena. She
knew this was the night of Ice's party and was worried that
something might've gone wrong.

"Hello?" Monique answered nervously.

"Is this Mo?" a very professional-sounding voice asked.

"This is she," Mo said with her heart pounding in her
chest.

"This is Michelle White. I'm a nurse at Harlem Hospital. I'm calling you about a Miss Dena Jones. Yours was the
last number dialed in her cell phone, do you know her?"

"Yes, that's my cousin. What's wrong?" Mo asked nervously.

"Well, she was brought into the emergency room about
an hour ago and—"

"That's obvious. Just tell me what happened!" Mo snapped.

Michelle ignored her indignant tone and kept it professional. "If you'd calm down I could tell you. She's alive, but in a bad way. She had several different types of drugs in her system, including heroin. Would it be possible for you to contact her family and have them come to the hospital as soon as possible? We're located on—" Mo hung up before she could finish her sentence.

Mo almost collapsed but managed to steady herself against her bedroom wall. She had just spoken to Dena and nothing seemed unusual, so the fact that she was in the hospital from a drug overdose, from heroin no less, seemed unreal. She knew Black Ice spelled trouble and was tight with herself for not doing more to come between him and Dena. Mo paced her bedroom for a minute trying to figure out what to do, but her nerves were too bad to think straight. She had to warn Dena's mother, but she didn't want to panic her until she knew more, and she was damn sure going to the hospital to find out.

Monique moved toward the window and saw Shannon sitting on a crate across the street. He was pouring liquor in front of a mural of Spooky, Nate, and Yvette that he had erected after the shoot-out. People warned him to stay off the block, but after losing his whole circle of people he didn't much give a fuck about the police catching him. Shannon was in a bad way and the news Mo was about to drop on him wouldn't make it any easier.

AFTER LEAVING THE CLUB, DON B and Stacks decided that they wanted to hit another spot and keep the party going, but True wasn't up for it. He had a long day ahead of him and needed to be well rested. In addition to a guest radio appearance at 9 a.m the next morning, he was supposed to be performing at halftime during the celebrity game. Don B protested and tried to keep him hanging, but True told him that he and Jah would hop in a cab. He'd had enough drama for the day and wanted to turn it in.

The ride to True's building was a short one, but gave both of the men time to think. Jah was glad to have gotten through another night of Hollywood bullshit and anxious to get back to Yoshi. He licked his lips at the thought of slipping between those thick yellow thighs and getting one off before going to sleep.

"How was that?" True asked, bringing Jah out of his thoughts.

"Huh, how was what?" Jah asked.

"That pussy? Didn't you say you had a joint downstairs?" True reminded him.

"Oh, it was cool," Jah told him, before going back to looking out the window. He could tell by the look on True's face that he didn't believe him, but he didn't press the issue.

"Jah, can I ask you a personal question?" True asked seriously.

"Depends on how personal it is."

"It's about Yoshi," True said. Jah raised his eyebrow. "Not like that," True assured him. "I mean, I see what you and her got, and I know its love . . . or at least, what I believe it to be, but how did you love her?"

"True, either I'm as high as you are, or your words ain't making no sense," Jah told him.

True searched for the right words. "I mean . . . Look, when you met Yoshi, she sort of had a reputation, right? But what I wanna know is how you were able to get past people trying to judge you?"

Jah wasn't going to answer the question, but seeing the sincerity in True's eyes he decided to let him in a bit. "Honestly, it's just something that happened," Jah confessed. "Every nigga in the hood knew who Yoshi was and every nigga wanted a piece of that, but that isn't what moved me. I dug who she was beneath 'China,' feel me?"

"Yeah," True said.

"What's with the funny-ass questions anyhow?" Jah asked suspiciously.

True turned his head towards the window when he spoke. "I was just asking. A long time ago I had a chick that I saw something in, but I never pressed it cause I knew niggaz was gonna look at me funny."

Jah had an idea who he was talking about, but didn't say. Instead, he just shrugged. "Sometimes you just gotta say fuck what people think and go with what you wanna do."

Before True could respond the taxi slammed on its breaks. A car had run the red light and came to a stop directly in front of them. The taxi driver blared the horn, but the violating car didn't move. Jah was about to say something to the driver when his window shattered. Jah didn't look to see who had attacked them or even reason why, he just snatched one of his pistols from the holster and started popping.

Charlie Rock managed to move out of the line of fire just as the bullets came whizzing through the shattered window. He backpedaled, returning fire with his good hand, managing to hit Jah low in the body. He heard the man scream, but had no way to tell how serious the injury was.

Fire shot up through Jah's gut where the bullet pierced flesh and muscle. He was wearing the vest, but the bullet had him just below the strap, where the skin was unprotected. Jah managed to sit up enough to try to go out the door, but as soon as he opened it the driver of the car that had cut them off started shooting. He lit up the whole front of the cab, killing the driver instantly.

Jah found himself in a bad way. He was pinned in the back of a cab, with bullets coming from two different directions. Though he had two guns on him, he was laying on the second one, trying not to get shot again or bleed to death from the first bullet. He looked to True, but the man seemed too stunned to do much more than curl up and pray he didn't take one. He was on his own. In a last attempt at survival, Jah kicked with his good leg, sending the door flying outward. Charlie raised his gun to fire, but Jah hit him twice in the stomach. Charlie dropped, but there was still Sha Boogie to deal with.

A bullet slamming into the seat cushion just above where True was crouching snapped him back to the here and now. Bullets and glass where flying everywhere, but his survival instincts kicked in. Using his free hand to open the door, True rolled out of the cab, blasting away with his P89. Firing more out of fear than intent to kill, he disabled the car, but Sha Boogie was still standing.

· · ·

SHA BOOGIE SAW HIS MAN go down and tried to take Jah's head off. He was about to move in, when he saw True trying to get busy on the other side. Seeing the object of his desire, he abandoned Jah and went around to the other side.

True was using his arm to cover his head, firing blind as he came spilling out of the back of the cab. Bullets struck the car at least three feet from where Sha Boogie was standing. Knowing that True was afraid only excited him more, as he advanced on the man, firing his pistol.

True saw Sha Boogie coming his way and felt his heart quicken. He had been a street cat all his life, but had never been in a real, live gun-fight. Jah seemed to be faring well on his end, but it wasn't True's cup of tea. If he got out of it he was going to let Big Dawg provide whatever security they deemed necessary. He tried to bolt from behind the door to the safety of a parked car, but took one in the side, sending him skidding against the curb and his gun skidding into the bushes. Seeing that his enemy was unarmed, Sha Boogie moved in for kill.

"Yeah, muthafucka, you thought I wasn't gonna get you back for that shit," Sha Boogie moved towards True, who was looking around frantically for his lost weapon. "At long last we get to settle an age-old debt."

"Muthafucka, I ain't never seen you a day in my life!" True spat. His whole body was on fire, but he was trying to buy enough time for help to come.

Sha's eyes took on a maddening glaze. "What? You changed the course of my whole fucking life and you got the nerve to say you don't know me." Sha leveled his gun at True's face. "Ten years ago you killed my father and now you're gonna die."

Through True's haze of pain he took a good look at the man. As Sha's features came into focus it all dawned on him. Though Sha Boogie was a little darker, he bore a striking resemblance to the man who had testified against True's mother. That man's death was the only blood that True had on his hands, and it was now coming back to bite him in the ass. Though he was in a great deal of pain, seeing the son of his mother's accuser drove him.

True tried to crawl towards Sha, but the pain was too intense. "Fuck ya snitching-ass pops, that nigga sent my mother to the joint. If I could've killed his bitch ass twice I would've!" True said, knowing he was going to die anyway, so he might as well get it off his chest.

"I'm glad you know it, so I ain't gotta tell you," Sha Boogie said, taking aim at True's face.

JAH GOT OUT OF THE car, gun dangling at his side. He had lost a lot of blood and knew it wouldn't be long before he fell out. He raised his gun and tried to draw a bead on Sha, but had trouble holding his arms steady. Pushing off the car he fired on True's assailant.

Just as Sha Boogie had fired on True, a bullet hit him in the neck, spinning him so he could catch the one to his stomach. Sha Boogie danced around for a minute trying to figure out what had just happened, before hitting the ground. As Sha Boogie's life drained away into the cracks of the pavement he croaked, "I got that nigga, Daddy!"

Though Sha Boogie had taken a fatal hit, so did True. A hole stuffed with what looked like ground beef decorated his shirt, where the Enyce emblem once was. He clutched at the hole as if his hands could stop the massive amounts of blood running out, but in the end it was a fight he couldn't win.

Jah limped around the side of the car to where True and Sha Boogie were laid out, trying his best to stay awake. Both men were sprawled out in pools of their own blood. Jah didn't know much about Sha Boogie, but he knew True was a kid that deserved to live. Yet the sad fact was that, in life, everything we do affects the grand scheme of things. Jah would make sure that people knew that True had gone out like a warrior, but other than that there was nothing he could do for him.

"Rest in peace, my dude," Jah said over True's body before limping away from the scene. He had gotten only a few feet when a bullet hit him in the back. He staggered, but didn't fall, spinning around to return fire, but only ended up getting hit three more times. Jah dropped to his knees and looked into the face of the man who had shot him.

"Dum-dums are nasty as hell, ain't they?" Charlie Rock limped over to Jah. He was bleeding heavily from his gut, but that didn't seem to affect his shooting arm. "You know, these are the only things Sha Boogie planned for that didn't go to shit." Charlie looked at his murdered friend, then to Jah. "Say goodnight, muthafucka!"

Jah saw the muzzle flash, followed by an intense pain in his cheek. He saw himself as ten years old again, riding the train with his brother Paul. "Never be like me, Jahlil, always be better," Paul said to him. For as much as his brother used to preach to him about not following in the family's footsteps, it seemed dying young was in their blood.

Charlie Rock limped off to the cab and tossed the driver out onto the curb, then he took the wheel. He looked at his man, Sha Boogie, and felt sad at his passing, but it was the very same thing in life that carried him over into death. As Charlie Rock pulled the cab out into traffic he thought about how he would miss his friend, but more importantly, he was free from Sha Boogie's insane quest.

Chapter 48

DENA WOKE UP THE NEXT MORNING IN A CAST-
iron bed. Her body felt like she had gone through twelve
rounds with Mike Tyson. Mo was sitting in a chair with her
feet propped, sleeping uncomfortably. She wondered how
long Mo had been there, but knowing her, she was there
probably ever since Dena had been admitted—whenever
that was.

Dena looked around the room and saw that all of her
family and friends were on deck. Her mother was in the next
bed sleeping soundly, while Nadine paced just outside the
door on her cell phone. Sharon was looking out the window
with a genuinely worried expression on her face. Her brother
Shannon was at her bedside saying prayers. When he saw
that she had woken up, his eyes lit up.

"Hey lil sis!" He took her hand. "How you feeling?"

"Like shit," Dena croaked. She hadn't realized how raw
her throat was until she tried to speak. Picking up on that,
Mo grabbed a pitcher of water and filled a plastic cup for
her. "How did I get here?" Dena sipped the water.

"The nurse said a white girl and her friend brought you
in then disappeared. They've treated you for the cuts
and . . . STDs," Mo said sadly.

"STDs? Why the hell would they—" Then it came back to Dena. Shorty had given her the Blue Diamond, which was surely laced, and it all went downhill from there. She couldn't remember the details, but what she did remember were the flashing faces of different men, and pain, a whole lot of pain. For the second time in less than a week someone who was supposed to love her had betrayed her. For as much as she hated to admit it, Mo was right about the pimp. Thinking of things she probably did under the influence of the drugs, Dena broke down.

"Its okay, D." Mo rubbed her back while Shannon wasn't quite sure what to do.

"No, its not okay, Mo," Dena sobbed. "You were right about Ice. I gave my heart to that man and he . . . God, I don't even wanna say it," she said shamefully.

"Dena." Mo took her hand. "You're with family. Tell us what he did to you."

Dena looked up at Mo through tearful eyes. Though it tasted like ash in her mouth, she shared the last few day's turn of events with her brother and best friends. She told them about Philly, the locked-door event, she even told them about the heroin. When the tale was completed, they were in tears.

"I'm so sorry, D." Mo hugged her.

Shannon just walked over into the corner and cried quietly. He felt like such a fuck-up, letting that happen to his little sister. He reasoned if he had spent more time watching her back than in the streets, then it wouldn't have happened. For as much as he hated himself, he hated Ice more.

The attending physician came into the room holding her clipboard and looking at the group over her blue-rimmed glasses. She was a plump, dark-skinned woman who wore her hair in a bun. "I see you're feeling a little better," she said to Dena."

"I wouldn't say all that, but I'm awake," Dena said, trying to make light of the situation.

"You've been through quite a bit, Ms. Jones, but I think you're going to recover. Now, I have some more serious business that I need to discuss with you, in private." She looked around the room.

"This is my family. You can talk in front of them," Dena said nervously. Shannon held one of her hands while Mo held the other.

The doctor was skeptical at first, but after Dena insisted again she spoke freely. "Well, as you may or may not know we've found multiple traces of semen inside you. Initially we thought you'd been raped, but during our exam we found no signs of forced entry."

"That's because they drugged me. I didn't know what I was doing!" Dena sobbed.

"Ms. Jones, calm down. From the different drugs we found in your system, I doubt if this happened willingly, regardless of what the charts say. Drug-induced or otherwise, rape is rape. But there's a bigger issue here."

"What the fuck could be bigger than my lil sister getting raped?" Shannon barked. He didn't mean to be hostile with the doctor, but he didn't know any other way to be at that point.

The doctor looked at him sadly. From her facial expression you could tell she wanted to cry. This was the part of her job she hated. "Ms. Jones, we've run tests on the different fluids found inside you and found that you've been infected with chlamydia, which we can treat, but we've also found traces of the HIV virus in one of the semen samples. So far you haven't tested reactive for the virus, but you'll have to come back every six months for testing. I'm sorry."

Shannon threw himself onto the floor, crying like a baby. Mo embraced her friend and shed heavy tears of her own. Nadine stopped talking on her phone and poked her head in the room to see what all the commotion was about.

"Ms. Jones, though you've been exposed it doesn't mean that you've contracted the virus. You may very well have dodged the bullet, but it's too soon to be certain." The doctor adjusted her glasses. "Even if it does show up later on this diagnosis is not the end of the world. Technology is so advanced these days that you could still live a healthy and normal life. There are—"

The doctor kept talking but Dena didn't listen. At that moment the whole world stopped moving. For all the bullshit the doctor was trying to tell her, it still didn't change the fact that she had loved a man and for this there was a good possibility that she was going to die. Dena had dreams of going to college and having kids one day, but one fuckup had changed all that.

No one had even noticed that Dena's mother was awake until they heard the sobbing coming from just off to their left. She had climbed out of the bed and had been listening as the doctor broke the news to her youngest child. Tears ran freely down her face and her legs began to tremble uncontrollably. Had it not been for Nadine holding her by the arm she'd have probably collapsed from the shock of what she'd heard. No parent wanted to entertain the thought of outliving their children, but it was suddenly a very real possibility for Ms. Jones.

Shannon managed to compose himself enough to get off the floor and moved to his sister's bedside. He tried to console her, but the words escaped him. What do you tell someone to soothe them when they'd just been handed a potential death sentence? Shannon knew that there were no words he could offer his little sister, but he had never been good with words anyhow. Shannon had always been a man of actions and his deeds would speak for him. For as much as he wanted to escape to the streets, as he was known to do, his family needed him at that moment so the streets would have to wait for their due. One thing he promised himself though was that they wouldn't have to wait long. Soothing his beast with promises of carnage and revenge, Shannon joined his family and friends as they prayed for Dena.

It's All a Part of the Game

IT SEEMED LIKE THERE WAS A DARK CLOUD hovering over Harlem that Sunday morning. The temperature had dropped almost twelve degrees lower from what it had been the whole week. Bitter winds whipped through the streets, pulling trash behind it like a game of Follow the Leader. The celebrity basketball game was still played in the park on 115th Street, the King Dome, for those not familiar, but it was a grim event.

The Big Dawg squad all wore black strips on their jerseys in honor of True and Jah. The celebration of the Don B and Stacks collabo turned into a celebration of True's life. His album would go on to sell more than five hundred thousand copies in its first week, partially due to the media coverage of his gruesome murder. Don B took little joy in the success. Though he had been hard on True, he only wanted to see him do well. When you're young, Black, and on top of your game, they'll always be people in the wings who want you to fall.

When the two squads took the floor, Don B had a sinking feeling about what the results of the game would be. Stacks's big secret was that he not only had the best all-around players from Texas on his team, but two of his starters played for the Houston Rockets. The ballers from Big Dawg put up a good fight, but in the end they were routed by twenty-five.

Lazy played horribly that afternoon. Cooter abused him on the court, going for a hot twenty to Lazy's six. He had been out all night stressing over the impending baby, and what he had done to his relationship. So, when game time rolled around he had neither the stamina nor willpower to put up any kind of real effort. To make matters worse, he ended up tearing the ligaments in his knee in the third quarter, ruining any dreams he had of being recruited to a top-ten school. Though college was still an option, his game would never be the same. Michelle was heartbroken by the prospect of her being an NBA wife flying out the window, but she would still have her man, even if Lazy did refuse to quit cheating on her.

When the Big Dawg took the floor it wasn't Billy at the helm. For as much as she looked forward to coaching in the highly publicized game, she was needed elsewhere. Yoshi was so broken up by Jah's murder that she was inconsolable. The doctors had given her something to make her sleep, but it did nothing for grief. Everybody feared that she was going to do something to herself, so Billy and Reese took turns sitting with her. Billy understood just what Yoshi was going through because she and the same kind of grief had walked hand in hand when Sol was killed.

From the moment Jah felt the rush of his first lick, life had dictated that the streets would claim him. Yoshi had believed that she could change what fate had written. And truth be told, she almost did. Though it was only for a short time, she had found happiness for herself and was able to pass it on to someone else. Jah was gone from this world, but never from her heart. At the end of their chapter he had died how he lived, with a gun in his hand.

Black Ice was beyond upset to lose his twenty-five thousand dollars. Over the course of the weekend he had lost three whores and a good chunk of his change. The morning after the locked-door, Wendy had stolen fifteen thousand dollars from his safe and disappeared with only the clothes on her back. Ice was mad as hell, but figured, with the eighteen-year-old beauty he had copped from an all-night diner, he would make three times that once he broke her in. Unfortunately he would never have a chance to see if she was built like that.

In the middle of the celebrity barbecue, a short kid who was built like a mailbox and who rocked his hair in messy cornrows, walked over to the grill where the pimp and his henchman were talking to a group of young ladies. There was something familiar about the young man, but Ice couldn't quite place him. Before he had a chance to ponder it further the park erupted in gunfire.

Shorty reached for his pistol, but the alcohol dulled his movements by a fraction of an inch which was all Shannon needed to gun him down. Shorty's head exploded like a melon when the bullet hit it. Ice tried to take cover but two bullets to the back immobilized him. Don B. and his people scattered leaving Ice at the mercy of the gunman.

"Turn yo bitch ass over!" Shannon kicked him in the ass, leaving a Timberland print on the rear of Ice's white linen shorts.

Ice was in a world of pain, but managed to roll over onto his side to face the man. "Dawg, I don't even know you. What the fuck is this about?" Ice asked, not bothering to hide the panic in his voice.

Shannon glared down at Black Ice. "This is about dreams, nigga. Dreams of a little girl that may never come true because of a slick-talking nigga."

Ice tried to plead. "Man, wait a second. I got ten grand in my truck. Let me live and you can have it!"

"Money?" Shannon chuckled. "Bitch nigga, I don't want ya money, I want ya fucking life. My little sister Dena wanted you to have this." Shannon leveled his gun. Ice opened his mouth to beg but a bullet ripping through the back of his throat silenced him. Shannon continued to squeeze the trigger until his gun was empty. While Ice lay motionless on the ground Shannon spat on him before walking calmly from the park. The debt had been settled. They say that even after Shannon was gone you could still hear Shorty's brains sizzling on the grill where they'd been deposited.

• • •

FOR A LONG TIME PEOPLE talked about the shootout at the Big Dawg game, but as with most things in the hood that news became old in light of more drama. Though Charlie Rock had managed to escape the scene of the triple murder, he couldn't escape his karma. He was last seen on the corner of Decatur and Ralph, being stuffed into the back of a car by Spider's older brother, Killer-Bo.